The Heart of Darkness

ODELIA FLORIS

The Chaucy Shire Medieval Mysteries
Book One

www.odeliafloris.com

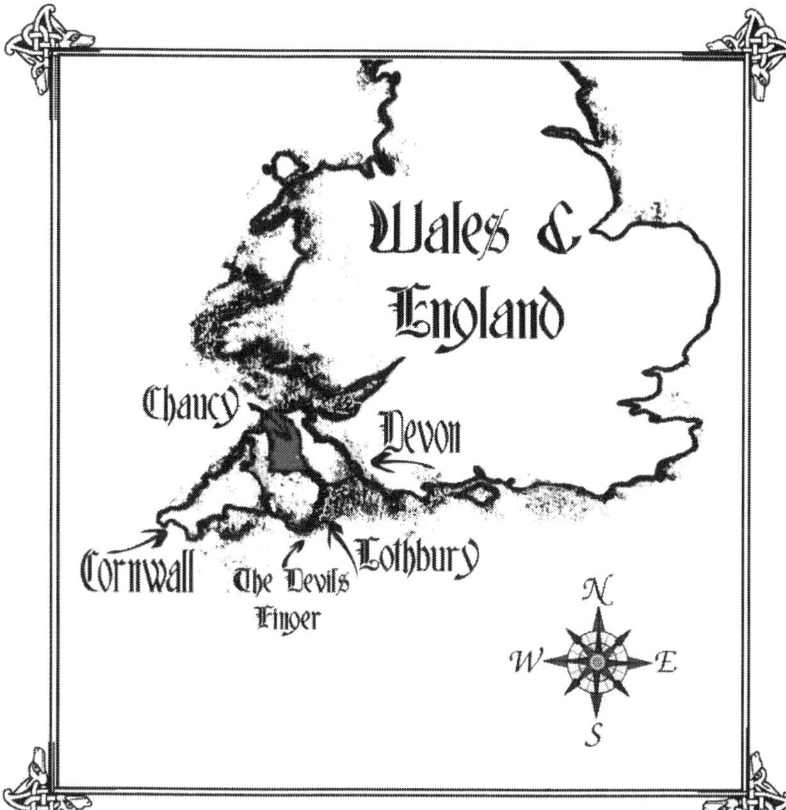

Chaucy & its
Neighbouring Shires

Also by Odelia Floris

Adult fiction:
Beguile Me Not
(A love story set in 1880s New Zealand)

Children's fiction:
The Little Demon Who Couldn't

Nonfiction:
Inspiration & Wisdom from the Pen of Ralph Waldo Emerson: Over 600 Quotes

I.

The Fall

Chauncy Shire, South West England, August 1430

LADY Sabina furiously snatched the instrument from her cousin Rowena's hand. 'I told you not to play my new lute!'

Feeling, as always, like a common little garden weed beside the tall, stately lily that was her cousin Lady Sabina, Rowena pushed back her thickly curling red hair with a jerk that served to keep her wounded feelings at bay. 'But you badly damaged my own lute, smashing it down on the edge of that table in frustration. It was hardly my lute's fault that you were having difficulty playing a new piece of music!'

The richly-dressed damsel haughtily placed the lute on a table behind her. 'Rowena, an inferior instrument cannot produce a sound satisfactory for someone as talented as I. Frustration was inevitable. And nay, generous as I am, you cannot touch my lute. My music master says that if someone of little skill plays this fine instrument, its sound will be damaged.'

The red-haired maiden drew herself as tall as possible in an attempt to compensate for her shortness. 'Then you should not play it.'

'Do you mean to insinuate that I play badly?'

Rowena put her small hands on her hips and glared up at her cousin. 'After suffering through many hours of music that sounded more like an instrument being tortured than played, I can tell you with absolute certainty that you do indeed play badly.'

Lady Sabina gasped, and before Rowena could duck she felt a stinging pain in her cheek as her cousin's hand hit it hard.

With eyes watering, the short, simply-dressed maiden clutched her smarting face with one hand while she considered her options for a moment. Then, with a swift swipe, she knocked off her cousin's tall, steeple-like hennin headdress. The hennin rolled across the bare wooden floorboards, its long, white gauze veil picking up a very satisfactory coating of dust as it went along.

Lady Sabina gasped in horror at the sight. When the headdress finally came to rest, she looked at Rowena again. Her icy blue eyes were cold, glinting daggers. 'Do not dare to lay a hand on me again,' she spat. 'Do not forget that I am your superior in rank, breeding and class. My father is a wealthy lord whereas *you* are the daughter of a mere troubadour, a penniless wondering minstrel. I'll make you pay for this, you insolent peasant!'

Lady Sabina screwed up her eyes and managed to squeeze some tears out. 'Mother, Mother, horrid cousin Rowena just hit me because she was using my things and I told her not to,' she cried, running into the next room. 'Tell her to stop being so vile!' Her voice sounded more like a whining child than the young woman of eighteen she really was.

A few moments later Rowena's aunt, Lady Cunningham, stormed in. Her daughter, who was snivelling loudly, followed. Anger filled Lady Cunningham's features. Without doubt she had once been beautiful, but now her face was hard and haggard, eroded by the slow poison of years spent nursing an intense disappointment at not rising from the lower nobility to a position at the royal court. She had made the mistake of marrying a man whose ambition was to amass wealth rather than climb the social ladder, wrongly thinking the drive he showed in business would naturally extend to social climbing.

'How can you be so cruel to your poor cousin after all we have done for you!' shrilled Lady Cunningham, jutting out her sharp chin and wagging a furious finger at Rowena. 'Your uncle and I have taken you in these twelve months despite fearing that, as your father was so lowly born, you might corrupt our own dear Sabina, you ungrateful child!'

Rowena pushed back the hair that had fallen over her face again. 'Corrupt her? I think her parents have done that themselves in the eighteen years I've not been here! She is the most spoilt, frivolous and silly girl I've yet been cursed enough to cross paths with!' Rowena was about to sharply remind her relatives that she was a woman of twenty-four, not a child, when she quickly thought better and shut her mouth.

Her aunt's hard grey eyes had narrowed to thin, hateful slits, while behind her, her child let out a histrionic wail of angst.

It was time to go. Rowena lifted the almost threadbare skirt of her faded red gown and made for the door. But before she could escape the unhappy room, her aunt suddenly lashed out with the belt she had quietly undone from about her waist.

Rowena made a desperate dive for the open doorway as the metal pendants and silver globes hanging on long chains from the belt whizzed past frighteningly close to her head. But the momentum she managed to get up was so great that when she burst out the upstairs solar and into the passageway, she could not make the turning. Her bare feet screeched as they slid on the wooden floor, and then there was an earth-shattering clang as she collided with the suit of armour displayed against the wall.

'Wait until Lord Cunningham gets back, by God and Saint Leroy he'll make you regret this! Do you hear; you'll wish your stupid, selfish mother had never had you!' came Lady Cunningham's scream.

Already unbalanced, Rowena went down like a tree that has

received the woodsman's final axe-blow. She caught her breath sharply as a piece of the armour suit she had landed on cut into her knee. Despite the pain, she wasted no time in scrambling back to her feet. She could hear her aunt's rapidly approaching footfalls and was in no mood for a second bout.

There was a tearing sound as she stumbled over the fallen armour, and she looked down to find part of her dress's hem in tatters. Oh well, what was another rip when a dress was already so full of patches and repairs? The only thing that mattered was getting outside; outside in the fresh air and the sunlight, in the freedom.

'Typical of my sister to do something like that,' Lady Cunningham's screech followed Rowena as she flew down the stairs. 'How much more selfish can you get than tearing yourself from the bosom of your loving family and then going and dropping dead, leaving a wild animal of an unmarried daughter to burden them with!'

Once outside Stoatley Manor, Rowena set off along the path that led down the valley to Willowmead, a small hamlet on the Cunningham lands.

Their lands covered a large area of the fertile, rolling hills of the Heathcote Downs, in the little shire of Chaucy. It was the largest estate in Chaucy, which was not saying a lot. Much of the shire's land was wild and poor, and hence of little interest to grand men. Of those few old families who could once have rightly thought themselves grand, the Cunninghams were the only ones who had not been weathered down by poor soils, mean harvests and slow trade.

Rowena did not intend to return to Stoatley until evening, by which time she hoped Lord Cunningham would have returned from his business in Hartfield, the shire's only market town, and gone up to his private chambers for the night. With a bit of luck, by the next morning he would have forgotten all about Lady

Cunningham's complaints about her. Lord Cunningham was rarely seen about at Stoatley during the day, spending most of his time either in Hartfield on business or shut away in his private chambers answering letters, reading the reports of his overseers and adding up his profits.

It was a perfect day to linger. The late summer's day was warm and mallow, and a soft breeze rippled through the golden cornfields like waves upon a lake and playfully tossed about Rowena's long red locks. She could hear the skylarks singing joyously as they swooped and soared in the air, high above the earth.

The young woman paused beside this field of gold and put a shielding hand above her eyes as she looked heavenwards. How wonderful it would feel to be as free as they! Local folklore had it that the larks flew so high that they reached the pearly gates of heaven, where they heard the angels singing, and as the birds swooped back towards earth they sung the angels' songs.

Still smiling at this charming thought, Rowena eventually continued on her leisurely way along the path, which finally arrived at the door of a humble little cottage. There, she stopped and knocked.

The door creaked slowly open and a mop-haired little boy paired out. When he saw who was standing on the front step, his eyes lit up with delight. 'Mama, Mama, it's Rowena!' he cried. Then his eyes alighted on the basket she was carrying. 'And look what she's brought us!'

Upon hearing this, his three brothers immediately rushed to join him. The delighted children grabbed Rowena by the hands and skirts; laughingly, she let them pull her inside.

Their mother Becky, a tall, robust-figured woman of twenty-nine, arose from a bench by the fireside holding a sleeping baby cradled in her arms. 'Oh Rowena, you're ever so good to us!'

'Well, it's the least I can do,' said Rowena, setting the basket down on the table.

The basket was immediately pounced on by eager little hands and all its contents examined with great excitement and strewn across the table. There were dusky plums, fat red strawberries, oat cakes, and most excitingly of all, little tarts filled with sweet berries. The delighted finders wasted no time in stuffing them into purple-lipped, gap-toothed little mouths.

Turning back to the children's' mother, Rowena frowned concernedly. 'How is poor Durwin?'

'He's mending remarkably fast, God be praised,' replied Becky, her full lips broadening into a wide smile that revealed a mouth of even, pearly-white teeth. 'The herbalist hermit-monk who has been attending to him is working a fair miracle. He said Durwin should have full use of his arm again soon.'

'The mason Durwin works for seems to be a decent soul, keeping his job for him to come back to. It would be an easy matter to find another stonemason's labourer.'

Becky smoothed back her mass of thick honey-blonde hair thoughtfully. 'Aye, that he is. Though I do believe he may feel a little remorseful about what happened to my Durwin. Accidents will happen, but them ropes they were using to lift the big stone blocks up to the top of the bell tower were too old. If they'd taken more care that last block would never have come crashing down on my Durwin's poor arm.'

'Quite. He was fortunate not be killed.'

Becky's earnest hazel eyes lifted heavenwards. 'I thank God every day for not recalling my Durwin to our heavenly home just yet, but it's been real hard feeding the five little ones on the few coins I had put away for lean times like this. Last week we didn't have enough to pay the rent. Old Miser Cunningham's sour little rent-man was not best pleased, but I managed to talk him into letting me owe him until this week.'

'Well you need be indebted no longer,' said the red-haired

maiden, holding out her hand. 'I've also brought you a little money so that you can pay the sheriff's tax collector and give the landlord his rent.'

Becky gratefully pocketed the money. 'May the Lord bless your good soul.'

The younger woman waved away her friend's gratitude. 'It's a mere trifle; just enough to keep the sheriff from turning up here bothering you because you can't pay your taxes.'

'Aye, we live in constant fear of that,' said Becky, glancing around anxiously as if expecting him to burst through her door at any moment. 'Folks say he is very harsh on those who don't pay their taxes on time, turning up the very next day with his men to seize what little they have. They also say he is most hard on anyone caught breaking the law. If a felony is committed, he is very zealous in his efforts to find the perpetrators; like a dog with a bone he is. And God have mercy on them if he catches them, because they ain't going to find no mercy in Sir Richard's dark heart!'

Rowena, though she had been living in the area for nearly a year, had not been out in society much and knew hardly anyone in Chaucy except for Stoatley estate's poorest families, whom she often took gifts of food (taken from the manor's kitchen when the Cunninghams were not looking). But she had heard the local sheriff's name mentioned by them with dread on more than one occasion.

'Has Sir Richard been sheriff of Chaucy for long?' she asked.

'It's been about three year now. My Durwin knows a few of the lads garrisoned at the sheriff's fortress. They say he gained some renown fighting the French at the battle of Agincourt, and further cemented his reputation by saving one of the king's most loyal barons from an assassination attempt, so was given the office by the king as a reward for his bravery. Old Henry can't have been that impressed with our Sir Richard though, seeing as

Chaucy is the measliest shire in all England. Except for the Heathcote Downs, we're naught but wild woods and barren moors here. Hardly any trade neither; just a few peasants scratching a living. You're never going to make much money fining and taxing us lot, however hard you try.'

'So is Sir Richard worse than the sheriff you had before?'

'Aye. You see, old sir Purcell, he just took his cut of the fines paid to the local shire court like he was entitled, creamed off a little, and left it at that. But this Sir Richard is not content with those rich pickings. Oh no. He had not been in office four moons before he raised the tax rate, and has done it three,' Becky raised three fingers, 'more times, since. Us poor folks had little enough before he came, but now we barely get by at all.' She shook her head despairingly. 'If the harvest were to fail we would starve for sure.'

'How despicable! He really must be completely heartless. But come.' Rowena smiled brightly, doing her best to distract the other woman from her gloomy thoughts. 'Let us not dwell on such worries today.' She took Becky companionably by the arm. 'Now, you must tell me how you are all getting on, and I insist on being told all the latest local news! Shall we sit outside on the bench at the front door? It's almost a crime to be indoors on such a lovely sunny day.'

Becky assented gladly, and very shortly the two women were seated on a wooden bench outside, leaning their backs against the sun-warmed wall of the little cottage.

After they had swapped news and chatted for a little while, a look of sadness crossed Rowena's normally cheerful face. 'When my mother died last September, I dreaded leaving Pennreth to come and live here with my aunt and uncle. I wished so much that my father had not died when I was six years old, and that the Cunninghams had not been my only surviving relatives. When I am sad and lonely, I often find my mind wandering back to

Pennreth in Cornwell and our little house above the sea. Sometimes, when I wake at night, I think I can hear the calls of the gulls and crash of the waves, but then I realise it is just a happy dream of carefree childhood days. From the day I arrived in Chaucy I have felt like an outsider, not quite a woman of gentle birth, but not a peasant either.'

'Never you fear, I'm always here to lend an ear to your sorrows,' said Becky, patting Rowena soothingly on the shoulder and handing her a handkerchief.

'I'm not a child, you know,' replied Rowena, unable to stop herself laughing at her friend's motherly tone. 'But thank you, Becky. You are a great comfort.' The red-haired damsel sighed. 'I do wish I could scrape enough money together to rent a room somewhere so I could move out of Stoatley Manor. I'm grateful my dear late mother taught me Latin as well as French and English, but although there is plenty of demand for those skills, the fact that I am a woman would be held against me. It is unlikely anyone would hire me.'

'You never know, you might find a man...you know, to marry,' Becky said cautiously.

'I'm sure I shall never find anyone. Lady Cunningham and Cousin Sabina are forever telling me that no man of gentle birth will ever look at me while my skin is so brown from all the time I spend out in the sun, because only lowly peasant maids have tanned skin. In fact, my beloved relatives doubt very much that any man would even manage to get past my shortness, unfashionable dress and total lack of social graces for long enough to realise how wild and stubborn I am. I always reply to this by saying that if a man found my browned face, simple dress and lack of conceit so off-putting I would not care, because I would rather remain a spinster all my life than marry a man such as that. Besides, how can I afford to buy the latest fashions on my small allowance? And I certainly don't want to plaster my face with that awful thick white powder so all my freckles won't show like Lady Sabina tells me I should because 'everybody's doing it'.'

'Don't be silly, dear,' said Becky. 'You're perfectly lovely, what with your beautiful mass of flaming red hair and emerald green eyes. As for being short, I think it gives you a sort of sweet elfin charm. You look like a fairy child, you do. No man in his right mind would think otherwise, of that I'm sure.'

'I'd marry you any day,' came a little voice from behind Rowena.

'How gallant of you, young sir,' she replied with a laugh, turning to meet the large round eyes of Becky's five-year-old son, who looked gravely down on her from the open cottage window.

* * * *

By the next day, Lord Cunningham had indeed forgotten about his wife's instructions to 'deal to that insolent girl, because poor dear Sabina is pained beyond words by her cruelty'. Lady Cunningham had gone on to say, as she often did, that 'this is what comes of marrying beneath one's self. I told my sister at the time, again and again, as did all the family: 'it is just a silly, childish infatuation. You must not marry him. Think of the children you might have. They will not be of good breeding, they will turn out bad sister, mark my words!' But being a stubborn, willful girl with no pity for her unfortunate relatives, who would have to live with the shame of such a connection, she completely ignores the pleas of her family, including those of her own mother, and just goes and marries the man regardless. She always did have a wildness about her, it has to be said; right from a young age, just like her daughter'.

The late summer's day had been hot and still. Lulled into

drowsiness by the placid heat, Rowena had left her fears of retribution behind at noon and spent the rest of the day watching the thunder clouds building over the western hills. It was now late afternoon and the dark clouds towered menacingly in the sky like giant fortresses in the air. Lightning flashed from them and the boom of thunder rolled across the valley. All of nature was still and silent, as if waiting in expectation for the rain.

As the thunderstorm came directly overhead, the first heavy drops of rain began to fall, making the leaves of the trees dance franticly up and down as the droplets thudded onto them.

'Rowena, shut the window at once!'

The young woman started at the sound of Lady Cunningham's shrill voice, then dutifully reached out to close the window. 'Yes, your ladyship.'

Lady Cunningham swept up to the window seat her niece sat on and started fussing with the curtains. 'What are you thinking of? Standing there at the open window letting all the rain pour into my solar!'

'Sorry, my lady.'

'I really despair at you, going around with your head in a daze all the time.'

From her vantage point at the second-storey window, Rowena saw Lord Cunningham coming riding up the road in great haste. He did not usually return home from his business in Hartfield until much later in the day. But seeing the thunder clouds building, he had no doubt decided it would be prudent to return home earlier than usual in order to avoid a soaking—although he had left it a little late.

Lord Cunningham roughly hauled his horse to a skidding stop in front of the manor's main door. 'Come here, you lazy scoundrel!' he bellowed, looking around for the servant boy who usually held his horse while he dismounted.

No one came. The rain began to come on more heavily. Lord

Cunningham's long, black brocade houp-pelande robe was rapidly becoming saturated with water.

'When I get my hands on you, boy, I'll give you a thrashing you'll never forget!' he screamed furiously, dismounting from his horse and hurrying inside, leaving the riderless horse standing miserably in the downpour, hindquarters swung into the storm and tail clamped tightly down.

Rowena chuckled quietly to herself. The stable boy had probably gathered his things and left secretly in the night. He would not be the first to have done so and very likely would not be the last. The Cunninghams worked their servants hard, paid them a pittance and showed little mercy.

A short while later, Lord Cunningham made a rare entrance into the upstairs solar where his wife and daughter were seated. He had changed out of his wet robe and into a dry but otherwise very similar robe. He had also put on a more elaborate, less practical cap with a long length of cloth trailing off it, which he wore draped about his shoulders. The cap may have been fancier, but it served its main purpose just the same, which was to hide its wearer's lack of hair. Underneath it, the top half of Lord Cunningham's head was as smooth and hairless as an egg. Despite still being on the right side of fifty, the years had not been kind to his body.

As soon as she noticed the solar's new occupant, Lady Sabina eagerly arose from her chair. 'Father, do look at my new gown!'

The latest purchase from Tailor Hamo's High-Fashion Damsel's Outfitters on Hartfield Market Square was a long-sleeved, high-waisted gold silk affair with a plunging neckline, a long train at the back and a full skirt so long Sabina had to lift it with one hand in order to walk.

Rowena drew herself deeper into the alcove of the window seat. She hated Sabina's constant preening, the way she insisted on showing off every new piece of finery.

Lady Sabina twirled around in the middle of the room so everyone could get a good look. 'Mother says that I look like a princess in it!'

Rowena used to always stop and salivate over the fabulous gowns on display in the front of the tailor's shop every time she passed, and daydream about owning such a marvel. But after accompanying her cousin for a fitting, she had gone off the idea. The way in which the skinny tailor, with his greasy, slicked-back hair, fawned over, flattered and inflated the vanity of his customers gave her the creeps. 'My lady, you look a marvel, a wonder! Queen Genevieve herself would not look better in this Persian silk! May I dare to suggest a little more mink fur? Oh, yes, oh my dearest lady, my poor, humble eyes can hardly bear to look upon such beauty!' he would cry ecstatically, almost falling at his customer's feet in worship.

Any notions Rowena might have had of scaling such giddy heights of fashion were well out of reach anyway. Her wealthy relatives gave her no financial assistance other than not charging her for food and giving her a small room at the top of the house, which required the climbing of three flights of stairs to reach. Rowena only had the money her mother had left her to live on, which was very little as they had been poor. She could only afford simple dresses, not the elaborate, richly embroidered gowns Lady Sabina wore.

Though they didn't seem very practical, Rowena consoled herself. If she were to wear a dress like that, its long hem would get wet and muddy in no time. Doubtless it would be torn on brambles too.

When he had finished dutifully admiring the dress, Lord Cunningham turned to his wife, who sat near the fireplace working on some sewing. 'I was over at the sheriff's castle earlier today. Sir Richard was telling me that his personal clerk, Thomas, has disappeared. When Sir Richard went around to Thomas's lodgings, he found all his money and possessions were still there. No sign of the man though. No one's seen him for days. It's as if he's vanished into thin air. Anyway, Sir Richard was not best pleased. Fair fuming, the man was. Said his clerk was indispensable, can't run the shire without one. But he's yet to find a replacement. Hard to find someone suitable at short notice, I suppose.'

'Indeed, my dear,' responded Lady Cunningham uninterestedly, barely glancing up from her sewing.

But Lady Sabina had been listening to the news with rapt attention. She cocked her head slyly to one side and put a long, slim finger to her blood-red lips.

Rowena stiffened with anticipation. Lady Sabina always did that when a cunning and spiteful plan was brewing in her head.

'Maybe *Rowena* could go over there and fill in as his clerk until a permanent replacement is found.' Lady Sabina shot a venomous look at her cousin. 'It would put all that *learning* she is so proud of to some use for once.'

Rowena caught her breath in horror. She had not met Sir Richard 'The Black Sheriff' Hastings and had no desire to do so. The local peasants said that in the three years he had been there he had proved to be hot-tempered, impatient, cruel and generally best avoided if at all possible. Lady Sabina, on the other hand, was most definitely in lust with Hartfield's sheriff. 'Isn't he simply the most marvellous beast you have ever set eyes on?' Lady Sabina had gushed to her friend Anne, after meeting him last winter. 'Indeed,' Anne had giggled. 'I certainly would not mind being ridden by him.' It had made Rowena cringe, and all Sabina and Anne's obscene giggling only served to make her add 'loved by vain and shallow women' to the list of things she held against Chaucy's sheriff.

Outside, the rain began to fall in torrents, spilling over the gutters and pouring down the windowpanes.

'Hmmm, not such a bad idea…' Lord Cunningham replied thoughtfully, before turning to his wife. 'What think you, my dear?'

'I think that is an excellent notion. It would give her something useful to do instead of wondering about the countryside all day like a wild animal,' Lady Cunningham replied with a disapproving sniff.

'Wouldn't it be unseemly…for a maiden to be with a man unchaperoned?' Rowena faltered from the window seat.

Lady Sabina haughtily tossed her gauze veil over her shoulder with an expert flick of the head. 'I am sure you need not fear on *that* account, Cousin. Sir Richard is a handsome man of good breeding who could have any lady he chooses. It is most unlikely that he would be interested in someone such as *you*.'

Rowena forced her face into a mask of stony calmness. Lady Sabina's cruel words might have stung like a slap in the face, but Rowena was determined that her cousin would not have the satisfaction of a hurt reaction.

Unlike Rowena, Lady Sabina was considered a great beauty among the circles she moved in and drew captivated eyes to her whenever she entered a room. She had a willowy, stick-thin figure with hipbones as sharp as her tongue, and was ridiculously tall. Her skin was as pale as freshly fallen snow, her eyes large and ice-blue, and her sculpted face, with its high, high cheekbones, gave her an arresting, otherworldly appearance.

'That's settled then,' said Lord Cunningham. 'Rowena, you will go over to Eaglestone Castle tomorrow morning to start work. I will send a boy over right away to inform Sir Richard he can expect a new personal clerk.'

The look Lady Sabina rested on her open-mouthed cousin could not have been more snake-like. 'I am *sure* our sheriff will be absolutely *delighted*.'

2.

The Darkness Comprehended it Not

THE HOUSE was silent except for the Cunninghams' servants, who were already beginning the day's work by scrubbing floors and fetching wood for the fires.

'Good morning, Mistress Pedley,' Rowena called out to the cook, who had just come into the kitchen rubbing the sleep out of her eyes.

The plump, pleasant-faced woman stifled a yawn. 'Morning, Mistress Rowena. There are some choice berries in the larder, just picked yesterday. I put a few aside for you.'

Rowena normally had her breakfast in the kitchen, much preferring to eat there than in the great hall with her relatives. But this morning she could not face the thought of eating anything. Her stomach, in sympathy with her state of mind, was feeling rather queasy. 'That's most thoughtful of you, but I think I shall have them when I get home later.'

Mistress Pedley gave a disapproving shake of the head. 'It doesn't do to be setting out of a morning on an empty belly.'

'Normally I would agree most heartily, but if I eat anything right now I feel sure I will be sick before I even get to Eaglestone Castle,' Rowena replied, donning a long bright blue cloak to ward off the chilly morning air.

'Oh yes,' said the cook, 'you are supposed to be going over to Eaglestone Castle to assist that sheriff—what's his name?'

'Sir Richard Hastings.'

'Aye, that's the one. Last night the serving maid was saying she'd heard Lady Sabina talking 'bout it.'

Rowena's small, plump hands froze halfway through their task of fastening the cloak's pin. 'Did Lady Sabina merely mention that I was going over to help out, or was there more?'

'Hildred said her ladyship was laughing 'bout how long you would last. Apparently, Lady Sabina reckoned you'd be lucky to last more than a day before the sheriff gave you the sack, or you decided to give yourself the sack.'

'And why was that?'

'Emmm...Hildred said she heard her Ladyship sayin' that Sir What's-It did not suffer fools gladly.'

The small hands pierced the broach through the thick cloth with a sudden stab and clicked it shut. 'Did she indeed? Well, you can tell Hildred that I shall be over at Eaglestone Castle every day until the sheriff finds a permanent clerk.' And with that, she picked up the bag containing her writing materials and walked out the door.

Eaglestone Castle was a brisk half-hour walk from Stoatley. The small path skirted the edge of several fields before going into the trees at the edge of the woods and emerging near the castle.

Rowena was anxious not to get off to a bad start with Sir Richard, so although she was familiar with the way to Eaglestone, she had set off extra early to make sure she was not late.

She was making good time. The first golden rays of sunlight were only just reaching the tops of the ancient oak, beech and elm trees that surrounded the manor house. The fresh morning air was damp and sweet-smelling after the previous day's rain, and birds made sweet melody all around.

Their songs lifted her spirits and helped to take her mind off

Eaglestone Castle and its dreaded inhabitant. But before long, Rowena could see the tall towers of the castle soaring high above the treetops, their pale grey stones bathed in the golden morning light.

When she emerged out into the meadow where the castle stood, she stopped to gaze up at it in awe. Although it did not occupy a lot of ground, Eaglestone Castle was built to impress. It was the perfect dream castle, the kind the imagination immediately populates with beautiful princesses, enchanted maidens, giants, sorceresses—and evil knights. The castle's three lacily decorated towers, which would have looked more at home on a cathedral than a castle, soared up towards heaven's blue vault with dizzying ambition. Atop the gatehouse flew a large white flag with a heraldic crest depicting a gold-armoured Saint George mounted on a white horse slaying a black, fire-breathing dragon. To complete the picture, each of the three towers was topped with a gaily fluttering flag. There was a white, a black and a red one.

Having feasted her eyes on the marvellous sight, Rowena moved off towards the gateway again. The path ran straight up to the moat that encircled the base of the castle walls and then followed it round to the gateway. Passing it, she wrinkled her nose at the fetid smell rising from the muddy, stagnant water pooled at the bottom of the almost dry moat. It clearly had seen better days.

Rowena crossed the lowered drawbridge that spanned the moat with great trepidation, passed through Eaglestone's giant arched gateway and emerged into a cobbled courtyard.

There was much bustle and noise in the courtyard. Armed men walked purposefully about or stood in groups talking loudly, while others sat polishing swords and armour. The new-comer felt very small and intimidated amongst all this activity and stood wavering, unsure of what to do next.

'Look out!' someone cried in warning.

Rowena suddenly realised the sound of galloping hooves were rapidly approaching from behind. She only just managed to leap aside in time to avoid being run down by three horsemen galloping in at full speed through the gates.

Once Rowena had calmed her frazzled nerves and regained a little composure, she continued across the yard, this time being careful to keep close to the walls. She did not know where the sheriff was to be found, and there were many doors leading inside.

The sensible thing to do would be to ask one of the soldiers. But she felt rather shy so hesitated, scanning the crowd for someone less intimidating. Her eyes quickly alighted on a pleasant-looking youth sitting against one of the walls polishing a chainmail coat. He looked a safe wager.

The maiden carefully scanned the courtyard for horsemen, and finding none, cautiously made her way over. 'Excuse me, young sire. I'm looking for the sheriff; do you know where I might find him?'

Two sharp blue eyes looked up at her. 'Yes, that I do, madam. Carry on across to those steps there.' He pointed at a large flight of stone steps across the courtyard from the gate. 'Go up them and through the big door at the top. There you will find a second flight of stairs. Sir Richard's chambers are at the top.'

The boy's directions were perfect, and Rowena was soon mounting the second flight of spiral stairs that led up what was clearly one of the tall towers. She walked slowly, wishing to delay the dreaded moment when she came face-to-face with Chaucy's most notorious man for as long as possible.

But as she ascended, her curiosity was roused by the sound of voices coming from the top of the stairs. The maiden quickened her pace until she could make out two men talking, then stopped to listen.

One was shouting angrily, ‘You let him get away! We go to all this bloody trouble ferreting out that low-life scum and he gets away because you only had one man covering the back door when you went in!’

‘I’m real sorry ’bout that, Sir Richard,’ replied the other man calmly, ‘but with all due respect, sir, I was a little short-handed, what with you needing all those men to investigate the missing maidens.’

‘This is my fault now, is it? I can’t be everywhere at once!’

There was a loud bang which sounded like a chair being kicked over.

Rowena started in fright and moved up a few more steps, anxious not to miss any of the drama unfolding above.

‘I’ve had enough!’ continued the furious voice, clearly Sir Richard’s. ‘Having that swine Cunningham turning up here yesterday and putting the squeeze on me about his damned money was bad enough, and now this!’

There was another loud bang, which sounded like the chair being kicked across the room.

The heart of the breathlessly listening Rowena thudded uncomfortably. The reports about how bad-tempered Sir Richard was had already been confirmed, and she had not even met the man. She desperately wanted to turn around and walk straight back out.

But no.

Gripping her satchel tightly in her clammy hands, she started to climb upwards. The thought of giving Lady Sabina the satisfaction of getting the better of her was unbearable.

As she neared the top, a well-built man of middle age came out the door and began descending the stairs, his sword jangling at each step as it bumped against his chainmail hauberk. With his weather-beaten, battle-scarred face and burly physique, he looked like a veteran of many campaigns. If his face had not looked so good-humoured, he would have been an intimidating sight.

Her fears that this might be Sir Richard were quickly laid to rest. The sheriff was said to be a younger man of about five and thirty, and his nickname referred not just to his character, but to his appearance also.

The soldier halted when they came opposite each other. 'I must warn you, madam,' he said quietly, 'Sir Richard's not in the best of moods this morning. If your business can wait, I'd leave it for another day.' His voice revealed him to be the man whom the sheriff had been raging at moments before.

She managed a nervous smile. 'I'm Rowena Walden. My uncle, Lord Cunningham, sent me over to help Sir Richard until he can find a new clerk.'

'Oh.' The man looked surprised. 'Sir said someone might be coming to fill in, but I wasn't expecting a—a—'

'A girl?' she suggested quietly.

'Well, to be honest, yes. I'm afraid his language and manners aren't always quite refined enough to be suitable for the presence of a young lady—or any lady, for that matter.'

Rowena was sure her eyes were as round as an owl's by now. 'Oh.'

'By the way, I'm Sergeant-at-Arms Leofwin Gallagher, an old army comrade of the sheriff's and his second in command here at the castle.' He removed his cap, revealing a head of close-cropped, tightly-curling brown hair, and bowed. 'Delighted to make your acquaintance, Mistress Rowena.'

'Likewise, sire,' she replied with a smile, surprised but delighted that the sergeant was so gallant despite his somewhat rough appearance, and curtsied lightly.

'I'd better let you on your way now,' said the warrior. 'You won't want to be late.'

She laughed nervously. 'No, I don't think that would be

good.'

He replaced his cap on his head. 'Well, God be with you.' And with that, he bid her good day and continued on his way.

She wistfully watched the delightful sergeant descend the stairs until he disappeared from sight, then, with a shaky sigh, started her slow ascent again.

Rowena arrived at the top of the stairs to discover the door wide open. She crept up to it as though approaching a wolf's lair and, with baited breath, paused in its arched stone doorway.

A broad-shouldered man was seated at a long wooden table at the far side of the round, sparsely furnished room. His head was bent over the parchment in front of him in concentration. In one large hand he held a quill pen, with the other he was counting out the small pile of gold coins lying on the table. Although Sir Richard was facing Rowena, he did not seem to have noticed her arrival.

She took advantage of the sheriff's absorption in the task before him to scrutinise his appearance. He was dressed in a doublet of shiny black leather, armoured on the chest and shoulders with metal studs arranged in intricate, swirling patterns. The sleeves were tightly laced from elbow to cuff, and the large hands they ended in were long-fingered and surprisingly refined, their pale blue veins standing out delicately in the muted light flooding through the window behind him. His glossy, raven-black hair was parted on the side and cut to fall softly onto the tops of his shoulders. To her great disappointment, she could not see much of his face, it being partly obscured by the locks of stiff black hair which had escaped from behind his ear and fallen forward.

She waited silently for a good while, hoping Sir Richard would notice her presence without her having to risk inciting him with a rude interruption.

Her hopes went unanswered. The slow, painstaking counting

and scratching just went on and on and on. Something would have to be done.

Rowena braced herself. 'Ahem'.

The writing stopped abruptly, and Sir Richard's head lifted with a start to reveal a pale, broodingly handsome face with sculpted, aquiline features, thin lips and dark eyes whose intense gaze seemed to pierce right through her. 'What do you want?' he growled.

Her courage began to desert her under Sir Richard's cold, questioning stare. 'Good day, sir. I—I—am Rowena Walden, my uncle, Lord Cunningham, sent me,' she managed to stammer. 'He said that you—needed a clerk.'

There was a sudden screech of quill on parchment as the hand holding it gave an involuntary jerk. But the stony, thin-lipped expression did not betray any of its wearer's emotions. 'Did he indeed?'

'Yes,' she replied a little more forcefully, beginning to get annoyed by Sir Richard's casual insolence.

He waved his leather-clad arm in the direction of a small table to his right, which was covered with large piles of parchment. 'There's your table.' He swept back the stray locks of hair. 'My previous clerk was a messy bastard, but he seemed to get the job done.'

And with that he returned to counting the money and scratching down the results on the parchment in front of him, taking no further heed of her.

Rowena went over to the small, rough-looking table and surveyed its piles with dismay. Self-consciously, she took off her cloak and, in the absence of any suitable furniture or hook, was forced to drop it on the floor.

After much deliberation the previous night, she had finally settled on wearing a long-sleeved bright green (or at least it used to be) gown with a figure-hugging bodice, tightly laced at the front. The style was flattering, if unfashionable, but the condition of it left much to be desired. Despite spending an hour the night before sewing together the tears in it with her smallest, most careful stitches, she was painfully aware of how dowdy she must look to someone as nicely dressed as Sir Richard.

But never mind. She was wanted for her skills and intelligence, not as a nice ornament. And surely she did not look uglier than his last clerk…

The castle's newest clerk sat down on the miserable wooden stool provided and began sifting through the papers in increasing panic. Most of them looked like payment demands, lists of expenses and account records. Rowena hadn't the faintest idea what to do with any of them.

She watched the sheriff out of the corner of her eye whilst trying to look as though she was busily occupied with the papers in front of her. With puzzlement, she noted that Sir Richard seemed to be counting the same pile of money over and over, and each time scratching down the result with a surprisingly shaky hand. Then he would frown blackly at the piece of parchment before beginning the laborious counting all over again. The cautiously watching maiden itched to offer the services of her able mathematical mind to the sheriff, but fear gagged her.

Finally, he finished counting the money and put it away in the small rosewood chest sitting on his table. Then he took out a number of scrolls and slowly got to his feet.

Her relief that he was finally doing something was short-lived. Not only did he have an unnerving stare and an insolent manner, which was bad enough, but now that he was standing he revealed himself to be tall—*very* tall. She hated the way that nearly everyone was able to look down on her. And Sir Richard would tower, absolutely *tower*, over her.

As the sheriff strode over to his new clerk, her relief was further tainted by the unnerving sight of an exceedingly large sword protruding from the long, intricately engraved leather and steel scabbard belted to his waist.

Rowena gave a huff of annoyance. Why in God's name did a sheriff, or any man for that matter, need to carry around an evil-looking thing like that in peacetime? It might be appropriate for a fully armed knight on the battlefield, but for anyone else to do so really was overkill.

Sir Richard stopped in front of the seated woman, who looked up at him nervously, desperately hoping he was going to give her a task that she could actually do.

'Read out these letters to me and take down the replies I dictate to you,' he said sullenly, putting the scrolls down in front of her.

While she read out the letters, Sir Richard paced up and down the room. From the small window that looked out over the town of Hartfield, across the middle of the room to his writing table and back again, the spurs strapped to his black, leather, mid-thigh length riding boots jingling as he walked.

The change of position gave Rowena a good view of his side profile. It proved to be just as arresting as the front. The forehead was noble and the long, aquiline nose truly magnificent.

So far the reports of him had turned out to be most accurate. He was indeed deeply handsome, deeply offensive and disturbingly sinister. His manner, his appearance, his brooding glare; it was as though he was made of fire and ice. And everyone knows what happens when you combine the two: a heck of a lot of steam arises and obscures everything.

Rowena pulled her eyes off him and forced them back onto the parchment before her. The first few letters were in Latin, but she saw that the remainder were in English. Why did the sheriff not read them himself?

'I have trouble reading and writing, alright! The letters all seem to jumble together on the page,' he snapped, in response to the look of surprise which she had been unable to conceal. He paused in front of the window for a moment and gazed bleakly out, a faraway look crossing his face. 'I never was much good at clever or cultured pursuits, as my father never tired of telling me. That bastard he hired to tutor me never did manage to beat much learning into me, hard as he tried,' he added grimly.

'Oh, I was not passing judgement on you, Sir Richard!' she said hastily, regretting her reaction.

'I would hope not,' he growled, suddenly turning away from the window. 'It's no business of a clerk to be going around passing judgement on people.'

He seemed to snap out of his thoughts of the past as if he greatly regretted having brought them to mind, and continued pacing up and down like a caged beast.

'Of course not, Sir Richard,' she replied meekly, and proceeded to read out the letters dutifully.

But inside she was quietly fuming at the insult.

.3.

Hell, Heaven and Uncertainty are Visited

ROWENA kept close to the walls, anxious to avoid coming as close to ending up as road-kill as she had when passing through the castle gates the first time. She had spent every day for the past two weeks at Eaglestone except for Sundays, and this morning had set off for Eaglestone at sunrise like she usually did.

For once they would not be expecting her. She had told Sir Richard she would not be coming this day because Lord Cunningham's sister and nephew were visiting, and her aunt had insisted Rowena be there. But Rowena had been playing a rough game of tag with her young cousin soon after he and his mother had arrived the previous evening when, right in front of Lady Cunningham and the lad's very refined mother, the both of them had fallen into the muddy pool at the bottom of the meadow behind Stoatley Manor.

The watching ladies had been so horrified by the state of their relatives when they emerged from the filthy water that, as soon as Master Eckersley had been scrubbed down by his nurse and smacked around the ear by his mother, he had been sent straight up to bed without his supper. As for Rowena, she had been ordered not to go anywhere near young Eckersley ever again, and Lady Cunningham had told her in no uncertain terms to keep out of sight and hearing for the remainder of her relatives' two-day visit.

This was just fine by her. Poor Eckersley seemed a nice lad, but his mother was a mean-spirited woman of very little brain who spent all her time gossiping and preening like a peacock.

'Good day, Rowena,' called a young soldier as she neared the castle's main door.

The garrison of soldiers stationed at the castle seemed to be much taken with their sheriff's new clerk. Often she was waylaid talking to them when going about her business around the castle.

'Greetings,' she said brightly. 'How is everything with you this morning, Will?'

'Good, but all the better for seeing you, as always,' he replied with a grin.

She gave him a playful shove. 'Stop it! I know you are only flattering me because you are hoping I'll increase the food rations again.'

'How can you be so cruel!' he cried, dramatically clapping his hand to his breast in anguish. 'You're an angel. You know how much we all love you. We worship the very ground you walk on.' He bowed low with much flourish, his hand still on his chest.

'Your words do me great honour, sire, but your heart is actually on the other side,' she replied laughingly, before continuing on her way up to the sheriff's office.

As she neared Sir Richard's public chamber, the sound of his and Gallagher's voices drifted out through the open door. 'That swine is up to something, I'm sure of it,' Sir Richard was saying. 'I can't comprehend any man doing such a thing without a reason. It must be a trap; he'll be hoping I will singe my wings on the flame he has so carefully placed in my way.'

'But why would he want to do that?' asked Gallagher.

'So he can squeeze me harder, that's why!'

'Surely not, sir. I mean, she hardly seems to be the kind.'

'That may well be, but she's bound to be under his control.

She is likely reporting my every move back to that loathsome dog as we speak.'

'Listen to me, sir; you can't get rid of her. He will see it as an insult, and if he blames her instead it will hardly be fair on the poor maid. You see the way they treat her.'

'I suppose you'rc right, old friend. God's bone's, sometimes I think the Devil is overseeing my torment personally! I wish I could find a way of getting rid of her...'

Rowena had been listening to this intense exchange as she climbed up towards the open doorway. She had not thought their subject matter sensitive until the last few sentences, when suddenly she realised their subject was almost certainly herself.

She stopped just as she reached the open door. Things were already awkward enough. Had they noticed? No. Perhaps it would be prudent to just quietly back out...

But as she took a step back, there was a loud creak as the floorboard her foot pressed onto let out a groan of protest. Four eyes were fixed on her in an instant.

Sir Richard could not have looked more horrified if he had been faced by his new clerk's ghost rather than her living body. 'What the hell are you doing here?' he gasped.

'I—I work here...'

'But you said you could not come in today!'

'Yes, but that was before I tumbled into a stagnant pond with my visiting cousin.'

Sir Richard's mouth opened as though he was about to speak, then silently closed again.

Rowena came into the room and put her satchel down on her table. 'My aunt changed her mind about my staying home after that, so I'm afraid you are going to be burdened with my presence instead.'

Her final words made the men exchange tense glances. The sergeant-at-arms' look was reproachful, while Sir Richard's was one of raw stress.

After a tense few moments during which none of the three could decide what to do next, the sheriff suddenly picked up the indigo blue cloak hanging over his chair and started putting it on as he strode towards the doorway. 'I just saw them bringing in a suspect, so I'm going down to the dungeons to question the felon—and Gallagher, get about your work. The crown does not pay you to stand around gawping at the castle floorboards.'

'Yes, Sir Richard,' Gallagher replied with a sigh, moving off after the sheriff.

As Sir Richard passed Rowena, she almost gagged at the wave of heavy, spicy, musky perfume which engulfed her. 'Rowena, I will attend to any letters later.'

'Of course, Sir Richard,' she managed to splutter.

But he seemed oblivious to her unfavourable reaction, and the sound of his jingling spurs and clattering sword was soon receding down the stairs.

After the knight and his deputy had left, Rowena sat staring silently at the cold, bare stone wall opposite for a long time.

So that was how it stood. Even though he was paying her the princely sum of absolutely nothing, her employer wanted rid of her. She had spent endless days scratching away on parchments, making sense of ridiculously chaotic financial records, and adding up lengthy expense lists until her head spun and her eyes ached. But she had done it willingly, happy in the belief that she was doing something useful for once instead of merely being the burden her relatives were forever complaining about. The knowledge that Gallagher pitied her was almost more painful than being thought a spy and a nuisance by Sir Richard.

Rowena smiled grimly. At least Lady Sabina's spiteful plan had failed. The silly cow had rather underestimated her father's influence. A poor knight could hardly be expected to send packing an underling personally provided to him by the most wealthy and powerful lord in the shire.

And the underling was not going to step down willingly. Sir Richard's efforts to freeze her into submission with his curt, frosty manner and wolfish glare only made her more determined to stay. All of these dust-covered, ink-blotted account records held a mystery, and she was determined to discover it.

'Sir Richard wants you to come down to the dungeons at once,' announced a young soldier who had just stuck his head around the door. 'He said to tell you to bring your writing things with you.'

'Did he say why?'

'I think he wants you to write some things down, milady.'

She started gathering quill, ink and parchment and putting them in her bag. 'Yes, I had guessed as much. *What* does he want me to write down?'

The soldier marched back out while she hurried along behind. 'He's been questioning some thief down there, so he probably wants you to take down some notes or something.'

Rowena had to skip down the stairs two steps at a time in order to keep up with his long stride. 'I see.'

But she did not see. As she tripped hastily along, Rowena still wondered why she was suddenly required in the dungeons. They were one of the few parts of the castle where she had not yet been and was yet to feel any desire to go.

The soldier led her down a long corridor and descended another flight of stone steps. As she reached the bottom, she was hit by an overpowering musty, damp stench of decay that had her fumbling for her handkerchief in the half-light, and once it was located, firmly holding it to her nose.

As her eyes adjusted to the lack of light, she saw that she was being led along a wide, subterranean vault. Large pillars spaced at regular intervals held up its arched roof, from which copious amounts of water dripped and trickled down onto the slimy, moss-covered stone floor.

Rowena felt like she had just entered some eerie underworld. The only sounds disturbing the deathly stillness were the ghostly echo of her and the soldier's footsteps, and the steady drip-drip of water droplets falling from the roof and landing in the puddles on the floor. She hugged herself in an effort to stop shivering. The sudden change from the warm, sunny day above to this cold, damp, subterranean world had given her the chills, and she half-expected some ghoul or demon to step out from behind a pillar at any moment.

When they were about halfway along the vault, a sudden scuffling noise broke out in a dark corner.

She stopped abruptly. 'What's that?'

But before the young man-at-arms could answer, the largest rat Rowena had ever seen scurried across the ground in front of them. Eaglestone's newest member of staff shrieked in fright and snatched up the hem of her dress, fearing the creature might think it a good place to hide.

The soldier took her firmly by the elbow and guided her onwards across the slippery flagstones. 'Don't worry, milady. The place is full of the vermin, but they're harmless enough—unless you are sleeping.'

Still casting wary glances about her, she let him shunt her along to the barred metal gate at the end of the vault. There he stopped, produced a large key, unlocked the gate with a loud click, and held it open for her.

She entered and found herself in a narrow passageway with a number of doors leading off it at regular intervals. The gate was swung shut and locked behind her, then the soldier escorted her to the one open door, from whence a weak light shone out.

'If you could just step in here, milady,' he instructed her.

She hesitated for a moment, dreading what she might find within, but then stepped reluctantly inside after the soldier.

The only light in the tiny stone cell came from a single flickering torch mounted on the wall. The scene it illuminated confirmed her worst fears. Sir Richard was seated at a rickety table glowering across at a terrified boy seated on the opposite side. The youth looked like he had taken a beating. He had a black eye, his face was smeared with blood and more ran down from his nose and onto his rough sackcloth jerkin.

Without removing his menacing stare from the trembling lad, Sir Richard pulled an upturned wooden crate to the table. 'Sit down and record the confession of this felon,' he ordered his new clerk.

But Rowena was rooted to the spot. She had heard of the rough treatment felons received at the hands of 'The Black Sheriff' often enough not to doubt it was true, yet she still felt disappointed. Sir Richard was surely better than this—or was it yet another of the animal's accursed ploys?

'Tell this lady what you told me,' the sheriff growled at the bloodied youth.

The prisoner lifted his blood-smeared face and looked up at Rowena with pleading eyes. 'Please, I'm innocent. I didn't do nothing. I didn't steal that bread.'

Sir Richard slammed his fist down on the table with a sudden violence that made his young clerk almost drop her satchel in fright. 'You just told me that you did!'

The miserable lad wiped the thick blood from his mouth with the back of his sleeve. 'I thought you was going to kill me if I didn't confess.'

At this, the sheriff jumped to his feet. Cringing near the door, Rowena clapped her hands over her ears at the loud bang of his stool hitting the floor.

The furious sheriff reached across the table and grabbed the lad by the collar with such force that he was lifted clean out of his seat. 'You're damn right I will!'

‘Sir Richard, let the boy go, I’m begging you!’ Rowena gasped, barely able to keep from turning away at the sight of such violence.

But Sir Richard ignored her. He gave the terrified boy a violent jerk and pulled him closer until their faces nearly touched. ‘Stop wasting my time, you thieving scoundrel!’

The prisoner winced at the shower of spittle hitting his face, but kept his mouth firmly shut.

‘Stop this! I can’t bear it, I can’t bear it!’ Rowena cried from the safety of the doorway, loath to let any scheming, devilish knight get between her and the exit.

She could just imagine it. So sorry about your niece, Lord Cunningham…don’t know how she managed to fall down that bottomless pit in the dungeons…must have wondered down there…a sheriff’s castle is really no place for a young girl…

Sir Richard took no notice of Rowena. ‘You confessed to this crime, so stop wasting my time!’ he shouted in the lad’s face.

The young clerk took a few desperately reluctant steps towards the enraged knight. ‘Stop. Please, please stop!’

The sheriff still took no notice.

‘Sir Richard, if you don’t stop trying to strangle that poor boy I’ll throw my inkpot at your head!’

Nothing.

The tin inkpot was aimed and sent on its way. It hit its target a ringing blow on the side of the head before clattering onto the stone floor.

Still nothing.

So his heart was not the only thing that was made of stone. She sunk gloomily onto the crate Sir Richard had drawn up to the table earlier. ‘I wish I had stayed in Cornwall. Nobody told me Hartfield was the address of the Seven Deadly Sins. Pennreth might have been a humble place, but at least there weren’t all these so-called ‘gentry’ who are just pagan swine!’

This finally got Sir Richard's attention. He loosened his grip and let the petrified boy fall back down. Then he turned his steely gaze towards the only woman on Eaglestone's clerical staff. The reflection of the flickering orange torch flames glittered in his dark eyes. 'My mistake, Mistress Rowena. I ought to have realised that a mere *girl* would not be able to handle this kind of work without becoming soft and sentimental.'

He spat the words out with a kind of casual insolence that seemed to say *I can't be bothered wasting insults on you when it is so obvious*. It incensed her. That spiteful cousin had really known what she was doing. Why go to the trouble of insulting someone yourself when you can farm the task out?

Rowena got to her feet, stalked up to her glowering overlord with the indignant air of an offended cat and halted in front of him. 'How do you know he is guilty? He might be telling the truth when he says he didn't do it.'

The sheriff's glittering dark eyes unflinchingly met the righteous challenge glaring up at him. 'Telling the truth? Hah! Not likely. That entire family are a pack of liars. His father was a felon if ever there was one. He was hanged by my predecessor four summers ago. He should have met his end on the gallows much sooner by rights, but the old fool had trouble making anything stick to that slippery knave.'

She stood on tiptoe in an effort to even out her serious height disadvantage a little. 'You can't go about beating people to a pulp just because they're related to convicted felons!'

He stretched himself up to his full height and more than killed off her gain. 'I'm telling you, the lad's guilty as sin.' The dark knight was as calm as an ice-covered pool now. 'This thieving knave deserved everything he got.'

She looked her adversary up and down distastefully. 'How can you say such things? Unless you behave with fairness and compassion, you're no better than the lowest criminal!'

The air of shock in the room was almost palpable. Sir Richard and the man-at-arms who had escorted Rowena down stared at her in silence. No one *ever* challenged the sheriff like that. They were far too in awe of his highly trained physical power and air of barely suppressed violence. But the fresh-faced country maid had already discovered the chink in Sir Richard's armour, and he knew it.

The plain fact of the matter was that, despite his hot temper and often morose attitude, Sir Richard was a man of honour in one respect. He abhorred any man who raised a hand against a woman, and Rowena felt confident he would not do her any violence, no matter how furious he was.

For what seemed an eternity, the two broad-shouldered warriors just stared at the young woman. And then stared some more.

Feeling desperately uncomfortable, Rowena looked down at her hands and cleared her throat.

The noise seemed to make Sir Richard recover a little from his stunned silence, although he still looked as if he needed more time to decide what he thought of the highly unexpected event. 'Ahem, so I take it you won't write down a confession for this—this—this *suspect* to sign?'

'Yes, you are correct.'

'What am I supposed to do now then? Let the crime go unpunished?' demanded the sheriff, through clenched teeth.

'Perhaps we could question him. If he did not do it, he might know who did.'

Sir Richard had a look of forced calmness about him as he picked the stool up from the floor and sat down. 'Very well, we shall try your way—though without the threat of a beating we'll never get anything out of the boy.'

Rowena looked earnestly across at the boy. 'You do know who did it, don't you?'

He faced her with a look of steely determination on his bruised and bloodied face. 'I won't tell you who it is 'cause then you'll punish them and it'll all be my fault 'cause I snitched on them.'

'I told—' began the sheriff, but was silenced by a kick in the shin delivered by a soft-shoed little foot.

Rowena could see the lad was not going to say anymore. She did not blame him for that or for any food he may have stolen. A starving pauper taking food was committing an act of self-preservation, not a felony.

She turned to the gloating Sir Richard. 'They were starving; look how thin the poor lad is. Surely you could just let him go? It's only a bit of bread, for goodness sake!'

The knight refused to look her in the eye. He bit his lip in silent reluctance, clearly loath to give in.

She placed a hand on his cheek and manually turned the scowling face towards her. 'Have you no pity in your heart?'

He nearly fell off his stool in shock at the unexpectedly bold move. 'If I just—just, God, what was I saying? Oh yes—ignore petty crime they'll get bolder! Next thing you know he'll be mugging innocent citizens at knife point.' He was getting into his stride again. 'I have to be seen to be harsh on felons!'

She kept her hand in place and smiled sweetly at him. 'If you sheriffs did not extort such high taxes and go around hanging families' only breadwinner, then poor people would not have to steal to keep from starving.'

He pushed his seat back until he was out of her reach and crossed his arms defensively. 'I only collect the taxes that I'm told to. It's part of my job to collect the king's taxes!'

'I have seen the figures,' she replied coolly. 'I know you are charging a higher tax rate than you ought to and keeping the extra money for yourself. They say all sheriffs are corrupt, and you are clearly no different.' Rowena calmly looked him in the eye. 'I'm not stupid. I know all about your finances, right down to the last penny.'

Sir Richard rose from his seat in dangerously tense silence and beckoned to her. 'A word—outside.'

She silently got up and followed him out.

It just had to be said. On her very first day she had noticed the horrifying amounts of money he was not so much skimming off as pouring off. His previous clerk had written it all down in the none-official account records he kept alongside the official one. She had hardly been able to believe Sir Richard did not know about this when he and his old clerk had so clearly been in league together on the fraud.

As soon as they were in the privacy of the passageway, the sheriff turned abruptly to face her. 'Someone's blackmailing me, extorting money from me. It's the only way I can raise the money to pay them, alright.' He spoke in a harsh whisper, and although Sir Richard's expression was veiled by the darkness, she could hear the desperation in his voice.

'Who are these villains who extort your money?'

'That's none of your damn business!' came the harsh reply. 'And you mustn't tell anyone about this. If it gets out that I have been charging too much tax, there'll be trouble!' As he spoke, Sir Richard turned his face towards the light coming from the doorway. Stress was written all over it.

She sighed. His position on this was non-negotiable, of that there was no doubt. 'Very well, I swear by the blood of Our Saviour that I will tell no one.'

This seemed to satisfy him, although not entirely. 'What about the lad? He heard what you said—you should have thought about that before you blurted it out!'

'Perhaps if you agreed to release the poor boy and drop all further inquiries he might promise to keep quiet?'

'It does not look like I have any choice in the matter,' he replied sullenly.

While the sheriff skulked in the passageway, his clerk hurried back into the cell. 'Soldier, get the torch!' she ordered a very surprised man-at-arms. 'We are letting this boy go, for he is innocent.'

Blinking uncertainly in the face of this unprecedented reversal, the man did as he was told, though not with his usual enthusiasm.

With a steadying hand firmly on the rather shaky boy's arm, Rowena followed Sir Richard and the torch-carrying soldier along the damp, gloomy passage. When they had climbed the stone steps and finally emerged blinkingly into the sunlight, Rowena breathed in the fresh air gratefully.

'Ah, there you are, sire!' said Sergeant Gallagher, coming down the stairs that led to the sheriff's chambers. 'I was about to go down to the dungeons to look for you.' When the sergeant came closer, he did not seem surprised to see the bruised, blood-smeared boy. He grimaced sympathetically at the youth. 'Ouch, that doesn't look too good.'

'It doesn't feel too good neither,' the miserable victim replied.

Gallagher grinned casually at Sir Richard. 'Walked into a door, did he?'

Sir Richard clenched his fist. 'Unless you've got something useful to say, Gallagher, just keep your damn mouth shut!'

The sergeant ignored Sir Richard. 'We really ought to take the lad to a healer.'

'I was thinking the same thing myself,' said Rowena. 'I have heard that there is a physician down in the town?'

'There is indeed,' Sir Richard muttered sourly. 'The man's a quack. I wouldn't go near the damn weasel even if I was dying, because the only thing I'd achieve by doing that would be to hasten my own death.'

'He's not far wrong there, madam. I wouldn't go to the man either,' said the sergeant. 'Many of the country folk go to a wise herbalist named Brother Jacob. He is a hermit-monk who lives in a cottage in the forest not far from here, and is spoken of very highly by all who know him. I can help you take the lad there, if you wish.'

Still feeling a little annoyed at Gallagher's seemingly casual attitude towards Sir Richard's behaviour, Rowena looked at him solemnly. 'I wish it, Sergeant.'

Once they were out of the castle, Sergeant Gallagher led Rowena and the lad along a twisting, narrow path that took them deeper and deeper into the forest until finally, just when Rowena was beginning to think that they were lost, the path suddenly opened out into a small clearing.

In the centre of the clearing stood a little stone cottage surrounded by beautifully tended garden beds filled with a colourful riot of herbs and flowers of every description, interspersed by narrow paths of yellow lime sand. The cottage had a steeply gabled roof covered by a thick layer of thatch and wooden shutters flanking the small windows on either side of the door.

The little home seemed most carefully and lovingly kept. It was immaculately clean, with not a thing out of place or in need of repair, while from the chimney a wisp of grey smoke curled gracefully into the air. A gentle breath of wind rippled through the garden, making the red daisies dance gaily on their tall, thin stems and sending a wave of sweetly scented air wafting deliciously over Rowena.

'How wonderful!' she exclaimed, stopping to savour the moment. 'And look at all the gay butterflies and busily humming little bees. Oh—and look at that fat fellow!' She laughed in delight at the sight of a very large bumblebee trying to squeeze into a nasturtium flower but failing on account of his size.

The battle-scarred soldier smiled indulgently. 'Aye, 'tis a pretty sight, to be sure.'

'That's all very well,' came the miserable voice of the lad from behind, 'but if your face was so swollen you could 'ardly see and you felt like you'd just been trampled by a herd of crazed oxen, you wouldn't care neither.'

Rowena, in her delight, had almost forgotten why she was there. But at this reminder, she started to walk towards the cottage once more.

When they reached the door, they found it was open. Rowena could see a figure clad in a pale grey monk's habit inside, kneeling on the floor in deep prayer before a small wooden crucifix hanging on the wall in front of him. He had his back to them and did not seem to have noticed their arrival. Reluctant to disturb him, the red-haired maiden paused on the doorstep.

But Gallagher stepped forward and knocked gently. 'Brother Jacob,' he called softly to the devoutly kneeling figure.

At this, the monk hastily crossed himself and rose to his feet. When he turned to face them, Rowena observed that he was a fairly short man of about sixty, round but not fat, with short, sandy-coloured hair and an almost child-like face which shone with gentle benevolence and simple good humour.

'You be welcome, friends, you be welcome! Come in,' he invited them warmly.

Upon stepping inside, Rowena was even more overcome with wonder than when she had seen the cottage from the outside. The shelves lining the walls were filled with earthenware pots and jars, and glass bottles of all shapes and sizes. From the roof-beams hung many bunches of drying herbs. There was a large wooden table in the centre of the room upon which sat a stone pestle and mortar, many pewter bowls, a small set of scales, a few lumps of golden beeswax, and scattered about the table were herbs and plants of every kind. There were long stalks of rosemary, piles of dried blue lavender flowers, straw-coloured chamomile flowers, pale silver southernwood leaves, fat red rosehips, fresh peppermint, and many more plants that she could not name.

While Rowena was still staring in wonder at the room's many unusual contents, Brother Jacob cast a professional eye over the boy's injuries. 'Sergeant, it looks like you have brought a patient to see me.' He smiled kindly at the lad. 'Come and take a seat over here, my son.'

Once his patient was seated, Brother Jacob got out a pewter bowl and set it down on the table. Then he started searching the shelves. 'Hmmm, now where did I put it...I'm sure it's here somewhere...' After searching through several shelves, he finally seized a small blue glass bottle with a cry of 'Ah, there you are!'

He pulled out the cork stopper and poured a measure of liquid into the bowl, then filled the rest of the bowl with water from the iron pot that simmered gently over a little fire in the corner.

As he was stirring the mix, Brother Jacob looked over to Sergeant Gallagher. 'Have you and your men been running down peasants again? Or perhaps he *slipped* on the cell floor?'

Although his tone was gravely serious, Rowena detected an impish twinkle in Brother Jacob's eyes.

'Be fair, brother!' Gallagher protested good-humouredly. 'That was just the once, and the fool ran out right in front of the sheriff's horse.'

Brother Jacob began washing the boy's face with the liquid he had prepared. 'So he 'slipped', did he?'

'Yes, well,' Sergeant Gallagher replied somewhat uncomfortably, 'he wasn't very talkative, so Sir Richard got a little impatient.'

There was no doubting Gallagher's loyalty to his comrade.

'Sir Richard does seem rather fond of walking on the dark side,' sighed the monk. 'Still, the good Lord loves all of his flock, even those whose hearts are filled with sin, for they need his love and forgiveness most of all.'

'Amen to that, brother,' said Gallagher. 'He is not a bad man at heart, just one who has lost his way a little.'

Brother Jacob smiled indulgently, although there was a definite hint of irony in his raised eyebrows. 'Yes indeed. Let us hope that he finds his way back onto the path of righteousness before too many more patients come my way.' He turned his attention onto Rowena, who had been hanging back, feeling a little shy in this wondrously strange place. While his soft grey eyes shone with a gentle kindness, their intense gaze seemed to miss nothing. 'Sergeant, you have not introduced your young friend.'

'Oh, do forgive me. This is Mistress Rowena Walden. She has been filling in as Sir Richard's clerk.'

Brother Jacob gave a courteous nod. 'Nice to finally make your acquaintance, Mistress Rowena.'

Rowena came forward and bobbed. 'I am honoured to meet you, brother.'

'That last clerk, now he was a put-upon looking fellow if ever I saw one. He looked as though he was carrying the whole world about on his back. Have you been getting on all right? Sir Richard has been acting in a manner befitting his station, I hope?'

'I had a little trouble finding my way around the castle at first, but all the soldiers were very kind, and as for Sir Richard, he is—he is just as I expected him to be.'

The monk had finished cleaning the lad's cuts and was now carefully dabbing on some ointment. 'One does not tame the wolf by running from its lair.'

Rowena smiled grimly. 'Quite so.'

'There you are, all done!' proclaimed Brother Jacob, wiping his hands with a cloth. 'Now, my son, you will keep out of trouble and stay away from the sheriff in future, won't you?'

'I'll try, brother,' the lad mumbled.

'If you and your family are ever starving, go to the abbey. Father Peter always gives alms to the poor.'

‘Thank you, brother.’

‘You are welcome, my son. It’s the least I can do.’

* * * *

‘Expenses, expenses and more bloody expenses,’ Sir Richard growled, gloomily sifting through the morning’s stack of payment demands piled on Rowena’s table. ‘Sometimes I marvel that I manage to pay the men at all.’

Rowena took out a few goose-quills. ‘I’ll make it work somehow. Last week we did not have enough to pay everyone, but I succeeded in talking that blacksmith out of charging you interest on the money you owe for shoeing the horses. I mean, twenty percent, that’s just daylight robbery!’

‘Damn weasel, I’d give him a good hiding if it wasn’t for the fact that he’d then refuse to shoe our horses, leaving me in even more you-know-what…’

Rowena turned her attention away from the quills she was cutting to a point with a small knife, and looked earnestly across at Sir Richard. ‘Why won’t you tell me who is blackmailing you? How can I help you if I don’t know who it is?’

He sunk despairingly into Rowena’s chair. ‘If he found out that I had told someone, there’d be hell to pay.’

‘I will not tell a soul; as God is God you have my word!’

‘I’d really rather not say. After all, as you said, we are getting by.’

She flung the quill pens down on the table in exasperation. ‘This man is bleeding you dry! You might just be managing to pay the weekly expenses, but the roof on the west tower needs fixing, the men need new weapons, and God only knows how you’ll be able to afford the work the moat so desperately needs.

It's so silted up that during a dry spell a man could walk right across and barely get his feet wet!'

Sir Richard nervously ran his fingers through his hair. 'Yes Rowena, I know.'

She opened the account book lying on the table in front of him. 'Look at all this money you're paying to your blackmailer. Ten thousand pounds,' she tapped an insistent ink-stained finger on the figure, 'in the last month alone!'

He stared grimly at the numbers. 'Good God.'

'You have to do something about it before you are ruined. Maybe you could sell off something?'

'I have told you before, there's nothing I can do except keep paying him off. I've already sold everything I can. I sold the small manor and estate near Willowmead that I bought when I came here three years ago, and the valuable suit of armour I still had from my jousting days.'

'But you don't have the money to keep paying. Unless,' she fixed a steely look on him, 'you are planning on marrying a rich lady? There seem to be plenty of foolish, empty-headed young damsels about who would willingly marry you tomorrow.'

'I assure you, I have no intention of marrying. But it's no matter; I'll just increase the taxes.'

Rowena stomped her foot in annoyance. 'Just increase the taxes? You've already increased the tax rate twice in the past year! The poor people are nearly starving as it is!' She punctuated this by slamming the account book shut and angrily turning away from him.

But as she did so, there was a loud clatter.

She snapped her eyes down. The goblet which had been sitting on the table was now lying on its side and water was spilling across the rough boards and pouring through the cracks.

There was a screech as Sir Richard hastily pushed his chair back.

Rowena clapped her hand to her mouth in horror. Most of the water had spilled into his lap. That dress, with its stupid long sleeves, might be pretty, but it certainly wasn't very practical. She was forever swiping things over with them.

'Good gracious, I'm so sorry!' she cried, pulling her handkerchief out of her pocket. 'Let me mop that up. I'm just so clumsy, always knocking things over and bumping into things. I don't know how I do it!'

The sheriff rolled his eyes in exasperation, but remained seated. He had resigned himself to Rowena's regular outbreaks of clumsiness two weeks ago.

In a fluster, she bent down and started franticly mopping at the wet spill on Sir Richard's thigh. Luckily most of the water had run off, as there was hardly any gap between his black leather doublet and tall riding boots.

Calming down a little, Rowena suddenly became aware of how close she was to him. Her hair was falling onto his shoulder, the smell of leather and his perfume filled her nose, and she could feel his hot breath on her cheek.

She paused abruptly and looked at him. She expected him to be angry with her, but he didn't look angry. Far from it—he was enjoying it!

She started back in shock and only just managed to avoid tripping over the end of his sword.

With a dark smirk playing on his lips, Sir Richard indicated a few remaining droplets. 'You've missed a bit just there.'

Rowena threw the handkerchief at him from a safe distance. 'Do it yourself.'

.4.

Pride Takes a Fall

SITTING on the bench against the outside wall of Becky's cottage later that day, Rowena put a dark, juicy raspberry into her mouth. Despite the bramble scratches on her arms, she was glad she had stopped on the way over to pick berries from the heavily laden brambles growing beside the path.

She leaned comfortably back against the wall and gave a sigh of contentment, enjoying the warmth of the late afternoon sunshine on her shoulders and the soft breeze playing in her hair. It was a lovely time of day. With the fierce heat of midday now but a memory, the air felt softer and mellower, and the light was less harsh. The first tinge of the glorious colours of autumn to come tinted a leaf here and there, and the golden wheat standing in the fields adjacent to the road was now fully ripe, its fat ears filled with the sun's goodness.

'The harvest should be starting any day now,' she said to Becky, who sat beside her.

'Yes, and what with all this rain we've been having, we need to get it in quick, before it spoils.' The blonde woman furrowed her brow anxiously. 'But all our men are still busy bringing in his lordship's grain. Us humble folk always have to wait until they've finished the harvest on the Stoatley lands before we have the time to bring in our own crops.'

'Is that where Durwin and the older boys are?'

'Aye. We usually all help with the harvest, but this year I'm stuck at home looking after the little ones. The girl who normally minds them while I'm out in the fields came down with something nasty and had to take to her bed.'

'Yes, you are a troublesome little man, aren't you?' Rowena cooed at baby James, holding him by his tiny hands and bouncing him on her knee. The delighted child gurgled happily back at her. 'Isn't he growing well? Every time I see him he seems to have doubled in size.'

'He is indeed, thanks to all the food you keep bringing us.'

'Ow!' cried Rowena, her attention diverted from the baby in her lap to his four-year-old brother, who, having eaten his fill of the berries and smeared a great deal of their purple juice onto his face in the process, had started experimentally pulling at her hair.

The little boy dropped the lock of tightly-curling red hair he held in his purple-stained little hand and gazed tentatively at the hair's owner in wide-eyed innocence.

'Peter, why don't you go and pick some marigolds? I will show you how to make a garland for your mother's hair with them.'

He nodded eagerly and skipped off to seek the bright orange flowers amongst the colourful jumble of plants growing around the cottage, many of them humble wild plants that had been collected from the surrounding countryside.

With peace reigning once again, Becky turned back to Rowena. 'You are looking unusually thoughtful today. Is something weighing on your mind?'

'It's nothing really…'

'I can tell something's bothering you, so out with it.'

Rowena glanced up at her friend. 'It's just earlier today…I caught Sir Richard looking at me and…' She trailed off as she gazed thoughtfully into the distance.

'And what?' demanded Becky.

'Well, I thought he was sort of eyeing me up, you know...'

'You think he might be sweet on you?'

'I'm not quite sure I would put it like that, but there was definitely a certain glint in his eye.'

Becky had been very alarmed when Rowena first told her that she was to be Sir Richard's new clerk, telling her to be 'most careful not to annoy him, and if he ever so much as looks at you funny, tell them Cunninghams he tried to make a fallen woman of you and refuse to go anywhere near him again'.

The older woman looked grave and wrapped her shawl more tightly around her shoulders, as if suddenly feeling cold even on this warm evening. 'Do you think he might be a danger to you?'

Becky's anxious look left Rowena in no doubt about her meaning.

'No!' she cried, though her strong words came more from shock at the idea than firm conviction.

'So, do you think he might want to marry you?'

Rowena felt even more shocked by this idea than the last one. 'No, surely Sir Richard doesn't have any such ideas! He has clearly stated that he has no intention of getting married, and if dire financial need fails to persuade an unwilling man to think of marriage, surely nothing can. Even if he is interested—which he isn't—I wouldn't want him anyway. He might have the looks to make any woman go weak at the knees, but he is hard and cruel. No woman wants to marry a rat, no matter how devastatingly handsome he is.'

'You are quite right there, dear. What really matters in a man is his character, not his status or ability to cut a fine figure.'

'The Black Sheriff may well have something of a wandering eye, but I'm sure I'm in no real danger of interesting him.'

'Don't say it like that!' her friend chided. 'You're a pretty maid and I'm sure that there are plenty of young men out there who would agree with me. Not every lad wants a lass who's face is so plastered in paint and what-not that he's likely to get stuck to it if he kisses her.'

'Yes, but not if they are from the nobility. All *they* care about is how fashionable a lady is and how magnificent a lineage she has. A maiden like me would have no chance if he was thinking of taking a wife. Sir Richard's father was very well-bred. He was at court, you know. Lady Sabina and about half the well-born damsels in the shire would marry him in a heartbeat. In the hope of meeting him, these damsels linger on the paths through the forest which he rides along and bat their eyelashes at him when he visits their manors on business, but apparently all to no avail. They are much more fashionable and have much larger fortunes than I. He could have anyone of them, so he is certainly not going to think of marrying *me*.'

Becky shook her head, still in disagreement. But she knew any more words from her upon the matter would just fall on deaf ears.

'He must have just been toying with me, teasing me and finding new ways to embarrass me and make my life difficult,' Rowena said firmly, her tone clearly signalling that she was having no more discussion on the matter. 'He makes no bones about the fact he doesn't like me, as I'm always interfering in things that are none of my business, and that he only puts up with me because he has to.'

Although she had silenced Becky's objections to her view that Sir Richard detested her, Rowena still could not shake off the doubts dwelling in her own mind. Everything she knew about men of that rank and everything she thought about herself told her that she was right…but then, that look in his eyes—no, I must have just imagined it. He'd never like me. Stop being silly, she scolded herself, coming out of her dreamy musings with a jolt.

Putting the line of thought firmly to one side, she turned to another, this time wondering who might be blackmailing Sir Richard and why, but she came to no conclusions.

'Look at all my pretty flowers,' a little voice demanded.

Rowena opened her eyes to find Becky's little son standing in front of her. He proudly placed his spoils at her feet: a basket now filled to overflowing with vivid orange marigold flowers.

'Oh Peter, they're lovely,' she cried, picking up the little basket. 'Here,' she patted the space on the bench next to her, 'come and sit beside Aunty Rowena.'

Young Peter was soon seated and proved a most diligent pupil, taking careful heed of 'Aunty' Rowena as she showed him how to fashion a garland from the cheerful blooms.

* * * *

'I'm not getting on that,' said Rowena, distrustfully eyeing the large grey horse Sergeant Gallagher held.

'Why not?' demanded the sheriff impatiently, already mounted on his horse.

'Because I cannot ride.'

Sir Richard stared down at her incredulously. 'I thought all educated ladies could ride!'

'Not this one.'

'How the hell are you supposed to get around on shire business if you refuse to ride?'

'Be fair, sir!' she protested. 'The reason I cannot ride is because I have never had the opportunity to learn, not lack of willingness on my part.'

'Surely your relatives have horses you can ride?'

'Yes, but none of them have ever offered to teach me how to ride. My cousin has occasionally tried to talk me into getting on her horse, but I have always declined because I'm sure she only offers in the hope that I will fall off and she can then laugh at me.'

'Surely your cousin would not do such a discourteous thing?' said Gallagher.

'You have not met her.'

'This horse is as quiet as a lamb, my lady,' Gallagher tried to reassure her. 'He'll be no trouble.'

But she remained unconvinced. The horse had begun pawing at the ground and did not seem at all quiet to her. 'If you think you're going to talk me into getting on that wild-eyed beast, you can think again.'

'That's well and good, my lady,' said the mild-mannered sergeant with a sigh, 'but how are you going to get over to Adderslee Farm with Sir Richard? It's much too far to walk, and he needs you to take down the notes—'

'Look,' Sir Richard interrupted, 'if you don't want to ride that horse, get up behind me on Lucifer. You are such a tiny thing he'll barely notice you're there.'

She stared up at him in horror. 'Did you just say that black beast is called *Lucifer?*'

'Don't ask me why. He was called that when I bought him.'

'You seriously expect me to get on a giant stallion called *Lucifer?*'

Sir Richard dismissively flicked a black-gauntleted hand and gave an impatient huff. 'We haven't got all day! I need to interrogate that sheep stealer we have got banged up in the dungeons when I get back from Adderslee. Stop fussing and just get on.'

'No, I can't.' Rowena could hear a note of panic creeping into her voice. 'I'm telling you, I really can't ride!'

'It's not my problem if you're afraid of horses. When I asked for a replacement clerk I did not ask for a *girl*. If they had just let me have a normal clerk like I wished, this sort of damn irritating thing would never be a problem.' The sheriff glared down at Rowena challengingly, as if to say *I dare you to prove me wrong*.

She knew he had got the better of her. Never one to back down willingly, she could not bear to say no now. 'Very well, I will do it if you insist.'

Clearly aware that he had won with the use of rather underhand tactics, Sir Richard smirked sardonically and nudged Lucifer forward. 'I'll just move him alongside this step so you can get on.'

She mounted the step and waited while Sir Richard attempted to manoeuvre his horse alongside it. 'If I fall off that thing and get killed, it will all be your fault.'

Lucifer was fresh out of his stable and keen to get going. Every time Sir Richard succeeded in getting him close enough for Rowena to mount, chewing maniacally on his bit and tossing his head, the tall horse side-stepped around until he faced her, leaving her unable to mount.

This did nothing for her already shaky nerves. If she had not felt so pressured by the sheriff, she would not have even considered getting on the skittish horse. But to her relief, Sergeant Gallagher decided to intervene before her nerves, which were momentarily fortified by anger, gave out.

'Let me give you a hand, sir,' he said, taking hold of Lucifer's bridle and holding the charger still. 'Here you are, Mistress Rowena.'

She shrugged helplessly. 'But he's still so high, Sir Richard! How am I supposed to jump all the way up there with my short legs?'

Sir Richard took his foot out of the stirrup near her. 'Stand right next to him, facing his ears, and put your foot in my stirrup.'

'But your stirrups are so long and I am so short. I will never make it up.'

He held out his hand. 'I'll pull you up.'

She certainly was not going to give him reason to insult her on account of her being a girl again. She took a deep breath, then took his hand and placed her foot in the stirrup. He gave her a quick nod and, as she sprung from the ground, pulled her up with ease.

Although she was now safely aboard, she did not feel much better. 'You will just walk slowly, won't you?'

'If you stop clinging to my shoulders like a monkey and put your arms around me to steady yourself, you'll be fine,' came his cross answer.

She immediately did as he suggested, locking her arms around his waist in a vice-like grip. 'I'm begging you to go slowly, Sir Richard. If I fall from here I'm sure I'll be able to say ten Hail Mary's before I hit the ground.'

'Nonsense! Stop making such a fuss.'

'Ready, sir?' asked the sergeant.

Sir Richard nodded.

Gallagher let the stallion go and stepped back. Lucifer surged forward immediately, and Rowena, taken by surprise, shrieked in fright.

'Don't do that, you'll frighten him!' Sir Richard hissed.

'Pardon me.'

'And for God's sake loosen your grip on me! At this rate, I'll be completely numb from the waist down by the time we get there.'

She loosened her grip slightly. 'Sorry, Sir Richard.'

Although Sir Richard restricted himself to a brisk walk, Rowena still felt terribly insecure. The considerable movement generated by the large horse's massive strides made her feel like a cork bobbing on a rough sea. She was also beginning to wish she had got on the horse astride rather than side-saddle. It might be considered unladylike, indeed, almost obscene, for a woman to ride astride, but it was better than getting killed.

Once they had negotiated the busy roads leading to and from Hartfield, the path turned into the forest. The trail ahead was straight, slightly uphill and empty of other travellers. Lucifer began to pull at the reins and toss his head.

'I always take this stretch of road at a canter; he's keen to go,' said the sheriff. 'Would it be alright if I let him have a little trot just to take the edge off him?'

'No, please don't let him trot!' she begged. 'I'm barely coping with walk!'

But just as Sir Richard was about to reply, a startled rabbit darted out of the undergrowth and across the path in front of them, and the already tense Lucifer instantly leapt to one side.

Rowena screamed in fright at the unexpected movement, startling the horse again, who jumped forward this time. Already unbalanced by the first jump, she started to fall.

She clung desperately to Sir Richard.

'Let go of me!' he shouted.

But it was too late. She felt him falling with her. Shutting her eyes, she braced for impact. After plunging down for what seemed like an age, but in reality was only a second or two, she hit the ground with a dull thud, face down.

Convinced she must have broken every bone in her body, she kept completely still and waited for the pain to set in. But it did not come—although the ground she had landed on did seem strangely lumpy and uneven…

She finally dared to open her eyes. She ought to have been looking at grass. But it did not look like grass, dirt, or any other such substance. She blinked hard, fearing she may have taken a knock to the head and started seeing things. But there was no doubt about it. What she was looking at was black and shiny with metal studs in it.

Then, coming from right by her head, she heard a choking

gasp. It suddenly dawned on her: she had just landed on top of Sir Richard!

Despite her dazed state, she quickly dragged herself off him.

Freed from her weight, he immediately bent forward with his hand clutched to his chest, gasping for air.

Feeling rather panicked by the thought that she might have just killed the sheriff of Chaucy, Rowena hauled herself to a sitting position and grasped him by the shoulders. 'Sir Richard, are you alright?'

But he had had the wind completely knocked out of him and seemed unable to speak.

Her face had gone all tingly from the sudden shock of the fall and her legs felt weak, but Rowena managed to move behind him and seize him by the shoulders, pulling him back towards herself. 'Lean back more, it will help!'

He did not resist, and fell weakly back against her. Unfortunately, she had not taken into account how heavy such a tall and well-muscled man was. She fell to the ground instantly under his considerable weight, with his head on her chest and half his upper body pinning her firmly down. He did not remove himself.

After only a few moments, Rowena could not bear to support him. 'Could you—could you just—maybe—lean against that tree—next to you!'

'You did say lean back more,' came the unhurried reply.

'Off—you're killing me!' she gasped.

'And that's my fault, is it? I told you to keep quiet.'

She pushed at him feebly. 'You've—made—your—point.'

He shifted a little of his weight onto his elbow, but kept his head in place. 'You might be a very insubordinate clerk, but you make a damn comfortable pillow.'

'I told you I couldn't ride! I should never have let you taunt me into getting on that skittish beast.'

'You could at least have let me go instead of pulling me off and using my body to break your fall. I wish I had landed on *you* instead.'

'Well I'm sorry for landing on you,' she said unconvincingly.

He finally rolled off her and sat up.

The put upon young clerk quickly pulled herself to her feet, keen to put some distance between herself and her crafty captor. 'Try and play the good nurse and all you do is end up standing in for soft furnishings!'

He felt his side and winced. 'I think you've cracked my damn rib.'

'That's your own fault for making me get on Lucifer!'

Sir Richard turned away with a ruffled air, as if her words were so ridiculous that they did not merit an answer.

Rowena suddenly put her hand to her neck. 'My pendant, it's gone!' she cried, feeling around her throat desperately for the familiar old friend. 'It must have been ripped off when I fell. Oh God, where is it—I have to find it!' She started franticly searching the leaf-covered ground.

A few anxious moments later Sir Richard called out, 'I think I have found it.' He held aloft a small raying sun of thin gold attached to a leather cord. 'It was snagged on my doublet.'

Rowena ran over to him. 'Thank God!' She took the necklace in her hand. 'Thank you. It is so precious to me. I couldn't bear to lose it.'

'A gift, was it?'

'Yes, it was a gift from my father to my mother. He died when I was very young and it was one of the only things she had to remember him by. Though we were very poor, she never sold it. On her deathbed she gave it to me—' Rowena paused for a moment, then added in a barely audible whisper, 'And when I wear it I feel like part of them is always with me.'

.5.

Death and the Maiden

LEANING against the window frame in the sheriff's chamber, Rowena gazed longingly out the open window. How wonderful it looked out there in the sunshine! Wouldn't it be lovely to be wondering through the forest on a day like this, or perhaps sitting on the bank of the brook where the blue forget-me-nots grew, dipping her toes in the cool water like she used to...

She turned back to the mountain of work still awaiting her on the table, and sighed. How much better than being in this cold, dark fortress, where rarely a ray of sunlight penetrated, slaving away on a thankless and seemingly never-ending task.

Presently, her thoughts were interrupted by the heavy tread of booted feet coming up the stairs. Although she was not expecting him to be about yet, the jingle of spurs announced them as belonging to Sir Richard, who promptly appeared through the door.

'A report has come of a fifteen-year-old girl being snatched and carried off by two horsemen near the hamlet of Dovers Dell. Gallagher and I are riding over there right away. It happened last night, but as the messenger was on foot, we didn't hear of until just now. Hopefully the villains' scent trail is still fresh enough for our bloodhounds to pick up.' Without waiting for a response, he started walking back out, hurriedly pulling on his gauntlets as he went. 'I'll be away for the rest of the day, so if there are any documents that require my attention, leave them until tomorrow,' he called out as he disappeared down the stairs.

Another kidnapping... Rowena had heard a fair amount of talk around Eaglestone about two twin girls of seventeen who disappeared whilst walking to a farm not far from Hartfield two months earlier. She remembered the Cunninghams mentioning it at the time, but they had been of the opinion that the girls had run off with some young man or other, just like the young peasant girl who went missing a few weeks before that. And the girls were from the lower orders anyway. Who cared if a few maidens went missing if they were not nobly born? 'Good riddance, I say,' had been Lady Cunningham's kindly sentiment on the matter.

* * * *

Sir Richard bounded down the stone steps and out into the castle courtyard, where Sergeant Gallagher and half a dozen mounted men-at-arms waited. Their horses, sensing the air of tension and urgency, fidgeted and chomped on their bits.

The sheriff leapt onto Lucifer, held saddled and ready to go by a pageboy, and urged the stallion into a gallop. The rest of his men followed, galloping out through the castle gates and over the lowered drawbridge, before disappearing down the road after him in a cloud of dust.

After a long, hard ride, the men finally arrived in Dovers Dell. The hamlet consisted of a small, ramshackle collection of cottages, widely spaced, with woven willow-fenced fields taking up the space between them. The cattle grazing in the fields looked up in surprise at the sight of the armed men clattering past, their sweating, foam-flicked horses steaming in the hot midday sun.

By the time the sheriff and his men reached the centre of the village, a small crowd had gathered. Except for an occasional whispered comment to a neighbour, the villagers stood sullenly staring in silence. A dog ran out barking at the strangers, causing some of the horses to nervously dance sideways. It was gruffly called back by its master.

Sir Richard rode up to the assembled villagers and halted in front of them. 'Who reported the maiden missing?' he demanded, scanning the crowd like a hawk after mice.

A balding man of late middle-age nervously stepped forward, clutching his cloth cap in his hands and bowing repeatedly. 'My name be Tom, and it be my lass that were snatched, my lord.' He kept his eyes on the ground, as if fearful that Sir Richard might be angered by someone so lowly looking upon him.

'It was reported that someone saw the girl being taken?'

'Argh, that be so,' said the girl's father, fidgeting with his cap. 'It were her friend Elsie that saw it.'

'Where is this girl? We need to speak with her.'

'Elsie, come over 'ere!' Tom called to a raggedly-dressed girl of about fifteen, who stood at the back of the crowd.

She dragged her feet as she slowly walked over with downcast eyes, and stopped a short way from Tom.

The grizzled peasant seized a reluctant Elsie by the hand and pulled her up to Sir Richard. 'Tell the sheriff what it were you saw!'

The raggedy girl sniffed loudly and wiped her nose with the back of her hand before nervously beginning. 'Well, me an' Mary—that's the lass that were snatched—was walkin' 'long the path in the woods. We'd been to see 'er Grandma, who ain't very well—'

Never mind that, tell me what happened to Mary!' Sir Richard interrupted, his patience beginning to wear thin.

‘Perhaps it would be easier if she just took us to the spot and explained to us what happened,’ Sergeant Gallagher suggested quietly.

‘Yes, that’s not a bad idea.’ Sir Richard turned to the girl. ‘Elsie, lead us to the place where you saw Mary being kidnapped.’

She sniffed again. ‘But there ain’t nothin’ to see there.’

‘Just show us the place and let us be the judge of that!’ Sir Richard replied curtly.

Gallagher, who had dismounted as soon as they had come up to the villagers, turned to Sir Richard. ‘Maybe it would be easier if you dismount from your horse and we follow her on foot, sir?’

Sir Richard wordlessly vaulted off Lucifer and motioned the girl forward.

Most of the crowd began to move off with them, but the sergeant held up his hand. ‘I’d be much obliged if the rest of you could stay back here. Too many people about might put the bloodhound off the scent, which will not help us find these felons.’

Elsie led the sheriff and his sergeant along the main street through Dovers Dell, which was a rutted dirt track that barely qualified as a road. When she reached the edge of the clearing, she turned sharply to the left and onto a smaller side path.

They had only been walking for a short while when the girl stopped. ‘This were the place Mary was.’

The path was fairly wide, but it did not look like many travellers used it, as the ground was overgrown in many places with grass and nettles.

‘And where were you when it happened?’ asked the sheriff.

‘I were some way ahead of ’er, cos she’d stopped to pick berries further back an’ hadn’t caught up yet.’

‘But you did see them take her?’

‘Aye. I ’eard the sound of horses comin’ an’ looked round an’ saw two men on 'orses trottin' towards us. When they reached Mary they came in real close like. I 'eard 'er scream, then one of 'em hit 'er over the 'ead an' dragged her up onto his 'orse like, then they was gone.'

'Which way did they go?'

She pointed up the road. 'That way.'

And that road goes south?'

The girl swept a few strands of matted hair out of her face and shrugged her shoulders. 'Dunno.'

'What did the men look like?'

'They was wearin' sort of long dark cloaks with the 'oods up.'

'Yes, and?'

'And what?'

'My God, what a bunch of inbred imbeciles…' Sir Richard muttered to his Sergeant, before turning back to the girl. 'Could you see their faces?'

'They 'ad cloths sort of tied round their faces.'

'I see. What colour were the horses they rode?'

'They was a sort of brown colour.'

Sir Richard turned to address his men. 'I don't think we are going to get any further here.' He paused to remount Lucifer, then wheeled the horse around. 'Let's set the dog on the scent. I can see the hoof prints of the villains' horses on the ground here. It doesn't look like any other horses have passed through recently, so we ought to have a good chance of catching their scent.'

With his nose intently sniffing the ground, the dog led the men along the road for a short distance before he veered off into the forest.

The closely-following men-at-arms managed to keep up a good pace as there was very little undergrowth, just a thick carpet of dry leaves underfoot. The woods they were being led through were filled with ancient trees, towering giants through whose massive canopy hardly any sunlight penetrated to the forest floor below.

After a while, the trees began to thin out and the undergrowth to thicken. Then, through a parting in the trees, a small lake came into view.

'I hope the bastards haven't ridden into the water,' the sheriff remarked to his sergeant. 'If they have, we'll have little chance of picking up their scent again.'

Much to everyone's disgust, the trail did indeed lead to the shore of the lake. There, after much sniffing around, the dog finally sat down whining, unable to find the scent.

'Spread out and search around the edges of the lake for any signs of them; there might be hoof prints in the muddy ground near the water,' Sir Richard ordered his men. 'And you, Will,' he gave the dog handler a nod, 'see if that mutt can find the place they came out of the water.'

'Yes, sir!' chorused the men.

But after many hours crashing through the thick undergrowth and much cursing, the sheriff and his men failed to find any sign of the kidnappers. Forced to admit defeat, they turned back the way they had come and wearily rode for Hartfield, both man and beast splattered with mud from trudging through the marshy ground and bleeding from bramble scratches.

* * * *

'Yes, everything is here,' Rowena informed the delivery driver who sat patiently on his ox-drawn cart, waiting while she checked that the food he had just delivered to the castle was all present and correct.

'God speed, lady.' He tipped his cap and urged the oxen

forward, the wooden wheels of the cart creaking in protest as it moved off.

Just as she was turning to go back inside, Rowena noticed a man walking into the courtyard. He was a respectable-looking man of about fifty, sombrely but neatly dressed in a long dark blue robe.

'Can I help you, sire?' she called to him.

His manner was tense and agitated. 'I need to see the sheriff at once!'

'I'm afraid Sir Richard's not here at the moment. I am his personal clerk, Rowena Walden. Perhaps I could pass on a message?'

The man shook his head. 'No, Mistress Walden. I need to see him now!'

'Sir Richard rode out to Dovers Dell this morning, and he said he wouldn't be back until late this afternoon.'

'So the rumour is true,' cried the grey-haired man, his eyes shining with a slightly unnerving intensity. 'There *has* been another kidnapping near Dovers Dell!'

'Yes, there was a report of a girl being carried off which Sir Richard has gone over to investigate. Do you have information about the crime, sire?'

'No, I am Walter Gray, father of the twin girls who disappeared two months ago. They were taken right near the edge of Hartfield. That wretched sheriff hasn't found a trace of them, not a single clue about where they might be or who took them. They were snatched barely half a mile from this castle. He's just useless, useless!' the man wailed, his face lined with anguish.

'I'm very sorry, sire,' Rowena said helplessly.

'I may be just a humble cloth merchant, but my goodwife and I loved our daughters dearly. My poor wife has hardly risen from her bed since our daughters were taken, so overcome with grief is she. They are our only daughters. We now have only our oldest son remaining, his brother having been taken by the plague that swept through the town two winters ago.' The man's voice broke as sobs racked through him, his thin body shaking with their violence.

Rowena felt completely useless, but managed to say reassuringly, 'I'm so sorry for your loss. Sir Richard will be doing everything he can. God willing, the felons might have left some new clues at Dovers Dell that expose their identity.'

* * * *

'Did you find the maiden that went missing?' Rowena asked Sir Richard hopefully, as he jumped off Lucifer at the foot of the steps leading up to Eaglestone's main entrance.

Sir Richard pushed his lank black hair back from his sweat-covered forehead. 'No, we did not.'

'Did you find out anything at all?'

He handed Lucifer's reins over to a pageboy. 'Not really.'

'Oh,' she replied, crestfallen. 'I was hoping you had found some clues that could lead to the felons who kidnapped those twins.'

The knight scowled down at her dangerously. 'Were you indeed? And what concern is that of yours?'

'Am I not entitled to have compassion for the poor parents of those maidens?'

'Not if you're just going to bug me about it!' Sir Richard replied sourly, pulling out a folded piece of paper that was tucked into his sword belt. 'A royal messenger handed me this at the gate. It's in that damned Latin, and he said it was urgent. What does it say?'

She took the paper and unfolded it. 'It says that you missed the deadline for sending in your tax payment, and if you don't send it this very instant, the king will send down some of his soldiers to make sure you do.'

'Hell, are you jesting?' He seized the paper and stared at it, even paler than usual. 'I know for certain that I never received any tax demand from the king recently!'

'It states here plainly that a letter was sent to you several weeks ago informing you of the new tax the king is charging all sheriffs.'

'So I received some tax demand and you did nothing about it?'

'I'm telling you, I've never seen anything about it until now, so if you'll excuse me, I'm going home!' And with that, she determinately marched off.

'What about the tax payment?' he shouted after her.

'Find thirty crowns and send it back with that letter,' she called over her shoulder. 'And if you can't find the money, there's nothing I can do to help you.'

He strode after her. 'Where do you think you are going? I need you to sort this damn thing—' he shook the letter furiously, 'out now!'

She stopped. 'You've already accused me of being incompetent, now sort it out yourself!'

Then she pushed away the letter he held out to her and started walking again, leaving the furious sheriff standing there scowling blackly at the offending letter in the courtyard, which had rapidly emptied at the sound of his bellowing.

* * * *

Rowena put down the heavy basket of pears and stood back to survey the bare boughs with satisfaction. That was the last of the orchard's fruit crop to be picked; the rest was already safely stowed away in the larder for the harsh winter months ahead.

As she was about to pick up the basket of fat, russet-tinged pears again and carry it back to the manor, she heard the crunch of approaching footsteps on the gravel path.

Could she never get a moment of peace without someone plaguing her? For a moment she contemplated quickly vaulting over the orchard wall to escape, but Sir Richard appeared from behind the trees before she had a chance to act.

'Ah, there you are,' he said, walking up to her. 'The kitchen wench said I'd find you here.'

She swatted away a buzzing wasp, muttering, 'Be off with you, you pest,' at the offending little creature.

Sir Richard looked ruffled. 'Excuse me?'

'I was talking to a wasp,' she snapped, sounding like she wished she had meant it for him. 'Anyway, what do you want? Can't you see I'm busy!'

The tall knight seemed unusually meek, as he did not react to her hostile words. Instead, he stood there silently for a few moments, fidgeting with his gauntlets.

She wiped her hands, sticky from the pears' sweet juice, on the skirt of her pale linen dress. 'Well, what is it you wanted? I have got things to be getting on with.'

He wrung his gloves tightly. 'I came over to—ahem—well, the thing is, Rowena, I'm sure that the local people know more about the kidnapping over at Dovers Dell then they're saying and...'

She gave a huff of impatience as he trailed off yet again.

'And Gallagher suggested,' he continued slowly, 'that maybe we'd find more out if—if you spoke to them.'

'After your insults yesterday, you now want me to trudge all the way over to Dovers Dell in the heat and do your job for you?'

'I—I—' he stammered, seeming barely able to force the words out. 'I *regret* what I said earlier. We're getting nowhere with the investigation and the people are getting restless—' He finally lifted his eyes from the ground. 'Will you help?'

She crossed her arms. 'Haven't you forgotten to add something to that?'

He looked confused. 'Forgotten something?'

'Yes.'

'Oh, I see...' He paused uncomfortably, his lips a thin line of annoyance.

Rowena stamped her foot. 'If a man cannot ask a lady a favour without being graceless and ill-mannered, he is certainly no gallant!'

As she started to angrily turn away, Sir Richard caught her by the arm. 'Rowena, stop! Will you help...please?'

Realising that this was as close to grovelling as Sir Richard was likely to come, and with the memory of the missing twins' father's desperate plea still haunting her, she knew she could not refuse with a clear conscience. 'Very well, I will help you. But with one condition: I'm not having any of your wild horse antics, so no trotting, cantering, bucking, falling off.'

'I promise to keep Lucifer to a walk—though I'm sure it will rain later, and if we do not hurry we are likely to get a soaking. If we don't get struck by lightning first...'

She looked across the valley to where the thunderclouds were building once more over the western hills, as they had done nearly every day for the past week. 'Yes, you are right.' She began walking back towards the manor with him. 'Those clouds are very dark and the air is heavy with the promise of rain already.'

Sir Richard wiped his brow with the sleeve of his shirt. 'It has been so damn hot and sticky lately.'

'It is wonderful to finally get rain after such a long, dry summer. I was beginning to think the drought would never break.'

'At least the farmers will have one less excuse for not paying their taxes on time,' he muttered. 'They are forever coming up with reasons why they've not been earning anything and can't afford it. The year was too wet, the year was too dry, the crops got blight, the wool prices were too low, the ale prices were too high… The way they carry on, you would think they were working for nothing!'

They had now reached the front of the manor, where Lucifer stood tethered, patiently waiting for his rider.

Rowena continued up the steps to the grand entrance. 'I'll just go in and let someone know where I'm going,' she called over her shoulder as she went inside.

She headed straight to the kitchen, where Mistress Pedley was almost always to be found toiling, red-faced from the heat of the fire that was always burning.

'Sir Richard needs me to ride over to Dovers Dell at once, so please tell Lady Cunningham where I have gone and that I'll be back later today!' she called to Mistress Pedley from the doorway, before turning and hurrying back towards the main door.

The cook looked up from the brace of birds she was butchering. 'Very good, Rowena—though remember what her ladyship said this morning 'bout getting back early today so that…' But her words faded as Rowena disappeared out the door, her mind firmly fixed on the task ahead of her.

A few moments later, Rowena was standing on Stoatley's front steps nervously looking at the mighty Lucifer.

'Sit with a leg on either side of him this time,' Sir Richard briskly instructed her. 'I will lift you on first,' he continued, 'then I'll mount myself.'

Before she could answer, he had put one arm around her waist and the other under her knees and lifted her off the ground. She gasped as he swung her high into the air as though she was no heavier than a child's doll, before placing her carefully down on Lucifer's broad back.

He then quickly gathered up the reins and mounted, agilely swinging his leg up over Lucifer's neck in order to avoid hitting Rowena, and set off down the road at a brisk walk.

After an uneventful two-hour ride, Rowena and Sir Richard finally neared Dovers Dell. Rowena had been terrified of falling off to begin with, but she was now so stiff and sore that all she could think of was reaching their destination as soon as possible so she could dismount.

At the sound of Lucifer's clattering hooves approaching, all the dogs in the hamlet began barking furiously. But when the heavily wooded path finally revealed the ramshackle collection of thatched huts and hovels, there was no one to be seen. Riding down the main road through Dovers Dell, the place seemed like a ghost town.

'That's strange,' said Sir Richard. 'Last time I was here with my men everyone came out to gawp at us. I wonder where they've all gone...'

'They can't have gone far; the chimneys are smoking, and look,' she pointed, 'there are children's toys lying on the ground near that cottage as if they were left only moments ago.'

As they came closer, the sound of a crying infant could clearly be heard. From another hovel a crash sounded, sending the flock of chickens scratching in the dirt outside it into squawks of alarm.

Sir Richard fingered his sword nervously. 'There are obviously still people here. I will dismount and knock on the door of this shack.'

'No,' said Rowena, 'I think the people are hiding because they are afraid. Let me go while you wait here.'

'But you are unarmed! If you go alone, you will be helpless if things get hostile.'

'The only reason we have come all this way is so that I can try to talk to them. If they are afraid, they will not say anything and our journey will have been in vain.'

'Very well... But I will stay close by. If there is any danger, retreat immediately. I've got enough troubles already without having to try to think of a good way of telling Lord Cunningham that his niece was stabbed to death in some revolting hovel in a remote village while I waited outside.'

Rowena smoothed the wrinkled skirt of her dress. 'Yes, yes, I get it!' She then walked cautiously up the muddy path leading to the hovel's rickety door. 'Good day,' she called out. 'Is anyone home?'

There was no reply, although she could still hear the baby crying.

She knocked on the door. 'Is there anyone in there?' We are not going to hurt you. I merely want to talk with you.'

The crude wooden door had such large gaps between its rough planks that she could see inside. But, although the dwelling was well lit by the sunlight shining in through the many cracks and holes in it, she could not see anyone. The baby's screams seemed to be coming from near the door, the only place that she could not see.

'Would you like me to kick the door in for you?' Sir Richard offered graciously.

'No thank you. You just stay out of this.' Rowena knocked again. 'Please open the door.'

She heard a few low whispers from inside, then a few moments later the protesting screech of a bolt being slowly drawn open.

The door creaked open a fraction.

'Thank you. Please, may I talk to you?'

The door finally opened and a young woman holding a baby in her arms stepped out.

Rowena smiled and held out her hand. 'Greetings, friend. My name is Rowena, and I have come here to help find Mary.'

The woman slowly extended a thin arm and clasped the offered hand weakly. 'I am Phoebe.'

'We are here to try and find the maidens who have gone missing. Do you know anything at all that might help us find Mary or the twins that were taken two months ago?'

Phoebe stared at Rowena, her hazel eyes round with fear, but did not reply.

'What are you so afraid of?' asked Rowena. 'I Promise nothing bad will happen to you or anyone in Dovers Dell if you tell us what you know.'

The woman jerked her head in Sir Richard's direction. 'Are you with 'im?'

'In a manner of speaking, but you have nothing to fear from him. He just wants to find the maidens.'

'How do I know what you're saying's true?'

'If you don't want the sheriff to know what it is you know, I won't tell him.'

Phoebe silently considered Rowena's words for a few moments before speaking. 'We was told by some armed men that were here before Mary were taken that they was working for Sir Richard. They said if we complained about it or told anyone else he would come back 'ere in the dead of night and torch our houses while we was sleeping inside '

Rowena could hardly believe what she was hearing. 'Surely you don't believe the sheriff would do something so terrible?'

'Well, 'e is a shifty-looking sod, that's for sure.'

'Just a moment, Phoebe,' said a worriedly frowning Rowena. 'I need to ask the sheriff about this.' She walked back to where Sir Richard was waiting. 'This woman says that the men who kidnapped Mary told the folk here that they worked for you, and that if they told anyone else about it, you would come back here and kill them.'

'Good God! You don't believe it, do you?'

'No, of course not!' she replied, a bit too enthusiastically. 'But why would the men say such a thing?'

'I don't know. Perhaps they are local men with a grudge against me.'

'Yes, they could be. How else would they even know your name?'

'Fair point. But I really can't think of anyone from Chaucy who could be taking these maidens.'

'I suppose that it is likely more people would have seen these men if they were from around these parts.'

Sir Richard swung himself off Lucifer. 'Look, I will talk to her, and tell her that I had nothing to do with these men or with the maidens being taken.'

'Very well, but go easy on her. We don't want to scare her or she might not talk—and for goodness sake keep that ridiculously large sword hidden under your cloak, because it really is an unnerving sight!'

'Alright, alright,' he muttered, annoyed by her scolding tone.

He followed his clerk up to the hovel's open door, where Phoebe waited just outside.

'I'll tell you what it were we've seen round these parts,' said the young peasant woman. 'But first answer me this: if it be really so that you ain't got nothing to do with them armed men that was here, how come your clerk was here with 'em? He said it were true that you was behind it all.'

Sir Richard took a step backwards and nearly collided with the doorframe. 'My old clerk, Thomas, was here?'

Rowena desperately hoped Phoebe had not noticed the clang of his sword as it clashed against the door.

'Aye, he were. And we know it were him 'cause some of the folks hereabouts 'ave seen Thomas in Hartfield and recognized him when they saw him.'

'I can assure you, I know nothing about Thomas being here and I certainly did not send him!'

Although the raggedly-dressed woman nodded, Rowena thought she still did not seem entirely convinced by Sir Richard's words.

'Do you know who the armed men that were with Thomas are?' Rowena asked.

'No. They was rough, brutal-looking men, well armed and all. We was much too frightened to speak to 'em, but from their voices it were clear they ain't from these parts.'

'And that's all you can tell us about them?'

Phoebe nodded again. 'They never stayed 'ere, only passed through a few times.'

'When was this?'

'First time we saw 'em were about two months back. They rode through a couple of times.'

'Was Thomas ever with them?'

'Aye, but we 'aven't see him 'ere for 'bout two moons. Them armed ruffians had been hanging 'bout the village for a few days before they carried Mary off. We'd seen that ratty little clerk of his,' Phoebe glared at Sir Richard, 'with 'em once or twice. 'E stole poor old Widow Jenkins' rooster, just grabbed 'old of it, rung its neck and slung it on his belt. As if we aren't poor enough without folks stealing from us!' She raised her eyes to heaven. 'May the good Lord save us from such servants of Satan.'

'Yes, I do recall Thomas bringing some dead fowl into my chamber around that time,' said Sir Richard. 'The heathen worm put it on the floor next to his table, where it left blood everywhere. Then I came along later and slipped in it.' He rubbed his temple and winced. 'Damn near knocked myself out on the edge of that table. I gave the knave a good clout round the ears next morning…'

'Do you know what Thomas was doing in Dovers Dell, Phoebe?' asked Rowena.

'That clerk seemed to be coming 'ere to meet with the men, don't know why, though.'

Rowena turned to Sir Richard. 'I think we have learned all we can here. Why don't we take a look at the place where Mary was kidnapped? These men may have been loitering around there for a while waiting for her. They might have dropped something that could give us a clue to who they are.'

He nodded. 'That's not a bad idea.'

Rowena travelled the short way along the path into the forest on foot, glad of a chance to stretch her legs after the long (for her anyway) ride. Sir Richard, mounted on Lucifer, reached the site ahead of her and had already dismounted and tethered the stallion to a tree by the time she got there.

'Right, let's give this place a thorough going-over,' he called to her as she came up to him. 'You search this side of the road and I'll search the other. Call out if you find anything.'

Rowena started her search at the edge of the overgrown road and moved out from there. The area running alongside the path was a wild tangle of blackberry, nettles, tall grasses, hawthorn and wild briar roses, able to grow there because the sunlight shone through where the trees had been cleared to make way for the road.

As Rowena got a little further from the road, she thought she could make out some impressions in the soft ground. They looked rather like the shape of a horseshoe, but with all the rain that had fallen, they were indistinct and she could not be sure if the marks really were hoof prints or just the activity of wild animals. The tracks led between the hawthorn and saplings for a short way then quickly faded when they reached a grassy clearing.

Rowena gave a huff of annoyance and stopped. 'Oh bother,' she said aloud. 'I've bashed my way through all those brambles for naught. Look at my poor hands,' she added in dismay, surveying her scratched, bleeding hands.

Rowena suddenly gasped. There were several tears in her dress, the largest of which extended much too high up the skirt for decency. 'Heavens, what a pretty picture I'll make when I get back to Stoatley! I just hope to high heaven that I can get up to my room without Aunt Cunningham seeing me…'

Then it suddenly occurred to her: if her dress got torn on the thorns of brambles and briar roses, their clothing might have got snagged too, leaving behind a scrap of material caught on a branch!

She immediately started looking around at the shrubs instead of the ground. Sure enough, there was a small scrap of rough, brown, sacking-like fabric caught on a blackberry bush just ahead of her.

She ran over to it. There, on the ground near it, were clear signs that someone had been there recently. The grass was trampled and some twigs on the surrounding trees were broken.

But a moment later Rowena gagged as the stench of rotting flesh hit her. A deer, or perhaps a wild pig, must have died nearby. She pulled her handkerchief out, and holding it over her nose, continued her search of the area.

The maiden followed the path of snapped branches deeper into the forest. But the smell only got stronger. She started to wonder if the marks had just been left by an animal, perhaps wounded by a hunter, that had crashed its way through the forest before dropping dead there.

Just when the stench was becoming unbearable and she was about to turn back, something pale on the ground under a bush caught her eye. She stooped down and took hold of it, but it was stuck. It felt hard and stiff. She could not make out what it was.

Rowena gave it another tug.

Still it would not come. She parted the undergrowth to get a better look at it. And there, staring up at her with frozen, glazed eyes, lay a pale, green-tinged corpse.

The thing she had been pulling on was the hand of the rotting body! She instantly snatched her hand back and screamed in horror.

'Rowena, what is it?' Sir Richard's cry reached her from back near the road.

But she was so shocked by the unexpected and grisly sight that she barely heard him.

'Rowena, are you alright?' he shouted again.

This time his voice was nearer, and she could hear him coming crashing towards her through the thick undergrowth.

Desperately trying to erase the image of the horrid, rotting face with its staring eyes from her mind, she leaned against a nearby tree and covered her face with a shaking hand—the hand she did *not* use to pull at the corpse.

A few moments later Sir Richard burst into the clearing, drawn sword in hand. 'What's wrong?' He quickly scanned the area for danger, ready to strike down any enemies in an instant.

'The most horrible, horrible thing, the grisliest thing I have ever set eyes on...' Words failed her, so she just pointed weakly at the thicket where the body lay.

'You found something in there?' Sir Richard walked over to the spot and parted the branches with his sword.

Rowena nodded, quickly covering her face again and turning away. She did not want to risk catching another glimpse of it.

'Good God,' cried the sheriff, 'it's that slimy knave, Thomas!'

She turned back in surprise. 'Thomas?'

'Yes, it's him all right. It explains why no one has seen him for four weeks. Looks like he's been dead about that long,' he said matter-of-factly, giving the corpse a poke with the toe of his boot, as if to satisfy himself that it was real.

But this was too much for Rowena. She felt a wave of nausea washing over her. 'Oh Lord,' she gasped to Sir Richard, who had come back over, 'I think I'm going to be sick.'

He rolled his eyes, clearly unfazed at the sight of the rotting body himself and unable to see what all the fuss was about.

She swiftly clapped her hand over her mouth to give herself time to duck behind the tree she was standing under, where she was violently sick.

To her relief, his relaxed attitude in the face of unsavoury experiences also seemed to extend to ladies throwing up. He barely paid any attention, simply continuing the conversation. 'I wonder what he was doing out on this remote road.' He casually leaned an arm against the tree. 'You got any ideas?'

'Argh,' she shuddered. 'Have you got a water flask with you? My mouth tastes foul.'

'Yes, but it is in Lucifer's saddle bag,' he replied absent-mindedly, walking back over to the thicket where the corpse lay. 'I think I might just pull him out so we can get a better look…'

She was a little surprised by his unchivalrous attitude in the face of feminine distress. Most men would have been only too glad of such an opportunity to show how strong and manly they were by enthusiastically comforting the stricken female.

'Is it too much to ask you to tear your attention away from that stinking corpse just for one moment and get me a drink of water?'

He seized the body by the feet and started pulling it out. 'God's bones, it's only a dead body! I've seen hundreds of the damn things when I was fighting in France.'

'Well, I haven't!'

'Never mind, you'll soon get used to it. The bastard can't do us any more harm now that he's dead.'

Holding her handkerchief firmly over her nose, Rowena

moved as far away from the corpse as she could without going back into the brambles that surrounded them.

In the meantime, Sir Richard had started going through the dead Thomas' clothing, searching for anything in his pockets.

'No, there's nothing here,' he announced shortly, getting back to his feet. 'The killers most likely took anything he had on him.'

Having recovered somewhat from the initial shock, Rowena managed to look at the corpse again, although only from a safe distance, and only from out of the corner of her eye. 'Can you tell how he was killed?'

'Yes, by a single sword-thrust through the heart. It doesn't look like he put up much of a fight; there's no sign of any other wounds on him.'

'Do you think he knew his killer?'

'Very likely. His killer would have to be standing right in front of him to deliver a cut like this.'

The sickly, cloying smell of rotting flesh hung heavily in the air despite Rowena's best attempts to block it out. Another wave of nausea threatened to engulf her. 'Can we go back now?' she asked weakly.

'Before we go, we ought to have a look on the ground around here in case the murderer dropped anything.'

She spat out the sour saliva that filled her mouth. 'Alright—but let's make it quick, because I can't take much more of this.'

'Don't be such a damn goose.'

They began a careful search of the area, she making sure to keep a good distance from the corpse. After only a few moments, Sir Richard held up something small and shiny.

She ran over. 'What is it?'

'Looks like some sort of brooch,' he replied, passing it to her.

The object was fairly large for a broach; perhaps the type of thing a man might use to pin his cloak together. It was made of iron, and engraved on the top side was a strange symbol.

She could not make out what it was beneath the dirt caked onto it, so tapped it against a nearby log to dislodge it and then blew away the last of the dust. Revealed was an image of a fierce bat with outstretched wings, and it beneath a human skull.

She passed the object back to Sir Richard. 'Do you think it might be some sort of heraldic crest?'

'Could well be.'

'Have you ever seen this emblem before?'

He frowned at the broach. 'I saw a great many coats of arms during my time fighting in France, but not this one.'

'We can show it to the soldiers at the castle; perhaps one of them will recognise it.'

'Yes, that's worth trying. Also, this road we are on leads to the town of Stonehaven, in the neighbouring shire. I shall ride over there as soon as I can and talk to the sheriff there. These villains might have passed through.'

.6.

Surprises from Demons, Angels and Unknowns

IT HAD been raining heavily for the past hour, and Rowena was completely soaked. After the ordeal of the trip to Dovers Dell, all she could think about was getting her heavy, sodden dress off. Sir Richard had dropped her off at the bottom of the hill so she could stretch her stiff muscles, aching from long hours spent in the saddle, by walking the short distance on foot. Now that she had reached the crest of the hill, Stoatley Manor was in view below.

As Rowena neared the manor's entrance, she broke into a jog. Desperate to get out of the rain, the young woman decided to go in through the front door. She usually entered through the back door because only the servants used it, meaning that she would not meet the Cunninghams.

She hastily pushed the big door open, burst in, slammed it shut and turned towards the stairs, but then stopped dead in her tracks. Every one of the Cunningham family stood staring at her, speechless with horror.

There were several moments of deafening silence, then a voice came from her right. 'What on earth is that *thing*?'

She turned towards the sound. Standing beside her aunt was a tall, thin man of about forty, dressed in the most outrageous manner. His black and yellow doublet had sleeves so long that they brushed the ground even though he was holding his hands to his waist. His hose had one red leg and one purple leg, and were accessorised by a very large, elaborate codpiece. When she turned her astonished gaze to his feet, she almost laughed out loud. His yellow leather shoes had toes so long that they looked as though he would hardly be able to walk in them.

She had never seen him before—then Rowena remembered: Lord Shrewsbury. The Cunninghams had been expecting a visitor, Lady Cunningham's distant cousin, Lord Shrewsbury!

So *that* was what Mistress Pedley had been trying to remind her about when she left that morning. Her aunt and Lady Sabina had been talking about almost nothing else for the past few weeks. And today was the day he was supposed to arrive.

Rowena suddenly realised what a sight she must look. Her pale-coloured dress was splashed with mud and torn—she quickly snatched the gaping hole in her skirt together. Furthermore, her hair was a wet tangle and her arms and face were covered in bramble scratches.

Rowena's aunt looked truly mortified by her sudden entrance and seemed unable to decide what to do. 'This is—' Lady Cunningham finally began, but was interrupted by Lord Shrewsbury.

'This is a filthy beggar-girl who should not have the insolence to come trespassing on your land. Be off with you!' He waved a long, thin-fingered hand at Rowena. 'Shoo, go on!'

Out of the corner of her eye, Rowena noticed Lady Cunningham covering her face with her hand in mortification.

She took no notice. 'I am Lady Cunningham's niece, Rowena Walden.'

Lord Shrewsbury gave his head an arch toss. 'Not just filthy but mad too, by God!'

Lady Cunningham looked even more tense and thin-lipped than usual. 'My lord, I regret to inform you that she is indeed my niece.'

'This ragged waif is your niece? My dear lady, surely you jest!'

Lady Cunningham sighed resignedly. 'No, I am afraid it is true. She is my sister's daughter.'

The gaudily dressed lord looked back at Rowena and gave a contemptuous sniff. 'Your *niece?* I can barely comprehend that such an elegant and noble lady as you could possibly be related to a thing like *that*.'

'It shames me to tell you that my sister made a very unwise marriage. This young lady's father was a very lowly-born man.'

Lord Shrewsbury looked disdainfully down his long, thin nose at Rowena. 'So I see.'

Even though she had only been in his company a short while, his affected falsetto voice was already beginning to grate.

Lady Cunningham wagged a finger. 'Breeding always shows through in the end, always. Vermin begets vermin.'

'Don't talk about him like that!' cried Rowena. 'I'm not ashamed of my father. He might not have been of noble birth, but he was a kind, honest man and I loved him!'

Lady Cunningham caught her breath with a hiss. 'I will have none of your nonsense, thank you. You are wrong and I am right and that is an end to it!'

Too tired to argue with her aunt, Rowena decided she had had enough trouble for one day. She lifted the muddy, dripping hem of her gown and started walking towards the stairs without another word or glance at the horrified gathering.

* * * *

'Rowena, kindly carry that jug of wine over with you,' Lady Cunningham ordered her niece.

'Do I have to go and sit with them? I need to go over to the castle soon, and would much rather just take a little bread and cheese to eat while I walk there.'

'Yes, you do have to go and eat with your cousin and Lord Shrewsbury. You have not spoken with our guest at all today. Come to think of it, you have barely been in his company at all in the two days that he has graced us with his presence,' her aunt replied shrilly. 'Am I to go to so much trouble convincing his lordship to come and honour us with his noble presence only to have you, ungrateful child, insult him by neglect?

'No, my lady,' Rowena murmured.

'You, who would benefit the most from social intercourse with one of such noble breeding, such refinement and style!'

'Sorry, my lady.'

'And it really is most improper for a young lady—although I do hesitate to call you that—to be wandering all over the countryside like some wild gypsy brat. I really must have a word with Lord Cunningham about that. I am sure that the sheriff can find a replacement for you somewhere. There are plenty of good-for-nothing's about he could employ.'

'I'm perfectly happy being his clerk.'

'I don't doubt it! Anything to avoid having to behave like a proper lady,' she spat. 'Now get out of my sight!'

'Yes, my lady.'

Rowena picked up the jug and reluctantly walked out of the kitchen and over to the table set up outside in the garden.

The table was spread with silver dishes containing every kind of rare and costly delicacy. Lady Cunningham had spared no expense in her efforts to impress Lord Shrewsbury. Rowena put the jug down on the table next to the empty one already there.

'Ah, a serving wench has brought us more wine at last!' cried Lord Shrewsbury, and giggled loudly at his own joke.

Standing near him, Lady Sabina and her friend Anne enthusiastically joined in.

'Well, she is dressed like one!' sniggered Lady Sabina.

This caused another burst of laughter from Anne and Lord Shrewsbury, who acted as though it was the funniest thing they had ever heard. But Rowena just bit her lip and stared into the distance. They were already as silly as a flock of squawking chickens without drinking any more wine...

Once Lord Shrewsbury, Lady Sabina and Anne had had their wine goblets refilled, they sat down and started to eat. Rowena chose the chair furthest away from the others and sat down too. Avoiding the roast swan, songbird pie and whole roast pig's head with an apple in its mouth, she chose instead a simple meal of bread, cheese, and a little ham.

In between picking at bits of food and praising it in the most flowery and excessive words possible, Lord Shrewsbury regaled Anne and Lady Sabina with stories of his time at court, spouting all sorts of pieces of scandalous gossip. The other two young ladies sat spellbound, hanging on his every word, but Rowena took very little notice. She was convinced that he had made most of the stories up. As for the gossip, she thought it sounded like a mix of malicious rumours, pointless nastiness and plain misinformation.

When the meal was almost finished, Rowena's interest was sparked by the mention of Sir Richard's name.

'Yes, shocking is it not,' Lord Shrewsbury was saying. 'Sir Richard visits twice a week without fail. And what is more, he does it in broad daylight, bold as brass.'

'Shocking!' echoed Anne, her eyes round with horror.

'What is shocking?' asked Rowena.

Lord Shrewsbury rolled his eyes in exasperation. 'Keep up, nitwit, for pity's sake.'

She ignored Anne and Lady Sabina's snickering. 'I'm sorry, my mind was wondering a little just then. What was it you were saying about Sir Richard?'

'That he visits a whore in Hartfield twice a week. He comes to her in broad daylight, making no attempt to conceal it.'

'How do you know that?'

'I have it on the best authority. A lady who lives right next door to the house of ill-repute told me—' He rolled his eyes. 'Imagine having to put up with *that*...'

Rowena was not sure how much longer she could listen to him and keep a civil tongue. 'Please, just tell me what she said.'

Lord Shrewsbury gave a disdainful sniff. 'Don't get your stays in a twist. One has to practise the art of conversation, you know—although I suppose one has to be patient where the lower orders are concerned, and not expect them to understand the *finer* things in life.'

'I'm not wearing stays.'

Lord Shrewsbury pulled a wry face. 'So *that* is why you look so fat.'

'I'm not fat! Now just tell me what this lady said.'

'If you say so...' he muttered aside to Lady Sabina, who giggled wildly. 'Yes, well,' he continued, 'this good lady—she was most respectable-looking you know, lovely brocade gown... anyway, she said the only occupants of the aforementioned house are a young lady and an older woman, who is no doubt her pimp. This neighbour—wearing a very nice fur she was too...must ask her where she got it...she has met the older woman but never the young one, who never goes out on foot. The only time she is seen is when she goes for a walk on her pony. But she is heavily veiled and never speaks to anyone. Obviously she is too ashamed to show her face in public.'

'Just because a young woman shuns society and rarely goes out does not mean that she is a prostitute,' said Rowena.

'Ah, but I have proof!' he cried triumphantly. 'Through a window, this neighbour glimpsed the young lady embracing Sir Richard. The good woman said that the lady was all over him—

kissing him,' he added, with a shudder.

'I still don't believe it. The dame could have been mistaken. She could hardly have got a good view from a glimpse of them through a window, and she said herself that she had never seen this maiden's face clearly.'

Lord Shrewsbury raised his carefully groomed eyebrows. 'Jealous, are we?'

'Certainly not!' Rowena replied in her most indignant tone, although, to her annoyance, she felt her cheeks grow warm.

'Yes, she is completely eaten up with jealousy. That is why she will not believe something which is clearly a fact beyond all doubt,' Lady Sabina chipped in nastily.

'No!' protested Rowena. 'I just think that one should not form such harsh judgements based on evidence which is no more than idle gossip. You have never even met the two ladies whom you are so quick to accuse. There might be a perfectly innocent explanation for their behaviour.'

'I've always thought you arrogant,' said Lady Sabina, 'but setting your cap at Sir Richard? That really is a folly beyond belief in one so lacking in beauty, grace and style.'

Lord Shrewsbury slowly licked his lips. 'Yes, that Sir Richard really is a magnificent beast…'

'I told you, I have not 'set my cap at him'. Even if I did have personal feelings for Sir Richard—which I don't—it would not change my views on this matter. Instead of talking all this nonsense, why don't you simply ask him why he goes to visit this young lady?'

Lord Shrewsbury gave Rowena a look that could have frozen saltwater. 'Kindly remember your station and refrain from speaking in that way.'

'Besides, Sir Richard is not here to ask,' added Lady Sabina, with a haughty toss of her head.

Rowena pointed down the valley, where she had just spotted

the sheriff coming riding towards them along the riverbank. 'But he will be shortly.'

'One does not say such things to a man's f-face!' spluttered a horrified-looking Lord Shrewsbury.

'Only behind his back?' snapped Rowena.

As he rode up to his clerk, Sir Richard's usual grim expression lifted to neutral, the closest she ever saw him get to a smile that was not a smirk. 'Greetings, Rowena.'

'Good day, Sir Richard. How goes it?'

He answered Rowena's polite query with a pained grimace, before dismounting and giving Anne and Lady Sabina a curt nod. 'Ladies.'

'Ah, Sir Richard!' cried Lord Shrewsbury, jumping to his feet and bowing elaborately. 'How wonderful to see you again!'

Sir Richard responded with a sullen glare.

'Remember,' said Lord Shrewsbury, 'we met in that back lane behind the Cockerel and Cow alehouse in Hartfield yesterday?'

'Indeed I do,' Sir Richard replied sourly, looking as if he wished he had forgotten. 'And did you manage to satisfy your appetite while you were there?'

Lord Shrewsbury squirmed uncomfortably. 'Yes, yes...I...ahem, had a very nice meal there...'

The nobleman's discomfort in the face of such a simple inquiry caused a few raised eyebrows among the ladies, although Rowena did think there was something wolfish and subtlety mocking about Sir Richard's manner towards him.

'Lord Shrewsbury has a question to ask you, Sir Richard,' she said to the knight, before turning to Lord Shrewsbury. 'Isn't that so, my lord?'

'No, no, it is really not important!' Lord Shrewsbury blustered, with a dismissive flick of the wrist.

But Rowena, bold with anger, ignored him. 'Yes, I think it is. Sir Richard, his lordship wants to know if it is true that you visit a certain young lady in Hartfield who he believes to be a prostitute.'

No sooner were the words out of her mouth when Sir Richard lunged at Lord Shrewsbury and grabbed him by the fur-lined collar. 'A prostitute? How dare you!' His face, which almost touched Shrewsbury's, was drawn into a furious, wolf-like snarl.

Anne and Lady Sabina screamed in terror, while the quaking lord just whimpered pitifully, his chalk-white face screwed up in horror beneath the spittle showering down on it.

Rowena clutched her hands to her head. Why could she not have just kept her mouth shut? 'Sir Richard, put the lord down at once!'

The sheriff took no notice of her. 'You keep your dirty little mind out of my business, Shrewsbury!' he snarled down at his captive.

'Put him down,' begged Rowena. 'You're frightening the ladies!'

Continuing to ignore the pleas for peace, Sir Richard gave the nobleman a violent jerk that tore half his collar off. 'You snivelling weed, the only filth around here is you!' And with that he slammed Lord Shrewsbury's head, face down, into the plate containing the remains of the roast swan.

To the relief of those watching, Sir Richard decided to leave it at that. He let Lord Shrewsbury go and turned away in disgust.

Lord Shrewsbury slowly lifted his head from the table. Beneath the coating of fat, gravy and meat scraps, his every feature was filled with revulsion and horror. 'Look what the animal's done to me!' he gasped.

Anne and Lady Sabina immediately rushed to his assistance with cries of sympathy and consolation, handkerchiefs at the ready, and began wiping the grease from his face and hair.

'And if you would like to know who the lady that I so boldly visit is, I invite you to come along when I visit her tomorrow,' Sir

Richard said calmly.

'No thank you,' murmured Anne and Lady Sabina.

Sir Richard rested a dark, steely eye on Lord Shrewsbury. 'How about you; would you like to come?'

'No, no, you just go ahead without me,' Lord Shrewsbury squeaked fearfully, retreating behind the ladies.

Rowena stepped forward. 'I would like to come.'

She could feel the horrified stares of the others boring into her, and thought she caught a whisper of *I can't believe she is prepared to go anywhere with such a maniac...*

Sir Richard gathered up Lucifer's reins and placed a foot in the stirrup. 'Meet me at the castle tomorrow morning at about ten.' He then swung himself effortlessly up onto the big stallion.

Rowena nodded. 'I will be there.'

The knight was about to ride off, but suddenly stopped. 'Oh, I almost forgot to give you these.' He got some parchments out of Lucifer's saddlebag and handed them down to her.

'I thought that you might not be able to come to the castle today, so I brought these over. They need seeing to urgently. If you could see to them now, I will send my pageboy Pepin over later to collect them.'

Rowena reached up and took them from him. 'Yes, of course. I will do it right away.'

'And heed this,' he added in a low voice. 'Do not leave Shrewsbury alone with the boy, not even for a moment.'

The grave manner in which this warning was delivered left its impression on Rowena. She could think of no reason why Shrewsbury might endanger thirteen-year-old Pepin, but was firmly resolved to heed Sir Richard regardless.

She nodded. 'Tell him to come in the servant's door and ask a servant to fetch me down to the kitchens. The Cunninghams' guests never go into the servants' part of the manor.'

* * * *

When Rowena left Stoatley the next morning, the sun was rising into a cloudless blue sky that promised another hot day.

The sun-kissed damsel was unusually pensive as she walked along the rarely-used country path. The rabbits who stopped to watch her pass barely received a single glance in return. She was mystified about whom the lady Sir Richard visited was, and the only mysteries she liked were ones she knew all about. She was aware that the sheriff always rode into Hartfield every Saturday and Wednesday, but she had never given his destination much thought.

The discomfort she felt at the thought of the handsome knight having a lover annoyed her as well. If a woman claimed, as she did, that she did not care a single straw about a man, then she ought not to feel anything at the idea that his heart might belong to another.

When Rowena reached Eaglestone Castle, Sir Richard was not yet down from his chambers. After calling out a cheerful good morning to everyone, she plonked herself down on one of the wooden crates sitting in the courtyard outside the armoury door, where a group of soldiers had gathered. There was a constant stream of banter as the men worked on cleaning their weapons and equipment, and frequent outbreaks of rowdy laughter.

'If you polish that dagger anymore, Will, you'll rub it clean away,' one old soldier was saying to a younger man.

'I like to have my weapons in good order,' replied the young man. 'A soldier never knows when his life might depend on them.'

'I know why you like to have them in good order—so that you can preen and admire your reflection in the shiny steel!' said the other.

'Oh Savaric, don't be so hard on the poor young man!' said Rowena. 'You know how hard it is to impress that barmaid in the Cockerel and Cow that he's got his eye on.'

'Aye,' the old soldier replied sourly. 'She's a real shrew, that's for sure. Last time I were in that alehouse she emptied a tankard of ale over me head just because I gave her a little squeeze. I don't drink there no more.'

'If Will is not looking his best he might share a similar fate, might he not?'

'Aye,' Savaric grumbled. 'But if I were you, Will, I'd steer clear of that one. She's nothing but trouble.'

'Ignore him, Will,' said Rowena. 'I think you'd make a lovely couple. And if a woman will not put up with nonsense from lecherous old men who can't keep their hands to themselves, I say good for her!'

Will ran his finger along the blade, testing its sharpness. 'You heard what the lady said, Savaric. Keep your paws off my lass.'

'Your lass?' scoffed the other man. 'Now you really are getting ahead of yourself! You've yet to get even a single kind word out of that one.'

'Yes, well, a woman has her standards and does not like to decide over-quickly. But she will eventually, just you wait and see'.

Sergeant Gallagher came out of the armoury and, seeing Rowena there, made his way over. After greeting her, he perched himself on the crate next to her. 'How is everything at Stoatley, madam?

Rowena had told the sergeant several times just to call her Rowena, but he stilled only ever addressed her as 'madam' or 'Mistress Rowena'.

'Well, we have this guest, Lord Shrewsbury, staying with us for the next four weeks. He is the most irritating, nasty little man

I have met in my entire life. I'm telling you, you would hardly think it was possible find so many different faults combined in one man! Anyway, the funniest thing happened when Sir Richard ran into him yesterday.'

Gallagher winced. 'This is not going to be good…'

Rowena then proceeded to recount the story of the incident with the swan scraps, right down to the smallest detail.

Her tale was received with uproarious laughter. Even Sergeant Gallagher could not resist a good chuckle.

'What's the joke?' The sheriff's voice came from behind her.

The seated men leapt from their seats and stood to attention.

'Oh, we were just hearing of a humorous little incident,' said Gallagher. 'You really wouldn't be interested, sir.'

Sir Richard gave the waiting men a curt nod. 'Don't let me keep you from your duties.'

'Sir!' chorused the soldiers, bowing sharply.

Then the men quietly disbanded and got back about their business.

'Shall we go, Rowena?' said Sir Richard.

She gave a nervous smile and nodded, still wavering between excitement at the promise of an interesting experience and dread at what she might find out.

He headed off, his large strides covering the ground with ease. She wordlessly followed him out the castle, having to hurry along at an uncomfortable pace that was between a run and walk in order to keep up with him. But she was much too relieved to have been spared the terrors of the massive Lucifer to even consider complaining.

With all the rain that had fallen recently, the road's dirt surface had changed from dry summer dust which blew over the surrounding fields in great clouds when the wind was up, into a treacherously slippery mud. They both carefully kept to the edges of the road to avoid the worst of it, Rowena hitching the hem of her dress well up to keep it out of the dirt.

Sir Richard seemed rather preoccupied, making no attempt to break the silence as they walked.

When they reached the outskirts of Hartfield, Sir Richard turned off the main route and into the part of town where many of the more well-to-do folk lived. The quiet lanes, with their pretty, well-spaced two-storey houses, were unfamiliar to Rowena. Preferring to avoid the noise, smell and bustle of the busy town, she never ventured into its rabbit warren of twisting streets and dark, narrow alleyways. The only part of Hartfield where she ever went was the market square on market days, which happened twice a week.

Presently, Sir Richard slowed in front of a tall, narrow timber-framed house with wattle and daub sides, which was surrounded by a hornbeam hedge of a little over head-height. In front of the hedge, a row of gillyflowers and periwinkles spilled over the rocks forming a garden edge and tumbling out onto the grassy lane.

Sir Richard turned into a gap in the hedge. 'Step this way, if you please.'

She followed him in.

He proceeded up the path winding through the large and sprawling garden surrounding the house, where lilies, peonies, violets, lavenders and roses grew in abundance. When he reached the front door, he opened it without knocking and entered.

The hall that Rowena nervously stepped into was small but pleasant. A copper tub filled with a large arrangement of flowers sat on a little table in the corner, which, along with a table, some simple wooden benches and one chair, were the room's only contents. There was no sign of anyone inside.

Sir Richard unbuckled his sword and dagger and placed them on the table. He then began undoing the laces on his leather doublet, something she had never seen him without before.

What could he possibly be doing?

Her baffled expression did not go unheeded by Sir Richard, who smiled wryly. 'She tells me that I feel like a scaly dragon wearing this.'

So it must be true! Surely he would not say something like that if he was not about to meet a lover?

As she followed Sir Richard through the house to the back door, she was filled with curiosity. What sort of woman did it take to capture and keep the heart of such a man? No doubt she was a great beauty…

But the sight which met Rowena's eyes as she stepped back outside was not what she had expected at all. There was indeed a damsel in the garden; a dark-haired slip of a maiden who looked no more than seventeen. She sat on a bank of creeping thyme under the dappled shade of a linden tree, surrounded by nodding flowers. The frail, sylph-like girl was dressed in a thin, flowing, white gown that made her appear so ethereal Rowena half expected her to dissolve into the air like a phantom.

At the sound of the door, the girl delightedly cried 'Richard, Richard!' in a high, girlish voice, and groped for something at her side.

Even though she seemed to be having trouble finding what she was searching for, the maiden did not lower her eyes to look for it.

Rowena thought it most strange until suddenly it dawned on her: the girl was blind!

The ethereal girl quickly found what she was searching for—a crutch leaning against the bank she sat on. Before Sir Richard could reach her, she had pulled herself to her feet and began limping towards him, leaning on the stick for support.

He hurried to meet her with outstretched arms. 'There's no need to get up, Everild, I'm here.'

Having reached him, the girl dropped her crutch and flung her arms around him. 'Oh, how lovely it is to see you, Richard! I have been sitting here listening for you all morning.'

Sir Richard warmly returned her embrace. 'It's good to see you too.'

'I know Aunty Amice says that sitting here waiting for you will not make you get here any faster,' the maiden gushed joyfully, 'but I am always so impatient for you to come I just can't help myself!'

He smiled fondly and kissed her cheek. 'Dearest Everild, always so cheerful.'

'How could I be anything but cheerful today? Wednesdays and Saturdays are my favouritest days!'

'Come, let's sit down. I want to hear about everything you've been doing since I last saw you.'

As soon as Sir Richard was seated, the girl deposited herself into his lap and clasped one of his large hands between her two tiny ones.

Sir Richard smiled down at the girl with a look of tenderness that Rowena had never seen in him before, had not thought he was even capable of until now. 'So come, tell me all about it.'

'I will tell you,' she said shyly, 'but first, won't you tell me who the lady you have brought with you is, or is it a secret?'

'Clever girl! How did you know?'

'I heard her footsteps and the rustle of her gown moving across the grass, silly.'

'But her feet barely made a sound on the soft ground.'

'Yes, that is because she is a small, light-footed lady,' the maiden replied as though she were stating the obvious. 'Now, are you going to tell me who she is?'

'Of course.' He motioned to Rowena, who was hanging back, to come over.

She obediently stepped forward.

'This is Rowena.'

'The cunning young lady who does all your accounts and clever things?' the girl asked.

Sir Richard laughed. 'Yes, that's right.'

Now able to see the ethereal girl from up close, Rowena noticed a pale scar running down one of her cheeks, and another, deeper scar across the bridge of her nose. The ugly marks stood out painfully in what was otherwise a delicately beautiful face.

Sir Richard then looked at Rowena. 'And this is Everild, my sister.'

His sister! No wonder he was so angry about the accusation that she was a prostitute. Rowena could understand that the poor maiden might not want people to see her face, but why had Sir Richard kept so quiet about his sister's existence?

'Delighted to meet you,' said Rowena, and was about to offer her hand, but stopped, unsure of how to act towards a blind person so as not to startle.

But Everild let go of Sir Richard and tentatively held out a little hand. 'Nice to meet you too, Rowena.'

Rowena warmly grasped Everild's hand, which, even on this hot day, still felt rather cold. 'I must say, your existence is a very well kept secret.' She darted a questioning glance at Sir Richard. 'I did not realise that your brother had any living relatives.'

Why did he have to be so mysterious? Surely he was not so ashamed of his sister that he did not want anyone to know about her?

But Sir Richard just looked away uneasily and Everild turned nervously back to him, creating an awkward silence.

Rowena regretted her annoyance instantly. 'Well, never mind that! Good things are worth waiting for.' She seated herself down next to them and smiled brightly. 'Now, Everild, I absolutely insist on knowing all about you.'

'I live here with Aunty Amice—well she's not really my aunt, but she's just as kind and good as a real one!'

'She looks after you, does she?'

'Yes. Richard hired her when we had to move out of the manor.'

'Sir Richard takes good care of you too?'

'Oh yes, the very best care.' She turned to Sir Richard and kissed his cheek. 'Richard is the nicest brother anyone could ever wish for!'

Rowena could not help smiling at the enthusiastic gesture, although Sir Richard looked rather embarrassed by his sister's glowing praise.

'That is good. I'm sure he loves you very much.'

Everild squeezed his hand. 'Yes, and I love him very much too.

Rowena could not help feeling a tinge of envy at the loving bond they shared. The man she knew alternated between sullen moroseness, heated fury and, for a little light relief, merciless teasing with a hint of sadism. She could hardly believe it was the same man.

Everild drew herself a little closer to her brother and whispered something in his ear.

'No, I'm sure she won't mind, dearest,' he replied.

Everild whispered to him again.

He smiled and nodded. 'Of course.' He looked to Rowena. 'Everild would like to know if you would mind if she felt your face. It's the only way she can get an idea of what you look like.'

'By all means. I don't mind a bit.'

Everild reached out her hand towards Rowena but moved it too far, missing her face.

Sir Richard quickly took hold of Everild's hand and placed it on Rowena's cheek.

Everild carefully moved her hand over Rowena's face, feeling her nose, her lips, her forehead, and lastly, her hair. When she was satisfied, she took hold of Sir Richard's hand again and snuggled up against him. 'What colour is Rowena's hair?'

'It's red-brown.'

'How lovely! And what about her colouring?'

'Her face is sun-browned and freckled, and her eyes are green.'

'How adorable,' Everild cried delightedly. 'I'm sure she looks just like she sounds—sweet, kind and cute as a kitten!'

Sir Richard squirmed a little and seemed unsure how to respond.

Everild gave his shoulders a shake. 'Do you not think I am right? Say something!'

He was careful to avoid looking at Rowena. 'Yes, of course you are right, sweet sister.'

'Wonderful!' She beamed up at him. 'So, Richard, when are you going to propose to her?'

'Everild!' Sir Richard yelped. The once menacing warrior now looked as if he wished the ground would open up and swallow him. 'We merely work together! Please, you are embarrassing my poor clerk.'

The visit did not last long after that, and in its meagre duration, Sir Richard took care to keep conversation well away from anything connected to his clerk.

As soon as he and Rowena were out of the door, Sir Richard began walking at a very fast pace. He clearly had still not recovered from the shock and embarrassment garnered by his sister's bold question. He had hardly looked at Rowena for the rest of the visit, and seemed keen to avoid her on the way home by keeping well ahead of her. Rowena could understand this. Springing a question like that was likely to rattle any man. But he now had got so far ahead of her that he was in danger of disappearing from view altogether.

'Sir Richard, please slow down!' she called to him. 'My legs are much shorter than yours; I really can't keep up!'

He came to a reluctant halt.

'Without you here I would be helplessly lost,' she gasped as she finally caught up with him. 'All these streets look the same. I wouldn't have a clue how to get back to the castle from here.'

He was still careful to avoid catching her eye, but did slow his pace considerably.

She could now walk alongside him. 'I really don't mind about what your sister said, so please, don't be embarrassed.'

'I'm not embarrassed!' he snapped, beginning to speed up again.

'Oh, wait for me!'

He reluctantly slowed. 'Pardon me.'

'Your sister is a lovely girl. You are very lucky to have her. I only wish that my own living relatives were half as nice.'

'She is an angel. How she came from such a brood of vipers as the Hastings God only knows! But what *is* clear is that I don't deserve her.'

'If you don't mind me asking; how did your sister get the scars on her face?'

The look with which he greeted this question suggested that he did mind. But he answered anyway. 'It happened when she was five years old. She was set upon by outlaws while travelling through a wild and lawless forest. They pulled her jewellery off, then slashed her across the face and stabbed her in the leg. She has been blind and lame ever since.' Sir Richard's voice had a hollow, emotionless tone as he told the story, as if he could not bear to think about it.

Sensing the pain the subject caused him, Rowena did not dig any further, although she felt sure that he was only telling her part of the story about what happened to Everild.

Rowena hesitated to ask the question his arrangements posed, but she could not keep silent. 'I ask this not out of idle curiosity,' she began cautiously, 'but because I am responsible for your finances. Why do you pay the lease of that house when your position as sheriff provides you with Eaglestone Castle, free of charge, to use as your own? It has more than enough space to house any number of relatives.'

'My sister would struggle to find her way around such a large pile, the stairs would be a constant danger, and most of all, I do not want her becoming entangled in any of the peril and evil that writhe about such men of war and disrepute as myself.'

The remainder of the walk back to Eaglestone Castle passed in a silence that was thoughtful on her part, and tensely self-flagellating on his.

* * * *

'Mistress Walden!'

Rowena quickly looked around to see who had called her name. It being a market day, the street was crowded with people. At first she was not sure who had called out, but then she recognised a man standing behind her among the many people filling Hartfield's main street. It was Walter Gray, the father of the kidnapped twins.

She nodded courteously. 'Sire, God give you good day.'

He doffed his soft velvet cap as he hurried towards her. 'Damsel, God keep you.'

She tried to look friendly and easy of mind, but was sure her shaky smile betrayed her nervousness. 'How is it with you?'

Still holding his cap, he gave a dismissive wave of the hand that suggested the answer was so obvious it did not merit saying. 'Have you discovered who these villains are yet?'

'No, but Sir Richard and his men rode over to Lothbury this morning. We think the felons might have passed through our neighbouring shire, so hopefully they will find some clues there.'

The man ran his fingers through his silver hair. They were shaking with agitation. 'Why did the sheriff not go over there days ago if he thinks that these evil rogues were seen there?'

'He did not find this out until two days ago, when I rode over to the scene of the latest kidnapping with him and we searched it again.'

'He has known about this new lead for two days and only now is he doing something about following it up?'

Rowena could see frustration and anger building in the man, but could think of little that she could say to pacify him. 'I'm truly sorry that we have not been able to bring your daughters back to you yet, sire, and I can understand your anger, but Sir Richard is trying his best to find the missing maidens.'

'Trying his best?' Walter Gray's already strained voice rose to a shout. 'That man does not care about my daughters! If he did, he would be putting some proper effort into trying to find them!'

'Please calm yourself, sire. I can assure you that Sir Richard is now doing everything he can to find your daughters.'

'You mean he wasn't doing everything he could before?'

'That's not what I meant—'

'That man is a complete failure as sheriff! He does nothing to protect the people of this shire from felons because he is too busy beating up starving petty thieves and finding new ways to squeeze more taxes out of us!'

A crowd had begun to gather at the sound of the shouting. Rowena knew Sir Richard would not be happy if he heard that there had been public accusations made against him. She just wished she could find a way to silence the man, or at least get him to somewhere where he would not be heard by half the town.

But the furious, grieving father had not even started. 'That Sir Richard is bent, corrupt!' He now addressed not just her, but the whole crowd. 'He's skimming off a great deal of the taxes we pay to him! Friends, I know how much the taxes demanded by the king are; the people of this shire are forced to pay half this much again!'

There was an angry growl from the people gathered there.

Rowena began to panic a little. But there was nothing she could do now. The situation was out of control.

'Many sheriffs are corrupt,' he continued, 'but the amount of money that our sheriff steals from us is unreasonable! If he does not even do his job of keeping the law, of keeping the people of this shire safe, why should we put up with this?'

'Why indeed!' shouted a young woman at the back of the crowd. 'Me sister nearly starved to death last winter when she was taken ill and couldn't work. She had no savings left because she'd paid them all to the sheriff's taxman!'

There was another growl of agreement from the crowd, louder this time.

'The time for passively tolerating this outrage is over!' cried Gray, punching the air. 'Now is the time for action!'

A great cheer erupted from the crowd, which was growing by the moment. Rowena was being pushed and jostled on every side, but escape was now impossible. The weight of the people pushing from the back, trying to get closer to the action, meant she could hardly move.

'The time has come for the people of this town to demand an end to this corruption and lawlessness!'

There was another cheer from the people, and many shouts of agreement.

Gray held up a piece of paper. 'This is a petition I am sending to the king, demanding that Sir Richard Hastings be removed from his position. If the king does not grant this request, then, my fellow citizens, we must take matters into our own hands. We must refuse to acknowledge him as our sheriff. We will refuse to pay our taxes to him!'

He paused until the thunderous cheer that roared forth from the crowd had died down. 'I know,' he continued, 'that I have every one of the good citizens of Hartfield and her neighbouring villages behind me in this!'

Cheers and shouts of 'Right you are, sire!' and 'Aye!' filled the streets.

Walter Gray raised his hand. 'I thank you, loyal friends!'

The cheering crowd surged towards Gray and lifted him up onto their shoulders, then poured down the street carrying him aloft.

Rowena seized hold of the signpost in front of her and clung to it. The tide of people swept passed her, at times pressing so hard she could scarcely breathe. She only just managed to keep hold of the pole and avoid being swept down the street with them.

Once the rowdy mob had gone, it was some time before she dared to loosen her grip.

.7.

Lightning Strikes Again and a Phoenix Arises

HURRY up and get out of the damn way!'

Hearing Sir Richard's by-now familiar bellow coming from the courtyard below, Rowena walked over to the window of the sheriff's office where, the day's work done, she had been preparing to leave for home.

The sheriff and his company were riding in through the gate, their progress slowed by a group of soldiers who had just come off duty and were exiting the castle en masse. The returning men and horses were covered in dust from the road and dripping with sweat.

When Sir Richard reached the centre of the courtyard, he dismounted and started shouting orders at his men. Judging from the mood he was in, they had not had a very successful day.

Wishing she had been ready to go sooner and thus avoided Sir Richard and his foul mood, Rowena tossed the last of her things into her leather satchel. Thinking quickly, she realised she might still be able to avoid him by getting down the stairs and waiting in a side room until he had gone up to his chambers.

But as she hurried down the stairs, just managing to take them two at a time, she heard his heavy tread and jingling spurs approaching. She paused in alarm, only halfway down the second flight. Realising there was nothing she could do, Rowena took a deep breath and continued slowly down.

A few heartbeats later, Sir Richard stood in the middle of the narrow staircase, blocking Rowena's path and forcing her to stop. 'I heard Walter Gray nearly started a riot in the street after *you* talked to him.'

Rowena crossed her arms and met his frosty, dagger-like glare, for once able to look him in the eye without having to tilt her head back, as the step evened out their considerable height difference. 'Yes, I did meet him in the street.'

'What did you say to him? You didn't say anything critical about me did you?' His voice had an edge that spelt danger.

She swept away some unruly red curls that had fallen over her face with a flick of her fingers. It had been a long and difficult day, much of it spent trying to make the accounts balance, and she was in no mood for being interrogated. 'No, I did not.'

'That old goat is always pestering me, trying to drag my name through the mud and shame me!' the dark knight muttered savagely.

Rowena felt her face becoming hot as her anger rose. 'Is that all you can think about? The poor man is completely grief-stricken and all you can think about is your stupid reputation, which is already virtually none existent!'

'The man almost started a riot after talking to you! What the hell did you say to him?'

'Just the truth. Nothing more, nothing less.'

He staggered slightly. 'You did what! Do you actually *want* me to be killed by an angry mob? Is that it?'

She gave a heatedly dismissive wave of the hand that had him ducking for fear she would take his eye out. 'No, I didn't tell him the truth about the money, just the investigation. But I almost wish I had now. You're causing the poor of this shire a lot of suffering with your harsh taxes!'

Sir Richard's dark eyes seemed to become blacker still and his lips tensed to a thin, hard line. The dangerous look of barely controlled violence in his eyes made her afraid, but she forced herself to stand and face him.

'I've had enough of you meddling in things that are not your concern,' he snarled. 'You are just my clerk; you have no right to pass judgement on me, you insolent little quill-pusher!'

She let out a snort of derision. 'Meddling? You have managed to get yourself a blackmailer—which is hardly surprising considering your foul temper and brutish manner—and made yourself as poor as a church mouse, yet still you expect me to find a way of paying all the expenses with your nonexistent funds!'

He eyed her with cold fury. 'I managed perfectly fine before you came along.'

She really was wasting her time here. As for continually allowing herself to be treated with such rudeness, it was simply wrong. How would Mother have felt if she had lived to see her daughter used like a serf? She could hear her oft-repeated words as if they had been spoken only yesterday: *self-respect is the very last thing you should let them take from you, daughter.*

Rowena glared back at Sir Richard in silence for a few moments as she considered her next words. Then she took a deep breath. 'Very well, as you do not welcome my presence here, I shall leave your employment.'

The sheriff's rigid fury had seemed likely to explode into violence at any moment, but these words sent a strange ripple across his face. 'I didn't say your work wasn't useful,' he replied hastily, in a hard tone that seemed to mask a deeper emotion. 'I just want you to keep out of things you know nothing about and which are none of your—'

'You just expect me to wordlessly put up with your behaviour,' she interrupted, 'behaviour which no woman should have to tolerate, especially from someone such as yourself—a knight who has taken an oath to adhere to the code of chivalry!

This code states that a knight should be charitable to the poor, protect the weak, behave in a courteous way, uphold the faith, and—' She drew herself to her full height. 'Honour and respect women. Yet you, Sir Richard, flagrantly and repeatedly break all of these promises!'

As soon as the words were out of Rowena's mouth, all of Sir Richard's frosty calmness disappeared in a flash. He leapt up onto the step directly below hers, so he now stood higher than her in spite of her extra step, and drew himself right up until their faces were almost touching. His breath came hot and fast onto her face. 'You are an insolent, hellishly irritating imp who knows nothing, absolutely nothing, about me, so don't tell me I'm a damn scoundrel!'

She flinched, desperately wanting to turn around and run back up the stairs, but instead settled for hurriedly hitching the skirt of her red velvet gown out of the way and climbing backwards onto the step above.

After taking a moment to calm herself, she mustered the courage to face the dark knight's enraged glare. 'You claim that my words are untrue, yet in the same breath you chose to speak in the most discourteous and dishonourable way!'

Still breathing hard, Sir Richard lifted a black-gauntleted hand and placed it slowly around Rowena's throat. His unblinking, coldly burning dark eyes never left hers. 'Are you saying that I am not worthy of knighthood?'

The long, leather-encased fingers resting on either side of her windpipe did not exert any pressure, yet their very stillness spoke of iron-hard strength. Fear did half the work Sir Richard threatened to inflict; she hardly dared breathe in case any movement on her part brought the menacing hand together.

Noticing that her arms were shaking violently, she clasped them tightly together behind her back. 'Sir Richard, please.'

He callously eyed his clerk for what seemed an eternity, then silently moved his thumb back to rest beside his fingers and began to lift his hand away.

The moment the petrifying fingers left her neck, Rowena's fear melted into a flood of anger. 'Any knight who behaves towards a lady in the way that you are doing right now brings shame upon himself and upon the man who made the error of dabbing him knight!'

She had been quick to speak—too quick. He had had not yet unhanded her, and while her indignant words were still echoing through the cold, dark stairwell, his powerful fingers were back around her throat in a flash. How she wished she had not spoken! But it was too late now.

'How—dare—you!' he choked, tightening his fingers around her neck. 'I curse the day that I met you!'

Rowena should not have been surprised at Sir Richard's sudden violence. She had been half-expecting something like this to happen ever since Lady Sabina had volunteered her for the unwanted position. Yet, for an unfathomable reason, she *was* surprised.

As his hands began to squeeze the life out of her, she went limp and stared back at him in shock. 'Why did I trust you?' she gasped. 'Why did I love…' But as the last of her breath left her body, her sentence trailed off unfinished.

Suddenly the choking hands were gone. Bereft of their support, Rowena fell to the ground at Sir Richard's feet. But the steep stairs allowed such violently arrived things no rest. She did not stop tumbling until she lay in a heap at the bottom.

Barely had she stopped falling when the maiden was already attempting to drag herself up. Half-blinded by her dishevelled hair, she groped franticly for a supportive wall. Something instantly was in her reaching hand, as though it had reached out to her—because it *had* reached out!

With a gasp, she pulled her hand free from Sir Richard's grasp.

'If you think that I'm just some weak, naive girl you can bully into submission, you, sir, are wrong!'

His tall figure darkened the passageway before her. 'I did not mean to hurt you. Let me help you—'

'No!' she cried, shrinking away from him.

Hastily, she pushed back the curtain of hair and wiped away the tears of pain filling her eyes.

The man now standing before Rowena looked truly concerned about her condition. All traces of rage were gone. He carefully held out his hand to her, as one might to a skittish animal. 'Please, allow me.'

Eyeing him fearfully, she dragged herself to her feet. 'Consider the position of clerk vacant.' Then she held out the satchel with a trembling hand. 'Here, this contains some of your papers.'

Sir Richard did not seem to notice what she held out. A sudden change had come over him, a strange, tortured look that was the closest thing to fear she had ever seen in him. He shook his head. 'No.'

'Take it.'

'No,' he repeated, a note of cold desperation streaking through his voice. 'No, you can't leave; I didn't say I wanted you to leave!'

Silently, she let her hand fall back down. Surely he did not actually *like* her? His manner towards her had ranged from open hostility to plain indifference, and never once had he thanked her or praised her. In all likelihood, he was just concerned about how his finances would fear without her expert touch. But no more could an answer be read in his eyes than the bottom of the deepest and blackest pool be seen by peering down from above. Only her own reflection met her sight.

She placed the satchel down on the floor, then slowly straightened up again. 'Good-bye, Sir Richard. It was interesting being insulted, abused and overworked by you. I shall never forget you as long as I live.'

He took a step towards her. 'No, Rowena, stop talking nonsense! You misunderstood me—I did not say I wanted rid of you!'

She retreated back several steps, never taking her eyes off the sheriff for even a moment. He had wanted rid of her from the day she first set foot in Eaglestone. He just could not be so insolent if he did not. And insolent he certainly was, even if he may possibly have had a little grudging respect for her deep down.

'Rowena, I will not lose my clerk over a misunderstanding.'

'I understand your brutality and insults perfectly, Sir Richard!'

He grudgingly held up his hands in surrender. 'Alright, I accept that I have been discourteous to you—'

'You are a beast, Sir Richard, a perfect beast! If you had the slightest bit of honour or decency, you would have informed me you did not require my services rather than trying to bully me into submission! I pray that I'm never foolish enough to set foot in this dark hall again. Now kindly let me pass, sir!'

Sir Richard did not move. His eyes seemed to be begging her not to go. 'Rowena, I—I—' he began, but faltered mid-sentence. An apology had clearly been on the tip of his tongue, but it was gone.

She stamped her foot. 'Your pride does you no credit—leave it for those worthy of harbouring the emotion!'

Rage flashed across his face once more. 'How dare you insult my honour like this! I will not stand for it!'

Rowena shrunk back against the wall. 'Sir Richard, if my words displease you, let me leave this place and never come back. I will do it willingly; you do not have to strangle me to death in order to get rid of me.'

He stepped directly in front of her. 'Will you not hear?' he said quietly, looking down at her with hollow eyes. 'I want you here. I want you to belong to me. If only those scornful words would be silent ever more…'

She caught her breath sharply as his hand touched upon her throat. Her earlier fear paled beside this new horror. His eyes had a terrible, vacant stare that made her blood run cold.

'Sir Richard, let me pass, I beg you.'

After the most terrifying few moments of her life, his eyelids flickered and he let his hand fall.

Seizing her chance, she quickly pushed past him and fled.

'Rowena, damn you!' she heard him bellow after her as she jumped down the next flight of stairs three at a time in her dash for the exit.

She did not look back.

Once Rowena was out of the castle, she broke into a run. She did not stop running until she reached Stoatley Manor, where she continued up to her room, bolted the door and flung herself onto her tiny bed.

* * * *

'Is it not simply delicious?' demanded Lady Sabina, giving a twirl to show off the new gown she was wearing.

'Yes darling, it is totally gorgeous,' agreed her friend Anne.

They had been excitedly gossiping and admiring each other's finery for over an hour. Seated in the solar with them, Rowena was desperately trying to finish the pile of handkerchiefs her aunt had told her to hem, so she could go outside.

Lady Sabina turned to her cousin. 'And what do you think, Rowena?'

'Ahem, yes, it's very nice,' she replied unconvincingly.

Lady Sabina tossed her head haughtily. 'Such a pity it would not suit you.'

'Yes darling, indeed it would not,' said Anne. 'Rowena's ruddy complexion would not be flattered by its colour. She is so tawny from the sun; the white would not suit her at all.'

Lady Sabina gave the dress another twirl. 'The gold embroidery on this gown would make her awful freckles stand out most terribly too.'

'That is before you even consider the fact that her rather *ample* bosom would burst right out of it,' added Anne.

'I cannot even begin to imagine how simply *awful* it must be to be so fat,' Lady Sabina said with a shudder.

Whilst Rowena was buxom, to say she was fat was both unkind and inaccurate. Not being the width of a twig did not make one fat. Rowena bit her lip, barely managing to stop herself from responding angrily to Sabina and Anne's taunting. She knew that if she did, her cousin would use it against her.

Forcing herself to remain calm, she continued sewing. 'Thank you for your concern, but I'm happy with the clothes I have and don't want your new dress.'

Rowena was now almost beginning to regret her outburst to Sir Richard four days ago. She wondered if she had been a little hasty. Being strangled by an evil sheriff was only marginally worse than spending endless days cooped up with Lady Cunningham, Lady Sabina, Anne, and a pile of sewing that the hours seemed to make bigger rather than smaller. At least *he* simply ignored her most of the time, and the job did have its moments.

She sighed. To think that this morning was an actual improvement on the previous one, when Lord Shrewsbury had *not* been out hawking... At least death at Sir Richard's hands had one bright side: it was quick. Unlike the slowly-dragging years it might take to die of boredom in Stoatley. As for the evil master himself... She paused her needle and frowned. For some annoying reason, she missed him a little. Maybe, like a foolish, goose-brained girl, she *had* been a tad in love with him after all. The beast. But not anymore—although, in fairness, some allowance needed to be made for the circumstances. He had been in an especially bad mood, and the subject of the kidnapped maidens' father had clearly touched a raw nerve. This was understandable. Someone already under strain would be likely to react badly if they found out that they had just been denounced by an angry mob which had nearly started a riot.

She tugged at her thread, which had got stuck yet again, and sighed. He might be bad tempered and brutish, she thought grimly, but at least he doesn't mock my appearance. And the work at the castle had been more interesting than sewing these stupid things!

But after the harsh words that had been spoken, she could not see how their relationship could possibly continue. He would never forgive her for the things she had said. Of that she felt sure. And neither could she forget. Such a cowardly and cruel attack was abominable. That look in his eyes…

'Ow!' she yelped, pricking her finger on the needle.

A large drop of red blood fell onto the white handkerchief in her hand. Wonderful. Now it was ruined. Lady Cunningham would not be happy.

'Do my eyes deceive or is that not a horse and rider galloping down the road to Stoatley?' Anne called to Lady Sabina, from her seat at the window.

Lady Sabina hurried over to the window. 'Yes, indeed it is, darling. I wonder who it might be.'

But Rowena just kept working on her sewing, hoping to finish the hemming so she could get out as quickly as possible and avoid having to suffer yet another of Lady Sabina's awful visitors.

Shortly, hoof beats sounded on the cobbles outside.

'I still cannot see who he is,' reported Anne. 'Although I am sure I have seen that black horse he is riding before somewhere; I cannot think where.'

'I do wish he would take down the hood of that wretched indigo cloak he has got pulled around his face, so we can see who he is,' added Sabina.

A man clad all in black except for an indigo cloak, and riding a black horse? Surely it wasn't him—Rowena rushed over to the window. Yes, it was.

'It's Sir Richard Hastings,' she said quietly.

Had he come to see Lord Cunningham? But Lord Cunningham was not at home—was Sir Richard still going to come in? Oh no, please don't come in!

Rowena listened intently. Muffled by distance and timber but still audible, the manor's great door clanked shut and the sound of voices came from the hall.

Yes, he had come in.

She knew it was her he had come to see. He was so angry when she had left him standing on the stairs. He would never forgive her for speaking to him like that, never. What could he possibly want? Her heart began to race. She did not want to see him, to speak to him. What would she say?

But she knew she could not get out without him seeing her, so remained seated where she was and waited, awful visions of Sir Richard dragging her out by the hair in front of Anne and Lady Sabina passing through her mind.

'Sir Richard?' cried Anne delightedly. 'I knew he was much taken with me when we met in Hartfield the other day. I could just tell! He was playing hard to get, you know, talking all rough and curt to me. He knows how wild we ladies go over a rogue. No doubt he saw me coming over to Stoatley and is coming to call on us, knowing I will be here.'

'You are wrong, Anne!' Lady Sabina said angrily. 'It is me he has come to see. Everyone knows I am the most beautiful lady in the district. It is only natural that a man as handsome as he is would choose the most beautiful lady of his acquaintance. He has just been biding his time, not wishing to appear desperate.'

'He's nearly here!' cried Anne. 'Quick, where's that mirror?' She began running around the room franticly searching for it. 'My hair needs fixing—I need to find it!' Anne finally noticed that Sabina had the mirror and was using it to smooth her own hair. 'Give that to me!' she screamed, trying to pull it off her friend.

A knock sounded on the door and a servant maid looked in. 'Sir Richard Hastings is here. Shall I show him up?'

'Yes, Millicent, show him up please,' said Rowena.

The other two ladies were still fighting over the hand mirror and had not noticed the servant.

Waiting for him to appear, Rowena breathed in deeply, trying in vain to slow her racing pulse. She could not deny she was drawn to him. There was something about him that she found deeply fascinating. Yet he was so angry, so sinister…

'Sir Richard Hastings!' announced the serving maid, flinging open the solar's large wooden door.

Upon hearing this, Anne and Lady Sabina immediately stopped fighting and, hurriedly attempting to smooth their dishevelled hair and clothes, sat down.

Sir Richard strode into the room.

Rowena immediately searched his face for any clues to his intentions. But she found nothing except a grim, stony mask.

Ignoring Anne and Lady Sabina's simpering greeting, he continued past them to where Rowena was seated by the fireplace at the far end of the room.

She rose to her feet and curtsied nervously. 'Sir Richard, greetings.'

'Good day.' He bowed stiffly. 'Rowena, I need to speak with you in private.'

She breathed a little easier. At least he was not going to humiliate her in front of Anne and Lady Sabina.

'Yes, of course,' she replied in a shaky voice. 'Perhaps we could walk in the garden?'

He gave a quick nod.

As she led the way, Rowena tried, not altogether successfully, to act normally in front of the other ladies. 'I was just about to go out there for a little fresh air when I saw you coming. The last of the summer flowers always put on such a pretty display,' she said in the most casual tone she could muster.

Sir Richard followed Rowena down the stairs and out the door in silence. She felt too desperately uncomfortable to look him in the eye, but could tell without even looking at him that he was in a state of agitation.

She felt sick with dread. What if he was so angry with her that he slandered her to Lord Cunningham, and her uncle threw her out? Where would she go then? At least a successful throttling attempt would not have left her with that worry to contend with...

Having reached the small wooden door that led into the walled garden, Rowena fumbled with the latch, her shaking hands unable to grasp it properly.

'Allow me.'

She started at the sound of his voice from behind, and quickly stepped back.

He swiftly unlatched the door and held it open for her.

As soon as they were enclosed in the privacy of the walled garden, Sir Richard started to speak. 'I have a great deal of respect for the work you do at Eaglestone Castle. I hope you can forgive me for not always having made that apparent to you.' His tone was grave and uneasy. As usual, he was uncomfortable in humility.

Made that apparent? Rowena thought angrily. That was an

understatement if ever I heard one! What he *has* made apparent is his dislike, mistrust and desire to silence me forever.

With her eyes fixed ahead of her, she continued walking nervously along the path in silence. She was too afraid to look at Sir Richard lest her hard-won composure should crumble.

'Rowena, I had a regard for you which I did not welcome. I am regretful if my manner towards you came across as one of coldness as a result.'

'A regard which you did not welcome?' Rowena gasped, his words stinging her painfully.

How could he be so cruel, coming here to add insult to injury? She angrily blinked away the tears that were beginning to fill her eyes and started walking faster, desperately wishing he would go away. How come he was always making her cry, damn him!

Sir Richard's long stride matched hers with ease. 'Pardon me, I did not say that very well,' he responded hastily, his stony discomfort heating a little.

Their fast pace had brought the unhappy pair to the end of the walk, where a low stone wall stood between them and the garden pool beyond. Rowena was distressed at being forced to halt, but she made up for it by crossing her arms and looking determinedly out over the placid green water, where hosts of jewel-like dragonflies darted and hovered on gauzy wings.

A hand was placed on her shoulder. 'What I meant was—' Sir Richard began earnestly.

'I understand your meaning perfectly!' she interrupted, angrily shaking his hand off. 'You think it is beneath you to have anything but contempt for a woman of lower birth who is neither fashionable nor beautiful in the eyes of your peers!'

'Rowena, look at me! I believed your intentions towards me to be dishonourable, believed that you wished to win my trust and confidence in order to betray me.'

She could not bear to look at him. 'I gave you no cause to

think me guilty of such vile intentions!'

Nothing except the lazy chirping of grass crickets and hum of bees reached Rowena's fearfully waiting ears. Then the soft creak of leather and muffled clink of metal which usually accompanied Sir Richard when he seated himself came from behind her. It was followed by a tense sigh.

'I'm ashamed, Rowena, ashamed...'

Surprise caused her to turn around instinctively. Sir Richard sat on a large flat boulder beside the path, resting his chin on his cupped hand as he stared gloomily at a marble statue of a sorrowing angel set amid a nearby drift of blue forget-me-nots. The angel's wings were folded in pained awkwardness, its face etched with distress and hands clutched tightly together.

'I'm sorry for what I said to you on the stairs, and to lay hands on you in such a manner was unspeakable,' he said quietly. 'I was in a bad temper, but you are right; the words I uttered and the way I acted were dishonourable and unworthy of any knight or man of honour. I'm a thoughtless bastard who is incapable of withstanding anything without flying into a murderous rage. God, how you must hate and despise me!'

The dejected, regret-filled words almost seemed to be addressed to the grieving angel, for Sir Richard did not remove his eyes from the angel's weeping marble eyes as he spoke.

With a puzzled eyebrow raised, Rowena slowly uncrossed her arms. A few moments' observation satisfied her that Sir Richard's remorse was genuine. Much better actors than he have failed to look so guilty and miserable.

'Your initial mistrust of me was understandable in the circumstances,' she said stiffly. 'Neither of us asked or wished for the presence of the other.' She took a cautious step towards the seated sheriff. 'I don't hate you entirely...I know the castle is not a place where ladies are expected, or indeed welcomed. You treated me as you would any man in that position, and as you never asked for or wished for any woman to darken your doorway, it was not altogether fair of me to condemn your failure to act towards a lady with all of the delicacy a knight ought to.'

His glittering black eyes suddenly turned from the sorrowing angel to his hesitant ex-assistant. 'I know I frighten you, and I'm sorry. From a young age, my world has been a soldier's world of brutality and violence. It is a world I have learned to survive in and feel at home in. But the noble virtues of patience, kindness and courtesy to others I have neither been taught nor ever shown any talent for. No wonder you cannot bear to look at me. What noble-minded woman could feel anything but revulsion at the sight of such a brute?'

She dropped the red rosehip she had been absent-mindedly squashing between her nervous fingers and finally dared to look him in the eyes. 'Forgive me for saying you are not worthy of knighthood. War is a brutal business that cannot fail to leave a man stained.'

He nodded and smiled weakly at her fingers, which had been stained red from the juice of the rosehip. 'Ever since the day I arrived as a page at Lord Mordred's castle and was beaten to a pulp by the older boys, all I wanted was to grow up and kill people. Many were the thrashings I received in boyhood, but the day I walked out of the chapel as Sir Richard, I swore to myself that only in death would I ever again leave a fight defeated. I have the blood of many men upon my hands, but to have laid even one finger on such a virtuous and blameless lady as you gives me guilt a hundredfold greater. Rowena, let me make amends by proving to you that I can be chivalrous.'

Her brow furrowed doubtfully. 'Oh?'

He slid off the boulder and came to rest on bended knee before a very surprised Rowena. 'Will you honour me with a token of your favour?'

Was this him asking her to be his lady-love, as Lady Sabina informed her was the fashion at court among the knights? She could not bring herself to believe that such a man could possibly admire her for who she was: a down-at-heel, clumsy and unfashionable young woman with no prospects. Was this some cruel jest? It had to be. He was too proud a man ever to lower himself like that.

Rowena blinked hard. She felt uncomfortable enough already without having the tears welling in her eyes overflowing down her face. 'I might not be a proper lady, but it is cruel of you to mock me like this, Sir Richard!'

He flinched like a man who had been struck across the face. 'I swear to you, I am entirely sincere! I promise I will loyally serve and honour you until my dying day.'

Still apprehensive, she searched his face for dishonest motives. His earnest expression gave no reasonable cause for doubt. 'I accept,' she murmured, colouring slightly with embarrassment at finding herself an actor in such a formal and unexpected ritual.

He seized her hand and pressed it to his lips with a passionate fervour. 'Sweet mistress of my heart, your fair example and peerless, lily-hued virtue shall be the light that illuminates my path and the undying flame of courage within my soul forever more!'

Rowena was too busy staring down in wide-eyed surprise to consider what she ought to do next. But Sir Richard's look of expectation soon became apparent to her. She smiled uncertainly and silently cursed herself for not paying enough attention to Anne's endless talk of knights and courtly love.

To her relief, he did not let her suffer for long. 'A token, my lady, I beg of you, that I might wear it as a sign of my devotion to you.'

'Of course!' she exclaimed, growing a little redder at her slowness.

Then she thought for a moment. Sleeves and veils were popular tokens, but she did not own a veil, and as for sleeves, the mere thought of giving him one of her piteous threadbare ones made her cringe. Just when she was about to resign herself to offering a crumpled and yellowed old handkerchief, Rowena realised she was already holding the answer between nervously fidgeting fingers. It was a finely carved green gemstone swan on the wing, and apart from her late mother's gold sun, the only other thing of any worth she owned.

'Take this,' she said, removing the pendant.

He swept his hair back from his neck—a clear signal that he wished her to put it on.

Once the pendant was in place, she took a step back. 'This was a gift from my father. I could never be parted from it, but while you wear it, it is still with me. Because you now belong to me, Sir Richard.

He kissed the token fervently. 'I shall treasure it always. This green jewel is the very same shade as your eyes. I pray that I will prove myself worthy in your eyes some day.'

8.

Fear in the Forest and at the Feast

HURRYING along the path late in the evening, Rowena pulled her cloak more tightly around her. She knew she ought to have left sooner.

Although it was full moon, she comforted herself, emerging from Eaglestone Castle's dark shadow and into the bright silver light. She would have left for home earlier, but because she had not done any work for four days, such a backlog had built up that, despite her early start, it had taken her all day and some of the evening to get through it all.

The path was lit clear as day by the moon, but she still felt uneasy. It was not far to Stoatley, only a brisk half hour walk. But the path passed into the forest for some of the way, where she knew it would be shaded from the moonlight by the dense tree canopy.

Still, there really was not much she could do now. Sir Richard had offered to put her up at the castle for the night but she had declined. Local gossips found enough reasons to condemn unmarried maidens as harlots without even having any real evidence. God knows what they would come up with if a girl gave them some proper fodder by sleeping overnight away from home. Probably conclude that she was an evil witch who had married the Devil himself and given birth to a goat...

Suddenly, a crunch sounded from near the edge of the road.

She started at the sound, but then laughed when she realised it was only a hedgehog cracking open a snail shell with its powerful teeth to get at the tasty morsel inside.

'Stop being silly!' she scolded herself aloud. 'There's no one here except for the creatures of the night searching for a meal.'

But in spite of her brave words, she still felt rather jumpy. Rowena normally loved to be outside at any time. She had often ventured out on a warm, moonlit evening and climbed up to the top of the valley. There, she would lie down on her back in the sweet-smelling grass, gaze up at the silent circling stars and listen to the sounds of the night: the chirp of crickets, the fox's bark, the song of the nightingale and the owl's haunting cry echoing across the valley below.

But on this moonlit evening, she would much rather have been safely indoors. She could not keep the thought of the violent, sinister men who had been seen in the shire out of her mind. Although not this close to the garrisoned castle, she reassured herself.

Nearing the dark forest, the sound of owls hooting amongst the trees made her shiver. Upon passing into the shadow of the trees, she had to stop for a moment to allow her eyes to adjust to the dimly-lit conditions. Barely able to make anything out in the darkness, she clutched the golden sun-pendent around her neck, its faint warmth giving her a little comfort.

As soon as she could see the path in front of her, she started hurrying onwards again. Rowena had not got far when she was seized by the overwhelming feeling that someone was watching her. At first she put it down to an overwrought mind combined with an overactive imagination, and managed to force herself to keep walking calmly forward, knowing that if she broke into a panicked run she would likely trip and fall on the dark path.

Then the unmistakable sound of a twig snapping rang out in the darkness to her left. The maiden instantly stopped and turned towards the direction from whence it came. But she could not see anything except dimly looming tree trunks.

'Is there anyone there?' she called out into the heavy darkness.

There was no answer. Deathly silence reigned in the black forest all around.

She was just about to start hurrying onwards when a loud crack sounded out. Panic gripped her. She was sure that only a man could cause such a large twig to snap. None of the wild animals who roamed the forest, except for deer, which would have taken fright by now, were anywhere near heavy enough.

Rowena scanned the darkness again. And there, among the dusky, towering trees she could just make out the shape of a human figure. She spun around, heart pounding, and started running back the way she had come.

Eaglestone castle was not far and offered her best chance of safety. She focused on the light at the end of the dark tunnel of trees, running towards it as fast as her short legs could carry her.

The sound of heavy, pounding footfalls followed. She dared to glance over her shoulder. A tall figure bounded after her, his long black cloak flying out behind him like the wings of a gigantic bat. He had a scarf tied around his face which left only his eyes showing, and in his hand she caught the cold glint of steel.

Rowena screamed in terror. Her pounding heart felt as if it was about to burst as she gasped for breath, and her lungs and throat burned. She could hear him gaining on her. His footfalls were becoming louder and louder and the sound of his heavy breaths getting closer.

Mustering every remaining drop of strength left in her, she made a last, desperate attempt to reach the end of the woodland path.

Just as she was bursting out into the open, a large, cold hand that felt as if it were made of iron seized her shoulder from behind. She screamed and fell to the ground, pulling her attacker down with her.

'Help!' she screamed as they rolled on the ground.

She pulled herself away and avoided being pinned under him, then struggled franticly to get to her feet. But it was no use. She could not free herself from the vice-like grip he had on her arm.

As they struggled on the ground, the creature fumbled for something caught in his cloak. The muffled clunk of metal came from near his hand. The dagger! He was trying to free the dagger caught in his cloak!

'Help, somebody please help me!'

But there was no one there, only the silent moon looking sadly down on the night.

'Please don't kill me, I'm too young to die!' she pleaded desperately.

His hard, glinting eyes regarded her with cold detachment. 'I have not come to kill you,' he rasped, 'only to fetch a little *gift* for your master.'

'A gift?' she gasped.

He chuckled caustically. 'I'm sure he will be delighted when he receives one of your *fingers* tomorrow morning. I would love to see his face when he opens the package!' He erupted into a wild cackle that ended in a coughing fit. 'I'm sure,' he continued once the fit had subsided, 'that he will not be late with his payment *again*.'

Rowena caught the flash of cold steel in her captor's large, bony hand. He had finally freed his dagger and was clutching it tightly.

'No, let me go!' she screamed, jerking franticly back.

He grasped her cloak's collar and used it as a ligature, drawing it tight about his victim's neck. Then he thrust his face in hers and breathed his foully reeking breath down on her. 'Now,' he hissed, 'which one would you like me to cut off?' He ended with another wild cackle.

She stared back at him, held in an almost trance-like state by the glint of the moon's reflection in his hard, cold eyes.

So this was where it had ended up. Sir Richard might not want to face the consequences of standing up to his blackmailer, but he was not the one being set upon and mutilated by some wheezing, crazed sadist with breath like a cesspit. It really wasn't fair. She had never wanted to go near Sir Richard. It was all Lady Sabina's doing. She had been weak, and Lady Sabina had played her like a fiddle. How Lady Sabina would laugh when she saw Rowena with a finger missing! Only criminals and soldiers had missing fingers. Rowena could hear Lady Sabina's taunts already.

'No!' she screamed suddenly, and with lightning-quick speed punched him in the throat.

The hard, glinting eyes bulged and flickered back at her in shock for a moment. He had clearly thought his victim had given up and resigned herself to her fate. He emitted a choking croak and scrabbled at his throat with a sinewy paw.

Seizing the chance, she grabbed a fist-sized stone lying nearby and hit him in the eye with it. The iron-like hand loosened its grip on her arm. She jerked free, scrambled to her feet and broke into a run.

This time she did not look back. With her body near the limit of its endurance, she felt sick and delirious. The world was spinning around her and she hardly knew where she was going. The only thing she could think of was keeping running until she reached safety.

The relief that washed over her as she finally stumbled in through the castle gates was immense. Most of the men had gone back to their quarters by now. Just a small night-watch was still on duty. But it was still only ten O'clock. Many of the men were eating, drinking, and judging by the noise coming from within the brightly lit castle, talking.

The moonlit courtyard was empty save for two large hounds

sitting near the armoury door. Seeing the woman enter, they leapt to their feet and began barking excitedly. Noticing the light coming from the armoury's open doorway, she headed towards it.

'Donner, Wilf, shut up!' came Sir Richard's shout from inside the armoury.

The two huge wolfhounds took no heed of their master and carried on barking.

'Shut up, you mongrels!'

The barking continued.

'Go and see what all the damn fuss is about, Gallagher. The daft mutts have probably just seen a rat again, but you never know,' Sir Richard grumbled.

'Yes, sir,' answered the sergeant.

The doorway darkened as Gallagher passed through. 'Rowena, is that you?'

She staggered on her feet, so exhausted she could barely stand.

'Sir Richard, come quickly!' called Gallagher.

Sir Richard was beside her in an instant. 'Rowena, what the hell happened?'

Rowena's vision swam as she reeled for a moment before starting to fall.

He seized her by the arms and pulled her upright. 'Are you hurt?'

Still gasping for breath, she could not speak, only managing to shake her head in reply.

Sir Richard kept a tight grip on her arm. 'Tell me what happened.'

'Evil in the forest—it was so horrible—I thought the vile thing was going to kill me!'

'Did you get attacked?'

She nodded. 'A man—in the forest—he—he—'

'Take your time, madam,' Gallagher said soothingly. 'Take as long as you need.'

'Through if we are to have any chance of catching this villain, you might not want to be too long about it,' Sir Richard added grimly.

'Perhaps we ought to go inside?' suggested Gallagher.

Still gasping hard, she nodded and gratefully mopped her hot face with the corner of her cloak.

Once through the armoury door, she had to shade her eyes for a moment while they adjusted to the brightness inside. The light of the two candles burning on a table in the centre of the room was greatly magnified by all the shining, brightly polished steel armour and weapons it bounced off.

The sergeant motioned to a long bench against the wall, underneath a row of hanging swords and daggers. 'Have a seat.'

Rowena collapsed onto the bench immediately, and once she was comfortably settled, began to feel a little better.

Sir Richard sat down next to her. 'Tell us about this villain in the forest.'

Gallagher handed her a goblet of water and took a seat on the other side of her.

'I was on my way home when, as I was passing through the woods, this lurking *thing* came out and—and—'

The sergeant gave her a reassuring smile. 'You are doing very well, madam.'

Sir Richard pushed his hair back. 'Yes, keep going.'

She managed to tell the two men the story of her terrifying meeting in the dark forest without having to stop again, finishing by saying, 'He told me that he was going to cut off one of my fingers and send it to you, Sir Richard, the next day.' She fixed a fierce glare on the sheriff. 'He said that you would not be late with your payments to him again.'

Sergeant Gallagher and Sir Richard exchanged glances. Sir Richard's was one of horror, but the sergeant's seemed to say *I told you so*.

It suddenly dawned on Rowena: Sergeant Gallagher knew who the blackmailer was! How could she have been so stupid? He and Sir Richard went way back—the sergeant probably knew all of Sir Richard's secrets. All this time she had been trying in vain to get him to tell her who it was when she could have asked Gallagher. What a fool to have believed that no one else knew the sheriff was being blackmailed and refrain from questioning anyone else about it for fear of betraying his secret!

'I'm sorry for being so frazzled earlier,' said Rowena. 'You hardened warriors must think me such a fool.'

'Not at all, madam,' said Gallagher.

Sir Richard cleared his throat. 'Well, you could have been a bit less—'

Gallagher darted a warning glance at him.

'No no, it's fine. Don't concern yourself about it,' the sheriff finished, earning an approving nod from his sergeant.

She looked at Sir Richard. 'I take it that the vile thug who attacked me was talking about the blackmail demands?'

Sir Richard looked away uncomfortably. 'Yes. I used up the last money I had paying that unexpected tax demand from the king. I had nothing left when the usual payment date came round. You were not here, so I didn't know what to do.'

'So you just didn't pay?'

He nodded. 'But I did warn him that I would be late with it, and assured him that I would pay as soon as I had the money.'

The look Rowena rested on Sir Richard turned accusing. 'The man in the forest, he looked a lot like the description the girl at Dovers Dell gave of the men who kidnapped her friend. He was wearing a long black cloak and had a cloth tied around his face.'

Sir Richard jumped to his feet. 'You charge me with having some secret knowledge of this?'

'There is little doubt in my mind that they must be linked,' she retorted. 'You can hardly claim that it's none of my business who's blackmailing you now, as they appear to have designs not only on your money, but also on *my* fingers. I don't know about you, but I'm rather fond of my fingers,' she stamped her foot, 'and would really hate to lose any!'

'I'm sorry,' Sir Richard muttered, sitting back down. 'You are right, it is your business. When I was fighting in France I did something I shouldn't have—'

'You're right there...' Gallagher mumbled under his breath.

Sir Richard shot his sergeant a black look before continuing. 'This blackmailer got hold of some letters. And this incriminating evidence—if certain people saw it I'd be in a lot of trouble.'

'Even more trouble than you are currently in?'

He nodded grimly. 'I'd lose my head on the executioner's block for sure.'

'What did you do that is so terrible?'

'It's really not important,' he answered irritably, shifting in his seat.

She knew from experience that it would be no use pressing him. 'Alright, don't tell me then. But do you know if there might be a link between the blackmailer and the kidnappers?'

'Not as far as I know.'

'So how come the same man appears to be working for your blackmailer *and* the kidnappers?'

'The man in the forest might have just been an assassin for hire who would do anyone's evil deeds for a fee,' suggested Gallagher.

'That would explain it,' agreed Sir Richard.

'You still have not told me who this blackmailer is. Sir Richard, I demand to know!'

The sheriff ran his fingers nervously through his hair. 'I really don't know if it would be a good idea for you to know that... The villain said I was on no account to tell anyone about it.'

'As God is God, I swear that I will not tell a living soul anything you tell me!'

'But I would be putting you in an impossible situation if I told you.'

'Why? Don't you trust me?'

'I really think you ought to tell her, sir,' urged Gallagher, a hint of impatience creeping into his normally unshakably calm exterior. 'We can depend on her loyalty, of that I am sure.'

Still Sir Richard hesitated.

'Sir, with all due respect, you have to tell her.'

The sheriff shook his head and said nothing.

Then Gallagher turned to Rowena. 'The blackmailer is your uncle, Lord Cunningham.'

'My uncle!' She could hardly believe her ears.

Sir Richard covered his face with his hands and groaned.

'Aye,' said Gallagher, 'your uncle.'

'He went and hired some low-life villain to go and mutilate his own niece, just so he could ring a bit more money out of someone!' she fumed, leaping up and starting to pace up and down the room. 'The rotten, rotten swine!'

'I knew that this would be the result if I told her who it was,' Sir Richard growled at Gallagher. 'How can you expect someone to know something like that and not confront the knave with it?'

'Not everyone is like you, sir,' answered the sergeant. 'Some people do have a little self-control.'

'You can count on me not going to Lord Cunningham with this, I assure you, Sir Richard,' she said, calming down a little.

'Thank God for that!' muttered Sir Richard. 'If his lordship found out I'd told you about it he would be furious—probably increase the demands twofold.'

Rowena stopped in front of the sheriff and his sergeant. 'Do you know where he keeps these incriminating letters?'

'Not for sure,' said Sir Richard, 'but most likely they are

somewhere in his rooms at Stoatley, locked in an iron strongbox.'

She rubbed her hands together thoughtfully, a plan beginning to take shape in her mind. 'So if you managed to get back those letters, he would have nothing to blackmail you with?'

Sir Richard nodded, but his brow was furrowed with concern. 'You're not thinking of doing anything foolhardy, are you?'

'No, certainly not...' she replied absent-mindedly, staring into the distance.

* * * *

Sitting on a low-hanging willow branch dangling her bare feet in the deliciously cool water below, Rowena's troubles seemed so far away. 'I think I shall reward myself with a nice cool dip when we have finished washing all these clothes,' she murmured thoughtfully.

Seated on the grassy bank nearby, Becky took a large bite out of her apple. 'Good idea. I could do with a cool-off too.'

'How soon these long, hazy summer days do pass...' sighed Rowena, gazing down contemplatively at the russet leaves floating lazily on the pool's calm surface.

'Aye, before you know it we'll be warming our numb fingers in front of smoking fires and wrapping up in our thickest shawls every time we step outside into the autumn mists and buffeting winds.'

'True, but I do love the autumn anyway. The way the forest blazes with colour is always a delight, and I still can't resist kicking up the fallen leaves when walking in the woods!'

'You are right; Mother Nature's autumn garments are indeed lovely.' Having finished her apple, Becky got up and started hanging the newly-washed clothes over the hawthorn bushes crowding the riverbank. 'Still, it's much harder to get your washing dry than on hot summer days like this.'

Rowena studied the rippling reflection dancing on the water's surface. The young woman looking up at her had laughing green eyes, a wide smile, a rounded face with a snub nose, and a tightly-curling mass of red hair that tumbled past rounded shoulders, while a few tendrils fell over pixyish ears. The dancing green eyes and long, exuberant mane met with approval, but the other features less so. The rounded face was felt to be chubby and lacking elegance, and as for the snub nose, it was deemed positively babyish.

'You know, I can hardly believe Sir Richard asked me to be his lady. Part of me still thinks he was only jesting about being my knight,' sighed the snub nose's disappointed owner.

'It sounded genuine enough from what you told me,' her friend replied.

'Yes, but I bear very little resemblance to Guinevere and the other ladies in the legends. They are always tall, willowy and perfectly poised, whereas I have about as much poise and elegance as a—well, I can't really think of anything that's as bumbling as me just off the top of my head. Why on earth would any knight want *me* to be his lady? I really am more likely to make a knight die laughing than inspire him to do heroic deeds in my honour.'

Becky could not help laughing at Rowena's deadpan expression as she delivered this glum verdict. 'Don't be so hard on yourself! You're a kind-hearted and loyal woman. That's the only thing that really matters.'

Rowena splashed her foot in the water and studied the resulting waves across her reflection gravely. 'I wager Sir Lancelot would not have been so in love with Queen Guinevere if she had not been so beautiful.'

'Yes, and think how much better things would have turned out for everyone then,' said Becky, who could always be relied on where being practical was concerned.

'I suppose so…'

What does Princess Sabina think of your new status?'

'She doesn't know—though I'm sure she will not fail to notice that he is wearing my green swan pendant next time she sees him. I was hoping he would wear it tucked inside his shirt; but no, he insists on wearing it on top for all to see.'

Becky took the last basket of unwashed clothes and put it down on a boulder at the water's edge. 'Aren't you going to lend me a hand?'

'Oh sorry,' said Rowena, sliding off her perch and wading over.

Becky vigorously wrung out the shirt she had just washed. 'Why don't you want anyone to see that Sir Richard is wearing your pendant? For myself, he has gone up greatly in my esteem since I heard that he liked you so much.'

'But the Cunninghams will make such a fuss when they find out.' Rowena picked up the wooden cloth-beating paddle. 'I hate fuss. Lady Sabina will go green with envy, beyond a shadow of a doubt. My cousin cannot bear it if anyone has something she doesn't. As far as I know, no knight has ever asked her to be his lady-love.'

'Don't be bothering yourself about her silliness. If she wants to get all eaten up with jealousy, just leave her to get on with it.'

Rowena splashed some water over the sheet and started beating it half-heartedly with the paddle. 'I suppose you are right. They might be finding out sooner than I thought though. The Cunninghams are having a gathering this evening; apparently they have an announcement to make. I really can't think what it might be. Anyway, all the local luminaries are invited, including Sir Richard.'

The blonde woman looked up from her work. 'I thought he never went to high society gatherings because he couldn't stand them.'

'No, normally he doesn't go. But this time he said he would come.'

Becky stood up and slowly straightened her back. 'Goodness me, crouching by the river like this really is hard on the old back and knees.' She picked up the basket, resting it against her hip as she carried it over to where the other clothes were spread out in the bright sunshine to dry.

Rowena followed her over and started helping her drape the wet garments over the bushes. 'I'm not sure why he is planning to come. I must say, his manner when I passed on Lady Cunningham's invitation seemed a little shifty. Perhaps he has an ulterior motive in accepting the invitation…'

* * * *

Rowena stopped in front of the mirror at the top of the stairs and paused to check her reflection.

She carefully tucked a stray red lock back into one of the two sections of hair from above her ears which she had plaited and fastened together with a gold cord at the back of her head.

Once she had adjusted one of the flowers woven into the braid, she stepped back for a final look. Her best gown did not look *too* bad. There had been few occasions to wear it, so it was still quite tidy despite its age. And the posy of flowers she had pinned on the bust was doing a good job of hiding the stain from that time Cousin Sabina had spilled wine over her at the midsummer dance. It seemed a little tighter than it did last time she wore it, though. Better keep that sweet tooth under control and keep fingers out of honey pot…

With that, she gave her leaf-green gown a final smooth, pulled her low-slung belt round to the centre, and moved off down the grand staircase.

The brightly-lit great hall came into view. The feast had not yet started, but already the high, vaulted hall was buzzing with laughing, chattering guests decked out in their most expensive finery. There were gentlemen carrying intricately engraved daggers and wearing rich furs, fine velvets and rakishly angled caps decorated with magnificent plumes. Ladies paraded about or stood elegantly chatting, dressed in long, trailing gowns of the costliest silks, trimmed with mink and topped by elaborate headdresses with fine gauze veils floating from them.

Rowena made her way through the glittering throng towards the large table stationed in the middle of the room. It was covered with a white brocade cloth and laid out with many pitchers of wine and a variety of fruits and cold meats for the guests to pick on. She took a handful of grapes and retreated to the edge of the room, preferring to keep to herself rather than mingle with the frighteningly fashionable crowd.

'Greetings, princess.' Sir Richard's velvety drawl from close behind took her by surprise.

She turned to find him grinning down at her. He had swapped his usual armour-reinforced leather doublet for a simple but elegant mid-thigh length one of dusky plum velvet; although he still wore his long riding boots—and yes, the green swan pendant.

'Oh hello, I didn't realise you were here already.'

A thick wave of exotic, spicy scent engulfed her as he stepped forward and took her hand. 'It does not do to be too predictable.' He bent forward and gave the small, plump hand a kiss that was a little too lingering for its owners liking in such a public place. 'When I first saw you I thought for a moment that an elfin queen had flitted in from the forest to join the party.'

Rowena gave him a playful slap on the wrist. 'Oh stop it! I know I look more like a cabbage-patch pixie. You are not going to get anywhere with *me* using flattery.'

'Flattery? My dear lady, you do me a great disservice! I speak only the truth.'

She laughed, enjoying his charming attentions despite her suspicion that he wanted something. 'You are frisky tonight. And looking very smart too. On the prowl, are you?'

He smiled dangerously. 'Absolutely.'

She raised a questioning eyebrow. 'Indeed; and are we after any prey in particular?'

'Yes—you.'

She had to work hard to keep her expression free of the panic his words unleashed in her heart. 'I always thought a wolf did not go after a scrawny fawn when there was a freshly killed hind before it already.'

'It might if the meat was more tender…' he purred, his voice lowered to a dark, velvety drawl.

When he was like this, Rowena had always found it hard to tell if he was being serious or just teasing her. She regarded him silently for a moment, trying to decide if that really was a hint of a smile playing on the corners of his lips. Yes, it was.

She tossed her head. 'If you think you are going to amuse yourself by spending all evening toying with me, you can think again.'

He turned away with a ruffled air. 'I try to be civil and all you do is mock me!'

'I believe 'tis you who mock *me*, Sir Richard.'

He suddenly laughed. 'Yes, you are right. You are such a delight to tease I just can't help myself. I do hope you can forgive me.'

She cocked her head to one side and placed a thoughtful finger to her pursed lip. 'Hmmm… I suppose I *might* forgive you, but it will depend on how you conduct yourself this evening. If you vex me I certainly shall not forgive you.'

'This evening, sweet lady, I shall not leave your side for a single moment. After all...' He gave her a sly sideways glance. 'Who would want to be anywhere else except at the side of the most beautiful and admirable damsel at the feast…?'

Her mind almost went blank with panic for a moment. This was the last thing she wanted or expected to hear from him. She desperately searched for an obstacle to place in his way. Ah yes, that might do it—

She put her hands on her hips and boldly looked up at him. 'It will make people think I'm wretchedly desperate if I'm always clinging on to you. I do not want to look like some love-sick girl hanging on a man all evening.'

He crossed his arms and calmly met her challenging look. 'That's alright then. I don't mind if *I* look like a love-sick idiot hanging on a girl all evening.'

Things were complicated enough as they were. Why did he always have to be so damn obstructive! She stamped her foot. 'If you insist on annoying me by following me around like a shadow I will not stand for it!'

He smirked like someone who did not doubt he would win and to whom resistance simply provided amusing sport. 'Indeed…and what are you going to do about it?'

'I—I will be such a shrew that you will not be able to bear being anywhere near me if I do not wish it!'

He moved in closer and stooped down to her ear. 'I shall be stuck to you all evening like pine-sap regardless, so don't think you will get rid of me, sweet mistress of my heart,' he whispered, his hair brushing against her cheek.

She looked down at the floor uneasily. 'Oh really, and why is that?'

He stepped in front of her. 'Because—' He placed a finger under her chin and tilted her head up so she could no longer avoid looking him in the eyes. 'You are planning some hare-brained attempt to steal the letters from Lord Cunningham this evening, while everybody is distracted by the feast.'

Her eyes widened. 'How did you know that?' she whispered back furiously. 'I haven't told anyone about my plan!'

'I guessed,' he replied, still keeping his voice low. 'You've been looking very shifty these last few days. I could tell something was brewing in that charming little head of yours.'

She felt like slapping him. So that was why he had turned up. The bastard! Why did he always have to be such a pain?

'Sir Richard!' cried Lady Sabina as she swept up to them, with Anne following along at her heel like a faithful lapdog. 'How delightful to see you!' She held a hand out to be kissed.

He took the offered hand and gave it a squeeze as he made a slight bow. 'My lady.'

She gave a piqued sniff at his reserved greeting, then glared coldly at Rowena, as if to say *how dare you be so intimate with him?* Lady Sabina turned her attention back to Sir Richard, bestowing her most coquettish smile on him. 'So then, what are you whispering about so secretively with Rowena?'

He looked at Lady Sabina in a less than flattering manner. 'If I wanted everyone to know that I wouldn't be whispering, would I?'

Lady Sabina looked up at him through seductively lowered eyelashes. 'But *I* am not everyone…'

'No, you are not, but you would *tell* everyone in less time than it takes for a fly to flap its wings twice.'

Anne squinted as she looked quizzically at the swan pendant displayed on top of his doublet. 'I have not seen you wearing that pendant before, but yet for some reason it seems strangely familiar…'

'No, I'm sure you're just imagining—' Rowena began, but was interrupted by Sir Richard.

'Yes, you have seen this before: hanging around Rowena's neck.'

Anne's normally round eyes became rounder still. 'Oh. *Oh. OH.*'

Standing so close to Sir Richard that her gown brushed against his leg, Lady Sabina twirled a lock of pale hair between her fingers and looked at him with slanted eyes. 'So, how much did you pay her for it?'

'I got a good price—' Rowena said quickly, but again he interrupted.

'She did get a good price; I got the pendant and she got a devoted knight.'

'You promised to be her knight? How romantic!' cried Anne, but she was quickly frozen into an awkward silence by a poisonous glance from Lady Sabina.

Lady Sabina looked like she had just bitten into a bad apple, but after a moment's stunned silence, she suddenly laughed and squeezed Sir Richard's upper arm. 'Really darling, you are *such* a tease. You must think I came down in the last rain shower, telling a tale like that!'

'I assure my lady that it is perfectly true.'

Lady Sabina slid her hand under his arm, smooth as a snake. 'Really…and why on earth would you want to do a thing like that?' The long white hand slid onto his chest. 'There are so many *other* ladies you could have asked…'

He took a step backwards. 'Because I like her the most, that is why.'

Lady Sabina took a step forward. 'You like *her* more than any other lady you know? Surely not. I simply refuse to believe that any knight could possibly want as his lady-love such a—' Lady Sabina leaned into him conspiratorially, 'well, to be perfectly honest, such a *tramp* of a girl. I mean, look at her.' She gave her cousin a look of scathing contempt. 'Is she fashionably dressed? Is she beautiful or elegant?'

Rowena felt her cheeks grow hot. What had she ever done to Sabina to make her torment her in this way? Was it too much to ask for a moment's peace?

Sir Richard's lips hardened into a thin, steely line. He plucked Lady Sabina's hand off his chest, his thumb and forefinger extended like a squeamish lady picking up something vile the cat had just brought in, and with a face to match.

If a man had done that to Rowena, she would have seriously considered becoming a nun.

He put a protective arm around Rowena. 'I do like her more than any other lady I know. Yes, there are times when she does look a little dishevelled, but that is because she is not afraid to exert herself when it is needed. Rowena has spirit and a keen wit; that is what I like about her. I can't bear these painted high-class ladies who sit around all day talking drivel, wasting time on trivial pursuits and primping themselves into the latest ridiculous fashion.'

Lady Sabina swallowed hard and gave a nervous laugh. 'Well, there really is no accounting for taste, I suppose!'

Her cousin looked so bewildered Rowena almost felt sorry for her. Almost, but not quite.

'Darling Sabina, do come over,' called Lady Cunningham. 'I think all the guests are here. Shall we tell everyone your wonderful news now?'

'Yes Mother, I'm coming!' answered Lady Sabina, looking very relieved at the interruption. She turned to go, but as she did so there was a loud rip. She stopped with a jerk and glared at the sheriff. 'Sir Richard, you are standing on my dress!'

He looked down unconcernedly. 'God's bones, so I am.' He removed his boot from the hem of her white silk gown. 'So sorry, dear lady. Do accept my humble apologies.'

Rowena had to work hard to keep a straight face.

Lady Sabina snatched the hem of her gown out of harm's way. 'You've ripped it!'

'Oh dear, so I have. You were standing so close to me that I did not realise my foot was on your skirt.'

Lady Sabina scrunched up her face like a baby that was about to cry. 'I won't look my best now!'

He gave a slight bow. 'Please accept my condolences.'

After throwing him a poisonous glare, she swept off furiously.

Now that Lady Sabina was out of earshot, Rowena burst out laughing. 'Oh Sir Richard, that was evil!'

He smiled modestly. 'Being a ruthless bastard has its moments...'

'If I may have your attention, everyone!' Lord Cunningham's voice sounded above the guests' laughter and chatter.

There was a mass move towards the front of the room. Rowena moved forward too, with Sir Richard close behind.

'Have you any idea what they were going to announce?' asked the sheriff.

'No, it is as much of a mystery to me as it is to you,' she replied, making her way to the front of the crowd so her view would not be obscured by the other guests, most of whom were much taller than she was.

Lord and Lady Cunningham stood in front of the great hall's grand fireplace, which was still the focal point of the room even though the fire was not lit on this mild evening. Standing next to them was Lady Sabina, and to Rowena's surprise, also Lord Shrewsbury. The four of them were all looking very pleased with themselves, especially Lady Sabina.

Rowena gave Sir Richard a nudge. 'What is that slimy knave doing up there?'

'God knows...'

Lord Cunningham raised a hand to silence the still-murmuring throng. After waiting a few moments for the noise to die out, he cleared his throat. 'Honoured guests, I thank you all for gracing Stoatley Manor with your presence this fine evening.' He raised a goblet. 'I would like to propose a toast to great friends!'

All the guests who had goblets in their hands raised them and chorused, 'To great friends!'

'When is the pompous scoundrel going to get to the point?' Rowena heard Sir Richard mutter crossly from close behind her.

Lord Cunningham clasped his hands together in front of himself and bowed. 'I thank you, I thank you, most noble guests. Now, you all will, I am sure, be waiting expectantly to hear the news I wish to convey to you, which is after all the reason I have brought all you fine people together this evening.'

Sir Richard sighed. 'If he doesn't hurry it up I think I shall be gracing the halls of hell before we find out…'

'Shush, someone will hear you,' Rowena whispered, moving her foot back and pressing it down as hard as she could on the toe of his boot.

She felt his large hands close around her and squeeze her ribs hard in response. She almost jumped forward in shock and barely managed to stifle a scream.

'Stop fooling around!' she hissed under her breath, knowing she would have a fit of giggles if he did not stop now.

The commotion earned them quite a few icy glares and 'Shhhs' from the guests around them, and the attention of Lady Cunningham, who shot Rowena a furious, disapproving look and shook her head vigorously.

'Silence, if you please!' Lord Cunningham called.

'Do carry on, my lord,' the sheriff said smoothly. 'I was merely amusing myself while I waited for you to get to the point.'

Lord Cunningham gave Sir Richard a disdainful glare before

continuing to talk, rubbing his large potbelly with a small, podgy hand decked with golden gem-encrusted rings as he did. 'I would appreciate the attention of you all. Lady Cunningham and I are proud, most proud and deeply honoured,' Lord Shrewsbury gave a self-satisfied smirk; 'to announce the betrothal of our beloved only daughter, Lady Sabina Cunningham, to—' he gave a dramatic pause, 'Lord Theobald Shrewsbury, the firstborn son of the Earl of Compton!'

There was an instant outbreak of applause in the hall, and many cries of congratulation, and exclamations of wonder and admiration.

Rowena was almost speechless. Lady Sabina betrothed to Lord Shrewsbury! She really had not seen that coming. Certainly, they got on like a haystack on fire, but he never looked like he was actually *wooing* Lady Sabina.

She turned to Sir Richard. 'What do you make of that?'

But Rowena got her answer sooner than she expected. Sir Richard had his handkerchief clapped over his mouth and was trying so hard not to laugh that he was almost choking.

'Sir Richard, what is so funny?'

He managed to compose himself enough to speak. 'Don't you know Lord Shrewsbury prefers the company of other men?'

'No he doesn't! He spends all his time with *women*. He hardly ever does anything with other men.'

This only made Sir Richard laugh harder.

She frowned at him. 'What is wrong with you? You really are puzzling me. Please try to make some sense!'

'God, you're naïve!' he gasped, shaking his head.

She put her hands on her hips and glared crossly up at him. 'Enlighten me then.'

'You are not entirely correct when you say he does not do anything with other men.'

'Really?' She was completely mystified now.

'Yes. When I was sixteen, I became the squire of a knight at the royal court. Lord Shrewsbury's family was at court too; his mother was lady-in-waiting to the queen, you see. He was five years older than me and already quite the young dandy. I never knew him personally, thank God, but I did hear about him—there was always a lot of gossip going around at court. He developed an inappropriate attachment to Lord March's thirteen-year-old ward. The object of his affections became a laughingstock among the squires and pages, and was taunted most cruelly.'

She shook her head sadly. 'How terrible. You, I hope, did not join in with this heartless bullying?'

'Of course I did! Don't you know me at all?'

'Oh Sir Richard, what a nasty way to treat a poor young girl!'

'You mean a poor young *boy*.'

Comprehension slowly dawned on her. 'Oh, I see…'

'The unfortunate youth shared none of Lord Shrewsbury's inclinations, and even if he had, his age would have still rendered the relationship indecent. But Lord March just told him to shut up and put up. No one wanted to incur the rage of the Earl of Compton's overindulged favourite child—especially not for the sake of a mere ward.'

'How horrible…'

'Yes. Secretly, we did feel bad for the page. But we were just too relieved that we were not the object of Lord Shrewsbury's desire in his stead. Luckily for the boy, it wasn't too long before Shrewsbury's eye was caught by another plaything and he lost interest.'

'Was this new infatuation any more willing?'

'Much more willing. It was the Duke of Huntley's son. Their interests were, well, very *similar*.'

'Thank goodness for that. But if he is not interested in ladies in that way, why does Lord Shrewsbury want to marry Lady

Sabina?'

'His father would want an heir.'

'That makes sense. But why not marry one of the ladies at court? The Cunninghams are a much less exalted bloodline than the Shrewsburys.'

'None of the eligible young ladies at court wanted to marry him. When I was there, Lord Shrewsbury's tastes were well known among the courtiers as well as the servants. Any lady who married him would have become a bit of a laughingstock. The only ones likely to willing take him on would be those who were not blessed with vast lands and a noble pedigree, or who had been tainted by scandal.'

'And Lady Sabina does not know this?'

'I doubt it, although I wouldn't be at all surprised if Lady Cunningham had heard some of the rumours.'

'Might it not have just been a phase which he has since outgrown?'

'I can tell you with total conviction that it is not. When I met him down the back alley of the Cow and Cockerel, he indecently propositioned me.'

Her jaw nearly hit the floor. 'He *what?*'

'And he didn't even wait for an answer before he started groping at me. It was quite something, let me tell you.'

She could not help giggling at the thought of the weedy little lord taking such an unwise liberty with the brawny knight. 'Did he mistake you for a prostitute or something?'

To her surprise, the humour of the incident did not seem to have been lost on Sir Richard. He chuckled darkly. 'No, he knows who I am. We met briefly when he visited the Cunninghams last year.'

'Surely no one could possibly think that your romantic interests have much in common with his?'

'I believe the misunderstanding might have arisen from what

Mistress Anne and your cousin told him.'

'Really, and what was that?'

'I understand they told him that, as I had shown no interest in them despite much encouragement on their part, my tastes must lie elsewhere.'

Rowena noticed that Lady Sabina and Lord Shrewsbury had nearly reached her as they made their way through the crowd arm-in-arm, receiving the congratulations and good wishes of the guests. She indicated the approaching danger with a nod in their direction, and gave Sir Richard a warning glance.

He nodded to show he understood. 'Fear not, I shan't say anything.'

'I'm glad to hear it, but I think I shall go and sit down for a little while anyway,' she said, moving off towards the chairs tucked away in a small alcove at the far end of the room.

* * * *

Later that evening, Rowena stepped outside into the walled garden adjacent the great hall

'Ah, that's better,' she murmured, taking a deep breath. 'It is awfully hot and stuffy in there.'

'Yes, it is,' said Sir Richard, who so far had not strayed more than a few feet from her.

She could see he was not going to be talked into leaving her side for a single moment that evening. But she knew this was her only real chance of getting the letters off Lord Cunningham. She was sure Lord Cunningham would not notice her bumping up against him in the crowd late in the evening, which would enable her to relieve him of his keys, and his almost certain state of total drunkenness would hopefully mean he would not realise they were gone. To ensure that she could search through his room undisturbed, she had brought a sleeping potion with her. She intended to slip it into the brandy nightcap he always had brought up to his room just before he went to bed.

But Sir Richard clearly intended to keep his wits about him. Despite her best efforts to ply him with alcohol, he was still only on his third drink. She was beginning to get desperate. The party would soon be drawing to a close and he was still stuck to her like a limpet. Every one of her attempts to throw him off had failed.

Now there was only one option left.

.9.

Nocturnal Nightmares See the Light of Day

NIGHT'S shadowy mantle covered the garden. Only the wistful stars sprinkled across heaven's dome and a little weak candlelight shining out through the hall's open door lightened her velvet embrace.

Rowena had spotted Sir Richard's half-empty goblet sitting beside him on the low stone wall where he sat. Grateful for night's dark veil, she slowly took a small glass bottle out of her pocket, and holding it out of her intended victim's sight behind her back, carefully drew out the stopper.

She then manoeuvred herself so that she stood beside the goblet with her back facing it. When he looked away, she let a few drops fall into the wine.

'Ah Rowena, the-there you are!' cried Lady Sabina, bursting out into the courtyard garden, clearly tipsy. 'Typical of you to be sulking in some corner instead of joining in like a normal p-p-person.'

Rowena quickly jammed the bottle back into her pocket. Why did Sabina always have to come flying in at the crucial moment?

Rowena gave a weak smile, her hands still clutched behind her. 'I'm not sulking out here—am I, Sir Richard?'

'No, not sulking,' he replied casually, 'just pacing around looking hot and frazzled.'

Lady Sabina flicked her veil over her shoulder with a toss of the head. 'Oh d-dear. But I suppose one must have p-p-patience with the poor unfortunates who have not been brought up properly and do not know h-how to behave at gatherings.'

The tall knight scowled darkly at Lady Sabina as he slowly got to his feet. 'Did you come out here for a reason?'

Lady Sabina shot him a peeved look before staggering over to her cousin, nearly falling more than once as she failed to keep her long skirts from under her feet. 'I have yet to receive Rowena's con-g-congratulations. Do I not h-have the right to speak to my cousin at my-my own betrothal feast?'

Sir Richard drained his goblet in one gulp. 'Yes, but only if you keep a civil tongue in your head.'

Lady Sabina took a swig of wine as she swung drunkenly around to face him. 'How d-d-dare you speak to me like that? I am about to be m-m-married to Lord Shrewsbury, you know. When I am his w-wife, you know, I will h-h-have hundreds of knights under m-m-my command, and if any of them d-d-dare, do you hear me? D-dare to speak to me like that, I shall have them fl-fl-flogged, publicly fl-fl-flogged.'

Sir Richard looked at her with open disgust. 'I thank you for the warning, my lady, but I have no intention of becoming one of Shrewsbury's minions.'

Rowena came to Lady Sabina's side and took her by the arm. 'Come, I think it's time you retired for the night.'

'N-n-n-no!' slurred Lady Sabina, shaking Rowena off. 'Stop treating m-m-me like a child.'

'You might want to consider not behaving like one then,' Sir Richard muttered under his breath.

But Lady Sabina did not seem to have heard him. 'Here.' She thrust her hand in front of Rowena. 'Look at my b-big betrothal ring. Take a g-g-good look, because you will not be getting one like this if you ever m-m-manage to find a man d-desperate enough to m-m-marry you.'

Rowena cast a disinterested eye over the gold ring, which was topped by the largest diamond she had ever seen. 'Yes, very nice.'

'I can s-see you are eaten up w-w-with jealousy, which I p-pray God will forgive you f-f-for. Your envy is understandable w-w-when I have met with such g-good fortune and you have n-n-nothing.'

'Good fortune?' Sir Richard was looking more bad-tempered by the moment. 'Wait until you've been married to the man for a while before you go around crowing about your good fortune!'

Lady Sabina lurched towards him. 'I can s-see you are angry because I am going to m-m-marry Lord Shrewsbury and not you,' she slurred, throwing her arms around his neck. 'But I w-will take pity on you, my love, and let you h-h-have one n-n-night of passion with me before I g-go.'

Sir Richard would not have looked more revolted if he had fallen into a cesspit. He roughly pushed her away. 'Get your hands off me, madam! If I have ever said or done anything which led you to believe I had some sort of romantic interest in you, I regret to inform you, madam, that you were badly mistaken.' As he spoke, he added insult to injury by dusting himself down like someone who had just been touched by a leper. 'Now for God's sake go and sober up before you embarrass yourself any further!'

Lady Sabina looked at him confusedly. 'What do you m-mean?'

Sir Richard pointed to the open door. 'Get you gone!'

Lady Sabina seized his hand and kissed it. 'Oh my l-love, let-let us go and sooth the p-pangs of our—'

Sir Richard pulled himself free of his unwanted conquest's drunken advances and jumped up onto the wall behind him. 'Rowena, can't you bloody do something about this crazed banshee before she damn-well ravishes me?'

Rowena, who had been watching the increasingly absurd scene

with a mixture of horror and mirth, shrugged her shoulders helplessly. 'What am I supposed to do? She never listens to *me*.'

Lady Sabina had now fallen to the ground and wrapped her arms around Sir Richard's leg.

'Just do something, I don't care what!' he ordered his clerk.

'Sir Richard Hastings, what in God's name are you doing to my daughter?' shrieked Lady Cunningham, storming out through the door.

Sir Richard let out a sigh of relief. 'Reinforcements, thank God!'

Lady Cunningham jabbed a bony finger at him. 'I demand that you explain yourself!'

'Madam, I'd be much obliged to you if you could please convince your daughter to give me my leg back.'

Lady Cunningham strode over to Lady Sabina and seized her by the arm. 'Sabina, what are you doing in this disgraceful position before that man? Get up at once!'

'Nooo!' the maiden wailed. 'He loves me, I know he does!'

Her mother's eyes were fierce with anger. 'Get up now!' she screamed, pulling Lady Sabina by the hair.

The drunken girl's weak resistance was easily overcome by the livid Lady Cunningham, who pulled her daughter to her feet and started dragging her towards the door. 'If either of you breathe so much as a single word to anyone about this incident I will have your heads! Do you hear me?' Lady Cunningham hissed at the two observers.

Rowena nodded, feeling rather intimidated by her aunt's venomous manner, but Sir Richard was too busy getting down from his place of safety to take much heed of the warning.

As soon as the Cunningham ladies were safely out the way, he sunk back down onto the garden wall. 'What do these crazed women think I am? A mindless piece of meat to pleasure themselves on? Ugly men have no idea how much trouble they avoid…'

She sighed. 'Yes, something like that.'

'Oh my head,' he groaned weakly, holding his head in his hands. 'It's swimming like a cork caught in a whirlpool. I shouldn't have had that third glass of wine. I know Cunningham's a miserly swine, but serving wine that would strip the hair off a sewer rat really is low…'

The sleeping potion was clearly taking effect. Rowena rubbed her hands together. At least something was going to plan.

'Rowena,' he murmured weakly, 'I think I'm going to faint…'

Knowing she would never be able to move him once he was asleep, she instantly jumped to her feet and started trying to pull him up. 'Just hold off on that until I can get you up to one of the guestrooms!'

'No, I'll…never make…make…it…' His head slumped closer and closer to his chest as he spoke.

'Sir Richard, no!'

He started sliding to the ground.

'Not here, for God's sake not here!' she begged, beginning to think she must have overdone the dose. She seized him by the shoulders and gave him a good shake. 'Wake up!'

This seemed to revive him a little. 'My head…feels…so…heavy…' he managed to gasp, before closing his eyes and beginning to topple over again.

She caught hold of him before he could slump down onto the hard paving stones and gave him another shake. But it had no effect. 'Sir Richard, wake up!' she cried, slapping him on the cheek.

He let out a low groan, but she could see he was too far gone now to be able to stand up again until the potion had worn off.

Gasping and puffing, she lowered his considerable weight to the ground.

'Need a hand there, Mistress Rowena?' a cheerful young voice interrupted her quiet panic.

She turned to see Herlewin, the new garden boy, eyeing the unconscious Sir Richard with a professional air. 'Thank goodness,' she gasped. 'I was beginning to think I'd have to leave him out here all night!'

'Wouldn't want to do that, would we now? Starts to get chilly at night this time of year. Looks a heavy one, though,' he added thoughtfully. 'Might have to get a bit of help in…'

'Yes, I can attest to his being very heavy indeed.'

'Been under him, have you?'

'No!' she yelped. 'I just meant that I'd already tried to move him.'

The strapping young man chuckled. 'I know you did.'

'Cheeky lout,' she retorted, but could not resist a giggle at the joke even though it had been at her own expense.

'Aldred!' he shouted. 'There's another one out here!'

The disgruntled-looking gardener shuffled out, his white hair almost standing on end. 'Is there no end to it?' he grumbled. 'I only just avoided having that last one chuck up on me. That's gratitude for you…'

'I'm sure this one will not cause you any grief, Aldred,' she tried to reassure him.

'That'd make a change…' he replied dubiously, taking hold of Sir Richard's arm.

Herlewin seized the unconscious knight's other arm, and after a nod from Aldred, the two men heaved. There was a flurry of groans and curses, most of them from the older man but a few from Herlewin too. Despite his impressive physique, he still had to work hard to lift Sir Richard up and drag him towards the door.

‘Please put him in the blue guestroom,’ she instructed them, relieved to finally have her master out of the way.

Now she could put her plan into action.

* * * *

It was well past midnight. If Rowena had not been so on edge, she would have been exhausted by now. She had been waiting in the dark, recessed window seat at the end of the upstairs corridor for what seemed like an age, but the distant tolling of the bells of Hartfield cathedral striking two informed her that it had in fact been only half an hour.

Her attempt to relieve Lord Cunningham of the keys he always wore dangling from his belt had been a delightful success. Once she had got Sir Richard out of the way (who she knew would have prevented her from trying to steal the letters from her uncle by force if necessary), it had been easy to take the keys.

The feast had gone on and on. She had lost count of the number of toasts that had been drunk and courses eaten. It had seemed like it would never end. But all the guests had finally staggered, giggled and slurred their way back to their guestrooms. And Lord Cunningham had fulfilled her prediction that he would be too groggy with wine to notice what she was up to. Slipping the sleeping draft into his brandy before the servant took it up to his room had been an easy matter. Her presence in the kitchens was a common sight and no one’s suspicions had been raised.

All she had to do now was wait for loud snores coming from her uncle’s bedchamber to signal it was safe to enter and begin the search. She intended to begin looking in the study first.

After some carefully casual questioning of the servants,

Rowena had discovered that the chamber he slept in led off the study, so she knew she had a good chance of finding the letters without having to search his bedroom while he slept.

Finally she heard the sound she had been waiting so impatiently for. By parting the heavy cloak wrapped around it, she let a small shaft of light shine from the lantern she carried. Then, with racing heart and shallow breath, she placed a shaky hand on the door latch, and praying that it would not creak, lifted it and pushed the door ever so slowly open.

The heavy oak door did not give her away. Hardly daring to breathe, Rowena tip-toed in and quickly surveyed the room for the most obvious place to begin her search. Her eyes alighted on two large wooden chests sitting on a table in the corner.

Yes, that seemed a likely hiding place. They had keyholes in them, but to her surprise, when she tried to open them they proved not to be locked. But the contents, a pile of paper scrolls, did look quite promising.

The nervous young woman started going through them one by one, unrolling each and giving it a quick scan. But they were all just account records for the estate.

She wiped her forehead with the back of her hand and sighed. It was going to be a long night.

What made the task even more daunting was that she was not even quite sure what she was really looking for. Despite her best efforts to make him, Sir Richard had never told her whom the letters were addressed to or what they were about. She was wary of missing the incriminating letters altogether. She knew he could not write very well, so it was likely he had got someone else to write them for him. This made her job much more difficult. Instead of simply checking if the handwriting was his, she had to look at the signature on every letter that looked a likely candidate.

After laboriously working her way through the contents of

both chests, she still had not found any letters that seemed compromising. She looked around the room, but there were no other documents or places where they might be kept. There was only one more place they might be: in his bedchamber.

She knew it was dangerous. Even the most resourceful person would struggle if pressed to come up with an acceptable reason for creeping around in the dead of night riffling through their uncle's bedchamber.

She stopped outside the bedchamber door, wavering indecisively. If she was caught red-handed, the consequences did not bear thinking about, but neither did the consequences if Sir Richard continued to be blackmailed. Aside from how irritable and strained it made the already moody knight, the danger of Walter Gray using Sir Richard's corruption to incite civil unrest was just too great.

Something had to be done, and it had to be done now. It had been such a stress getting this far that she could not bear the thought of turning back now.

She took a deep breath and inched the bedchamber door slowly, carefully open.

* * * *

'Just a moment!' Rowena called in answer to the knock that had just sounded on the door.

She wiped the stewed apple smeared around baby James's face off with a cloth, and hurried over to his older brother Peter, who sat howling on the floor surrounded by the sticks, bits of wood and tied cloth dolls he was using as toys.

She crouched beside the little boy. 'Shush honey, it's alright. Show me which hand you hurt.'

'The-this one,' he wailed pitifully, holding out a red little hand. 'The b-block fell on it!'

The knock sounded again, louder and more insistent this time.

'I said I'd be with you shortly!' she shouted above the din in the cottage.

Peter's howls were promptly joined by his little brother's. Distressed by Peter's anguish and his own lack of attention, he banged the spoon Rowena had been using to feed him with on the table, where he was seated in his little chair, and cried 'Mama, Mamaaaa!'

'Rowena, can I come in?'

She recognised the voice outside instantly as belonging to Sir Richard.

'Oh no…' she groaned aloud, at her wit's end. With one weary hand she leaned against the nearby windowsill, and with the other cradled her hot, flustered head. 'Yes, just let yourself in,' she called weakly.

There was a click as he unlatched the door. She lifted her head to see him step inside and duck his head to fit under the low doorway. His state of mind was written all over his face.

It was not a good one, and she had not expected anything less. The last time she had seen him was when he was being half dragged, half carried towards the guest quarters by Aldred and Herlewin the previous evening.

Rowena let her head sink into her cupped hands with a sigh. Why did he have to choose the very worst time to turn up? Like right now, when she was surrounded by crying, out of control children and—she glanced down at the sorry sight that was her dress—smeared in stewed fruit.

'Rowena…' he growled at her.

She met his accusing glare with resignation. 'Yes, what is it?'

'You know what.'

Young Peter, seeing that his attempts to get 'Aunty' Rowena's attention by pulling at her skirts were having no effect, started to howl even louder. Baby James followed his older brother's example, and brought his screams up a pitch too.

The two children had both been in a difficult mood ever since she got there, and at this moment she felt like joining in with the children's screams herself. Ignoring the screaming children and growling sheriff, she took a deep breath and tried to block out the noise for long enough to calm herself a little.

Then baby James decided to throw his bowl of stewed fruit onto the floor for good measure.

'Oh Jamie, no!' she gasped, as the pewter bowl shattered on the floor. 'Why did I offer to look after them while Becky was bringing in the harvest?' she groaned, collapsing onto the nearest stool. 'They are like little angels when she's here, but I look after them for a mere hour and they turn into the spawn of Satan!' She wiped her sticky hands on her skirt and sighed. 'I'm already at my wit's end, Sir Richard, so please, whatever you do, don't start bugging me about last night.'

A spark of anger flashed in Sir Richard's eyes. Gripping the edge of the table with white-knuckled hands, he shut his eyes and tightened his lips to a thin, hard line.

Rowena braced herself for the inferno, but it did not come. Instead, he opened his eyes after a few silent moments and went over to the still-crying Peter. To the watching damsel's great surprise, he gathered the little boy in his arms and lifted him up.

Peter seemed rather surprised too. He quickly stopped his crying and gazed at the towering stranger intently, a mixture of fear and wonder in his eyes.

The powerfully-built warrior smiled kindly at the little child. 'What is the matter, young sire?'

'I squished my little pinkies,' Peter replied, regarding the injured hand gravely.

'Now that is bad,' Sir Richard said sympathetically. 'Do you think your little fingers might hurt less if I showed you something special? How would you like to see my sword?'

The little boy looked up at him in wide-eyed wonder. 'You have a s-sword?'

'Yes, I'm wearing it now,' Sir Richard replied, setting Peter back down. 'I'll show you.'

Now that Peter had stopped bawling and she could actually hear herself think, Rowena got up and went over to baby James, whose earlier screams had subsided to a low sob. She lifted him out of his chair and started to rock him gently in her arms.

Meanwhile, Sir Richard was unbuckling his sword belt as Peter stood watching with rapt interest.

Once it was off, Sir Richard held out the sheathed sword to Peter with one hand. 'Here, see if you can hold it.'

The little boy looked at it with awed reverence. 'Aunty Rowena is always telling me stories about knights and dragons and princesses. Is your sword magic?'

Sir Richard laughed. 'Magic?'

Peter crossed his arms and gazed up at the huge warrior with a look of graveness on his chubby little face that made Rowena smile. 'Yes. In Aunty Rowena's stories there is sometimes a sword that burns with fl-ames or fights on its own.'

'No, I'm afraid my sword does neither of those things.'

'I just thinked it might because *you* look like one of the knights in her stories.'

'Thank you, young sire. I am indeed a knight,' Sir Richard answered, a little too smugly for the liking of the watching Rowena.

The awe-struck child gaped speechlessly for a moment. 'A *knight?*' he finally asked. 'A proper knight like the king makes?'

'Yes, that's right; the king did make me a knight.'

Peter held out his hands. 'Can I hold your sword?'

'You can try, but I warn you, it's very heavy.' Sir Richard

carefully lowered the sword into little Peter's eagerly waiting hands.

As soon as the child had the full weight of the massive blade in his chubby little hands, he nearly fell to the ground. Sir Richard quickly took the weight again.

'Lordy!' gasped the little boy, looking worshipfully up at Sir Richard. 'You are as strong as a giant!'

'That's because he *is* a giant, honey,' Rowena chipped in, feeling relieved that the children had finally settled down, but somewhat cross and more than a little embarrassed that the menacing and often abrasive Sir Richard had triumphed where she had been failing so miserably.

She looked down on the now quietly-settled baby James. 'He must be tired now. I think I might put him back to bed. Just bear with me a moment while I step outside—I moved his cot outside under the birch tree in the garden so he will not get so hot.' She held out her hand to Peter. 'Come, let's go and put Jamie in his cot.'

The little boy pouted and clung to the table leg. 'No, I don't want to go.'

'Are there knights in Rowena's stories who protect the weak?' Sir Richard asked the reluctant traveller.

Peter nodded his round, mop-haired little head sagely.

'Well, why don't you go out with Rowena and act as sentry while your little brother sleeps, like a real knight?'

The boy nodded eagerly.

Sir Richard handed Peter one of the long twigs lying on top of the woodpile near the hearth. 'Here, now you have a sword too. Perhaps *your* sword will be a magic sword?'

Peter's face lit up with delight as he took hold of it. 'Yes! My sword makes monsters and evil knights turn into ashes if I touch them with it,' he declared boldly, swinging the stick in his hand.

'Shall we go and put your brother to bed now?' suggested

Rowena.

Peter nodded vigorously, making his golden curls bounce playfully. 'Yes, I will escort you out, but—' he looked up at Sir Richard, 'first he must make me a knight.'

Sir Richard smiled good-humouredly. 'Of course.' He drew his huge sword out of its scabbard. 'Now you must kneel before me on bended knee.'

Peter solemnly kneeled before the warrior.

Sir Richard lightly touched the little boy on each shoulder, while Rowena held her breath at the sight of the massive steel blade coming so close to the dear little head.

'Arise, Sir Peter!'

The little boy could not have looked more proud. He got up and solemnly turned his big eyes up at Rowena. 'Now we can go. I shall go first, like a knight ought, to protect weak damsels and babies from bad things.'

Rowena laughed with delight and let him lead the way, which he did with full knightly dignity, shoulders back and 'sword' held in front as he marched out the door with his pleased minder following behind carrying his baby brother.

That Sir Richard really was a case of still waters running deep…

.10.

The Revelation of the Night

ROWENA came back inside to find Sir Richard had pulled out a bench and sat down at the big table in the centre of the room.

When she had settled herself down on a stool at the other end of the table, he crossed his arms and fixed a reproachful look on her. 'You know, Rowena, red hair is not the only thing you have in common with the fox.'

She put on her most innocent expression. 'Oh?'

'No. You also have the same low, animal cunning.'

'To be showered with such lofty compliments…' she cooed in mock-gratification.

The reproachful dark eyes were unrelenting. 'I thought I knew you, but no. You might have the feeble body and sweet manner of a woman, but you have the heart of a damn fox that sneaks into the hencoop and kills the unsuspecting fowls in their sleep!'

'Are you insulting me or just trying to tell me that you are a chicken?' she inquired matter-of-factly.

'Don't take that tone; I know what you did to me!'

'Yes, I tried to help you.'

'You tricked me into drinking God knows what—probably something they give to horses when they're castrating them—and then had me hauled away like a piece of meat and thrown in some damn flea-infested corner of the servant's quarters!'

'I did tell them to take you up to one of the guest rooms, but perhaps they were already all full.'

'What if you had given me too much of that stuff? You could have killed me!'

'I assure you, Sir Richard, the sleeping potion I gave you was perfectly safe.'

He gave an unconvinced grunt in reply.

She rested her chin on her hand and looked slyly across at him. 'You have yet to ask me if I found the letters...'

He suddenly sat bolt upright. 'Are you telling me you actually *found* them?'

'I think I did.'

He jumped to his feet. 'Where are they? Why didn't you tell me you had them?'

'I have them concealed on my person, and you did not ask.'

He held out his hand. 'Show them to me!'

'Bear with me a moment while I get them out...' she said, turning her back to him for a moment while she pulled the letters out through the neck of her dress.

He looked on admiringly. 'Good choice. No one would think of looking down *there* for them.'

She gave a slightly embarrassed laugh. 'I've had them stuffed down the front of my dress ever since I found them last night, even while I was sleeping, in case Lord Cunningham discovered they were missing and had the manor turned over in an attempt to find them. I did not want to burn them until I had shown them to you, because I wish to make sure that these are the letters in question, and—' she shot him an indignant look, 'because I'm sure you would not believe that I really had found the letters unless you saw them with your own eyes.'

As soon as they were presented to him, Sir Richard seized hold of the four letters and tensely ran his eyes over each one.

'Yes, these are the letters—they are all here,' he said when he had finished, and let out a long sigh of relief.

‘Thank goodness! I doubt I could have managed a second attempt if they were not.’

He sat for several minutes silently staring at the letters in his hands, as if unsure if they were real or just phantoms conjured up by a desperate and overwrought mind.

‘You know, Sir Richard,’ she began tentatively, ‘I couldn’t help reading the letters…’

At this, he immediately snapped out of his reverie and a rather panicked look came over him. ‘Yes, and?’

Rowena could sense the unwelcome nature of her statement from his defensive, prickly tone. But it would take a lot more than that to put her off asking him the question that had been burning in her mind ever since she had read the letters the previous night.

The letters had been in a small, locked iron chest under the bed of the soundly snoring Lord Cunningham. She had been on the verge of giving up the search and going back to bed, when the metal chest had glimmered in the lamplight and given its presence away. She had almost been too afraid to pull it out from right underneath her sleeping uncle, but the promise it held of ending Sir Richard’s financial woes and greatly unburdening Chaucy’s poorer citizens had made her bold.

The instant she set eyes on the letters she had known they were what she was looking for. They had Sir Richard’s familiar shaky signature at the bottom, were addressed to a lady called Morgana de Wintore—and contained English military secrets.

She looked calmly across the table at him. ‘Sir Richard, why did you not tell me you were a French spy?’

He pushed his dark hair back from his face, something he always did when he was at his most stressed, and bit his lip silently.

‘I believed that you upheld the rules of war, that you were loyal to your comrades. But now I find out that you were a…’

She paused, reluctant to say that most distasteful of words.

'A traitor,' he finished for her, in a voice that was hollow and empty.

'Yes, a traitor.' She spat the word out as if it tasted foul in her mouth.

He cleared his throat and darted a glance at her, then fixed his eyes back on the gauntlets he was wringing nervously together in his hands. 'I'm afraid I got rather entangled with this lady, Morgana de Wintore,' he began reluctantly. 'It was years ago. I was only about four and twenty at the time. Morgan turned out to be a French spy. She manipulated me into passing on anything I knew about King Henry's army in return for her faithfulness.'

'Did it work?' asked Rowena.

'Did what work?'

'Spying for Lady Cruelty in return for her love—did she forsake all others and keep herself only unto you?'

Bitterness passed over his face. 'Yes. For about two weeks.'

'So you then stopped spying for her?' his companion asked hopefully.

The sheriff nodded. 'These letters here are the only ones I passed on to her.'

'Did the English realise that someone was betraying them to the enemy?'

Sir Richard threw the gauntlets onto the table and wiped away the sweat beading on his brow. 'Oh yes. The tactical plans I passed on to the French did not cause the English a great deal of trouble, but they were furious that one of their own had betrayed them.'

'And they no doubt wish very much to flush out the traitor and remove his head from his body,' she added gloomily.

'Can you see now why I was so reluctant for you to search for the letters?'

She frowned crossly. 'No, actually, I do not. Unless you

thought I would betray you, I really do not see what you would have to fear. And if you *did* think that, I would be sorely wounded. You might not have been above such things, but I would never even consider betraying a friend or comrade.'

'I did not for a moment think that you do would do such a thing!' he hurriedly defended himself.

'What then?'

There was a long pause.

'Sir Richard, tell me what you thought.'

'I thought you would be furious with me if you found out what I had done,' he replied in a quiet voice.

She sighed and sunk her head down to rest on her arms, which were crossed on the table in front of her. 'If I fancied myself angry with you, I think I would really be angry with myself for having believed you were something which you are not. No, Sir Richard, I'm not angry with you. I knew you were a dark horse and I would expect nothing less from you.'

Looking both relieved and somewhat ashamed, he smiled nervously. 'I'm glad you're being so good about it. I was terribly afraid you would fly into one of your righteous rages and denounce me like some vengeful angel who, upon weighing the soul of a mortal, had found it greatly lacking.'

She gave a low laugh. 'Frankly, I don't have the energy to get into a righteous rage even if I wanted to—though I am sure that if a vengeful angel *did* weigh your soul it would indeed find it greatly lacking,' she added sharply.

He eyed her cautiously. 'Or perhaps I spoke too soon…'

She yawned sleepily. 'No, you are quite safe—for now.'

He nodded and gave a satisfied smile, then got up and walked over to the hearth. There the knight held out the incriminating letters which had cast a terrible shadow over his life ever since they had been written. 'I've dreamed of this moment for many a long year…' he whispered, throwing them into the flames.

The sheriff's clerk was glad too. It was such a relief to have finally put an end to the nightmare that was Sir Richard's overstretched finances.

He watched the letters burn until nothing but ashes remained, then turned away and came over to where Rowena sat.

'I owe you my undying gratitude for risking your position and reputation for me in this way,' he said earnestly, taking her hand in his. 'I want to thank you for it with all my heart.'

She felt her cheeks grow warm in the face of a sentiment that she was so unfamiliar with having directed at her. 'It's really nothing. I have no position or reputation to speak of anyway.'

'It was not 'nothing'. What you did was very brave, and I want you to know that—'

'Really, Sir Richard,' she protested, 'there's no need—'

He silenced her by placing a finger on her lips. 'Hush. I know you are determined to disagree, but I will not be contradicted on this point,' he said with a smile.

She felt her blush deepen a little, but nodded acceptance.

He lifted his finger from her lips and took her other hand in his too. 'I want you to know that I consider myself deeply in your debt for this. Anytime you need or want anything from me, consider it done, no matter how great or small it might be.'

'You are very kind. I don't know what to say…'

He laughed and gave her hands a gentle squeeze. ''Yes' would do nicely.'

She smiled slyly at him. 'Your wish is my command, master.'

'Hmmm…now I think you mean to tease me.'

'And *I* think that you will find teasing is *your* special talent,' she said archly, beginning to think it might be wise to free herself from his grip.

He eyed her dangerously. 'Oh really?'

She quickly got to her feet. 'Oh no, you're getting that dreadful predatory look in your eyes again, like you did at the feast last night. Causing a shocking scene like that, right in front of anyone who is anyone for miles around—I really must severely tell you off for doing such a thing! You know, I was that close to breaking into an uncontrollable fit of giggles.' She gave an indignant sniff. 'In future, I shall be making sure that your hands are where I can see them at public gatherings.'

He smiled darkly down at her. 'If you don't stop your scolding *you* might end up being the one jumping to a place of safety like a maid who has seen a mouse this time, because I can think of a *very* good way of silencing you.'

'Oh yes, in all the excitement of stealing the letters I had forgotten all about that! It really was the funniest thing I have ever seen!' she cried, laughing heartily at the memory.

'You thought it was funny, did you? I'm set upon by some crazed, drink-sodden girl and all you can do is laugh.' He made a lunge for her waist. 'I'll teach you not to laugh at me like that, madam!'

She shrieked and skipped to the side in just time to avoid being caught. 'No you won't!'

'I wouldn't be so sure about that, little lady,' he replied, advancing on her again. 'You're always out-foxing me and making me look a fool, and I think it's time I taught you a lesson.'

Rowena was not sure what punishment Sir Richard had in mind, but the look in his eyes did not bode well. She backed away from him rapidly, determined not to be caught.

He kept pace with her retreat. 'So, do you still think my predicament last night was funny?'

'Yes I do, and I can't wait to tell everyone at Eaglestone all about it!' she replied rather boldly considering her odds.

He lunged for her again. 'That does it!'

But this time her nimble dodge only found her in a corner, firmly trapped and staring straight at Sir Richard's naked chest through the opening in his leather doublet and shirt, both undone to near his waist in the heat.

He placed a hand on the wall on either side of her, removing any chance of escape she might have had, and leaned over her.

'I capture the castle…' he whispered, in deep, darkly honeyed tones that washed over her like a caress.

The heady, overpowering scent of musky, spicy perfume mixed with the smell of leather and his sweat made her feel giddy.

She leaned her head back against the cool stone wall and looked up at him with a smile of resignation. 'Yes, Sir Richard, I think you are the victor this time. But it is hardly a noble victory, as your size is so much greater than mine.'

He looked down on her in smug triumph. 'If looked at purely from the point of brute strength, perhaps. But if one adds your foxy cunning to the scales, I think it becomes much more balanced.'

'But you did not give me a chance to think about cheating, so I think my point still stands.'

He gave a low, bemused laugh. 'You do not give in easily, do you?'

She tilted her chin up defiantly. 'You may have gained an easy victory over my body, but you will find my spirit a much harder opponent. I doubt you stand any real chance at all.'

'Fighting words indeed, my lady…' he murmured, moving in closer.

Rowena let out a gasp as the pressure of his hard, muscular body pressed against her. His panting breath was hot on her cheek and she could feel his pulse throbbing through the thin cloth separating them. Her own heart began to race and her bosom heaved against his firm abdomen as she breathed faster and more deeply.

'I'm not quite sure that your body and your mind are in complete agreement here, madam…' came his low, velvety purr.

She looked up at him. His liquidly dark, heavy-lidded eyes fixed on hers with a seductive intensity that made her feel weak.

'I think you might have just called my bluff, Sir Richard,' she gasped breathlessly. 'I feel…like I'm going to faint…'

He smiled his slow, dark smile. 'So, you finally admit defeat?'

She had always thought herself immune to his physical charms, but now she felt like she was drowning in a sea of throbbing, sweating maleness. If he did not remove his hard, heaving body from hers soon and stop breathing over her like that, she was sure she was going to faint or have a heart seizure—or both.

Still panting, she nodded. 'Yes—'

One large, strong hand slid around her waist, while the other came to rest on her bare chest, rather close to her gown's low neckline.

Feeling even giddier, she watched with hypnotically fixed eyes as a heavy bead of sweat ran slowly down the hard, smooth contours of his naked chest.

'I do wish it wasn't so stiflingly hot…' she gasped.

'Are you talking about me or the weather?'

'I had meant to refer to the latter, but I think the sentiment extends to the former too.'

He laughed sardonically. 'I must say, even *I* did not expect the crafty fox to be overcome quite so easily…'

Rowena pulled her eyes up. 'Neither did she.'

But the new view was even worse than the previous one. He had fixed his burning black eyes on hers and bought his parted lips down to hover just above her own lips. Hypnotically, she held his gaze as his burning velvet lips first brushed against hers, then pressed a firm kiss upon them.

She could barely think at all. Why did those eyes have to be so darkly, deeply seductive? Those eyes, they were pools of liquid black—pools of ruin! What was she thinking of, letting some devilish knight whom she barely knew have his way with her? God's bones!

She suddenly put both hands to his chest and pushed back. 'You, sir, are taking a great liberty!'

He lifted his head, but she felt his body stiffen in resistance to her push. 'The kind of liberty *you* made free to take with *my* person?'

She set her jaw firmly and tightened her lips as she tried to meet the challenge in his eyes defiantly. It was a failure. She felt her cheeks glow hot, and when he lifted a dark eyebrow in amused satisfaction, she had to look down. That slightly sadistic smile playing on his lips spoke of gratification at a victory achieved and a power exercised. If she allowed him to exercise it anymore, her city would surely fall.

She stopped pushing, but kept her hands braced against him 'I'm sorry for what I did to you at the feast, *master*. Now will you release your underling, or does this master demand more of his minions than a Christian knight ought to?'

He tilted his head to one side and regarded her darkly. Feeling that he mistrusted the sincerity of his clerk's sudden fit of meekness, she kept her eyes lowered. A wolf with bared teeth poised at its vanquished foe's throat only invites defiance from fools.

After a few moments' consideration, he stepped back. 'Pardon me. I did not mean to offend your modesty.'

She irately smoothed her dishevelled hair. 'My modesty? Did you think I would have loose virtues because I'm some poor, common maid?'

'No!'

She hitched the fallen neckline of her gown back onto her shoulder with an angry jerk. 'Oh, so this is your habit with *all* women then, is it?'

He took an aghast step back that nearly had him flying over a stool. 'If you are suggesting that I am a ravisher of women, I will consider it a grave insult to my honour!'

'I was not suggesting that you are a ravisher of women's bodies, but of their hearts. Where the heart leads the body is likely to follow!'

'Madam, I swear by Our Lady that my soul is free of the sin which you accuse me of. I have never in my life stained the virtue of any maiden!'

She shot Sir Richard a cross look as she stepped carefully past him enroute to the centre of the room. 'And then you decided it was about time you did. I really must be tired,' she added under her breath, 'letting a man like *you* anywhere near me without so much as a betrothal between us.'

He bowed stiffly. 'I beg your pardon, sweet lady. I did not intend for things to get out of hand.'

Still in a huff, she stooped to pick up the broken pieces of pewter bowl lying scattered on the floor. 'The only thing that got out of hand is *you*.'

The knight gave a silent and rather unwilling nod of acceptance at this latest rebuff from his clerk.

Starting to feel ever so slightly guilty at Sir Richard's remorseful face, she dropped the pieces of broken bowl in a pail by the door and turned to him with a more open expression. 'Never mind, accidents will happen.'

He seemed less than comfortable with her verdict, but nodded anyway.

Rowena smiled wryly to herself. No doubt he had decided it would be wisest to stop digging. Deciding it was best to put the matter to bed quickly, she smiled politely across at Sir Richard. 'Pray, let's talk of other things. Tell me, how are your investigations going?'

He carefully drew a bench out, sat down and rocked it onto its back legs. 'Well, I had been hoping that Thomas's killer would be found before the upcoming sitting of the shire court, so the people could be satisfied some progress was being made. The court is only a few days away now; it looks like I'll have to pass an unsolved verdict when the case comes up. All the citizens of Hartfield will be keenly noting the outcome of this court-day to see if I have solved any of these crimes. I hope Gray doesn't use it to start some damn riot…'

Rowena perched herself on the edge of the stout table. 'But at least you will be able to announce the much lower new tax rate. I'm sure that will go a long way towards silencing any discontented mutterings—don't rock that bench back like that, you will break it! The sort of furniture humble folk can afford is not up to such punishment.'

He let all four of the bench's legs rest back on the ground. 'Pardon me. This bench is so low it's going to give me stiff knees. Yes, you are right about the taxes. That was, after all, Gray's main rallying cry.'

'It is not the bench which is low but your legs which are long.'

He leaned back against the wall behind and swung his boots up to rest on the table. 'True.'

She promptly shoved them back off. 'No, off!'

There was a decidedly miffed air about the tall knight as he rearranged himself on the tiny bench. 'I already feel henpecked and you are not even my wife!'

His clerk gave a piqued sniff. 'No, thank goodness. Having to put up with that sort of thing every day of her life really can drive a woman to the edge of reason. Now, you were saying about the investigation?'

'Yes, the investigation…the trail has just gone cold. We have not found a single witness or new piece of evidence since you and I searched the scene of the last kidnapping at Dovers Dell. I have had every one of my available men out on the case. They have been going around to all the dwellings that are anywhere near where the maidens were taken from, or where the felons might have passed through. I gave my men orders to take the broach we found at Dovers Dell and show it to all the folk they talked to in the hope one of them might recognise it, but there has been nothing.'

'So what are you going to do now?'

'I don't know. As it has now been such a long time since the first maidens were taken, there is a good chance we will never find them. My men and I have scrutinised every possible lead and clue. There is nothing left that we can do.'

'Oh don't say that! I can't bear to think what dreadful fate might have befallen those poor girls. They were kidnapped, not murdered. They're probably still alive somewhere.'

'Yes, but they are likely a very long way from here by now.'

'Please don't give up, Sir Richard. For the maidens' sake you must not give up hope. Someone *must* have seen or heard something.'

'But there is nothing left for us to do that has not already been done before. We have scoured every corner of this shire. Lucifer has covered so many miles in these past weeks that he has worn through his shoes at twice his normal rate. My backside shall be glad when this is over too,' he added, shifting uncomfortably on the hard seat.

'Despite what some of Hartfield's citizens say, I know you have been working very hard. But I'm sure there must still be something that can be done. Have you thought about what the felons may have in mind for the maidens?'

'I have heard some rumours about slave traders near the coast. I talked to a pilgrim awhile back who had just docked at the seaport in Dead Men's Cove, which is on Lothbury's south coast. He had heard talk in the local alehouse about slave ships docking there at night to take supplies on board, and some said also children who had been sold to them by their parents. But the ship's main cargo was said to be folk who had been captured by the pirates roaming the waters of the channel.'

'Where do these slave ships take the poor souls to be sold?'

'Almost certainly the East. Turkey, Persia and the like. White slaves are said to fetch a high price over there. There is a great demand for them among the wealthy sultans and princes.'

'Do you think young women would be especially sought-after by slave traders?'

He nodded. 'A pretty girl would almost certainly fetch the highest price of all at the Eastern slave markets.'

'From what we've been told, it seems that all of the victims were comely young maidens. This is a very promising lead. Why don't you ride over to this Dead Men's Cove and look into it?'

'It is in the next shire; I have no jurisdiction there. I'm supposed to go to the sheriff of any shire outside my own and pass on any suspicions of felony being committed there for him to investigate.'

'Well, why don't you do that then?'

'I did. It was pointless. He flatly denied there was anything shady going on in his shire. The slimy knave is clearly as bent as a thumbscrew—he wouldn't even let me finish speaking before he was saying 'how dare you come over into my shire accusing me of corruption!' I never said anything to him about corruption, but after his guilty reaction I was left in no doubt that he's bent. If there is anything underhand going on in his patch, he will be getting his cut.'

'Oh dear...' she sighed, but her attention was not on Sir Richard anymore. The cottage door, left open to allow what little breeze there was to pass through, had just darkened with the figure of a worried Becky, who looked as if she had just entered her home to find a wolf seated at her table.

Becky pointed to the seated sheriff, who had not noticed her yet as he was seated with his back to her. 'What's this?' she mouthed silently to Rowena.

Rowena hopped down from the table edge. 'Becky, it's barely midday; surely you have not finished the harvest already?'

Becky cautiously stepped inside, eyeing Sir Richard like he was a wild animal that might jump up and bite her at any moment. 'No, we ain't finished. I just forgot the food basket.'

The sheriff turned to see who it was, then quickly got to his feet.

Rowena gave her friend a reassuring smile. 'This is our sheriff, Sir Richard Hastings.'

He bowed. 'Dame, our Lord give you good day.'

'And this is my friend Becky, whose house this is.'

Becky replied to his polite greeting with a curt nod. 'What might you be doing here, Sir Richard?'

He placed a casual hand on Rowena's shoulder, which caused Becky to visibly stiffen. 'I came over to talk to my clerk.'

Rowena raised her eyebrows. 'Talk to? I think scold would be a more accurate word.'

Becky's eyes narrowed. 'He's not been bothering you, has he?'

Sir Richard laughed. 'Goodwife, you need have no fears on that account. It is me you should pity. Rowena is forever proving the superiority of her wits over mine.'

Becky shook her head, looking a little startled.

'That's not true at all!' cried Rowena, giving him a playful slap on the hand.

He winced and rubbed his hand. 'Look at the way she abuses me.'

'Don't take any heed of anything he says, Becky. Now, Sir Richard, have you not got sheriff's business to be getting on with?'

'Yes, I do indeed. Very nice to make your acquaintance, Dame Becky,' he said, picking up his gauntlets and starting to move towards the door. 'Oh yes.' He stopped and turned back towards the women. 'I have some news about the tax rates which you will want to know.'

Becky let out an audible groan. 'They ain't going up again, are they? How are us poor folks to live when we are forced to give most of our earnings to—'

He raised a silencing hand. 'Madam, I beg that you let me finish. The news I wish to tell you is that the tax rate will be going down, not up.'

The blonde dame put a cynical hand to her hip. 'By how much?'

'The new tax rate, which will be officially announced and take effect at the next shire court hearing, is to be a third of the current tax rate.'

Becky's jaw dropped low enough to fit a pie in whole. 'By all the saints in heaven!' But her cynicism quickly returned. 'For how long?'

'Permanently, I hope,' he replied with a smile.

.11.

Lest your Heart's Blood Should Run Cold

IT REALLY was most odd. The hour when Sir Richard normally started work for the day was already long past, yet it seemed none of the guards had seen him that morning. Rowena threw her cloak across a chair and hurried back down the stairs. In the dim light, she saw someone sitting on the last step.

This someone was not tall enough to be a man, which meant it had to be Pepin, the castle's only pageboy. He had been asked about the whereabouts of the master already, so she just swept her skirt aside and made to pass by. But something long, thin and hard contacted sharply with her shin and barred any further progress.

'Pepin, what are you doing polishing Sir Richard's sword right in the middle of this dark, narrow stair?' she demanded crossly. 'For heaven's sake have a care!'

'Sorry, my lady,' he muttered, sulkily moving the blade aside.

'Where is Sergeant Gallagher? I want to ask him if he knows where Sir Richard is.'

'I asked him. He don't know.'

'I wager you nearly killed the sergeant with your booby-trap first!'

'It ain't my fault if everybody in this place insists on going round with their eyes fixed on the rafters—and nobody told me not to sit here!'

'Well, I'm telling you now. And make an effort to talk properly; you're not in your father's tannery anymore!' she called over her shoulder as she ran back upstairs.

When Rowena returned to the sheriff's chamber, she hoped that he might have come down from his private sleeping quarters on the floor above. But the chamber was just as empty as when she had left it.

She climbed the little spiral stairs that led to his living quarters and knocked on the door again. 'Sir Richard, are you in there?'

There was no answer. For about the fiftieth time since arriving at Eaglestone Castle an hour ago, she wondered if she should just enter his private chambers anyway. She felt uneasy about doing so. No one except him ever went in there. An uninvited intrusion into his inner sanctum might not be well received. And the massive stone walls were so thick it was impossible to hear what was going on in the next room. What if he had a lady in there with him? Now that really would be embarrassing...

Things had been a little uncomfortable between the sheriff and his young clerk since their scorching encounter the previous week. Neither party had mentioned the incident, but Rowena felt sure Sir Richard was as annoyed with both himself and his clerk as she was herself.

Rowena gave a huff of impatience. If only there was a way of hearing what was going on inside—of course, the keyhole!

She stooped down and looked through it. Blackness was all she could see. Damn, the key was in the lock.

She clutched her hands to her head in exasperation, then suddenly cried 'that'll do it!' She swiftly pulled a long hair pin out from her coiffure, inserted it into the keyhole and gave it a good poke.

There was a clatter on the other side of the door as the key fell out. But when she peered in again, she was only met with more disappointment. The sole things visible through the tiny hole were the wall opposite, the bare wooden floorboards, and right on the periphery of her sight, what looked like an overturned chair, though she could not say for sure. Nothing startling there. Messy living quarters were hardly a rarity where bachelors are concerned.

She knocked as loudly as she could. 'Sir Richard!' she shouted, before putting her ear to the keyhole to listen for any reply.

At first there was only silence, but then a faint, muffled sound reached her ears.

'Sir Richard, are you in there?' she called again.

Rowena held her breath—yes, there it was again. A sound had definitely come from within, and it sounded like…a snore? No it did not, it was a groan!

She instantly jumped to her feet and groped for the door latch in the dark stairwell, then once it was found, burst into the room.

She franticly scanned the chamber, which was sparsely furnished with a pair of uncomfortable-looking chairs and a battered iron trunk. 'Sir Richard, where are you?'

The groans were clearly audible now, but there was still no one to be seen. The bedchamber—he must be in the bedchamber!

Her head filled with scenes of horror and carnage as she ran over to the closed door leading off the chamber and pulled it open. Her throat was so constricted with panic at the thought of what she might find that she could only breathe in shallow, rasping gasps.

At first she could not see anyone in the dimly-lit bedchamber, but her attention was immediately drawn to the floor on the other side of the bed by a low groan.

Rowena instantly rushed over. A large pool of dark, oozing blood covered the floor, and a motionless Sir Richard lay face down beside it with his hands tied behind his back.

She threw herself to her knees beside him and started franticly untying the cord. 'Sir Richard, are you alright? Say something!'

There was a muffled, choking groan in reply.

She seized him by the shoulder, almost sobbing with dread and panic. 'No, please, oh blessed Lord no!'

He groaned again and just managed to lift his hand off the floor and weakly indicate his head.

'Oh God, you're gagged. I'm sorry!' She placed shaking fingers on the cloth tightly bound around his head and started fumbling with its impossibly tight knot.

'It's no good, I can't get this thing undone!' she cried, despairing after a few fruitless attempts.

He turned his head to the side a little and looked up at her, then back to the floor beside his hand.

'What is it?'

He repeated the action.

This time she followed his eyes. A dagger was lying on the floor nearby. She snatched hold of it, took a deep breath to steady her shaking hands, and carefully slit the gag with the razor-sharp blade.

'I was beginning to think you'd never come!' he gasped.

She cast a panicked eye over his body, searching for the source of all the blood pooling on the floor beside him. 'Is this blood yours? Are you hurt?'

'Calm down, would you. I'm not dead yet...'

But his weak, rasping voice only added to the terror already generated by his blue-tinged, deathly pale face. Then she suddenly noticed a large dark red stain on his left upper arm. 'Your arm!'

Sir Richard put his hand over the centre of the blood-soaked area and winced as he pressed down hard. 'Yes, the blood is mine. I've been stabbed,' he said matter-of-factly, as though such things were a normal, everyday occurrence.

'But there is so much blood on the floor here; surely it can't all be yours or there'd be none left!'

He gave a humourless, pained laugh. 'Don't worry, there's still plenty more left where that came from.'

But she hardly heard him. She was too busy looking around for something to bind around the wound from which blood was still welling up through the fingers of the hand Sir Richard held over it. Her eyes alighted on the edge of the bed sheet that was visible from under the cover.

'Don't rip those! I only just bought the damn things.'

'You're lying on the floor bleeding to death and all you can think about is the cost of bed linen!' she replied through gritted teeth, ripping a long strip off the sheet. 'For goodness sake stop being such a stoical martyr and let me get on with my panicking! Now hold your arm up and let me get this around it.'

He obediently raised the arm. 'It really does look worse than it is.'

She lifted his hand off the wound and started to wrap the long linen strip around his arm. 'Who did this to you?'

'I could not sleep last night, so I went out on the battlements at the top of the tower. When I came back and walked into here, some damn scurvy knave who was lurking behind the bed-curtains jumped me from behind. I think the rotten scoundrel was looking for those God-damned letters. I managed to get my dagger out, but he had the advantage of surprise. There was a bit of a scuffle, during which the villainous knave stabbed me. The force of it made me lose my balance and hit my head on the post of that accursed bed frame. After that, everything went black until I woke about an hour ago.'

Rowena looked up from the bandage she was putting the final knot in. 'To think you were lying up here all alone bleeding while I was just in the room below you.' She placed her hand on his forehead. It was clammy and icy cold. The young woman frowned anxiously and bit her lip. 'Why did I not think to come up sooner? Still,' she added, shaking herself out of the mood, 'my regrets are no use to you now. I must get you to a physician. Do you think you can get up?'

'I'll try.' He grimaced as, with her help, he dragged himself up to lean on the elbow of his right arm, but stopped there, breathing heavily. 'I've been drifting in and out of consciousness since I first came to. If I get up and start to fall you're not going to be much use. Go and find Gallagher.'

'Yes, good idea.' She placed a concerned hand on his forehead. 'You will be alright while I'm gone, won't you?'

He gave a quick nod. 'Yes, yes, you just go. I promise not to drop dead while you're away.'

Her frown deepened and she held up an admonishing finger. 'Don't jest about that sort of thing. It's not funny.'

He took her finger and gave it a squeeze. 'Alright, in addition to not dropping dead in your absence, I also promise to keep my soldier's gallows humour to myself.'

* * * *

When she had finally, with the aid of Gallagher's brawn, got Sir Richard to the site of Brother Jacob's cottage, Rowena felt able to relax a little. She had sent Pepin ahead to let the monk know the injured sheriff was coming, while she herself accompanied the wounded man and his comrade.

To his clerk's castigation, the stoical knight had swiftly dismissed any suggestion of having a cart bring him to the herbalist's cottage, and insisted on walking the short distance there himself.

Brother Jacob stood in his cottage's open doorway waiting for the patient to arrive. He hurried forward to meet the party as soon as they came into view through the trees. 'Do allow me to relieve you, Mistress Rowena.'

She stepped back, only too happy to relinquish her role as a crutch. 'Thank you, brother.'

But Sir Richard waved away the offer of help. 'No really, brother, I can stand by myself. I don't need to burden someone of your dignified years with my weight.'

Brother Jacob respected this and let the wounded man walk the remainder of the way using only his sergeant's broad shoulder for support.

Once inside, the monk gestured towards a chair. 'Take a seat and make yourself as comfortable as you can.'

While Gallagher and Rowena hovered anxiously at his side, Sir Richard lowered himself into the chair with a relieved sigh.

'I will manage from here,' said Brother Jacob. 'Why don't you two take a seat as well? I am sure you both deserve it by now.'

'I think I might just wait outside,' said Gallagher.

'By all means,' replied Brother Jacob, in his warm and softly-spoken manner.

'Do you mind if I stay?' asked Rowena.

'I do not use witchcraft or any odd quackery here that I don't want seen, so feel free.' He looked to Sir Richard. 'As long as that is alright with you?'

'I don't mind—providing she doesn't faint or stand there cringing with horror.'

'I promise not to do anything like that,' Rowena replied quickly, even though she did not feel entirely confident that she would not.

'Now, let us have a look at this arm first,' Brother Jacob murmured, pushing back the sleeves of his dove-grey monk's habit. 'Did you lose much blood?' he asked, beginning to unwind the bandage.

Sir Richard nodded grimly. 'Yes, quite a lot.'

'There was a colossal pool of blood where I found him lying,' added Rowena. 'When I first saw it I thought he must be at death's door for sure.'

The monk smiled indulgently. 'There is a lot more blood in the body than many people give it credit for, but,' he added, casting a professional eye over the knight's pale features, 'judging by the colour of you, Sir Richard, I think you have lost a dangerous amount.'

Sir Richard did not look particularly concerned. 'I know, but it's not the first time.'

Brother Jacob finished removing the blood-soaked bandage and placed it in a bowl on the nearby table. 'Now, I need to get this shirt off. Do you think you can get it over your head, or shall I cut it off?'

'No, don't cut it! I've had enough of my linen ruined for one day,' growled Sir Richard, shooting an admonishing look at Rowena.

She silently replied with a wry look of her own. Why couldn't he just be plain grateful for once?

'When I lift this pad off your wound, quickly get the arm out of the shirt,' instructed Brother Jacob.

The knight removed his arm from the right sleeve and lifted his shirt over his head. Then he slipped it off his wounded left arm, while the monk lifted the cloth off and hastily pressed it back down on the wound as blood started to well.

Upon seeing Sir Richard's naked upper body for the first time, Rowena had to clap her hand over her mouth to stifle a gasp of horrified surprise. From her position perched on a high stool behind him, she had an uninterrupted view of his back. It was covered in scars. She had never seen anything like it. There were too many of the long, pale scars to count. And most of them ran parallel like... She furrowed her brows in concentration. Yes, like wounds gained in a flogging.

'If you stare like that for much longer, you're going to bore a hole in my back.'

She started at the sound of Sir Richard's grimly-spoken words (he could not possibly see her from where he was seated), and gulped. 'I was not st—'

'Yes you were.'

She cleared her throat and shifted uncomfortably. 'Pardon me. I did not, ahem, mean to.'

'I'm used to it. Everyone does it,' he replied stonily, still with his back to her.

'I think this is the point when you put the poor young lady out of her misery and tell her how you got all those impressive scars,' murmured Brother Jacob.

Sir Richard gave a dry chuckle. The monk's subtle telling-off was clearly not lost on him. 'Alright, if you really must know, Rowena. I was set upon by some bastard swine that had it in for me. He was intending to kill me in some slow and highly original fashion, but I escaped from his dungeon having only been flogged to a pulp, as the fool guarding me turned his back on me. You'd be surprised how easy it is to ring a man's neck...'

Although her curiosity was not satisfied by this brief but brutal explanation, she was too wary of his prickly reaction to ask any more about it. He clearly did not want to talk to her about it. No surprises there then.

'How...awful,' she replied awkwardly.

Brother Jacob sighed and shook his head sadly. 'Such evil, such evil...'

'It was revenge, and I can't say I didn't deserve it.' Sir Richard's harsh whisper was barely audible to her.

Brother Jacob held the cloth he had used to clean the wound above a bowl and wrung the bloody water out of it. 'A man who takes the task of retribution into his own hands and sins in the name of revenge is no less a sinner than he who strikes the first blow. Does such a man not prove how little faith he has that the heavenly hosts will see to it that justice is done? Does he not show his arrogance by daring to believe he has the right to pass such a judgement on his fellow man? My son, he who strikes another man in revenge is unchristian, for he scorns the Saviour's love and forgiveness, and blasphemes against our heavenly Father.'

Sir Richard had listened respectfully with his head bowed down while Brother Jacob delivered the little sermon. Whether in shame or concentration Rowena was not sure.

After a moment's silence, he looked up at the monk, who was now carefully patting the wound dry. 'Thank you, brother. Knowing that he is going to hell just as surely as I am is some comfort.'

Brother Jacob smiled kindly, and placed a fatherly hand on his patient's shoulder. 'You are welcome, my son. But I think you did not quite take that the right way. Our Saviour died for us. If we repent and atone, God will forgive.'

Sir Richard nodded slowly and unsurely. 'Yes, I suppose you are right.'

Brother Jacob smiled ruefully. The other man's doubting look had not escaped his notice. 'I *am* right.' He wiped his hand on a cloth. 'This wound is going to need stitching. I hope you do not have a weak stomach, Mistress Rowena.'

'Don't worry about me. As long as the body is fresh I'm alright.'

Brother Jacob bustled around busily getting out the things he needed for the job. 'I'm afraid it will hurt rather a lot, Sir Richard,' he said over his shoulder, searching his shelves for something, 'but I cannot do it unless you keep still. Do you think you will manage?'

Sir Richard flicked a dismissive hand. 'I'll be fine, absolutely fine.'

'Are you sure? Perhaps you would like to hold the young lady's hand while I do it? Some people find that helps take their mind off the pain.'

'Well…I suppose I *might* find it hard going,' said Sir Richard, a shadow of a smile playing on the corners of his mouth.

She gave Sir Richard a disbelieving look. 'Oh really?'

There was no way he needed a woman to hold his hand in order to cope with a little pain. But still, it would not hurt to indulge him just this once…

She moved off her stool and came over. 'Alright, where do you want your angel of mercy?'

'If you sat down here on my right side, that would be perfect,' Sir Richard replied smugly.

She drew up a stool and did as she was asked.

He placed his hand in her lap. 'Here it is.'

'But Brother Jacob has not started yet.'

He put on his best pained face. 'It hurts in anticipation, you heartless maid!'

She could not help laughing at this. 'Very well.' She took his hand. 'As you are clearly such a coward in the face of pain, I shall take pity on you.'

Hmmm…the view was not bad here. All that time Sir Richard spent honing his fighting skills down in the field at the back of the castle might be a waste of time for a sheriff, who was rarely called upon to do any serious fighting, but it did make him look *very* impressive without his shirt on. She cast an admiring eye over his lean, muscular torso and bulging biceps. Yes, very nice…

Then she suddenly became aware that her admiration was not going unnoticed. Sir Richard was looking directly across at her with a self-satisfied smirk on his face.

She instantly snapped her eyes down. 'Ahem, I was just…' she started, and then trailed off. If it had not worked the first time, it was hardly going to work now.

He grinned. 'Feel free. Don't let me put you off.'

Holding a needle and thread, Brother Jacob turned back to his patient. 'I'm ready to start now, so brace yourself. This wound is going to require quite a few stitches. If it gets too much and you would like a rest, just let me know. '

Rowena tightened her grip on Sir Richard's hand in anticipation, but when the monk made the first stitch, he did not react at all.

'Is that alright?' asked a frowning Brother Jacob.

'Oh, you've started—yes, yes, it's fine,' he replied casually.

'So you are indeed as hard as you look...' murmured Brother Jacob, without taking his intensely focused eyes off the job at hand.

'I must say, Sir Richard,' said Rowena, 'I am impressed. I think *you* are the one who should be holding *my* hand.'

Brother Jacob soon finished stitching the wound, his task made easy by Sir Richard's high pain threshold. He did not complain or so much as flinch once for the duration.

The monk finished off by carefully bandaging the wounded arm, and placing it in a cloth sling, which did not thrill the patient. 'Do I really have to wear this damn thing?' he asked.

'Yes, you do,' came the firm reply. 'If you do not, your wound might start bleeding afresh. If it is kept still it will heal more quickly.'

Sir Richard's only reply to this unwelcome news was a sullen grunt.

'Now, did you not hit your head as well? The boy who came to warn me you were coming said that you hit your head and blacked out.'

The injured man nodded and indicated a large purple bruise on his temple that extended into his hairline. 'I was out cold for a while, but I'm fine now.'

Brother Jacob took a careful look at the area. 'Hmmm…quite a lot of bruising here… Does it hurt?'

'It wouldn't if you weren't poking at it.'

Brother Jacob quickly removed his hands. 'I do beg your pardon. And does your head ache at all?'

'A little.'

'I see…'

The monk moved over to the shelves that covered the entire back wall of the room, and started searching through the bottles and jars lining them. 'I have got just the salve for this kind of thing. I made it only the other day, but I seem to have lost it already…' He searched for a while longer until finally, right on the very topmost shelf, he found the pot he was looking for. 'Ah,' he cried, lifting it down, 'you can't hide from me up there, little pot!'

He then sat the little terracotta jar down on his big worktable and removed its waxed cloth cover.

Sir Richard eyed it distastefully. 'Are you going to smear that on my head?'

Brother Jacob turned to his patient, pot in hand. 'Yes. It will do that nasty bruise a world of good.'

'But it's sticky. It'll get all stuck in my hair.'

Brother Jacob scooped up a good gob of the thick, golden-yellow ointment with his finger. 'It will do your magnificent black locks nothing but good, I assure you.'

'Whatever you say…' grumbled Sir Richard, a rather bad grace about him.

Once the ointment had been smoothed on, a task Brother Jacob carried out with the utmost care and delicacy, the monk wiped the excess off his hands. 'I cannot make you do this against your will, but I strongly advise that you rest here for a day or two. Blows to the head are sometimes worse than they appear at first, and you are weak from blood-loss. I have a little ward here, in the next-door room. You would be quite comfortable.'

'But I can't!' replied the sheriff. 'I've got so many things to do; the new tax payments to organise, the upcoming court day, kidnappings to solve—'

Rowena squeezed his hand, which still rested in hers. 'Stop. You are wounded, you need to rest. I can do most of the things that need doing urgently. And anyway, it's only for a day or two.'

'What if something goes wrong? I won't be there.'

'If I need you, I will know where to find you, won't I? Now stop being such a bad patient and do as Brother Jacob advises. If you were around the castle I would only be in a twitter all the time, thinking you might be about to kick the bucket at any moment.'

The reluctant patient held up his one free hand in surrender. 'Alright, I will do it. But only if you promise to tell me instantly if there are any new developments.'

'Of course I will tell you if anything important happens.'

Brother Jacob put away the last of the things he had taken out, then opened the door leading to the next room. 'If you would care to step this way.'

The room Brother Jacob ushered Sir Richard and Rowena into was large and square, with plastered walls washed in the same pale yellow limewash as the front room was. There were four beds, two against each wall on the right and left of the door, facing each other. A deliciously cool breeze wafted in through the open window, playfully tossing about the muslin curtains and riffling through the crisp white sheets hanging down from the beds.

'This looks lovely,' said Rowena. 'I'm sure you will be very comfortable in here, Sir Richard.'

'I'd much rather be back at Eaglestone…' he growled.

.12.

Vengeance is Thine

'WHAT is that you are reading?'

Rowena held up the book she had been reading as she walked along to show Sir Richard.

He frowned in concentration as he stared at it. 'The… the…romance?'

She gave a nod and smiled encouragingly. 'Yes, very good.'

'The romance…of Percival and…and—no, it's no good!' he finished, throwing up his hands in frustration.

'It says 'the romance of Percival and the grail quest.' Why won't you let me teach you how to read better? 'It's nowhere near as difficult to learn as you seem to think.'

Sir Richard clicked to Lucifer to encourage on his big warhorse, who was ambling sleepily along behind them, head drooping and eyes half shut.

Once the stallion had woken a little and picked his pace up, Sir Richard turned his attention back to his human companion. 'It might seem easy to a clever maid like you, but I'm a soldier, not a scholar. Book learning has never come easily to me.'

'Nonsense. I'm telling you, anyone can learn if they put their mind to it. You've just not had a decent teacher, that's all.'

He clicked to Lucifer, who was pulling on his reins as he trailed behind again. 'Come on, boy. I know it's the end of a long day and you wish you were back in your meadow now, but for God's sake try and keep awake for another half hour! Yes, I suppose I could make a little time. But I must warn you, I'm a very bad pupil and am sure to try your patience greatly.'

'You always try my patience greatly.'

He laughed softly, choosing to tolerate the poke. 'Perhaps you might have time to tell Everild some of the stories you are always reading? I'm sure she would like that. She was always interested in myths and poetry and the like. But I was always much too busy running around pretending to kill things and win tournaments, and of course rescue damsels in distress.'

'I will gladly tell her some of my stories. Although I'm sure she will be even more delighted when her brother can read her favourite tales to her—ah, now do you mind if we take a little detour to the church at the nunnery? It is a year to the day since my mother departed this world, and I must go to the church to light a candle and pray for her. Her grave is in Cornwall in a little churchyard near the village where we lived, high up on the edge of the cliffs overlooking the sea. It's three day's journey from here, so I have not been back there since I came here to live with my relatives.'

'I did not know you had been bereaved so recently. I'm sorry. You must miss her very much,' he replied carefully, turning into the road that led up to the Holy Convent of the Martyrdom of St Agnes.

'I miss her more than I can say. Sometimes I think of it and I'm sad, but then I remember how she always longed for the day when she could finally be reunited with my father, and I'm happy that she could finally leave behind her grief and the hard life we led. My mother married my father, a lowly-born troubadour, much against the wishes of her family, so they cast her out without a penny. Her father refused to give her the dowry that was rightfully hers. But she never really recovered from the death of my father after only seven years of marriage...her health was always fragile after that. All the carding and spinning she had to take in so she could make ends meet did nothing to help. I did everything I could to ease her burden, but I was only a child…and her family never forgave her—never visited us or gave us so much as a penny, even though we barely had enough to eat at times,' she added bitterly, the memory of the pale ghost her mother had been reduced to in the end arising painfully.

'Do you hate them for it?'

'No. They might have denied my mother her rightful inheritance and driven her into an early grave through their hard-heartedness, but I will not let them poison my soul with hatred. That is one thing I will never let them do to me.'

He nodded, staring meditatively down at the ground as he walked alongside her.

She forced a smile. 'I think I'd better end my tale of woe. You're starting to look rather depressed there. Now, let us talk of something more cheerful. How about a game of riddles?' She did not wait for an answer before beginning. 'I race over hill and dale, over sea and over shore, yet I have neither feet nor boat. What am I?'

'Hmmm…' he mused thoughtfully. 'A bird?'

'Good guess, but a bird *does* have feet.'

'By Our Lady, you are a clever thing! Let me see…moves over land and sea with neither feet nor boat…ah!' he cried suddenly, 'I know; it's the wind!'

She applauded quietly. 'Very good! Now it's your turn.'

'Whoa! Slow down there, old friend,' Sir Richard chided Lucifer. Having woken up again now that he realised they were headed in an exciting new direction, the black stallion had started overtaking his master.

With his horse back under control, Sir Richard thought silently for a moment, and then a smile slowly spread over his face. 'What is green, red, pink and brown, can change from overcast skies and rain showers to bright sunshine in a heartbeat, and is wiser in the evening than in the morning?'

She bit her lip thoughtfully. 'Well, *that* is a hard one… Can you give me any more clues?'

He shook his head laughingly, clearly delighted at her struggles.

She suddenly eyed him suspiciously. 'You are not cheating, are you? There really is a proper answer to this riddle?'

'Me cheat? My dear lady, how could you think such a thing!'

She spent several more minutes in deep, brow-furrowing thought while Sir Richard laughed down at her with a smug confidence that displayed little faith in her ability to find the answer.

'I give up, you mean wretch!' she cried at last, sure that he had given her an unsolvable riddle.

He laughed heartily. 'The answer, my love—' he snubbed her nose, 'is you!'

'Me?'

'Yes. Your eyes are green, your hair is red, your lips are pink, your freckles are brown, your mood can change from tears and vexation to sunny smiles in a heartbeat, and you are wiser in the evening than in the morning because you are always going around with your head in a book!'

'How clever of you! I would never have guessed that even if I'd thought on it until Doomsday!'

When they reached the top of the rise that was the site of the small collection of stone buildings that made up the Holy Convent of the Martyrdom of St Agnes, Rowena went up to the door of the little stone church and stopped. 'You might be obliged to have me escorted to and from Eaglestone Castle for my safety, but don't feel obliged to come in if you do not wish to. You can just wait out here. I will not be long.'

He hooked Lucifer's reins over the hitching rail nearby. 'No, I think I'll come in with you.'

All the other well-to-do folk in and around Hartfield, including Sir Richard and the Cunninghams, went to St Luke's Cathedral in the centre of Hartfield. St Luke's was a much larger and grander church, but Rowena always attended mass at the Church of St Agnes. Apart from her and the twenty or so nuns at the convent, the only other people who came to little St Agnes' were the peasants living nearby.

This suited Rowena perfectly. She liked the intimacy of the tiny church, its quiet rural setting, and above all, the simple, pious congregation. No dressing to impress that dashing young man who always sat in row four or parading about showing off the latest addition to the jewellery box here.

Rowena opened the small wooden door and stepped through into the church, leaving it open for Sir Richard to follow.

After a few moments of hesitation, he stepped in after her. He ducked his head from habit, although there was no danger with this doorway; the high, pointed arch provided him with more than enough headroom.

The sight which met him upon entering the church needed only a choir of angels to make it truly heavenly. The low, golden light of the setting sun streaming in through the coloured glass windows flooded the whitewashed interior of the church in radiant, jewel-like hues of purple, cobalt blue, yellow, green and red. A light haze of incense smoke caught the sunbeams and wafted them into nebulous, swirling patterns that shimmered in the air, and Rowena was kneeling at the front of the church before the altar, her mass of red-brown curls, backlit by the sun, creating a glowing golden halo around her head.

Not wishing to disturb the holy peace that seemed to pervade the place, he slipped into a pew as silently as he could. He then leaned back and breathed deeply of the air, which was thick with the heavy, spicy aroma of incense and the warm, honeyed sweetness of burning beeswax candles.

Rowena crossed herself and rose to her feet, then went over to the small table near the altar, where she took one of the little candles heaped on it. She lit it in the flame of the large candle burning on the altar, and put it with the small group of other burning candles placed at the feet of a statue of the Virgin Mary gracing one front corner of the church.

Sinking to her knees before it, she intently watched the red-gold flame, which at first danced wildly in the air created by her movements, then burned straight and still when the turbulence ceased.

Lighting a candle in memory of her mother always filled Rowena with a peaceful, comforting warmth. The way the flame's light shone into the darkness reminded her of her mother's love, how it had always radiated from her heart, casting its warmth on everyone around her. And it brought to mind the way in which, deep in her own heart, the flame of her love for her mother always burned brightly, truly and unceasingly. Even though she was not with her in body, Rowena always felt her mother to be with her in spirit, watching over her, guiding her and loving her.

She gazed up at the Madonna's serene, wisdom-filled countenance, clasped her hands together and whispered:

In God's power, through Christ's light,
With the grace of the Holy Spirit;
I send you my love, I send you my thoughts.
You watch over me always—my love streams to you in spirit realms.

Rowena then arose, stepped back and slipped into a pew, where she sat in silent contemplation.

But after only a few moments, her peace was interrupted by a choking sob coming from behind. She quickly turned and looked.

Seated a few rows back from her, Sir Richard was bowed over, his pale hands clutching the back of the pew in front of him with white-knuckled intensity, shaking as violent sobs racked through him.

She leapt up instantly. 'Sir Richard, what's wrong?'

'Oh God!'

The agony in his voice went through her heart like a steel blade. 'Are you hurt?' What's the matter? she demanded with raising panic, running to his side.

He did not lift him head from where it was buried in his arms, and sobs possessed his body.

She sat down beside him and placed her hands on his shoulders. 'Please tell me, Sir Richard.'

'The stain, the stain of sin on my soul!' he choked, clutching his hands together so tightly that the nails dug into his flesh. 'No.' He drew back from her. 'I don't deserve to be in a holy place like this—'

He made as though to get up, but she held onto him. 'Stay, please. This house is open to saint and sinner alike.'

He let her detain him. 'It is my fault that Everild was blinded and maimed; I was with her when it happened. Why, why did I get so impatient and ride ahead of her like that? She was but a little child mounted on a small pony; of course she could not go as fast as I—and—' He paused for a moment, so overcome he could barely speak. 'And if I had stayed with her like I promised to, the outlaws would never have set upon her. I can still hear her screams ringing in my ears!' he cried desperately, covering his face with shaking hands.

Rowena clasped her short arms around the wretched knight's broad shoulders as best she could. 'You were hardly more than a boy! Please, you must forgive yourself.'

He lifted his head and looked bleakly into space. 'And Morgana...' He lifted a hand, as if reaching out to a ghostly apparition. 'I killed her...'

'Killed her?' Rowena kept her hands on his shoulders, but did shrink back a little, unable to disguise her horror.

The gaunt look on his face was unnerving. 'Yes. Soon after I returned from fighting in France I fell in love with a beautiful lady, the only child of the lord whose castle I was a guest in at the time. She was terribly proud and disdainful, believing that no man alive was good enough for her. She saw this as no sin, for she prided herself on her cold-heartedness. She loved nothing more than to have a brave knight grovelling helplessly at her feet. I was enthralled by her from the moment I first set eyes on her, but she would not accept my love. The more deeds of valour and knightly prowess I did in her honour, the more she mocked me. She had many noble knights in her spell. First she would allow one suitor to be at her side and bask in her smiles and kisses, and then she would cast him off like a worn shoe and move onto another, leaving her other would-be lovers filled with agonising jealousy as she indulged her latest favourite.'

Rowena listened with rapt attention, uneasy about where the chilling tale would end.

'It was hell,' he continued grimly. 'But then I found out she was spying for the French. Well—you know what happened. But then…'

'Yes, do carry on,' she prompted breathlessly, gripping the folds of his leather doublet tightly to keep her hands from shaking.

He swallowed hard and looked down at the floor. 'What I did not tell you before is that when she broke her promise to be faithful to me in return, I—' He swallowed hard. 'I told her that if she would not be faithful, I would betray her to the English. She just laughed in my face. I was so *angry*. I just wanted to punish her, make her taste the pain she bestowed so plentifully on me.'

'But you did not actually *kill* this lady yourself?'

He raised his deathly pale face. 'No, I did not wield the executioner's axe with my own hands. But I might as well have done!' His head fell back onto his arms. 'The guilt, it is a filthy stain on my soul which, no matter how hard I try, I can never wash off. It is a devil that gnaws at me relentlessly day and night!'

'Did you know that they would execute her?' she asked cautiously, almost too afraid of what his answer might be.

'Yes—no, I don't know!'

'Surely you only meant to teach her not to toy with you?'

With a quivering hand, Sir Richard pushed back the curtain of black hair which had fallen over his face. 'I was so hurt and angry…I really don't know what I was thinking. But you are right; I did not wish to have her killed, just punished. How foolish to think that they would not kill her because she was from a noble family!'

He turned to her with a wild desperation she had never seen in his eyes before. 'I am the one who caused her death. She haunts me!' Fingernails dug into fleshy palm with a violence that threatened to draw blood. 'At night when I lie there in the dark silence, sleep does not come. Instead I am visited nightly by visions of her that arise torturously before my guilty soul. Visions of her in her muddied white shift, almost mad with fear at the fate she awaited in her prison cell that chill, grey dawn. Oh she was not proud, disdainful Lady Morgana anymore.'

His trembling lips thinned to a hard, bitter line of pain. 'She begged me, *begged me*, to find a way of saving her. She grovelled and pleaded and cried on her knees before me. I told her captors I had been wrong, that she was not a spy; but it was useless. They had searched her rooms and found incriminating letters. She would not listen when I told her that there was nothing I could do to save her now. Still she begged to live…' Staring into space with hollow eyes, he rubbed his forehead with a shaking hand, if trying to erase the memory from his mind. 'I meant to punish her, but the pathetic shadow I succeeded in reducing her to gave me no pleasure! If I had not seen her with my own eyes, I would not have believed it to be possible. There was not one shred of human dignity left in her. Even her stony-eyed jailer was embarrassed to look upon her. If ever someone faced death with fear, it was her…'

'What you did was terrible, but you acted in the heat of the moment,' Rowena tried to comfort him. 'You did not mean to cause her death—'

'I desecrate a place like this by daring to enter with my polluted soul!' he suddenly cried. 'My heart is black with evil. I am not worthy; I must leave here—'

He made to rise again, but she clung to him. 'The good shepherd rejoices more when the one lost sheep returns to the fold than at all the other sheep. I pray you; do not lose faith in the mercy of God.'

He suddenly went very still. 'This darkness—I wish I could cut it from me…'

The glint of steel in his hand caught her eye. 'No, Sir Richard, put the dagger away!'

He clutched the naked blade between his trembling hands. 'Cut it from me…' His low, harsh whisper was barely audible as a trickle of blood ran out from between his hands and dripped onto the white skirt of Rowena's gown.

With detached interest he watched the bright red stain spread as it soaked into the fabric.

She clasped his hands between her own. 'Please stop.' Tears stung her eyes as she felt his warm blood seeping between her fingers. 'You must forgive yourself. Please, I'm begging you, let the blade go!'

After an excruciating few moments, he loosened his grip and let the blade fall onto the flagstones below with a clatter. His dark eyes, full of grief and longing, met hers. 'How can I cut my heart of darkness from me?'

She quickly took out her handkerchief and bound it around his bleeding palm. 'If the budding stem scorns the light and reaches instead for dank, mouldy places, it pales, withers, and is eaten up by foul canker and worm. You cannot cut your evils and failings from you, but you can transform them into something beautiful and good if you will but reach for the light.'

He nodded thoughtfully. 'Is there anything you do not have a ready answer for?'

She smiled. 'No. I'm like the legendary Sybil at the oracle in ancient Delphi, and if any wise words I tell turn out not to be true, it is because you interpreted it all wrong.'

He weakly returned her smile. 'And you certainly never run out of witticisms.' He bent down, picked his dagger off the floor and put it back in its scabbard. 'I'm sorry for frightening you like that. I don't know what came over me—oh no, your gown!' He suddenly seemed to notice what had happened. 'I've bled all over you. Hell, I'm sorry.'

She waved his concern aside, too relieved he had decided not hurt himself further to care. 'It's no matter. This gown has seen better days. One more stain is going to make little difference.'

He passed her his handkerchief. 'Here, as you have given me yours, you can use mine to mop up the worst of the blood.'

'Thank you.' She took it and dabbed half-heartedly at the bright red stain, which had now spread to the size of her hand.

This job was taking a heavy toll on her wardrobe. If her aunt thought she looked like a wild gypsy maid before, now that her niece was the sheriff's clerk, she thought she looked like a beggar-child. Rowena sighed. Never mind…

Already looking surprisingly calm, Sir Richard got to his feet. 'I have detained you here long enough. Shall we go?'

She passed him back his handkerchief and nodded. 'You don't have to escort me to and from the castle yourself all the time, you know. I know how busy you are; I'm sure one of your soldiers could do it sometimes. And furthermore, I have no intention of having any more nocturnal adventures in the forest.'

He offered her his arm. 'No, it's fine. I like escorting you home.'

She tucked her hand underneath the offered arm and leaned into Sir Richard as they walked down the aisle towards the door. The silence between sheriff and clerk was as golden as the just-emerged sun after a tempest's passing.

But the peace did not last long. A few minutes later, the sheriff was to be found facing a new problem.

'What are you going to do about it, young man? I demand an answer!' shouted the new problem.

Sir Richard retreated back a step, but Abbess Hawisa kept pace with him, her large finger, strong and stout as the rest of her, still jabbing at his chest, glowering face still thrust in his.

'Well, I—'

'Come on young man, spit it out!' the abbess of the Holy Convent of the Martyrdom of St Agnes commanded him.

He stood his ground this time. Although Abbess Hawisa was a tall woman, her height did not match the towering knight's, and he took full advantage of it to glare grimly down at her. 'If I may, I would like to speak to the nun who reported these lurking men watching her,' he replied, much more firmly this time in order to subdue the abbess, who was ready to go in for the kill the moment she caught a whiff of weakness.

She put her hands on her broad hips and looked him up and down disapprovingly. 'This is a closed order. The sisters here do not have any contact with the outside world. Especially not with men,' she added with a distasteful sniff. 'But as it is of such grave importance, I will allow you to speak with Sister Alice briefly, in my presence.'

'Thank you, abbess. And do you know how long ago it was

that Sister Alice saw these men?' he asked, in the most tactful and professional manner he could muster.

'Sister Alice usually goes down to the spring to draw up water at half-seven in the evening, to clean the dairy when she has finished the milking. It must have been around then.' Abbess Hawisa moved off the front step of the church, where she had accosted the sheriff as he and Rowena were exiting. 'Come!' she barked, leading the way towards the convent's main building.

The sheriff moved off with her, closely followed by Rowena.

The abbess entered the door leading into the cloister. 'We at St Agnes's have of course heard the dreadful tales of young girls being carried off never to be seen again. Sister Alice's nerves have always been weak, and the tales played on her mind terribly. I must warn you that the poor child is still in a dreadful state of shock.'

The sheriff and his young clerk were led along a cool, echoing cloister which faced onto a courtyard garden.

Abbess Hawisa stopped in front of the closed door right at the far end. 'If you would kindly wait outside, child,' she ordered Rowena, but then suddenly her eyes narrowed. 'What is that all over your dress?'

Rowena cringed under the abbess's fierce, disapproving look. 'It's—it's, ahem, blood.'

'And what is it doing smeared all down your front? Did you murder someone on your way here?'

The interrogative and bitingly sarcastic older woman made Rowena feel like a bad child who had just done something unspeakable. For once she wished she was even smaller, so small that she could crawl under a stone and hide. She swallowed hard 'It's n-not mine. Sir Richard cut himself and some of the blood spilt onto me.'

Abbess Hawisa, who already stood uncomfortably close to Rowena, moved even closer. 'And what were you doing standing so close to him?'

'I—I—' squirmed Rowena, as she tried unsuccessfully to come up with something more suitable than 'the sheriff of Chaucy bled all over me while I was trying to talk him out of cutting himself in your church'.

Much to her relief, Sir Richard decided to come to her aid. 'I'm afraid it was my fault.' He produced the wounded hand. 'She was binding her handkerchief around the wound on my hand, and we did not realise I was bleeding so much.'

'Hmmm.' The Abbess gave another one of her disapproving sniffs, but it seemed she could find no further impropriety to pick on.

Sir Richard paused before the cell door the Abbess held open for him. 'I wish Rowena to be present when I'm speaking with this nun.'

Abbess Hawisa did not look pleased by the request, but gave a reluctant grunt of assent anyway.

Once the abbess and Sir Richard had passed into the cell, Rowena followed. Seated on the tiny cell's equally tiny bed was a hysterical nun who looked about twenty, and offering words of comfort and a shoulder to cry on was another nun, this one of about twice her years.

The abbess motioned at the frail, pale-faced younger woman. 'This is Sister Alice, who saw the lurking villains.' Then she indicated the other nun. 'And this is Sister Elfreda, who did not see the lurking villains.'

Sister Alice lifted her head from Sister Elfreda's shoulder, looked at her visitors and let out a little scream. 'No, no I can't—make them go away, Sister Elfreda!'

'Don't be afraid, sister,' said Sir Richard. 'I only want a little information.'

But Sister Alice only clung more tightly to her companion. 'Make them go away, I beg you!'

Feeling that the tiny cell was overcrowded enough without her adding to the problem, Rowena stayed back and observed from the doorway.

Sir Richard carefully seated himself next to the terrified young nun and gave her his most reassuring smile. 'Calm yourself, madam. I'm not going to hurt you. I merely wish to hear your story.'

This seemed to have the desired effect. Sister Alice went quiet and studied the intimidating intruder shyly, before seeming to decide he did not sound as frightening as he looked. She nodded timidly.

'So tell me, what happened?'

She took a moment to pluck up the courage to speak, but after an encouraging nod from Sister Elfreda, she began. 'I was going down to the spring to fetch water at about half past seven, when I caught a glimpse of something moving in the trees near the path.' Her soft, girlish voice was almost a whisper. 'I thought it was a deer, so carried on to the spring and filled my pail. But when I was coming back…'

'You are doing very well, sister. Please continue.'

Sister Alice wiped her tearful eyes with the corner of her veil. 'When I passed that place, I saw it again. I looked more carefully this time and…I thought I could make out a cloaked figure with a cloth tied around his face—and I was so afraid!' The tears started to flow again. 'But don't they always say not to panic and run if you think a dog is about to attack? So I just kept walking!' Her words ended abruptly as she started sobbing hysterically.

Sir Richard cleared his throat uncomfortably and shoved back his hair. Hysterical nuns were clearly one area where he felt out of his depth. He looked helplessly at Rowena, but she had nothing to offer besides a sympathetic shrug.

'Sister, there's no need to be afraid. You are safe now,' he said rather awkwardly, and placed a comforting hand on her arm.

Sister Alice shrieked in fright and shrunk away from him the instant he touched her.

He snatched back the hand like he had burnt it.

'Do not touch!' the abbess bellowed at the sheriff, advancing on him.

For a moment, Rowena thought Abbess Hawisa was going to slap Sir Richard, but instead she stopped less than a half-foot from him, and wagged her finger violently in his face. 'Kindly keep your hands to yourself, young man!'

Meeting Abbess Hawisa's furious look with a stony, thin-lipped scowl of his own, Sir Richard slowly rose up to his full height and, without removing his unblinking glare from her eyes for a moment, he closed his hand around the offending finger. 'And *I* would appreciate it, madam, if you would keep *your* hands to yourself.'

Rowena thought she heard a titter from Sister Elfreda, but it quickly turned into a cough.

The abbess blinked up at the towering, darkly menacing knight in astonishment. Her lips moved, but no words came out. After a few moments, she gave up and stared at him in silence.

Sir Richard moved the abbess's finger down to her side and released it. 'Very good.' He gave her a frosty smile. 'I think we will get on much better now that that little misunderstanding has been resolved. So,' he addressed everyone in the cell this time, 'who would be so kind as to show Rowena and I where this suspicious figure lurked?'

'I am happy to lead you there,' said Sister Elfreda.

He gave a gracious nod and gestured towards the door. 'Excellent. Please lead the way, sister.'

.13.

Sir Richard has a Brush with Vice, Virtue and a Cooking Pot

ONCE outside, Sister Elfreda led the two visitors along a gravel path that snaked towards the vegetable plot, then skirted around it before ending at the door of a lean-to at the cloister's back wall. The path was bordered on both sides by a neatly clipped lavender hedge that released wafts of warm, soporific fragrance as the women's skirts brushed past it.

Upon reaching the end of the gravel path, Sister Elfreda stopped. 'Here is the dairy. The spring is down the path at the bottom of this meadow.'

The tall nun then moved off along a faint path leading through the tall meadow grasses. Dotted everywhere were bright yellow buttercups, golden dandelions and red, silky-petalled field poppies that hovered like butterflies above the thick summer pasture. Once she had put some distance between herself and the cloister, Sister Elfreda slowed a little to allow Sir Richard and Rowena to come alongside her.

Rowena was now able to study their guide's face properly for the first time. The nun had a refined, even-featured face with a thin, straight nose and a noble forehead. Her expression bore the serenity of the moon in the midnight sky and her dove-grey eyes shone with the mysterious, faraway light of the morning star.

The observer's verdict was most favourable. Sister Elfreda

made a truly admirable nun, being a lady who looked as though her mind was in heaven even while her body dwelt on earth.

'I am sorry about Abbess Hawisa's behaviour towards you both earlier,' said Sister Elfreda, frowning slightly. 'Unfortunately she tends to be a little territorial and controlling. I do hope you were not too offended.'

'You get use to dealing with difficult characters in my line of work,' Sir Richard replied brusquely.

The nun put a friendly hand on Rowena's arm. 'I am especially sorry to you, madam. I know how uncomfortable our abbess made you.'

Rowena tried to look as unconcerned as possible, not wishing to hurt Sister Elfreda's feelings as she was being so kind and helpful. 'It's alright, I really didn't mind,' she lied.

'And as soon as she gets home she is going to make a straw effigy of the abbess and stick pins in it...' Sir Richard added smoothly.

His horrified clerk breathed in sharply. Normally she would have given him a dig in the ribs or kick in the shin for taking such a liberty, but Sister Elfreda walked between them. 'I would—would never do such a thing!' she stammered desperately.

She was surprised by an easy laugh from their guide. 'I'm ashamed to admit I feel like doing that too sometimes,' said Sister Elfreda. 'Abbess Hawisa has little faith in the human soul's ability to resist the sins of the flesh, particularly where the young are concerned, and,' she looked sympathetically at Sir Richard, 'is very sure in her view that all men have only one thing on their minds.'

'I do indeed have only one thing on my mind these days: finding the felons who've been carrying off these maidens in Chaucy,' the knight muttered sourly.

Sister Elfreda's serenity appeared unruffled. Still smiling her wide, all-knowing smile, she touched Sir Richard lightly on the arm. 'Yes, I am sure you have, darling. I for one do not share her views on such matters.'

Silence reigned for a good few moments before Sir Richard turned to the serene sister thoughtfully. 'If you don't mind me saying so, Sister Alice seems a rather over-excitable young woman. Do you think that what she reported was really there, or might it merely be the offspring of a fearful imagination?'

'I wondered myself at first,' said Sister Elfreda. 'But her tale seems consistent enough.'

Having reached the far side of the meadow, the nun mounted a stile that spanned the fence dividing it from a grassy lane beyond. She had to hitch the skirt of her habit up to her knees so it did not hinder her while she stepped over the top bar, but she did not seem overly concerned about revealing so much naked leg in front of her male companion.

Rowena waited until Sir Richard had negotiated the stile, and then mounted it herself. From this vantage point, she could see that the wide laneway led down into a wooded valley, from whence the trickling of running water sounded.

'It must be a hard task for a girl as small and frail as Sister Alice to carry water all the way from down there and over this stile,' said Sir Richard, giving Rowena a gallant but unnecessary hand as she jumped nimbly down.

'Indeed it is,' replied Sister Elfreda. 'But the abbess insists that all the sisters here work hard, regardless of their stature or talents.'

'I wager it's not a common sight to see *her* lugging water up here.'

Sister Elfreda smiled dryly. 'I am afraid our blessed mother superior gave up such menial tasks long ago.' She pointed to a small gap in the dense foliage crowding both sides of the path, about halfway down to the spring at the bottom of the valley. 'Here is the place.'

Upon reaching the spot Sister Elfreda had pointed out, Sir Richard parted the saplings and pushed through, carefully holding them so they did not whip back in the face of the closely-following Rowena.

About fifty feet back from the path, the saplings and brambles gave way to clear, leaf-strewn forest floor as the towering woodland giants cast their heavy shade. Only the odd beam of dappled light from the setting sun penetrated the thick greenwood.

There was an abundance of evidence to suggest someone had been there recently. The brown, red and gold September leaves littering the forest floor were scuffed and scattered, and the damp black soil liberally dotted with horse hoof prints.

Sir Richard knelt beside the disturbed ground. 'Yes, definitely two horses, I would say.'

'How can you tell that?' asked his assistant.

'Because there are two different sets of hoof prints, silly!'

'Yes, but how can you tell that they do not belong to the *same* horse?'

'Because horses have different sized feet, just like us. One of these sets of hoof prints is larger than the other.'

'I see—' She suddenly paused to sniff the air, then frowned worriedly. 'Can you smell that? I'm sure I can smell dead meat…'

He tested the air too. 'You're right. It does smell of rotting meat.'

Rowena crossed her arms and turned up her nose. 'This time you can look, because I certainly am *not*. Being a wild, free-spirited country maid is all well and good, but sometimes you just want a man for the task.'

The knight got to his feet. 'Fine. You just stand there and be a weak female while I go look.'

Sir Richard started a quick search of the undergrowth. 'Here, come and see what I've found!' he called a few moments later, from near a thicket of briar roses.

She held the end of her sleeve firmly over her nose. 'No, I don't want to.'

He looked over his shoulder at her and laughed at her distastefully wrinkled face. 'It's safe, honestly.'

I suppose he does look genuine enough, she thought reluctantly, before taking a deep breath and holding it while she cautiously sidled over to the spot.

'A dead rabbit. Why didn't you just tell me it was a dead rabbit?'

He smirked darkly down on his irritated young clerk and crossed his arms. 'Because it is so much more amusing to tease you, my sweet cinnamon…'

* * * *

'I'm sure it must have been the felons,' said Rowena. 'The description fitted them perfectly, and the lone girl passing along a thickly wooded, remote path is obviously their favourite prey.'

Sir Richard sidestepped to avoid colliding with a woman carrying a towering load of fire-kindling through the bustling market. 'I agree, Rowena. It most definitely sounded like them.'

'Do you think they'll try to carry off one of the nuns again, or might they have been scared off?' Rowena almost had to shout to be heard above the cries of the hawkers and stallholders touting their wares, and the squawking, clucking chickens in wicker baskets awaiting sale.

'Please sir, spare a penny for a stavin' orphan!' came a little voice from behind them.

'What?' Sir Richard looked about for the speaker, and then

turned around in response to a tug at his doublet.

Staring fearfully but hopefully up at the knight and his companion was a raggedly-dressed, barefooted boy of about seven. His white teeth stood out sharply against his dirt-smeared little face, and he looked up at them from beneath a tatty but jauntily-angled cap.

'Please my lord,' he said, holding out an empty bowl.

Sir Richard reached into the purse tied to his belt, took out a generous handful of coins and deposited them in the bowl. 'Here you go, son.'

The thin, dirty little face lit up with delight. 'Aw, thank ye sir!' The grubby little hand hopefully clutching its begging bowl then moved in front of Rowena. 'Please mistress, spare a penny for a stavin' orphan!'

'I'm afraid I don't have a lot...' she muttered, fingering the few coins in her purse reluctantly.

The poor maid had been saving up her meagre allowance for weeks, and today was the day she was taking it into Hartfield to buy cloth for two new dresses to replace her torn, stained and faded old ones.

The urchin rattled his begging bowl and looked up at her with sad, soulful eyes. 'Please mistress, spare a penny!'

She sighed. What the heck. Her clothes might be a bit tatty, but they still had a long way to go before they rivalled this poor child's.

She took her purse out of her pocket and tipped its entire contents into his bowl. 'Take these.'

The little beggar looked at his haul in disbelief, his eyes shining with joy. 'God bless ye, God bless ye! Me twin sister'll be beside herself!' he cried, flashing his benefactors an ear-to-ear grin before running off excitedly.

Rowena smiled. 'Aw, bless him.'

Even Sir Richard allowed himself an indulgent smile before

turning back to his clerk. ‘Now, what was it you were asking me? Ah yes! Will they try again at the convent…I’m surprised they did not carry it through, as Sister Alice did not show them that she’d noticed they were there. Perhaps they were just scouting in preparation for setting an ambush.’

‘Yes, I think it’s likely they were. And that means it is an opportunity to catch them we cannot afford to miss.’

‘But how? If the felons get the slightest inkling that we are waiting to seize them, they’ll disappear back into the forest without a trace like they always do.’

‘You are quite right, and that’s where my cunning plan comes in.’

He lifted his black velvet cap off and ran his fingers through his hair. ‘Oh no, you’ve got that look on your face again! I wager it’s going to be a dangerous plan…’

She gave a miffed toss of the head. ‘It is better to have a dangerous plan than no plan at all!’

He groaned. ‘Alright, let’s hear your ridiculously dangerous, hare-brained plan.’

‘Well, I was thinking—’

‘Always a dangerous thing…’ he muttered beneath his breath.

She jabbed an elbow in his ribs. ‘Shut up. What I was thinking is this: if I disguise myself in a nun’s habit and pretend to be Sister Alice going down to the spring to get water, the villains might try to carry me off.’

‘So your plan is to get kidnapped in place of Sister Alice? How is losing another clerk going to help me get any closer to arresting these felonious bastards?’

‘Because, goose-head, you and your men will be lying in ambush, ready to fall on the felons when they try to carry me off.’

He shook his head firmly. ‘No, it’s far too dangerous. And anyway, who knows when they are planning to strike? We might be waiting for eons.'

'I agree that it could be risky, but if the ambush has been set up properly, and you and your men are the skilled soldiers you claim to be, then I believe it's worth it. Only think; you might finally catch the villains—'

'Good God!' Pulling Rowena after him, Sir Richard suddenly dived into a narrow, filthy alley and flattened himself against the side wall of the alehouse it ran between. 'By Jove's codlings, that was a close thing!' he gasped, looking furtively back out into the marketplace.

She looked around at her unexpected new surroundings with confusion. 'W-what?'

'I damn near run into that—no, don't look, he might see you!' He pushed her back against the wall. 'It's that rogue, Gray.'

'Walter Gray, the father of the—'

'Oi, what ya think ya doin' on my patch, ya brazen cow!' a female voice suddenly screeched.

And before Rowena could make out what was happening, a young woman dressed only in a flimsy red slip had seized her by the hair and started trying to pull her out of the alley, all the while screaming threats and abuse.

'Lay off, would you!' Sir Richard shouted, seizing Rowena's attacker from behind and pulling her off. 'This lady here is a virtuous woman!'

The garishly made-up woman was so intent on her frantic attack that the sheriff had to lift her up until her feet barely touched the ground in order to restrain her. 'God in high heaven, listen to me, would you! She's not a harlot!'

The knight's words finally seemed to sink in. The young woman stopped her violent kicking and screaming. 'She ain't?'

'No, I certainly am not!' Rowena replied, indignantly dusting herself down and smoothing her hair back into place.

The sharp-faced woman grinned guiltily. 'Aw, beg pardon, lady. Didn't realise.'

Rowena eyed her crossly, keeping well back. 'You could have asked *before* trying to kill me.'

But the dishevelled woman's attention had already moved onto a more interesting place.

She lifted the hem of her dress until her leg was bared to mid-thigh, gave her greasy blonde hair a saucy toss and looked flirtatiously up at Sir Richard. 'Ya might 'ave read her wrong, but luckily for you, sir, relief ain't far away. Two shillings, round the back o' the Cockerel and Cow?' She ran her tongue suggestively around her lips. 'Come on, ya know ya want to…'

He glared down at her stonily. 'Do you know who I am, madam?'

She flicked a dismissive hand. 'Aw, don't worry, ya can count on me ta be real discreet. We never tell anyone if we do it with dignitaries. In fact, many of me best customers are quite,' she winked, 'well known…'

'I think you might just have succeeded in persuading me,' said the sheriff.

'Come and let me show ya a good time then…' she purred, taking him by the hand.

'No,' he replied calmly. 'What you succeeded in persuading me of was that it might be a good idea to arrest you.'

'Ya what?' she gaped.

'Yes.' His hand suddenly tightened around her wrist. 'Allow me to introduce myself. I am Sir Richard Hastings, sheriff of Chaucy. And you, madam, are breaking the law.'

She would have looked less horrified if he had turned out to be the Devil himself. 'The sheriff!' she screeched, franticly trying to free herself from his vice-like grip.

He let her jerk helplessly on the end of his arm for a good while before finally releasing her.

She instantly bolted up the alley shouting, 'Girls, girls, the law is 'ere!'

But Sir Richard did not follow her. Instead, he just stood there leaning casually against the alehouse with a dark smirk on his face.

'So that's what you do for a little light relief, is it?' said Rowena.

'No, I've given up arresting them. We use to haul them in for breaking the peace, public drunkenness and lewdness, and throw them in the dungeons until the next court-day. They'd usually be convicted, fined and released. But the very next day they'd be out working twice as hard so they could still afford their pimp's extortions and their drink habit. The cells get filled to overflowing in no time if you go and arrest every bit of riff-raff about. These women are not going to stop selling their bodies unless men stop wanting to buy them. And I'd swear some of those tarts were making more money in jail than they were out...'

Rowena nodded grimly. 'Yes. Last week, because of an error with their taxes, I had to enter that revolting cesspit of vice otherwise known as the Boar and Ring alehouse. There was no shortage of flabby, watery-eyed, lecherous fools wanting to go up for a toss in the hay with the pox-ridden whores filling the place. It was revolting. Honestly, the age of some of them! Once a man gets to a certain age, he really ought to give up leering and lusting over the pert flesh of women young enough to be his own granddaughters, and start thinking about preventing his vice-ridden soul from burning in hell.'

She shuddered in revulsion, still feeling tainted by all the leering looks of the dirty old and not-so-old men that had followed her every move from the moment she entered the place. 'Argh! I'm telling you, next time I have to go into that vile joint to sort out their dodgy taxes I'm taking you with me, so you can slam the head of anyone who looks at me funny against a hard surface. You are good at that. And on the subject of vile filth: can we get out of this seedy alley, or have you not finished cowering yet?'

'Let me have a look…' He inched along the alehouse wall until he was right near the corner, and then stuck his head out furtively, carefully scanning left and right. 'Looks like it's clear now.'

While she queued impatiently behind, he ventured out slowly, searching the crowded marketplace with the alertness of a hawk. But no sooner was Sir Richard out of the alley, when there was a loud commotion and a massive runaway hog swept him off his feet as it tried to charge between his legs. The sheriff disappeared from view as he reached for an overhead beam laden with the wares of a stall selling pots. Rowena then heard a loud, tinny dong followed by string of expletives from Sir Richard.

She crept out of the alley, looking rather furtive herself now.

'Damn, cursed beast!' she heard him swearing furiously from behind the hanging wares of the cooking-pot stall.

She cautiously made her way over. When things were not going well for him it was generally wise to keep clear.

She found Sir Richard rubbing the top of his head crossly and cursing under his breath. 'Sometimes I'd swear God was playing a practical joke on me!' he muttered savagely. 'I mean, who the hell expects a damn hog to come at them like that, and for these bloody things to be in the way too!' He gave the large cauldron hanging level with his head an angry shove that set it clanging loudly against its neighbours.

This proved to be the last straw for the already upset young stallholder, a pretty girl of about fifteen with wheaten hair tied back in a red handkerchief. The suntanned face puckered up, and tears overflowed the forget-me-not blue eyes and rolled down the freckled cheeks.

'Now look what you've done!' Rowena hissed at the hapless

perpetrator.

But before he could respond, Sir Richard was forced to hurriedly flatten himself against the pot stall and wait while the hog's owners rushed past in hot pursuit.

The three stocky, red-faced farmers puffing after it were swearing even more lustily than Sir Richard had been. Rowena had heard plenty of bad language from the men at Eaglestone Castle, but the obscenities coming out of the mouths of the pursuing farmers made even her wince. After dodging around the basket of apples spilled by the fleeing hog, narrowly avoiding tripping over a stray mutt, and pushing a frail, haunch-backed old woman into a stack of wicker chicken coups, the foul-mouthed farmers were gone.

After shouting a few good wishes such as, 'May you rot in hell, you loathsome oafs!' and 'I hope you get the black plague ten times over, dung-face!' after the farmers, Sir Richard looked first at his unimpressed clerk, then at the weeping young stallholder.

He shrugged helplessly at Rowena. 'What am I supposed to do? Women are better with crying; why don't you do something?'

He received a withering look in reply.

A rather shame-faced sheriff turned back to the sobbing girl. 'Forgive me, I didn't mean to upset you,' he offered uncomfortably.

But this only seemed to make the wheaten-haired girl cry more. 'N-nothing I ever do is right,' she wailed. 'I try so h-hard to do things right, but I just g-get scolded!'

'Don't cry,' the sheriff pleaded rather desperately. 'It was not your fault I hit my head, it's mine for being so tall.'

'It's always Lylie do this and Lylie do that, and Lylie why are ya such a lazy, stupid slut! I'm just useless and everybody h-hates me!' sobbed the stallholder.

'I told you I was no good at this!' the sheriff hissed at Rowena, by now looking rather panicked at the river of tears he had unwittingly started.

She glared back at him unsympathetically. 'Try harder.'

'Alright, alright.' He moved around to the girl's side of the stall. 'I was cursing my bad luck, not you!'

'I bring b-bad luck with me everywhere; nothing never g-goes right where I am!'

After casting a final look on his clerk that condemned her for putting him through this, Sir Richard drew the still-sobbing pot seller behind the back of the stall, out of sight of the gawking eyes that were beginning to be cast on the drama. There he sat her on a wooden crate and sank down beside her.

Rowena was then surprised to see the stallholder fling her arms around Sir Richard, bury her face against his chest and sob as if her heart was about to break.

After scanning to see that no one but Rowena was watching, he let the girl cry on his shoulder. The look on his face made it clear that she was tolerated rather than welcomed.

Rowena shot him a meaningful glare.

What? he mouthed silently back.

She rolled her eyes.

Once he had sent a peeved look Rowena's way, he put his arms around the girl, rather awkwardly, as someone might a fragile thing liable to crumple at the slightest pressure. 'Hush now…'

This earned him a nod of approval from his clerk. At least he was trying.

When her rivers dried up at last, the stallholder lifted her head from her sheriff's now tear-soaked doublet. 'I didn't mean to be so trying,' she whispered, suddenly overcome with shyness.

'Don't worry,' he replied, 'I'm used to it. I'm always making women cry. The mere sight of me does the trick in many cases.'

She smiled a watery smile. 'If I told my stepmother I'd been crying on the shoulder of the Black Sheriff she would slap me for being a liar.'

'Well, the post has demanded that I turn my hand to a far greater number of things than I ever dreamed it would. So—Lylie, isn't it?'

She nodded.

'Will I ever shake off that title?'

'Even if you changed the black horse, the black clothes and the black scowl so familiar to the folk of Hartfield, they're so used to calling you the Black Sheriff that I doubt they'd ever stop.'

'Do you come to the market every week to sell your wares?'

She nodded miserably. 'Me stepmother comes too, but she always leaves me to it while she goes and drinks in the alehouse. When she returns at the end of the day, she always scolds and slaps me for not making enough money. But what am I supposed to do if thieves steal things while I'm busy trying to fend off dirty old men? Or know when folks give me the wrong money and I'm not learned enough to tell? I've tried to find a job as a live-in servant so I can escape, but the only place who offered to take me on was the Boar and Ring. Even a simple country lass like me knows 'tis more than likely they had jobs beyond sweeping and cleaning in mind for me.'

Rowena stepped a little closer. 'Sir Richard, wasn't I telling you only the other day that we could do with a cleaner at the castle?'

'Yes, I do recall that. Can we afford it?'

'I would not have suggested it if we couldn't.'

He turned back to the young stallholder. 'Would you like a job at Eaglestone Castle? The rats are large and the pay is small, but you will not be ill-used.'

Lylie nodded eagerly, her eyes now shining with joy instead of tears. 'When can I start?'

* * * *

Sir Richard held a bundle of clothes out to Rowena. 'I am still not entirely convinced that this isn't a hare-brained idea, you know.'

'That is well and good,' she replied, taking the clothes, 'but do you have any better ideas?'

He pushed his hair back with nervous fingers and sighed. 'No…no, I don't. Sergeant Gallagher and about half a dozen men-at-arms are set up in ambush. I intend to wait here until you are ready to set out on the woodland path, then I shall join my men.'

Rowena pulled the black nun's habit over her head and struggled for a moment to find the sleeves and head-opening amid all the voluminous cloth.

'Yes, just pull it down,' he said, giving the garment a helping tug.

As she finally emerged from the heavy woollen folds, a knock sounded on the door.

Sister Elfreda's celestial countenance glided into view around the door of the cell where Rowena was changing into her disguise. 'It is still a little early for Sister Alice's normal trip down to the spring; you are welcome to wait here until it is time.'

After thanking the nun, who had shown her and the sheriff every kindness and given all possible assistance, Rowena returned to frowning at the white wimple she was holding.

Sister Elfreda hurried to her aid with a cheerful smile. 'I can put that on for you.'

'You are too kind, sister.'

The nun quickly set about putting it on Rowena. 'It is a brave thing you are doing. All of us here at St Agnes's are very grateful that you are willing to do this.' Sister Elfreda smiled her heavenly smile at the seated sheriff. 'And I must say, Sir Richard, we were pleasantly surprised that you were prepared to go to so much effort over this. Although it was taken with a grain of salt (admittedly some took a larger grain than others) we have heard a lot of talk among the local people about how you are not going to any trouble to look into the kidnappings and the murder of your clerk, Thomas.'

He grimaced sourly. 'There are a few people who seem to think that if they put pressure on me by spreading false rumours about how I'm corrupt and never bother investigating any crimes, preferring to arrest the first suspect I come across and nail it on them, it'll help the felons get caught.'

With nimble fingers, the serene nun tucked the last bit of the wimple into place. 'From what I have heard, our sheriff being corrupt was *not* mere malicious rumour.'

'It is now.'

The graceful Sister Elfreda turned to Sir Richard and smiled warmly. 'Well done. The humble folk of this shire must be very relieved. Now, is there anything else I can do for either of you?'

Rowena tugged at the unfamiliar and rather awkward-feeling new headdress. 'No, thank you kindly.'

Sister Elfreda clasped her hands together in front of her. 'I will pray for your safety and success. May Our Lady and the holy Saint Agnes bless and protect you.' And with that she was gone, leaving the scent of lavender and rose oil hanging in the warm air.

After the nun's departure, silence reigned for several minutes. Rowena paced back and forth in the tiny cell while Sir Richard lounged in the room's only seat.

'I like your new costume,' he broke the tense silence at last. 'It makes you look terribly saintly.'

She stopped in front of him. 'Oh, that's good. If I'm killed protecting nuns from evil villains perhaps they'll confer sainthood on me and say hundreds of masses for my soul.'

'Why are you talking like that? You seemed so confident about this before.'

'It's this wretched waiting, I can't bear it!' she cried suddenly, clutching her clammy hands together and continuing her nervous pacing. 'And how come you are occupying the only chair in this spartan place? she added. 'It's not very gentlemanly!'

'You are welcome to sit.'

'How can I?' she snapped crossly. 'You are sitting on the only chair.'

He smiled and held out his hand to her. 'Come here; I want to ask you something.'

She came up to him. 'Oh Lord! It might only be half an hour we need to wait, but it seems more like half a day,' she moaned, feeling more frazzled by the moment.

He took her hand and patted his knee. 'Here, you can sit on my lap.'

She raised her eyebrows. 'I'm sure I can.'

He smiled up at her, entreating her to comply.

'Oh alright, I'll humour you just this once…' Now with a hand in each of his, she let him draw her towards him and hopped onto his knees so she faced him.

'There is something I have wanted to ask you for some time,' he began earnestly. 'What you are about to do could be dangerous, so I don't wish to delay any longer even though I still don't know how to say this.'

She held her breath in anticipation. He was not much given to emotional speeches. This was most unusual…

He glanced down at her hands, clasped in his. 'As I said, my crude skills are inadequate for this, but—' his dark, intense eyes met hers, 'I will do my best, poor as that is sure to be.

Rowena—'

'Yes?'

'I love you. Marry me, Rowena! Let me taste that undeserved happiness!'

.14.

The Spirit's Morning Call

ROWENA stared back at him in silence. Then she looked down uncomfortably. 'Sir Richard, if you marry me you will become a commoner. Your honour and your family's name would be debased. In the eyes of your peers you will be nothing. Your relatives—they will cast you out. I saw what that did to my mother—' She paused to swallow the painful lump in her throat. 'And I will not—cannot—allow myself to be the cause of such a fate to anyone I care for.'

He pressed her hand passionately to his lips. 'Be my mistress then! Even if you were not my wife in the eyes of the world, in my doting eyes you would be. I would give to you every fidelity and provision that a wife has the right to expect.'

She shrunk back a little. 'Sir Richard, no! I—I—' She found herself desperately searching for words. 'I care for you, but—'

'But you're afraid of me,' he finished for her grimly. 'You think me a brute still. You mistrust me... God, to be seen so in the eyes of the lady I love!'

'I'm sorry; I cannot deny that it is true. At times, you have the sheer, primal beastliness of a starving wolf.'

He squeezed her hands tightly. 'Your eyes speak what your lips will not, Rowena. Tell me that you do not love me, and I will never talk to you of this again!'

'Sir, do not ask that of me, for I do not know the answer—oh, you are hurting me; loosen your hold, I beg!'

'Forgive me, beloved!' he gasped, letting her hands go. 'I'm like a giant hand capturing a beautiful butterfly and—' he paused for a moment, overcome with emotion, 'crushing its wings so it cannot fly.'

'You know as well as I that there is a dark, tortured, twisted corner of your heart where no light falls—a place from which your anger can suddenly leap out like a wolf from the dark depths of the forest. I feel I cannot trust you as one should a husband, nor entirely rely on you. It is a foolish woman who takes a lion into her chamber and believes herself safe from its bite.'

He stared bleakly over her shoulder, his face bathed in the golden light of the sinking sun which flooded in through the cell's only small, high window. 'I understand. I must not expect any fair, wise and virtuous woman to love a brute like me…' As he spoke, a lone tear overflowed the dark, glistening pools and rolled slowly down the pale cheek.

'Oh Richard, please don't take it like that!' she cried, and kissed his cold cheek. 'Only a bit of you is a brute, not all of you! Forgive the harsh words I must speak…'

The glittering dark eyes remained locked on the wall behind her. 'In that moment of unredeemable shame when I had my vile hand about your throat, you gave me cause to believe that, previous to that unpardonable act, I held a place in your affections I now do not…' His voice was almost a whisper.

She pushed the stiff dark hair back from the pale, quivering face. 'I was naive. I believed, like the woman who thinks her tame lion's taste for flesh will not extend to herself, that you would not harm me. The marks upon my throat took two weeks to fade.'

In a flash, the dark eyes found her gaze. 'Do you think I don't love you enough?'

'I know you love me as truly as it is possible for you to. But it is easy to love those things that are being good to us, and that do not thwart us or try us. A heart filled with love finds something to love in everyone, no matter their agreeableness or usefulness. '

All trace of the tears were removed with one pass of the back of a large hand. 'You are right. I should not have let my anxiety for your safety draw me into asking for your hand. Forgive me for taking such a liberty.' His voice was a hard monotone.

She knew from experience that it would not be any use trying to talk Sir Richard out of his bleak mood. If he was just left alone, it would usually lift before long. But it was still hard seeing him like that and knowing she had been the cause of it.

Seeing how high the golden tongues of sunlight had climbed up the silver birch visible through the window, Rowena was reminded of the time. It must be almost half past seven.

That still left just enough time to have a snack. She reached into her pocket and fished for the apple she had dropped in earlier. But the rosy red fruit never got to her mouth, because just then, the door suddenly burst open.

'Sir Richard, what are you doing with that nun in your lap?' screamed a livid Abbess Hawisa. 'You wanton, fornicating devil, I'll ruin you for this! Your name will be mud! Do you hear me? Mud!'

Holding the apple suspended midway to its destination, Rowena froze in shock. She did not dare look behind her.

But Sir Richard looked boldly up at the unexpected visitor and casually leaned back in his chair. 'When was it that you gained the gift of being able to see through solid objects? Were you born with it, or did it develop as your saintliness increased?'

Although Rowena could not see the abbess, she could tell Sir Richard's unexpected reaction had left her stumped.

'What...what do you mean?' Abbess Hawisa stammered furiously. 'I'm ordering you to get that nun out of your lap at once!'

Sir Richard smirked darkly. 'Perhaps you would like to show the abbess her mistake?' he suggested to Rowena.

The petrified young woman slowly climbed off her sheriff's knees and turned around.

Abbess Hawisa, puffed up like a bullfrog with anger, deflated immediately. 'Oh.'

Sir Richard got up, put his hand on Rowena's shoulder and looked the abbess calmly in the eye. 'Rowena and I are going to be married.'

Abbess Hawisa did not linger long after that, and neither did the sheriff and his clerk, who maintained an ill-boding silence until she was clear of the convent.

'Married! Why would you say a thing like that?' Rowena demanded as she hurried along the lavender-lined path after Sir Richard, almost having to break into a jog to keep up with his long stride.

'Because we are. You just don't know it yet,' came the matter-of-fact answer.

'What right have you to tell the abbess a thing like that?' The unexpected announcement had made Rowena cross, and being forced to address all her questions to the back of Sir Richard's head was making it worse.

'I wished to spare you from shame.'

'But it's a lie! Abbess Hawisa will go and tell everyone we're betrothed, and I will be a lot more shamed then!'

'But it's not a lie, because—' He suddenly stopped and spun around to face her. 'I *am* going to marry you.'

'What—'

But he interrupted her. 'I think I should leave you here and go to join Gallagher at the ambush. Here.' He held the wooden pail he was carrying out to her. 'You'll need this, 'sister'.'

They were halfway across the meadow now. She took the pail in her hand, suddenly becoming subdued at this reminder of the task ahead of her. 'Yes, you'd better get into position now.'

She turned to go, but he caught her by the arm. 'Wait a moment—' He tucked a rebellious red curl back under her wimple. 'There, now you are perfect.'

She bit her lip nervously, her annoyance suddenly forgotten. 'I just hope our plan is perfect too.'

'God's blessing and mercy be with you, my love.' Then he planted a kiss on her forehead and was gone.

He really could be charmingly insufferable... Rowena shook her head fondly as she watched him move swiftly across the meadow to the woods bordering it and disappear into the trees.

Suddenly feeling very small and very alone, she clutched the pail's rope handle tightly. The sun now dipped low in the sky, and the only sound on the empty path was a distant blackbird's song. The forest seemed strangely silent, as if holding its breath in anticipation.

She kissed the thin golden sun-pendent hanging around her neck and determinedly set off. Her eyes were fixed on the stile at the bottom of the meadow. Once she was in the lane, she took deep breaths to slow her pounding heart and focused on putting one foot in front of the other.

As the young woman walked, her imagination conjured up terrifying visions of death and disaster, and her mind swirled with doubts. He had been right; it *was* a ridiculous idea. She was all alone on this empty path with night falling...she had not thought it through properly—had only thought of the relief it would be to catch the felons.

The terrifying reality of being the bait in such a honey-trap hit her with blood-chilling, hair-raising, clammy-handed force. She needed every bit of self-control she possessed to prevent herself from turning back.

And she was desperate to search the wooded bank to her left where the sheriff and his men said they would be lying in wait.

Just the merest glimpse or sound would have brought her great comfort, but she knew she could not look there lest it gave away their position.

After the hardest two hundred paces she had ever walked, she reached the place at the bottom of the dell where water bubbled up from between mossy limestone boulders and splashed down into a small rocky pool. A narrow set of steps led the last few paces down the steep bank surrounding the spring.

Rowena hurried down, and had to catch hold of a sapling to prevent herself taking a tumble in her breathless, panicked carelessness. Pulling her scattered mind together, she continued on.

When she reached the water's edge, she quickly filled her pail with the cold, crystal-clear water and started hurrying back.

Rowena spilled a considerable amount of the water by bumping the pail against her legs as she hauled it up the steps. Now back on the even-surfaced lane, the going was much easier.

But the added weight of the water put a heavy demand on her already scarce breaths, and she was forced to stop scuttling along like an agitated beetle and walk at a more normal pace. After all, she had to remind herself, the whole point of this was that the felons would try to carry her off.

Now she was halfway back to the stile. Realising this, she fearfully looked around. Was not this the very place where Sister Alice had seen the sinister figure watching? Rowena's heart was in her mouth. The suspense was almost unbearable.

Suddenly, a commotion erupted in the undergrowth. There was a strange, croaking cry and a flapping sound accompanying the frantic movement coming from right near the lane.

Rowena started so violently that she dropped the pail to the ground with a thud that sloshed copious amounts of water over her skirt. She nearly fell flat on her face in sheer fright. Out of the corner of her eye she saw something rise above the vegetation.

Just as she was about to scream in terror, she realised what she was looking at. It was a pheasant. It was an accursed squawking, flapping pheasant hen.

Muttering disgusted insults at the offending bird, she picked up her now almost empty pail and carried on.

She was too annoyed by the incident with the bird to be bothered working herself into much of a panic. If she got kidnapped, she got kidnapped. There was going to be no more shrieking like a silly, air-headed girl. How the soldiers would laugh...

The rest of the walk to the stile was uneventful, and when Rowena reached it, she was not sure if she was relieved or disappointed that no one had tried to carry her off.

* * * *

'I'm sure that that fiendish abbess was just using the hysterical nun's fevered imaginings as an excuse to bully me,' Sir Richard growled to his sergeant. 'I'm telling you; she's really got it in for me.'

Their horses were tethered about twenty feet back from the edge of the steep, forested bank where he and Gallagher, camouflaged as best they could, acted as lookouts.

Lying on his belly in the undergrowth at the top of the bank overlooking the path, Sergeant Gallagher swatted away a bloodthirsty midge looking to make an evening meal out of him. 'Aye, that woman is a real battleaxe,' he whispered back. 'But there *were* the hoof prints in the woods. I doubt she could conjure them up just to irk you, Sir Richard.'

The sheriff shifted uncomfortably. 'Yes, but they could have belonged to the horses of lovers meeting in secret under cover of darkness, or hunters after the deer that emerge into the forest clearing at sundown.'

Having to lay front down in the damp leaves without moving a muscle for a good hour every evening for the last four days was starting to get to Sir Richard. It really had been a stupid idea that was never going to work. Even if that jittery nun had been right about the men in the woods watching her, the chances of them having been spooked was high. Hiding eight men-at-arms on foot, plus himself, Sergeant Gallagher and the two horses was not easy.

Still, it had been awfully funny seeing Rowena take fright at that pheasant... He chuckled quietly at the memory.

'Here she comes,' Gallagher murmured, as Rowena reappeared from the spring's rocky dell.

With her pail now full, she started back up the road. The young woman walked much more slowly than she had the first time she made the journey.

It had been decided unanimously by all concerned that this would be the last time the trap would be tried. There had been no sign of anything unusual the previous four times the ambush had been set, and everyone was losing patience with the whole thing.

'Is that rust I can see on your sword?' Sir Richard pointed a dangerously tense finger at the offending sight.

'Aye, just a touch. The armoury has become rather damp lately, what with all the rain leaking in through the holes in the roof.'

'What sort of excuse is that?' the sheriff whispered furiously at his relaxed-looking sergeant. 'You are a leader; you are supposed to act as an example to the men! How can you expect them to keep their own weapons in good order when they have such a shoddy example before them?'

'Sorry about that, sir,' Gallagher replied carefully but casually.

'Show some respect!' snapped the knight. 'This company is

getting soft and slack!'

'With all due respect, Sir Richard, I can hardly jump to attention, because that really would give our position away.'

'Give our position away to whom? Lurking pheasants? This whole damn thing is a complete waste of time.' He slammed his fist into the ground. 'God, why can't we catch these bastards!'

'Sir—'

'Somewhere up there God is just laughing at us—'

'Sir!' hissed Gallagher, tugging urgently at Sir Richard's sleeve.

'What, in God's name what?' the sheriff bellowed, making no attempt to keep his voice down.

'Look!' Gallagher pointed down to the road. 'There's something happening!'

Sir Richard was on his feet in an instant. 'Bloody hell!'

Down below them two black-cloaked horsemen, with hoods drawn low and only their eyes showing above the cloths hiding their faces, were rapidly approaching Rowena from behind. She had dropped her pail and was running for her life.

But it was no use. The black horsemen were already almost upon her. Galloping abreast, they drew level with her, one on each side.

'Help, Sir Richard, help me!' her terrified scream echoed through the forest.

The sheriff and his sergeant leapt onto their horses and urged them vigorously forward.

'Go, go, go!' they shouted to their waiting men.

But it was too late. From their vantage point up on the bank, Sir Richard and Gallagher saw one of the galloping horsemen seize Rowena by the arm and pull her over the front of his horse without slowing his break-neck speed for a moment.

The lightning speed and flawless skill with which the move was carried out was truly astounding. By the time Sir Richard was charging down the bank, the villains were already disappearing around the first bend in the road in a cloud of dust.

The sheriff shouted strongly-worded encouragement (some might say abuse) as he urged his men to the pursuit.

It did not achieve much. The men laying in ambush behind a thicket further up the road had drawn their weapons and rushed out immediately upon hearing the pounding hoofbeats coming their way. The galloping horsemen swept past the foot-soldiers, passing so close to one that he was knocked to the ground. The men were forced to beat a hasty retreat as their commander and his sergeant came thundering down the narrow lane in hot pursuit of the disappearing kidnappers.

Some muffled, breathless screams came from the victim, and her would-be rescuers could see her legs kicking franticly. But when the horse she had been pulled over gave a small buck of protest at the disturbance, her legs quickly stopped moving.

The fleeing felons were mounted on lean, long-legged horses that swallowed the ground before them with ease. Poor Lucifer, with his big, muscular body, thick, feathered legs and huge hooves, was more suited to carrying a heavily armed knight into battle than racing across country at high speed.

The warhorse could sense the urgency of his rider, and give it everything he had. Though more comfortable at a canter, the horse willingly lengthened his strides into a flat, rapid gallop.

The thunder of hooves and the loud rhythm of Lucifer's massive breaths keeping time with his strides filled Sir Richard's ears. Lucifer's thick black mane whipped in his face as he stood in the stirrups and leaned forward to ease some weight off the stallion's back.

But despite Lucifer's big-hearted effort, his rider could see they were falling further and further behind the felons, and that Rowena was slipping further and further away from him. The one person apart from his sister he had ever truly loved...

Mercifully, the forest path the fleeing horsemen led their pursuers along was straight for the most part. When they disappeared around a bend in the path, it was not long before Sir Richard and Gallagher caught sight of them again in the distance.

After about twenty minutes hard riding, the black-cloaked horsemen disappeared around a long corner, and when Sir Richard and Gallagher rounded the bend themselves there was only empty road ahead. They urged their horses on, hoping the long curve would straighten out at last, but instead found themselves at a fork in the path.

Sir Richard sat back down in his saddle and Lucifer obediently skidded to a stop. The knight wheeled his horse around to face his sergeant, who was coming charging along a little way behind on his grey horse.

'Which way?' Sir Richard cried, dropping his reins and throwing his hands into the air. 'What in God's name do we do now?'

His mind was devoid of everything except blind panic. The thought of losing Rowena through his own mistake was too much. He would not, could not, think that he might never again see her dear, kind face and the laughing green eyes he loved so much. How afraid she must be. For someone whose main experience of horses was falling off the towering Lucifer, this would be hell.

Just like Everild had, Rowena trusted him to protect her. He let them both down. The sheriff felt choked by the horror of it.

Gallagher pointed down the turning to the right. 'I can see wet ground down here!'

Sir Richard was cantering in that direction before his sergeant had even finished speaking. Wet ground was good. Wet ground meant hoof prints.

And there were hoof prints. Two sets of galloping horse-hoof prints perfectly cast in the wet, sticky clay.

'This way, Gallagher! I've found the bastards' trail!'

The chase was on again.

The road started to widen and the forest to thin. Peasants working the fields that the thundering horsemen passed looked up from their labours to watch, and women came to the door of their cottages and stared, wondering at the strange sight for a moment before returning to the endless duties awaiting them.

Whether it was after a long or a little while Sir Richard could not say, but the path eventually ended in a flat clearing at the edge of a lake. They had reached the shores of the unimaginatively but aptly named Deeplake.

The two pursuers franticly scanned the dusty clearing, but could see neither their quarry nor any other roads leading on from there. The only thing of note to be seen in the lonely, desolate place was a small pier leading out over the dark, still waters of the lake.

Sir Richard jumped off the sweating, foam-flicked Lucifer, hurried fearfully to the water's edge and looked out.

And yes, there was the boat that ferried people and cargo across the narrow middle of the long, thin lake, saving them a full day's travel. And in it were the two horsemen.

The boat was already out of earshot and its sail hoisted high up on the mast. It would be at least two hours before the boat had dropped off her passengers and returned.

By which time Rowena and her kidnappers would be long gone.

.15.

Desolation

AFTER letting Lucifer's reins drop from his hand, Sir Richard fell to his knees in the dust.

His heart felt like it had been ripped from his body and trampled in the dry, dusty road. Unable to bear the sight of the boat carrying his beloved away from him becoming ever fainter as the ghostly mists claimed it, he covered his face with his hands and collapsed sobbing in the road.

A few moments later, he suddenly lifted his head to listen. Was it just his overwrought mind, or was that really the faint, answering cry of his beloved, carried by the breeze across the dark, deep water that separated them?

'Rowena!' he cried desperately at the hazy shape still just visible through the hovering mists. 'Rowena!'

But the only answer was the hollow echo of his own voice calling mockingly back to him as it bounced across the dark surface of Deeplake.

He let out a scream of agonised despair that scarcely sounded human. The pain of losing Rowena was far greater than any of the many physical pains he had endured. He felt as though his soul was falling down a bottomless pit of inner darkness. It was worse than any physical hell.

Sprawled in the dirt, Sir Richard howled and sobbed and beat his fists on the hard, sun-baked clay. Even if he had cried enough tears to fill Deeplake, he still felt as though he would not have expressed all of his grief and pain.

Growing more concerned by the moment, Sergeant Gallagher quickly dismounted from his horse.

Even Lucifer was being made restless by his master. The big warhorse flicked an uncertain ear towards the sound and nickered nervously.

'I promise you, sir, we will find her,' Gallagher said as he reached the sobbing, pathetic figure on the ground. He knelt down and put a hand on his comrade's shaking shoulder. 'We will follow them. Even if we have to travel to the very gates of hell, we will follow them. Don't despair; we will find her.'

The distraught knight took no heed. His head did not lift even a fraction above the road's dust.

Sergeant Gallagher took a firmer grip on Sir Richard and gave him a good jerk. 'Come on! Pull yourself together, man. No matter how many tears you shed, nothing good is going to grow out of it.'

Sir Richard slowly dragged himself into a sitting position and drew his knees up to his chin. A dust-streaked curtain of dishevelled hair fell over his ghostly-pale face.

His eyes were dark, hollow pits of despair. 'If we don't find her I will kill myself. The only thing I ever bring to those I love is death and destruction. It would be better for everyone if I was dead.'

'With all due respect, sir, stop talking trash. I've been fighting shoulder-to-shoulder with you for more than fifteen years and I'm still alive. I won't deny that we might have caught the felons before they fled if we hadn't been so busy discussing weapon maintenance. But what's done is done. The true test of a warrior is how he finishes, not how he starts.'

'But we will never catch them up. By the time we get across this accursed lake they'll have long since vanished into the wilds like they always do. And Rowena with them…' he added in a whisper, staring fixedly out over the misty waters as if hoping she might arise from their cold, dark depths.

'Eaglestone is less than an hour from here; we will ride back to the castle to get some supplies together and tell the men what's happening. And then we will come straight back here and wait for the ferry to return and take us across. The ferryman will be able to tell us which way the villains went.'

'But it will be dark by the time we get back here. The ferryman will not want to take us across in the dark.'

'Look, there is a full moon tonight.' Gallagher pointed to the bright orb peeping above the treetops to the east. 'As for the ferryman, he will not refuse to take his sheriff across on official business, no matter if it be day or night.'

'But we will still never catch them...' came the hopeless moan of despair.

'Now look here, sir; stop wallowing in self-pity and get up!' ordered the sergeant, who was uncomfortable with having to be so tough-talking and was starting to resent the sheriff for forcing him to be.

The knight ignored him.

Gallagher seized Sir Richard's arm and attempted to pull him up. 'With all due respect, sir, get off your rear end and pull yourself together!'

'Leave me be.'

Gallagher pulled harder. 'No man has ever truly lost everything because there is always hope. And hope never deserts a man unless he throws it away himself. Now get up!'

'I said, leave me be!'

Gallagher kicked him in the ribs. 'And I said get up!'

Fire flashed in the dark eyes again. Sir Richard leapt to his feet and gave his sergeant an angry shove. 'Damn you! Don't you dare do that to me!'

A stone could not have been calmer than the endlessly-patient

Gallagher. He had never lost his temper and was not about to do so now. 'If you don't want someone else giving you a kick, do it yourself.'

Sir Richard breathed hotly in his sergeant's face for a moment, but decided not to take the matter any further. He stepped back and picked up his horse's reins. 'Alright, you win. Let's get going.'

By the time Sir Richard and Gallagher returned to the shores of Deeplake, it was well and truly dark. But now sailing high in the indigo sky, the silent moon cast a rippling silver path over the waters.

The way back through the rapidly darkening forest had been hard going. Shaded from the moon's light, they had almost wondered off the path a number of times, and the low-hanging branches that would suddenly loom out of the blackness in front of them had forced them to traverse the thickest parts of the forest on foot.

The sheriff and his sergeant rode their horses up to the water's edge and looked out over the moonlit lake, anxiously searching for the ferry. To the great relief of both men, the boat was spotted silently moving towards the pier, the gentle but constant breeze blowing in from the east filling its sail.

Sir Richard and Gallagher urged their mounts forward onto the small pier's wooden boards. Well used to the many strange sights, sounds and obstacles to be encountered in a warhorse's life, the horses stepped on without hesitation.

After a short but impatient wait, the ferry was finally moored. There was a lantern hanging at the boat's bow, and illuminated by its light, a lone ferryman. He was almost invisible beneath his heavy cloak, the hood drawn low against the chilly night wind blowing unhindered across Deeplake.

'The ferry doesn't sail again until the morrow,' he rasped, hardly bothering to glance up at the anxiously waiting travellers.

'I'm the sheriff of this shire. We are on the trail of some felons and we need to cross now,' said the tall knight.

Without saying a word, the ferryman put the gangplank down and waited for the unwanted cargo to board.

When the ferry moored at the other shore after a tense, wordless passage, Sir Richard deemed it safe enough to question the silent, surly ferryman, as there was now no risk of him refusing to take them across.

'Tell us about your last passengers!' he demanded roughly.

The heavily cloaked figure shrugged. 'They paid their fare and didn't cause any bother.'

'How many were there? Did they have a young lady with them?'

'No, there were just two men—'

Sir Richard's heart jumped into his mouth. 'What! No woman?'

'No. But there was a big, sacking-bound bundle with them. It seemed quite heavy. Its length would have been a foot or two less than yours, and it was sort of lumpy and uneven.'

Sir Richard took a menacing step towards the ferryman. 'Did it seem like there was anything alive inside this bundle?'

A shifty, evasive look came over the ferryman. 'I couldn't really say. It was dark, and it's not my job to be going around prodding at passengers' baggage.'

'Were you not suspicious?' growled the sheriff.

The ferryman coughed uneasily. 'I don't get paid for being suspicious.'

A well-filled purse was dangled tantalizingly in front of the ferryman. 'Oh really…?'

Small, greedy eyes followed the purse's movement. 'I do remember now. It definitely looked the shape and size a woman could be,' he replied, clutching out for the money.

But the purse was snatched away before the covetous hand

could close around it. 'No, not good enough, I'm afraid. But if you had been a good citizen and done something about the poor maid bundled up like a sack of rags, it would be a different story.' He brought his face right up to the other man's. 'Now, you leech, tell me where these men went!'

Blinking his hard little eyes, the ferryman took a step back. 'They slung the bundle—'

'You mean the maiden.'

'Yes, that—and they rode off along the road going south.'

* * * *

The road leading south was much wider and more frequently used than the forest tracks they had travelled at the beginning of the pursuit. Sir Richard and Sergeant Gallagher were relieved that the road led past open meadows, and only occasionally passed into shade where a lone forest giant had been left standing at the side of the road, unclaimed by the axe that had felled the rest of its kind to make way for pastures long ago.

Although the country they were passing through was not very familiar to him, Sir Richard knew it was the southern edge of the Heathcote Downs, where his shire would soon end and become Lothbury, the shire between Chaucy and the South Coast.

With the full moon lighting up the country bright as day, they were able to ride at a brisk trot. But after a while, Gallagher turned to Sir Richard. 'It must be well past midnight by now. I think we should stop and rest until dawn.'

Sir Richard kept riding determinedly onwards. 'No. The villains will get further ahead of us.' The thought of doing anything that might widen the distance between him and Rowena was unbearable.

'Surely they will be forced to stop awhile somewhere too,' said the sergeant. 'In the dark, we might miss signs of their passing or roads they may have turned down. If we don't catch up with the villains very soon, we will be forced to stop during daylight hours to rest the horses. Why travel at night when you can travel in daylight?'

Although stopping was the last thing Sir Richard felt like doing, he could see the sense of his sergeant's suggestion. They were passing a hay meadow which had been recently cut, and the hay was heaped into a few large haystacks by the road. 'Yes, you're right, we ought to stop. This field seems as good a place as any.'

The horses were soon tethered near one of the haystacks and their bridles, saddles and saddlebags removed. After giving the hardworking horses a rub down with a handful of hay to dry them off, the two men sat down beside the haystack.

After a meal of bread, cheese and apples, the weary soldiers sunk onto their hay pillows and wrapped their blankets tightly around themselves. The cool wind blowing from the north had a bite that heralded the coming of autumn.

Judging by the gentle, rhythmic snores coming from his direction, Sir Richard could tell his ever-relaxed sergeant had fallen asleep almost as soon as his head hit the hay. He himself, however, was not so fortunate. Tired as his limbs were, his fear-filled mind would give him no rest. If he drifted off into drowsy near-sleep, his tortured thoughts would jumble together in a whirling, twisted mass that was part dream, part memory and part thought.

* * * *

The inside of the room was dark. Every inch had been searched with groping, frantic hands. But no door could be found. A pale, eerie blue light began to fill the cell. Standing an arm's length away was a white-faced young woman. Her dishevelled hair cascaded over her thin, trembling shoulders and down to her waist. Her white slip was smeared with dark stains. Blood covered her nose and hands. Tears had washed thin rivers down her dusty cheeks. The ghostly, waif-like damsel fell to her knees.

She threw back her head and screamed, 'Help me, save me!' The wrenching, half-crazed cry grew louder and louder until it was not just coming from her throat, but from all sides. Sharp, clawing talons suddenly bit into living flesh with searing agony.

Sir Richard woke from his nightmare with a start.

The first rosy blush of the fresh-faced dawn coloured the eastern sky. The setting moon and the last of the stars still shone faintly from the translucent, pale blue heavens, and down the valley a crowing cock heralded the new day.

The knight shivered in the chill, damp morning air and shook the dewdrops from his hair. Pulling himself to a sitting position, he leaned back against the haystack and quickly wiped the sleep from his eyes.

Why did that nightmare keep haunting him? It had visited him on many a lonely, tortured night, reviving the memory of Morgana de Wintore as she had been when he visited her on the morning of her execution. A memory he was desperate to forget but that refused to leave him.

Sir Richard splashed bracingly cold water from a nearby goblet over his face, calling in wakefulness to banish the nighttime demons. He then pulled himself to his feet and stretched his stiff limbs. At nearly thirty-six, and with the brutal abuse of a warrior's hard life behind him, his body was starting to complain about spending a cold night on hard ground out in the open.

He stirred the still-snoring Gallagher with his foot. 'Rise and shine, comrade!'

It was almost indecent of the man to be sleeping next to a tormented dreamer with such a peaceful smile on his face…

Gallagher rolled onto his back and slowly opened his eyes. 'Ah, morning…and I was having such a nice sleep…'

The men soon had their saddlebags packed and their horses ready, and were out on the road again. As the fertile farmland of the rolling downs gave way to steeper, stonier hills and wooded gorges, the road became narrower. The prosperous farms they had passed at regular intervals in the darkness thinned to the odd cottage or shepherd's hut.

The fear that the felons might be hiding at a farm or have doubled back on themselves in the night weighed heavily on both men's minds, but remained unsaid. Neither of them wanted to encourage such dark thoughts.

* * * *

It was nearly noon, and they had yet to pass another traveller on the lonely road. They were trotting towards the base of a mountain range that reared steeply up in front of them, when Sir Richard thought he could see someone amongst the trees the path passed into.

He urged Lucifer into a faster trot. His mood had been getting blacker and bleaker all morning as the empty miles had passed. But now he felt a sudden, joyous surge of hope, for standing in the road before him was a barefooted young country maid surrounded by a flock of geese, which she was driving along the path towards him.

He halted sharply in front of her. 'Have you seen any travellers on horseback pass this way lately?'

The raven-haired girl rested her hands atop the long staff she carried and glared up at him. She might have been barefoot and dressed in the simple garb of a peasant, but she eyed him with the regal air of a royal princess. 'Look what you've done to me geese; they be all scattered now!' The black-eyed goose-girl pointed an indigent finger at her squawking flock, most of which had run into the roadside trees in alarm at the fast-approaching horseman. 'You just think you can do whatever you wish, Sir High-and-Mighty! Coming here on your great beast, scattering me geese like it don't matter and setting about interrogating me without so much as bidding me good day!'

The excitement of at last finding someone who might have seen Rowena had still not worn off. He hardly heard her complaints. 'Have you seen—'

But the scornful goose-girl quickly interrupted him. 'I ain't talking to you no more, for you be rude.' And with that, the pouting girl, filled with the sort of indigent anger only a maid of her years could wear, turned away from him and flounced off in a huff.

'No—I'm sorry!' he called after her desperately.

The unimpressed goose-girl turned her black eyes back on him and gave her head a disdainful toss. 'Sorry ain't no use to me! Sorry can't herd them geese back together!'

His joyous new mood was now well and truly gone. He gave a deflated sigh as he watched the indignant girl storm off. There went a young lady who took herself very seriously…

He jumped off Lucifer. It was about time he took her just as seriously.

'Let me help you,' he called to the goose-girl, hurrying after her.

The only reply he received was a sullen glare from the glittering black eyes.

He ignored this less than enthusiastic response and started trying to herd the honking geese back together.

Gallagher just looked on in quiet amusement from a safe distance. When Sir Richard crossed paths with someone as difficult as he was himself, it was best to just stand clear and avoid the wreckage…

The knight threw himself at the task with great energy. His feet slipped from under him on the wet, mossy ground beneath the trees more than once, but he did not let that stop him. After a quick dust-down, he would be back at the geese.

And he took great care not to let a single expletive, curse or complaint slip from his lips, however much he felt like ringing the honking, flapping damn birds' necks. There was no way there was going to be a repeat of an incident like the one in the marketplace. Comforting that young stallholder had been harder than fighting two armed men at once—though if badly upset, this maid looked more likely to kill than cry.

When all the fowls were shepherded back into a flock again, Sir Richard turned his attention back to the raven-haired maid. 'Now madam, perhaps I can start again. God give you good day, damsel.' He bowed low. 'Have you seen anyone pass here?'

Although she did not look actively impressed, the maid did not actually look unimpressed now. 'When I was getting me geese sorted for taking to market at sun-up, two men and a maiden rode past in haste. They were going the same way as you.'

His heart leapt for joy within him. 'You did! And what did they look like?'

'The two men were wearing black cloaks, and quickly put their hoods down when they spotted me, and the maiden was dressed in a black robe a bit like a nun's habit, though without the head bit. The horse she rode was being led by one of them men.'

A wave of hope and relief surged over him. 'Thank you, thank you, thank you!'

‘It’s no bother,’ she replied aloofly, as though helping knight-errands was an everyday occurrence for her.

Sir Richard flung his arms around her in a big hug that lifted her clean off the ground, and kissed her. ‘I bloody love you!’

And with that he leapt onto Lucifer and cantered off down the road, leaving the goose-girl staring speechlessly at the receding back of the tall dark stranger.

.16.

Men of Iron

ALL AFTERNOON Sir Richard and Sergeant Gallagher had steadily climbed the mountain range that formed the southern boundary of Chaucy Shire, dividing it from its neighbour, Lothbury.

The mountains were steep and rocky, in many places rising as sheer cliff faces. White veils of water cascaded over several of these precipices and plunged down into misty gorges below. The path was exceedingly narrow. Often, there was only enough space for travellers to move in single file, and in many places the track had a sheer rock face on one side and a plunging precipice on the other. Eagles glided on the warm air currents rising from the sun-warmed rocks below, and cawing ravens circled the cliff tops which towered into the sky like castles. It took only a little imagination to see lords and ladies walking high up on their battlements or gazing out from arched windows.

As the sun sunk lower in the western sky, the menacing, inky storm clouds that had been rolling in from the north finally caught up with the two travellers. Keen to get off the mountaintop before night, they moved as fast as they dared on the dizzyingly high trail. Already over the highest point of the narrow mountain pass, they were relieved when the path ahead snaked down into a gorge with a flat grassy bank along its river. There they could stop for the night.

By the time they reached the bottom of the gorge, storm

clouds smothered the mountaintop in a thick, dark shroud. All the birds had fallen silent. The only sound to be heard was the eerie moaning of the wind whistling around the lonely peaks.

Gallagher pointed at a large overhang of rock at the bottom of the cliff face. 'That will do nicely.'

The two men quickly made for the place. There were signs that many travellers before them had camped under the rock's protection. Its roof was black with the soot of their camp fires.

With the first heavy drops of rain beginning to fall, Sir Richard and Gallagher hurried to get the horses unsaddled and tethered, and to gather enough of the dead wood lying on the riverbank before it became soaked.

With the help of some dry moss and a flint stone, a cheerful blaze was soon burning in the rock alcove, keeping the rapidly falling darkness at bay. A short while later, the two wayfarers were hungrily tucking into a trout which had been caught in a well-stocked pool during a short early afternoon stop, and washing it down with hot rosehip and elderflower tea.

Outside, the storm began to rage. The boom of thunder crashed forth from the sky and rolled through the gorge, amplified as it echoed off the rocks. Occasionally a bolt of lightning struck the mountaintop and briefly lit the black night bright as day with its strange blue-white light.

Then the wind got up. It howled and moaned and raged around the high, desolate pass all night long, sounding at times like the cries of revelling demons and evil spirits shrieking in the stormy darkness, and at other moments like the cries of the damned. Rain poured down in torrents. Blown about savagely by the wind, it swirled first one way, then another.

The travellers were very grateful for their simple but solid shelter. Too low for a man to stand upright in but long enough to lie down in, it kept out most of the storm. What little rain did blow in was kept off by the oilcloth Sir Richard and Sergeant

Gallagher had put over their legs.

The noise of the raging storm was such that Sir Richard held little hope of getting any sleep that night. He pulled his blanket tightly around himself and settled his head down on the saddle blanket he was using as a pillow.

Lying next to him, it was a different matter for Sergeant Gallagher. After only a short while, calm snores came from his direction. Was there any limit to that man's ability to sleep?

Sir Richard was determined to get as much rest as he could before the hard miles ahead of them the following day. He tried to block out the sounds coming from outside, but kept hearing Rowena's voice in the moaning wind, seeing her face in the swirling rain when it was lit up the lightning, and hearing her light, quick footfalls coming towards him in the drumming rain beating down on the rock.

Eventually he fell into a fitful sleep. And this time he dreamt that Rowena came to him as he lay sleeping. Holding a burning candle, she glided into the room dressed all in white and hovered over him. Watching, just silently, peacefully watching.

A few hours later, Sir Richard crawled blinkingly out into the dawn light. The only clouds to be seen in the sky were a benign scattering of light, fluffy ones tinted brilliant gold by the rising sun. The lone sign left behind by the night's storm was a change in the tune of the river. The bright, lively chatter of the previous day had turned into an angry roar as the grey-brown floodwaters jostled for space, racing through the narrow gorge in their headlong dash for the ocean.

He took a deep breath of the sweet, damp air and stretched his arms up. It was a relief to be out of the cramped cave and able to stand fully upright, *without* hitting his head like he had done when he first got up.

But then he turned to look at the grassy patch by the cliff face, where he had tethered the horses to a rowan tree the evening before. They were gone.

'Gallagher, Gallagher, wake up!' he shouted.

In an instant the sergeant was sitting bolt upright with a drawn sword in his hand, looking around franticly for the villains who were trying to murder him in his sleep. 'What, what?'

'The horses—they're gone!'

The sword was tossed aside. 'No!' Gallagher quickly crawled out.

Sir Richard ran towards the place, filled with sickening dread. He found the rope he had tied the horses to. It had snapped.

He held the broken end up. 'It looks like the horses got spooked by the thunder and bolted in the night!'

The only place the horses could have gone apart from back up the narrow track they had come down the previous evening was downstream along the riverbank. There was a path leading down through trees, with clearings in many places where the forest had been heavily grazed by deer.

Sir Richard hurried along the path, with the now fully awake Gallagher close behind. The dread filling him was intense. There were so many sheer faces the panicked horses could have plunged over. In spite of their good night vision, the horses would have had very poor visibility in the mist and rain. The path wound around a sink-hole.

When he peered down into it, the hole proved to be about as deep as he was tall, and at the bottom was a scattering of bleached white bones. But it was not wide enough at the top for a horse to fit in, although a horse could easily break a leg if it stumbled over it.

Hurrying on more franticly than ever, he suddenly turned a bend to find himself face-to-face with Lucifer. The gleaming black charger was standing in a clearing in knee-deep pasture, with a large mouthful of grass between his teeth and his friend grazing nearby.

Lucifer stopped his chewing for a few moments while he silently regarded the newcomer with his big brown eyes, then flicked his tail and went back to his grazing.

* * * *

'A crossroads.'

'Aye, a crossroads.'

Halted in front of the sign, Sir Richard eyed it distastefully. 'What are we going to do now?'

Sergeant Gallagher removed his cloth cap and scratched his head thoughtfully. 'There's a crude hill curved on one arm and what looks like some waves on the other, so I'm guessing straight ahead leads to the coast and left to the hills.'

'This might be the first crossroads we've come across since we passed the goose-girl, but the felons could easily have taken some other shortcut or detour over these open moors in an attempt to throw us off their trail.'

Gallagher replaced his cap. 'Aye, that they might have. Only a fool would go wandering off the path on such a featureless and bog-dotted moor, but if they know these moors well they may have taken the risk.'

'And we have not passed a single soul ever since we got off that damn mountain and onto this lonely, god-forsaken moor. A full two days!' Sir Richard ran his shaking fingers through his hair. 'We might as well give it up and go home...'

'We're sure to pass some shepherds tending all these sheep. You can see for miles across this open country; one of them will have seen the felons pass.'

'Very optimistic of you, but these moors go on forever. We'd be very lucky to come across anyone who has seen them.'

'Maybe, but I think the felons will be making for the coast. I can't see that they would go to some remote country area. No, they will be taking this road to the sea.'

Several hours later, Gallagher and Sir Richard were still travelling the same wild and lonely road.

Slumped tiredly on Lucifer, the knight had the dull, drooping look of a man who had given up hope. 'But we've already asked two shepherds without luck, and he's over on the next hill,' he moaned. 'We've wasted enough time this morning as it is.'

Gallagher turned his horse off the road and started heading to the right. 'Come on, sir, it's worth a try.'

The tall knight muttered darkly under his breath but followed anyway.

The lone figure Sir Richard and Sergeant Gallagher had spotted was perched on a rock atop the long, steady rise to the right. On this very misty morning, they had only caught sight of the shepherd when the thick mists around the hilltop had parted a short while ago.

The dense mists were always moving and changing. At dawn, the mountains they descended two days previously had been completely hidden from view in a blanket of fog. Then, as the sun climbed higher, the fog had lowered to reveal the mountaintops floating like islands in a white sea of mist. Sometimes the mists thinned to reveal a tantalising glimpse of blue sky or distant moorland, but only to come stealthily stealing back and surround the travellers once more.

The two comrades-in-arms steered their mounts down into the marshy, turf-covered dell separating the road from the broad hill the shepherd had been seen on.

But as they climbed up the opposite side, a thick blanket of fog descended. In moments the visibility was less than twenty paces on all sides, and any sense of direction was lost. The travellers quickly came to a halt and dismounted from their horses.

'It was foolish to go wandering off the road in these misty wilds,' Sir Richard grumbled. 'You hear of wayfarers who get lost in the mist on lonely moors like this and wonder round and round in circles for days on end until they finally die.'

His sergeant had to work hard to keep a straight face. 'I can't say I have heard any credible stories of that kind myself. After all, how can these poor souls who got lost in the mists tell such a tale if they're dead?'

'That may be,' came the glum, unconvinced reply of one determined to be gloomy, 'but even if we don't become hopelessly lost, we're sure to be swallowed up by one of the bottomless mires these places are always covered in, or fall into a cave like the one in that gorge. Perhaps, many years hence, a lone shepherd will come across our bleached bones, picked clean by the ravens…'

Gallagher sighed wearily. To many more days spent in such melancholy company and even he would be in danger of losing the will to live.

With the corner of his cloak, Sir Richard wiped off the water droplets clinging to his hair. 'God, I'm so tired …'

Gallagher suddenly lifted a finger. 'Listen—'

Sir Richard listened. Drifting towards them through the mist was the faint, faraway sound of music. At first he felt like he was dreaming, but when he moved towards it, the sound of a pipe playing a haunting melody could clearly be heard.

He stumbled blindly towards the heavenly music.

The sound came nearer and nearer and still he could see no one. But then the mist drifted apart to reveal a handsome golden-haired youth playing a small pipe, sitting cross-legged on a large, flat boulder.

The knight stared spellbound at the sight. He scarcely dared to believe he was not dreaming, and was afraid to make a sound for fear the beautiful youth might prove to be a phantom conjured up by his own desperate mind, and fade into the swirling mist.

When the golden-haired youth had finished his achingly beautiful tune, he lowered his pipe from his lips and looked directly at the arrivals with startling violet-blue eyes. He did not seem surprised in the slightest at seeing the two strangers emerge from the mist. If anything, Sir Richard fancied the youth looked as if he had been waiting for them.

He might have had the face of a satyr or elf, but the dazzling youth was dressed as a shepherd. Over a simple green woollen tunic he wore a white sheepskin vest, and resting against the rock he sat on was a wooden shepherd's crook.

'Greetings, wayfaring strangers,' said the youth.

'Good morn, shepherd,' replied the knight.

'I can tell you that those whom you seek did pass this way, Sir Knight,' said the youth.

Sir Richard could only blink at the divine shepherd in astonishment. How could he possibly know the seeker's question before it was asked? What was he, a mind reader? He was certainly looking at Sir Richard as though he could see right into him...

The youth smiled. 'I know because I saw an unhappy lady and two ruffians pass by in great haste not six hours hence, casting the furtive backward glance of the wrong-doer fleeing his pursuers.'

'And which—'

'They were going south.'

Sir Richard's state of mind was now such that if the golden shepherd had unfurled angel's wings before his very eyes and taken flight, he would only have been mildly surprised. He bowed low. 'I thank you, kind shepherd! I thank you a hundred times over!'

The golden shepherd smiled his bewitching smile and inclined his head in acknowledgement. 'Follow the north wind and you will find her.'

Sir Richard took an astonished step back and bowed again. He did not doubt a word the all-knowing golden youth said.

'May the guiding light walk beside you on every step of your journey, and may the road level beneath your feet and the wind be ever at your back,' said the beautiful shepherd.

The knight backed humbly away, bowing and muttering his grateful thanks. When he looked up again, the golden-haired youth had been reclaimed by the mist.

With his soul now brimming with hope, the knight swung up onto Lucifer and briskly made for the road, which was now clearly visible down below.

As the two comrades departed, the haunting melody struck up again and drifted after them on the faint breeze which was beginning to blow away the mists. All except for the mist embracing the top of the mount from whence the golden shepherd's music came.

* * * *

'So, this is the road's destination.' Sir Richard reined Lucifer in on the brow of the hill leading down to the ocean.

For several silent moments he and Gallagher feasted their eyes on the welcome sight of the little seaside town of Hamlin, which was crammed onto the scarce land betwixt cliff and sea. The cries of the many gulls wheeling overhead and perched on the town's roofs provided the unmistakable sound of the seashore.

He and Gallagher had been riding hard ever since their meeting with the golden-haired shepherd the morning of the previous day. Riding all of the day and half of the night, at every crossroads they had taken the road going south.

Dusk was now fast approaching. Sir Richard watched the last

rays of the setting sun disappear as it dipped into the burning sea in a fiery golden haze. This was the end of the road for them. Of that he felt sure. Somewhere in or around this small bay and its little fishing port, the villains were lying low. And tomorrow he was going to track the loathsome scum down and flush them out of their hole. But first he needed to find an inn to put up for the night in.

He urged Lucifer forward down the steep path leading into the town.

The place did not smell as bad as most of the inland towns. The usual foul smells were mixed with the fresh, salty sea air and the watery aroma of seaweed. Many of Hamlin's buildings were three or four storeys high, squeezed up because there was no room to spread out on the thin strip of flat land between the high, rocky cliffs behind and the seashore in front.

The narrow main street running in a straight line from the seashore to the road out of town was empty except for a few dogs that barked half-heartedly at the two passers-by, and a small group of young boys playing a game with pebbles on a game board they had drawn onto the bare earth with a stick. Alerted to the new arrivals by the dogs, the boys stopped their game and stared at the strangers.

Sir Richard and Sergeant Gallagher called out a friendly greeting as they walked by, but the boys just stared back in silence.

When they were about halfway down the street, Gallagher pointed to a sign hanging at the corner of one of the narrow lanes and alleys leading off it. 'Here, that looks to be the sign of an inn or tavern.'

Sir Richard looked to where his friend pointed. The wooden signboard had a crudely carved and painted flying pig on it, telling the illiterate patrons (which were probably all of them) that the name of the establishment was the Flying Pig. The arrow next to it pointed down an alley so narrow two large men would struggle to pass in it without pushing against each other.

'Yes,' said the knight, 'let's see if they have any lodgings.'

They slung their horses' reins over a nearby hitching-rail and turned into the tiny alley, with Sir Richard leading the charge.

The narrow alley was empty of everything except the stench of urine and vomit, which hung heavily in the air. The overhanging upper storeys of the tall buildings made the dark lane almost tunnel-like, but the two men did not have to go in far. A sign of a flying pig above it announced that the third door along belonged to the establishment advertised at the alley entrance.

Sir Richard stopped outside. The small, battered wooden door was a little below street level, with three rough stone steps leading down to it. The one small, dirty window opening onto the alley shone a little light out, and the sound of raised voices, drunken singing and rowdy laughter came from within.

'It seems a rough place, though a popular one too, which is usually a good sign,' muttered the knight, more to himself than to his comrade.

While Gallagher waited outside, Sir Richard descended the steps, opened the door and stepped inside. He ducked his head just in time to avoid hitting it on the doorframe.

The first thing that struck him was the smell. The place reeked of stale ale, sweating bodies and rancid meat fat. He drew his lips into a thin, unimpressed line. A quick scan of the public room proved it was small, low-ceilinged and dimly-lit, and that the dirty rushes covering the floor were littered with bones, some with dogs gnawing on them. Benches and tables as rough and battered as the door were packed in tightly, and almost every place at the benches was filled by coarse, roughly-dressed patrons.

Despite the earliness of the hour, a few were already slumped face-down on tables or passed out on the floor while the less intoxicated patrons stepped over them. Others sat in groups at the tables singing lewd, rude songs. Many were talking loudly and coarsely. Some, flushed red with drink, argued angrily in a dark back corner.

Sir Richard had only been standing there for a few moments when the room fell silent. It had started when the drinkers nearest the door noticed the presence of the stranger, and the wave of silence spread from there right through to the darkest, dingiest back corner like the ripple of a pebble dropped in water. Even the two drunken churls rolling around fighting on the floor stopped and got slowly and menacingly to their feet.

Every eye in the room was fixed on Sir Richard. None were friendly, but the alehouse-keeper's was most disturbing of all. He was a swarthy hulk of a man with a large scar starting at his upper lip, pulling it into a constant sneer, and going right up his cheek, and long, greasy hair falling past his shoulders. The top half that showed above the bar he stood behind was dressed in just a sleeveless vest of thick leather which showed off his huge, bulging arms and hairy barrel-chest. He glared at the strange new arrival like a bull that had just spotted an intruder in his field, and rested two ham-like fists that ended in metal-studded leather wrist guards on the bar top in front of him.

It had clearly been a mistake to head into the first inn they came across. If he and Gallagher stayed the night in this place, they would be leaving in the morning having gained a lot of new friends—a lot of very tiny biting, sucking, jumping, maddening-itch causing new friends—and having lost every last one of their possessions, right down to the last stitch of clothing on their backs.

If they were lucky, that is. If Lady Luck chose not to smile on them, they would probably never leave this cesspit of vice at all. There was bound to be a cellar they threw the bodies down.

Without taking his hard, unblinking glare off the roomful of ruffians, Sir Richard slowly backed towards the door. Never turn and run from a menacing dog, especially not a rabid fighting dog…

He felt behind for the door, pushed it open and backed out, returning the stares of the den of thieves and drunks with as good as he got. Once outside, he quickly slammed the door shut.

'So, did they have any rooms?' asked Gallagher.

'I think we ought to, ahem, continue our search for a bed for the night elsewhere. Somewhere we're not likely to be murdered in our sleep, for instance.'

'Pigs will fly before I spend a night in that alehouse…' Sir Richard grumbled to his sergeant as they exited the vile alleyway.

.17.

Entombment

THIS looks much more promising,' said Sir Richard, looking up at the narrow three-storied building he and Gallagher stood before.

Proudly looking out to sea, it was the largest and grandest building they had passed in Hamlin so far. The small bay's golden-pebbled beach was situated a stones throw from the front door, below a retaining wall lifting the street about ten feet above the seashore below. The inn had a wide set of steps leading up to its double doors, and a large window on each side of them, through which an inviting golden light shone out into the dusky street. Above the door was a carving of a mermaid with long hair cascading down over her naked torso, and below the mermaid a leafy branch was hung to notify passers-by that wine could be bought within.

'The Mermaid,' Gallagher said thoughtfully. 'Aye, it does look a more promising place.'

After tethering their horses to the rail outside, the two weary men climbed the steps and entered.

The Mermaid was much more spacious and brightly-lit than the Flying Pig, and far cleaner. A cheerful blaze crackled in the fireplace halfway along one sidewall, keeping at bay the nip in the night air that announced the onset of autumn. The wooden floorboards were swept clean and the fist-hole free tables occupied by respectable-looking patrons, who mulled over mugs of ale or talked in lively groups. There was no sign of drunken excess and the place was warm, welcoming and humming with the buzz of jovial conversation. A few inquiring eyes were turned on the strangers, but they quickly went back to their ale, wine or companions.

'Good even to 'ee, sirs!' a pretty, buxom blonde woman called to them cheerfully from behind the bar. She looked to be about forty, and was dressed in a tight, low-cut gown that showed off her ample bosom to good advantage.

Sir Richard came up to her. 'Good evening, dame.'

'How might I be able to help 'ee, good sirs?' inquired the smiling lady.

'We need lodgings for the night.'

'Aye, that I can provide. Them three rooms up on the top floor were vacated just this morn.' The lady cast an appreciative eye over the raven-haired knight. 'You look the sort of man to travel in style. I'm guessing 'ee have horses with 'ee? Tom can take them round to the stables.'

There was no doubt the buxom inn-keeper was rather impressed by her newest guest. She had a definite twinkle in her soot-paint framed eyes and was kittenishly toying with a blonde lock.

Unwilling for there to be any fault with this inn, Sir Richard quickly reassured himself that she probably flirted with most of her male customers. After all, she was a comely woman, and it would be good for business.

'Thank you, dame. Yes, we did arrive on horseback. Can you ask your man to bring our saddle bags up to our lodgings too, please?'

'Certainly can, sir, no trouble at all!'

'And I don't suppose it would be possible for me to have a bath prepared in my chamber? We've been on the road for six days, sleeping rough under the stars. I'm filthy and smell bad enough to make a sewer rat gag.'

She nodded vigorously. 'Consider it done. And if there's anything else we can get for 'ee fine gentlemen, just sing out and 'twill be seen to in a jiffy.' She pulled her eyes off the darkly handsome knight for a moment and turned to a young woman busily filling ale pots. 'Bessie, tell Tom to take the two horses hitched out front round to the stables. And 'ee heard what the two gentlemen require. Go and see to it if 'ee please! So,' she turned her wide smile back on her guests, 'from whence do 'ee come?'

'We've come from Hartfield. I'm Sir Richard Hastings, the sheriff of Chaucy, and this is my deputy, Sergeant Gallagher. We are here on a business matter.'

'And I am Merewen, the owner of the Mermaid. My, we are honoured! We rarely have such noble folks as 'ee staying at our humble establishment. But I must not be holding up such important men with my tittle-tattle. 'Ee have had a hard journey and will be wanting to get up to your chambers. Will 'ee be wanting supper later?'

'Yes, we're ravenous. We ate the last of our provisions this morning. There was only a little dry bread and salted fish left, but after we shared it with a blind beggar we came across, it did not go far.'

'I will have my fish-wife's special ready for 'ee the moment 'ee are come down. Famous for miles around, is my fish-wife's pie. Monessa!' Merewen called to a serving-maid. 'Show these two exalted gentlemen up to their lodgings!'

Scarcely had the words left the innkeeper's mouth, when a bright, rosy-cheeked girl was politely ushering the two travel-stained warriors upstairs.

After climbing two flights of stairs, she led them along a passageway. Stopping outside a door, she held it open and smiled at her tallest charge. 'This is you, my lord.'

* * * *

The lodgings really were rather nice. The chamber was small, with the ceiling sloping steeply at the front under the gabled roof, but as long as he was careful to avoid hitting his head by keeping clear of that bit, it was fine. There was a clean, neatly made bed with a very satisfactory mattress of well fluffed-up straw stuffed into a cloth case, which had proved to be quite comfortable when he tested it.

Sir Richard walked over to the window looking out to sea. The view more than made up for it being an attic room. He could see for miles across the darkening ocean and out over the little harbour down below, where Hamlin's small fishing fleet was anchored. In the far distance, he could just make out a rocky headland on either side of the entrance to Brightwater Cove.

The knight continued unlacing his shirt. Yes, it was good to have decent lodgings for once.

He turned from the window and went over to the bench he had laid his cloak, sword, dagger and doublet on, and slipped off the rest of his clothes. He had been pleased to find the round half-barrel of a bathtub was generously sized. Small bathtubs were one of his pet peeves. There was nothing worse than trying to bathe in something that was little more than a glorified puddle.

He dipped an exploratory toe into the steaming water. The temperature was nice, not too hot. He stepped in and lowered himself into the steaming water with a sigh of contentment, then leaned back and closed his eyes.

But just as he was relaxing, the door swung open and Merewen bustled in carrying a heavy, steaming pail in one hand and some small sundries in the other.

He was too startled to notice what they were. He pulled his knees up towards his chest with a speed that nearly sent a wave over the top of the tub, and quickly spread his outstretched hands over the most intimate parts of his anatomy. By God! Couldn't she at least knock?

'Here's another pail of hot water, just to get 'ee really toasty!' she announced breezily, and started pouring it into the bathtub without waiting for a response.

Merewen might have been completely comfortable with her guest's state of undress, but he hardly knew where to look. He was not used to women bursting into his private chambers without so much as a by-your-leave.

'Thank you, madam,' he stammered, looking longingly at his clothes.

'It's no trouble at all,' she beamed, setting down the empty pail. 'Now, I brought 'ee a cake of best Spanish hard soap, which I keep for special occasions. I bought a case of it from a Mediterranean trader who passed through here last year. Best olive oil, it is. And here's a drying cloth—' She produced a big length of white linen. 'And a few herbs to ease them aches of the road and make 'ee smell sweet—don't want them sewer rats fainting!'

She scattered a handful of leaves and flowers into the water, and a fresh, deliciously sweet aroma rose instantly into the steamy air.

'Thank you, madam,' he said, with a better grace. 'You run an exemplary establishment.'

'And I'll just get rid of those down to the laundry.' She scooped up the clothes lying on the bench. 'A spare shirt and hose, 'ee do have one, don't 'ee?' she asked, in response to his rather alarmed look.

He shifted uncomfortably but carefully. 'Ahem, yes I do, but there are in my saddle bags, which do not seem to have been brought up to my room yet.'

'I'll see to it right away!' said the cheerful innkeeper, heading out the door with his clothes bundled under her arm.

The energy and enthusiasm of the indomitable Merewen seemed limitless.

He regretfully watched his garments disappear. 'My gratitude, madam, has no damn limits…'

When Merewen had closed the door behind her, Sir Richard leaned back again and tried to relax, though still kept his hands close to his groin in case they were needed at short notice again. The threat of the blasé dame's return was ever-present and he was determined not to be caught out again.

A short while later, Sir Richard entered the public room of the Mermaid inn. He seated himself down on a bench beside the well-scrubbed Gallagher, at a table in the large room's front corner.

With a sigh of satisfaction, he felt his smooth chin. He had hated the dark, rough stubble that had grown in the last week. Shaving was difficult and potentially painful enough at the best of times with the thin, curved knife and poorly-leathering soap usually available. Shaving with that on the side of the road without the assistance of a mirror was just asking for a cut throat.

Merewen's expensive Spanish olive oil soap had made a nice change from the cheap mutton-fat based soap he used back home, and he had made full use of her generosity, giving his hair a good leather with it too.

The indefatigable innkeeper had not caused him any further embarrassment either, a fact for which he was eternally grateful. Instead, a blessedly demure girl had knocked (he wished Merewen would take a leaf out of her book) and, upon hearing his 'come in', had opened the door a little way, stuck her arm through the doorway and deposited his saddlebags on the floor just inside.

Sir Richard had only been seated for a few moments when a young serving-maid arrived at their table carrying a steaming plateful of food in each hand.

She set the deliciously aromatic meals down in front of them and placing a spoon next to each plate. 'Here 'ee go, sirs.'

Both men conveyed their thanks and tucked in like hungry wolves.

The food tasted just as good as the mouth-watering aroma promised. The meal consisted of a thick-crusted pie filled with a succulent mix of herring, oysters, mussels and lobster in a creamy sauce flavoured with mustard, onions and parsley, served alongside a big helping of boiled turnip.

When the men were mopping up the last of the delicious juices with the hunks of dark rye bread that accompanied the meal, their cheery, buxom hostess came bustling over. 'Was it to your liking, sirs?'

The sheriff and his sergeant both gave a hearty assent.

'Glad to hear it, glad to hear it!' Merewen beamed, coming up behind the bench they were seated at and slipping in between them. Once she had settled herself comfortably on the bench, she turned smilingly to Sir Richard, who had moved over as much as possible. 'So, are 'ee going to tell us what 'ee are doing here, or is it a secret official mission 'ee are not at liberty to talk about?'

'We are here to look for two men who were travelling over the Ragnell Pass and south along the high road over the moors,' replied Sir Richard. 'They were mounted and about half a day ahead of us.'

'But are 'ee not rather overstepping the boundary of your shire and with it the limits of your authority?'

'Strictly speaking, yes. But when I came to the sheriff of your shire with my concerns that felons were coming over the border and committing crime in Chaucy before disappearing back to the safety of this shire, he just told me I was mad, that there were no men in his shire fitting the description of the felons terrorising my people. But I know they are here. Gallagher and I managed to follow them over the border this time.'

Merewen sighed and shook her head. 'Our sheriff does naught about crime. 'E's hardly ever seen outside of Dead Man's Cove, where he has his lair. Us folks here have certainly never seen him. We're just left to fend for ourselves.'

'Is there any inhabited land further south than Hamlin?'

'Aye, there is the thin headland stretching out into the sea between our Brightwater Cove and Dead Man's round the corner. It's called the Devil's Finger, and right at the tip, just offshore, there is what 'ee could call either a very small island or a very large boulder, called Skull Rock, and on that there's a castle. It was built on the end of the headland over eighty year ago as a coastal defence in case the French tried to invade, but about thirty year back, part of the headland fell into the sea, making it into an island and pulling half the castle in with it. After that it was abandoned by its original builders because, in addition to the damage, it was now right hard to get at. The only way onto the rock is by boat, but with rogue seas and gales being so frequent around the exposed headland, it can be safely reached but a few days a year.'

Both Sir Richard and Sergeant Gallagher were listening to their hostess with rapt attention, but Merewen paused for a moment to beckon over Bessie, the girl who had brought the food over. 'These gentlemen have finished their meal.' She held the two empty plates out to the serving-maid.

Bessie took the plates off her mistress. 'Would either of 'ee like a drink?' she asked the two guests.

'I'll have a pot of mead, please,' said Gallagher.

'Certainly, and what about you, my lord?' Bessie turned to the taller man.

He had never liked ale. The thick, soup-like consistency was hardly thirst-quenching, and he felt the taste left a lot to be desired too. As for wine, he had never been able to look at it in quite the same way since Rowena had drugged (or as he would say, poisoned,) his drink at the Cunninghams' feast. The headache and grogginess had lingered for days. He had not drunk wine since.

'I'll just have some water—if it's clean.'

'Very good, sire,' she said, before hurrying off.

'You were saying about the castle at Devil's Finger, madam?' Gallagher prompted Merewen.

'Aye,' she continued, only too glad to have such a captive audience for her tale. 'It must be about ten year ago that the castle started being rebuilt. Our lads saw it from out at sea when they passed around Devil's in their fishing boats. Us Hamlin folk knew naught about it—neither who the men mending the castle were nor what they wanted it for, and no one from the castle ever comes here. Occasionally, in the light of a full moon, a ship will be spotted anchoring near the rock. But the ships never come into Hamlin's port. We were well-mystified, I can tell 'ee. Some of the old wives began to weave dark tales of the goings-on up at the rock. Round the fireplace on dark winter's nights, when the wind howls outside and the ships are tossed at sea, they tell of how the rock is inhabited by demons, witches and evil spirits. And they tell of how, every year on Allhallows Eve, every demon for miles around, some say right down to Land's End, comes flocking to the rock in dark, flapping, screeching swarms that darken the face of the moon, and how steeple-hatted witches come flying in from the four corners of the earth on broomsticks or ragwort stalks and alight atop the castle. Upon the stroke of midnight, the rock cracks open right the way down to hell and the Devil himself steps out.'

'Some tale...' muttered Sir Richard.

'And have any of the local people ever come across the

mysterious, secretive rebuilders of the castle on the rock?' asked Gallagher. 'Is there any real evidence to support this old wives' tale that the castle's new inhabitants are evil spirits?'

Merewen paused while Bessie set her guests' drinks down before them. 'Aye,' she began, when the serving-maid had gone. 'A few years back a young lass went wandering out onto the Devil's Finger looking for flowers to make herself a garland for the dance on St John's Eve. The old women had warned the young folk not to go onto the Devil's Finger, but the maid's companions said she kept finding the prettiest wild flowers growing right at the edge of the cliff-top where the sheep did not graze. In spite of her friends' pleas not to, she went further and further along the headland, uttering cries of delight as she found all manner of rare treasures for her garland. Her companions were too afraid to follow, and eventually she disappeared from view. She was never seen again. Her poor distraught father got together a group of brave young lads to search the cliffs, but no trace of her did they find. Some Hamlin folk say she fell from the cliff-top and into the sea, others say it was the demons who took her.'

'Hmmm…interesting,' Sir Richard said thoughtfully, exchanging a glance with Gallagher.

Both men were thinking the same thing. The tale of young maidens out on their own in the wilds being carried off was a familiar one.

'And there's more,' said Merewen, in a low, fearful voice. 'Last Michaelmas, one of our fishing vessels was out at the mouth of Brightwater Cove when it was caught in a sudden storm that blew up out of nowhere. The brave men fought valiantly to keep their boat away from the Devil's Finger, but it weren't no manner of use. They were wrecked on the boulders lying under the water just off Skull Rock. Five of the six fishermen on board were washed onto Skull Rock, while the sixth clung to drifting wreckage offshore. And the things he saw…' She crossed herself as her voice trailed off in a horrified whisper.

Sir Richard and Sergeant Gallagher instinctively drew in closer to her, waiting with baited breath to hear the terrible tale's ending. 'What did he see?'

'When the five poor, shipwrecked souls got up out of the raging sea below Skull Rock, some armed figures descended down from the castle and murdered them!' Merewen kept her voice at a low whisper, as if it was too horrible to say aloud. 'The sea ran red with their blood! It's said their screams can still be heard at Devil's Finger on a stormy night… No one has ever gone anywhere near the place from that day to this…'

Sir Richard stared at her in horror. 'Good God!'

The mere thought of such a heinous crime outraged him. Killing an unarmed man was against the laws of chivalry and an absolute abomination. But the tale also brought a stab of personal guilt to his conscience.

The battle of Agincourt had lasted only one hour. Despite being exhausted and heavily outnumbered, the English army of some nine hundred unmounted men-at-arms, of which he was one, and five thousand archers, had defeated the French force with a loss of only three hundred men. The huge force of heavily armoured French cavalry suffered greatly under the hail of English arrows. Their first charge had retreated and collided with the advance of eight thousand of their own men-at-arms and quickly become bogged down in the mud, where they were forced to engage in hand-to-hand combat with the British archers.

The French defeat had been total. Six thousand of them were killed in what amounted to little more than a slaughter by the English army. One thousand were taken prisoner—one thousand of the least fortunate. Afraid the prisoners might rebel, the English king had ordered them killed. But the knights and men-at-arms would not carry out the unchivalrous cold-blooded murder. Sir Richard had been appalled by the request. Unfortunately for the prisoners, the English archers had been a lot less appalled. Many of them were felons who had been forced into the army, or desperate poor men from the lowest orders who had joined for the money. They did not let an inconvenient little thing like mercy or moral scruples get in their way. The massacre had been quickly and willingly carried out.

Along with his two companions, Sir Richard gazed contemplatively into the distance with the faraway look of one dwelling deep in memories of the past which still cast long shadows over the present.

Seven thousand French warriors died in the mud of Agincourt, including much of the flower of French chivalry, and with them the newly-dubbed Sir Richard Hastings's desire to fight for his king. Henry V was a vain, glory-seeking, murdering swine who he hoped—no, *knew*—would rot in hell for eternity.

Sir Richard shared the opinion of the many knights and men-at-arms who thought killing a man with a bow was unchivalrous. There was no glory in fighting an enemy unless you could see the whites of his eyes and smell his blood as you delivered the death-blow, as you extinguished life, that prolific but precious thing filled with untold wonder.

Yes, killing from a distance was a cowardly, despicable thing and anyone who did it was a vile worm who did not deserve to be called a warrior. Disgusted with modern warfare and with King Henry, whom he thought had no business invading another peoples' country, Sir Richard had been left bitter and disillusioned mere months after finally achieving his boyhood dream of becoming a knight.

''Ee look weary,' Merewen interrupted his reminiscences at last. 'I think 'tis time I let 'ee get up to bed.'

He pulled himself back into the present. 'Yes, you're right; it's time we turned in.' He smiled at his hostess. 'Thank you,

Dame Merewen, you have been a great help.'

'It's no trouble at all.'

* * * *

A short while after the sound of seagulls and ocean waves rhythmically breaking onto the shore had alerted Rowena to the fact that she was now nearing the coast, the cart stopped for some time.

Rowena had managed to scratch a hole in a part of the enclosed cart's floor that was afflicted with dry-rot, and shortly after she saw it was dark outside, the cart lurched forward again.

It travelled a short distance, the waves becoming ever louder, and stopped again as if waiting for something. The sound of the sea crashing onto rocks was now deafening, and she could see bright moonlight falling onto the sandy ground beneath the cart.

Rowena hated the cart. It was basically a large wooden box on wheels. There was only enough room to stand up if you bent almost double, and the only comfort provided was a little straw to sit on. The two days of bumping, jerking, bone-rattling travel in the stiflingly airless near darkness, with only the constant squeaking of the wheels for company, had been sheer misery. Even when they stopped for a few hours at night, she could still hear the squeaking and rattling of the cart ringing in her ears.

Being handcuffed and set on a horse as it travelled that high mountain pass had been terrifying, but at least she had been able to take in the view and breathe clean air.

Although she would have been glad of the cart's shelter that night of the storm. Her two captors had refused to stop at the cave in the gorge, and when the storm struck, the three of them were high up on the mountain. The few stunted bushes had provided virtually no cover, and by midnight, the trickle running down the rock-face they sheltered against turned into a torrent. While the captors spent the night hanging onto their terrified horses, she had lain, bound hand and foot, in the pouring water. She had never been so cold. To have been struck down by one of the lightning bolts exploding all around had started to look like it would be a merciful release. The very memory made her shiver.

Rowena heard footsteps padding softly around to the cart's bolted door. She shrunk into the corner furthest from the door and crouched there, almost shaking as the key clicked in the lock and the bolt was drawn back.

The door screeched open and a dark, hooded figure stood there in the moonlight, his eyes glittering at her and a length of rope held taught in his hard, bony hands.

He then stepped into the cart.

She did not attempt to fight him or escape. She knew there were at least four of them. Resistance would be futile and was only likely to end in her getting hurt.

'Turn around and put your hands behind your back!' he ordered her roughly.

Rowena did as she was told.

The rope bit painfully into her wrists as it was wound tightly around them, and a cloth bag was placed over her head and knotted securely in place.

Then she was half lifted, half pulled out of the cart. The wind was strong and cold. She shivered, wishing not for the first time that she was wearing a cloak. But she enjoyed the salty freshness of the air none the less.

Having no sight was a frighteningly disorientating experience, and when she was suddenly grasped around the upper legs and swung up onto a broad shoulder, she let out an involuntary shriek and kicked her still-free feet vigorously.

A hand instantly seized her feet and bound her legs together.

Then the man carrying her started walking.

The sound of waves crashing onto rocks started to get even louder. The captive guessed that she was being carried to the edge of a cliff face with the raging sea below.

She felt a rising wave of panic. Why were they carrying her to a cliff's edge? Upon first hearing the sound of the sea, she had thought they were going to put her on a ship. But you cannot board a ship from a wave-bettered cliff. The only reason for carrying things to the edge of cliff faces overlooking the ocean was to throw them over.

Her head told her no one would haul their kidnap victim for days across country just to throw them into the sea. If they had wanted to kill her, they could easily have slit her throat and buried her deep in the forest back in Chaucy.

But her heart would not listen to the cold voice of reason.

The waves now sounded as though they were directly below, and she could feel the sea-spray falling on her bare hands. 'Please, no!' she screamed. 'I'm begging you to let me live; I'll never tell anyone what happened if you just let me go!'

She was given a rough jerk that made her scream. 'Shut your stupid mouth, bitch! You're worth more to us alive than dead.'

The rhythm of her captor's strides changed, becoming shorter and jerkier. She was almost certain he was carrying her down a steep path. A steep path down the cliffs to the sea.

Her panic subsided somewhat, but she was still fearful. The path was probably very narrow, and likely there was a steep drop down into the raging sea on one side. She kept very, very still, not wishing to cause her carrier to lose his balance and send them both plunging to almost certain death in the boiling waters or on hard rocks below.

After a heart-stopping descent, her captor's gait evened out again. His feet made hardly any sound as he moved slowly and rather laboriously across the ground. She was certain he was now walking on a sandy beach.

Then he started wading into the sea. The roar of the breakers was deafening.

Surely he was not carrying her out to a boat?

His pace slowed as he waded deeper into the sea. Rowena felt water on her skin as the salty spray being thrown up by the waves hitting her bearer soaked through her clothes.

The sea became deeper still, and water closed over her feet, then her ankles, and then was nearly up to her knees. When a big wave came along, she was drenched with water. The now-sodden cloth bag covering her face was beginning to suffocate her.

'This bag—I'm drowning in here—I can't breathe!' she gasped, starting to panic again.

'Stop your whining, woman!' came the gruff, unsympathetic response.

Rowena made a determined effort to calm herself. The more she panicked the faster her heart would beat, and the faster her heart beat the more air she would require.

To her immense and everlasting relief, the sea did not get any deeper, and a short while later she was being carried up some steps.

She was then dumped onto her feet.

The sound of voices could be heard not far off. Two men talking, she thought, but could not make out what they were saying above the roar of the sea. The rope bound around her ankles was cut, and she was marched abruptly forwards by a rough hand placed on her shoulder.

She could tell she was now inside. The sound of the waves was muffled, and her footfalls and those of the men with her sounded loudly on the stone floor and echoed hollowly around.

After being pushed along endless corridors and through numerous chambers, and dragged up countless flights of steps with a ruffian's hand under each arm, they came to a halt. There was a metallic jingling, followed by the sound of a key turning in a lock, and a heavy door creaked reluctantly open.

The cord binding her wrists was then cut, the wet bag undone and whipped off her head, and she was pushed violently from behind.

Rowena was thrown forward and landed in a heap on the cold, hard flagstones. Mocking jeers rang out as the door slammed shut behind her.

The lock clicked and someone on the other side said, 'They'll be queuing up for her,' as their footsteps and scornful laughter receded into the distance.

Rowena slowly lifted her face up off the floor. From a window high above, a small beam of moonlight cut through the darkness. When her eyes had adjusted themselves to the conditions, she saw she was in a high-ceilinged stone chamber. The roar of the sea came from far below and the mournful cry of gulls sounded through the stone walls on all sides.

The seagulls were like old friends to her. She loved hearing their cries above the sound of waves. They reminded her of her girlhood in Cornwell. One day an ancient mariner had told her how the souls of sailors drowned at sea turn into seabirds and sail the ocean currents forever. Sitting high up on the cliffs above her mother's cottage, she had spent many happy hours watching the waves rolling in and the seabirds circling, pondering the wizened old seaman's strange, haunting tale. Oh to see such happy, happy hours again…

Then a noise suddenly reached her ears.

She spun round to face the dark corner from whence it came.

In the dim light were four shadowy figures dressed in long robes.

Rowena quickly got to her feet. 'Who are you?' she cried out fearfully, shrinking against the wall.

The ghostly figures moved towards her. When they reached

the centre of the chamber, the beam of moonlight fell on their faces. They were deathly pale, wan-faced maidens with hollow, staring eyes whose vacant expression contained more than a hint of madness.

Rowena shot like a frightened mouse into the corner furthest from the ghoulish maidens. 'I said, who are you?' Her words echoed back to her, repeating over and over in hollow, ringing tones.

But still the deathly maidens advanced.

.18.

The Castle of the Skull Receives a Ludicrous Challenge

THE RHYTHMIC sound of waves lapping the pebbled shore outside had lulled Sir Richard to sleep like a soothing lullaby. He had not had a sleep that satisfying for he could not remember how long.

Riding along the seashore on Lucifer in the dawn light with his sergeant beside him, if not actually cheerful, he felt a sense of buoyant optimism that he could not explain. He was sure the castle at the end of the Devil's Finger must be the lair of the felons who dared to come raiding in his shire so boldly.

And now their day of reckoning had come. The vile bastards would not be carrying any more poor maidens off if he had anything to do with it. No. This was the pagans' twilight hour.

When they reached the end of the small beach in front of Hamlin, the two men turned their horses up onto the path leading out along the cliffs of Brightwater Cove and round to the Devil's Finger.

The flat, sandy ground provided an excellent surface, so Sir Richard urged his well-rested steed into a canter. He was eager to see the dreaded castle with its rumoured hellish occupants for himself.

As Lucifer bounded along the sandy cliff-top with rocking, perfectly controlled strides, Sir Richard revelled in the feel of a good horse beneath him, bracing, salt-laden air in his lungs and the wind in his hair.

The big horse quickly swallowed up the distance, and before Sir Richard expected it, a castle came into view ahead.

It was not a large castle, but it covered the whole top of the rock jutting up out of the boiling sea at the end of the headland. Perched precariously on its very own rock, the heavy stone fortress looked menacingly out over everything around it as if to say, 'No one enters *me* without permission'.

The Devil's Finger narrowed to less than fifteen paces wide at its tip before plunging more than two hundred feet down a sheer cliff-face to the roaring sea below. Sir Richard rode right up to the edge of the point.

Facing him at eye level from across the raging waters, he almost felt as though the castle was watching him. The two round towers set at the front corners each had a high-up window that gave it the appearance of possessing a pair of eyes, and the large iron gate in the middle that of a mouth.

The gate opened out onto what clearly used to be the causeway to the mainland, but was now ruined rubble that stretched some precarious fifty paces towards the point of Devil's Finger before plunging down into the sea. In the centre of the castle was a tall tower with a roof rising to a point. It looked like a hat sitting atop the watching castle.

It really was uncanny, and it gave him the creeps. No wonder Hamlin's old wives told such terrifying tales about the place.

A short while later, Gallagher reached the spot too and halted next to his comrade. He stared out at the place in grim silence for a good while, and then pointed a finger. 'Isn't that a flag flying from the top of that central tower?'

Sir Richard looked hard. 'Yes, I do believe you are right there, old friend.' He squinted across at it even harder. 'Yes—it's a banner; a red background with a black skull, and—' He looked some more. 'A black bat with outstretched wings above, just like this.' He produced the broach Rowena had found near the body of the murdered Thomas.

'Aye, so it is…'

When the knight fixed his eyes on the castle again, something else caught his attention. Surely that red thing had not been fluttering from the central tower's high window when he was looking at it only moments before?

'Gallagher, what's that thing blowing in the wind just below the roof of that tower?'

His sergeant shielded his eyes from the sunlight with his hand and looked intently over at the place. 'Aye, there's definitely something there… You know,' he declared firmly after another long, hard look, 'I do believe that thing flying from the window is the sleeve of the gown Rowena was wearing the day she was carried off.'

'By the Virgin's bones, you must have the eyesight of an eagle!'

Sir Richard stared so hard at the thing he started to see stars, but all he could make out was a red blur—hang on, Gallagher was right, though; she had been wearing a red velvet gown of just such a colour under that nun's habit!

After staring at the castle in silence for a good while longer, both men finally turned for Hamlin.

As Sir Richard rode away from the menacing fortress, he felt the unnerving sensation of malevolent eyes watching his departing figure intently. He kept looking back over his shoulder, but there was no sign of any human figures either on the battlements or at the windows, just the red flag with the black skull and bat flapping furiously and defiantly in the wind.

* * * *

Seated on a bench in the front corner of the Mermaid Inn, Sir Richard had been brooding thoughtfully for the past two hours over a mug of the rather nice spiced, honey-sweetened drink Merewen served. The golden late afternoon sunlight streaming in through the front window opposite him was pleasantly warm, but he still felt a chill run down his back when he thought of the castle on Skull Rock and of Rowena being held captive there.

He was now more certain than ever that it was the lair of the villains who had been terrorising Chaucy and who had carried off Rowena. But the problem was that the fortress looked to be truly impenetrable. Even an army would be hard-pressed to breach the place.

Seated opposite him across the table, Sergeant Gallagher looked equally thoughtful as he mulled over his mead, and from her station behind the bar, where she was filling pottery mugs with ale from the cask lying atop the counter, Merewen was talking animatedly to a weather-beaten old mariner.

Ever since Sir Richard and Sergeant Gallagher had told her the tale of their travels and purpose in Hamlin, and of the kidnapped Chaucy maidens, she had been relating the story to every single one of her customers. By the next day, there would not be one man, woman or child in Hamlin who had not heard the tale at least once.

The odd word of Merewen's drifted over to the seated Hartfield men. 'War heroes…young brave… (Sir Richard assumed that was himself) Will be rescuing captive maidens…taking on demons…cleansing that place of evil…'

After a good while of listening to this, the pressure started to get too much for Sir Richard. The people of Hamlin would not be talking about him in such glowing terms if he was forced to go home with his tail between his legs having done no more than stare the foul fortress in the face. And it hardly took a lion-heart to do that.

The castle seemed like an unreachable prison that was impossible to break into. He and Gallagher had talked it over all afternoon and failed to come up with any plausible plans for rescuing Rowena.

But just as he was about to get out of his seat and slink outside, an old man slipped silently onto the bench beside him. The venerable gentleman looked as old as Father Time himself, with a fuzz of snow-white hair that had the appearance of fluffy clouds encircling the summit of some ancient, sacred peak.

The old man sat beside the knight in companionable silence for a while, but at last he spoke. 'I know about a way you might be able to get inside that castle.' His voice was very feeble, and as he spoke he did not look at the knight seated beside him.

Sir Richard's attention was fixed on the old man in an instant. He looked at him like a treasure-hunter who had just unearthed a king's ransom. 'You do?'

'Aye. My trade was that of a mason. I worked on building that castle on yonder headland.'

'You did?' cried the delighted knight. 'Tell me more!'

'When we built the fort we put in shafts on the outside walls for the privies to drain down into the sea. The shafts were large enough for a man to fit through, and the rough stones mean it can be climbed. Of course, I do not know if they are still there. It was many, many years ago now, and the new occupants may have changed it when they rebuilt the damaged sides. '

'Where are these shafts situated?' Sir Richard asked intently.

'There were four of them, one on each of the castle's sides. We made them a little long, and at low-tide water was sometimes forced up them like a blowhole when the seas were particularly rough.' The old man chuckled, but had to stop when it brought on a coughing fit. 'Ahem, aye, the men garrisoned there were not too impressed by that...'

‘So are the ends of the shafts always submerged beneath the waterline?’ asked Gallagher.

‘No, when the tide is right out they used to be about a man’s height above,’ answered the white-haired old man. ‘But if you are to try to enter the castle via the privy shafts, you’ll have to be a very strong swimmer. ‘The currents are strong, and violent waves pound the rocks on all but the calmest days.’

‘I’m a good swimmer,’ said Sir Richard. ‘I served my time as a page and then squire at a castle on a small island off the coast. We boys used to race each other to see who could swim around the island fastest—it’s a wonder none of us drowned. What I’m worried about is how we can get the maidens back if we manage to find them. Is there any way of getting from Skull Rock to the headland without the need for swimming?’

‘Well,’ said the old man, ‘when the rock causeway fell down it left that area higher. When the great tides of the equinox come, for a week or so in spring and autumn it is possible to wade out to the rock. Before the Evil Ones came, young lads would wade over at low tide to hunt the seabirds nesting on the rock. But—’ he wagged an ancient, wrinkled finger, ‘if the swell is high or the sea stormy, it’s powerful enough to sweep even a strong man off the underwater causeway. Girls with water-logged dresses?’ He shook his head feebly. ‘Very risky, very risky…’

* * * *

The next morning, all alone in the early dawn light except for the crying gulls overhead, Sir Richard and Lucifer stood on the tip of Devil’s Finger and stared across at the castle on Skull Rock.

Squatting gloatingly on its rock, the castle seemed to stare back.

'If you think you're safe, sitting there in smug self-satisfaction with your thick walls and your boiling sea of a moat,' he shouted across at it, 'let me tell you something: you are wrong!'

But it just sat there silently, brooding and gloating, and gloating and brooding.

All alone out on the wind-swept headland, Sir Richard stared across at the castle for a good while longer. His eyes were fixed on the faint red blur fluttering high up on the tower.

'You are not having her!' he shouted, shaking his fist at the fortress. 'Do you hear me? Not having her!'

And with those defiant words still being carried across the boiling sea by the wind, the lone knight wheeled his black horse around and galloped off along the headland towards the rising sun.

By sundown that day, everyone in Hamlin had heard the news: the brave Chaucy warriors; Sir Richard Hastings, rescuer of damsels, slayer of dragons and doer of valiant knightly deeds; and Leofwin Gallagher of Hartfield, defender of the Faith, veteran of numerous victorious campaigns and faithful unto death, were to take on the castle on Skull Rock and its demonic occupants that very night. It had spread like wildfire after Gallagher told Merewen that morning, and it was now the talk of the town.

As for the man of the moment himself, Sir Richard Hastings, rescuer of damsels etc, he had spent most of the day trying to hide without looking like he was trying to hide.

Every time he had come down from his chamber he had been accosted by well-wishers and admirers. So up there he had stayed, venturing down only briefly at noon to feed. But now that evening was coming on, he thought it would be wise to go out for a ride, get a little fresh air and exercise to help limber up for the effort ahead and clear his mind at the same time.

He exited his room and headed for the stairs. To his relief, the only person he met on his way down was Monessa, the demure serving-maid. She just curtsied reverently and waited for him to pass with down-cast eyes, too in awe to look at the exalted hero. He managed to sneak through the Mermaid's public room and out the backdoor to the stables without exciting much attention.

His desperate desire to rescue Rowena was pressure enough without the weight of public expectation being added on. The thought that he might never see her again was so unbearable that he was careful to push it down every time it arose, which was about fifty times an hour.

If he had dwelt on what it would really be like to have the woman he hoped to marry kidnapped and carried off to some far-flung heathen land where she would be sold to some decadent prince like a pound of flour, all because he had been a careless, hot-tempered idiot who had been more interested in a spot of rust on a sword than her safety, he would not have been able to function.

Sir Richard felt deeply unworthy of all the praise that was being heaped on him by the folk of Hamlin. The way Merewen rattled on about what a great hero he was made him cringe. He had tried repeatedly to inform her that he was just a humble sheriff, a poor, lowly knight doing what any knight would do.

But had she listened? Not a chance. If anything, his indomitable hostess had gained an even greater admiration for him. Not only was the knight a fearless and honourable warrior, but a modest one too!

He almost groaned aloud at the memory.

After a quick word with Tom the stable-boy, Lucifer was soon brought around saddled and ready to ride. Sir Richard swung himself up onto the big stallion and clattered out of the stable yard.

From the street he turned left, around to the side of Brightwater Cove across the bay from Devil's Finger.

Sir Richard dismounted and walked the last half-mile home on foot to give the sweating, blowing Lucifer a chance to cool down and dry off after their long canter along the cliff tops to the head of the cove. Just before he entered the town, he stopped on the bank overlooking the pebbled beach to watch the waves dashing playfully onto the shore and the sun's orange disc slipping down into the burning sea.

The rhythm of his horse contentedly munching on the salt-laden grasses growing amongst the tough seaside daisies and the sound of waves rolling in and out was a soothing lullaby that calmed his fraught mind. The way in which Mother Nature could always be relied upon to follow the same cycle was a reassuring fixture in an often uncertain world.

He was deep in his philosophic reverie when a little voice came unexpectedly from nearby. 'Are you the brave knight who is going to vanquish the monsters?'

He could not help smiling when he looked down to find a girl of no more than ten looking gravely up at him, her hands folded neatly in front of her like a proper lady. 'Yes, I am he.'

'It is nice to meet you,' said the little lady, curtsying primly. She then held out a tiny, dainty hand to be kissed. 'My name is Daisy.'

Giving his most gracious and courtly bow, he gently took the little hand in his big one and kissed it. 'Enchanted to make your acquaintance, Mistress Daisy.'

The little damsel smiled delightedly. 'You are very gallant, Sir Richard.'

'And you are very pretty, Mistress Daisy.'

'Do you have a lady-love, Sir Richard?' asked the little lady.

A cloud crossed the dark warrior's face. 'Yes, Mistress Daisy, that I do. But she was carried off by evil men who are holding her captive in the castle on Skull Rock. See here—' He showed her the green swan pendant he wore. 'My lady-love gave this to me.'

'You must be very sad,' said the little lady. 'Will you let me be your lady until you get her back?'

Having such a tiny lady-love would be most unusual, but he could not possibly decline a gracious request from such an elegant and well-mannered little damsel. 'Madam, I accept,' he replied, bowing low.

Her smile grew even wider. 'And now I must give you something as a token of my love.' She reached into her pocket and took something out, which she then proudly presented to her knight.

He took the offered token and brought it up to examine. It was a bent, rusty hairpin. Sir Richard bowed even lower and more elaborately than before. 'I thank you for your most generous token, Mistress Daisy. I will treasure it.'

The little lady gave a regal nod of approval. 'Thank you. I will pray for your success.' And with that, she walked primly off.

He watched her go with a bemused smile on his lips. He had never met such a well-mannered and lady-like little girl before. She really was charming.

When she had disappeared from view among the houses, the knight looked down at the token in his hand again. It was a poor, worthless thing that was fit for nothing.

But while most other men would have tossed it into the sea without a second thought, Sir Richard did something different. He reached inside his doublet and carefully tucked the token into his breast pocket as though the bent, rusty pin was his most treasured possession.

* * * *

The wait was over. From his lookout high up on the cliff, Sir Richard could now see the rock emerging from the frothing, moonlit sea.

The local men had told him that when it was fully above water, it marked the tide's lowest ebb. He and Gallagher had decided they would allow themselves one hour to get into the castle, find any captives and get them down to the water, ready to cross the causeway when the tide was at its lowest.

But they had no idea how many captives there were, or even if there were any at all. A ship could have already carried Rowena far away over the watery depths—Sir Richard quickly pushed the horrifying thought away. 'Let's go.'

'Aye, 'tis time,' agreed Gallagher, moving off down the narrow cliff path after his comrade.

A group of locals who knew had pointed out the way down to the sea below the Devil's Finger. It was via the little path running down a place where the sheer rock-face gave way to steep, sandy soil.

When they reached the beach, the two men made their way along the small strip of sand which had been left high and dry by the retreating tide, right at the base of the towering cliff.

'We need to leave our swords here,' Sir Richard said to Gallagher, once they had reached the tip of the Devil's Finger.

The sergeant began to unbuckle his huge blade. 'Aye. This ledge just here on the cliff looks a good place to leave them until we return.'

One the knight had safely stowed his sword, he began unbuttoning his leather doublet. 'We need to leave behind everything heavy or likely to encumber us in the water.'

He took the bent, rusting hairpin out before putting his doublet up onto the rock ledge alongside his sword. He then unclipped the chain of Rowena's swan and threaded the hairpin on by the hole in its head, to hang alongside the green pendant.

Then the two men wordlessly waded into the rough, white-capped surf pounding the beach.

The water's bitter coldness took Sir Richard's breath away. It was frigid. If they were in the sea for any length of time the cold would sap their strength and freeze their muscles, which in the turbulent seas surrounding the point would likely spell death.

It did not take long for the freezing water to reach up to the men's chests. Every time a wave came it passed right over their heads. Soon their feet could not find any solid ground and they were forced to start swimming.

The powerful knight struck out strongly for the side of the castle on the leeside of the gale. The waters would hopefully be less rough there because the breakers would not be hitting the rocks head-on.

The currents were fearfully strong, threatening to drag the two figures, dwarfed by the gigantic cliffs and surging waves, off course and dash them on the jagged rocks rearing above the foaming sea all around. But, although the pull of the current and the buffeting of the raging sea were strong, the will and single-minded determination of the two warriors was stronger.

Ignoring burning muscles and overworked lungs that made every breath a stab of agony, the two men fought their way over to the castle.

When they reached it, they clung to the rock face at the base of the castle walls while they caught their breath for a moment.

'I feel sick,' Sir Richard spluttered. 'I've swallowed enough seawater to float a ship!'

'Aye, me too,' gasped his comrade, only just managing not to be pulled off the rock by the vigorous swell.

Sir Richard jerked his thumb towards a point a little further along the wall. 'That looks like the outlet just there.'

They had judged the tide perfectly. The large shaft up the castle wall was clear of the sea, but not so high it could not be reached.

When Sir Richard and Gallagher had recovered a little, they

swam along the rock face until they reached the drain, keeping a careful watch for the big breakers which rolled in regularly, lest they be dashed against the unforgiving stones.

Now directly beneath the opening, Sir Richard could see it was more than big enough for a man to fit in. There was a shelf of rock jutting out below that proved a very useful aid, allowing him to get his head and shoulders up into the drain.

Much to his relief, the only thing he could smell was the briny scent of the ocean and the fresh tang of sea plants, which he could feel growing thickly on the walls up to the high tide-line.

'Yes, this looks good,' he called down to the anxiously waiting Gallagher. 'It does not seem to be in use, so I'm going up.'

'Very good, sir. Shout out when you reach the top.'

It was pitch black inside the vertical tunnel and the sides were covered with slimy algae, but as the old man in the Mermaid had promised, there were enough grooves and pieces of stone jutting out to provide footholds. The going was desperately slow, but little by little the determined warrior pulled himself up by feeling for holds in the darkness.

By the time Sir Richard thought he must be nearing the top, he could feel sticky blood covering his smarting hands and shoulders where the stones had grazed off the skin.

His body was screaming out for relief when his hands suddenly met a wooden board blocking any further progress above.

Knowing that this must be the top, he mustered all his remaining strength for one final effort. Freeing his hands by bracing his back against one wall and his legs on the one opposite, he pushed the board with all his might.

It felt soft and crumbly with dry rot, but although it gave slightly, it would not yield.

Letting out a roar of furious desperation, the knight punched it violently. His fist went straight through, showering him with a cloud of rotten wood crumbs that he felt stick to his sweat-covered body. Several more punches and he was through.

A dim light shone from the opening, and when he dragged his agonised body out of the shaft, he found himself in a small room with a cross-shaped opening in the outside wall, designed for defenders to fire arrows through. The beam of silver moonlight shining in through the arrow-slit pierced into the dark interior and cast a perfect silver cross on the stone floor.

The bloodied knight had barely taken in these new surroundings when he suddenly collapsed on the floor, and the world went dark.

.19.

Hope is Faithful

FROM her lookout high up in the tower, Rowena scanned the foaming moonlit sea below. She had been intently watching two shapes bobbing in the raging waves as they moved closer to the rock of her prison fortress, trying to decide if they were seals, wooden logs or men. The sea was so violent that they surely could not possibly be men who were making their way through the waters so determinedly, yet the figures really did seem to have arms.

Then an especially large wave passed over them.

The unhappy prisoner rubbed her eyes in a vain attempt to sharpen her sight, but hard as she looked at the spot in the frothing surf where the two figures had been before, she could no longer see anything there.

They must have been seals after all.

She turned her eyes from the sea and let out a long-held breath that was part sigh, part sob. The dark prison, with its lone, barred window set high up in the wall, was becoming unbearable. The long days and even longer nights of her captivity had started to meld into one, and she had lost count of the number of days that had passed since she was carried off by the Evil Ones, for that was what she had named her captors in the absence of them revealing their identities or intentions.

The only break in the dreadful, fear-filled monotony was when the daily meal of stale bread and distastefully under-done turnips was hastily thrust in through the bars of the gate. However much she pleaded, the jailer who brought the food would not tell her what fate lay in store. His only answer was always a cruel, smugly knowing leer that was worse than any words.

With her hands closed around the bars and her face pressed up against their cold, unforgiving hardness, the young captive looked out over the raging seas once more.

The strong, salt-laden wind coming off the sea cooled her hot cheeks and dried the tears of a heart overflowing with sadness as it yearned to be free. Free like the seabirds circling overhead as they rode the buffeting air currents unhindered, voicing cries which were no longer simply meaningless shrieks to the captive maiden, but cries of hope, of the hope that one day she would again be free like they were.

Rowena never thought she would say it, but she desperately missed Chaucy and all the new friends she had made there. And she never thought she would have reason to say this: Sir Richard had been right. He might not know much, but he did know about fighting, warfare and ambushes. She should have listened when he said it was a hare-brained idea.

But there was no point in such bitter regrets now. Sir Richard was a brave man and there was no doubt he would have given chase. But no mortal could possibly get into this prison.

She leaned against the cold iron bars and closed her eyes. She was beyond human help now.

But the young woman was disturbed after only a short while by the cry of an unfamiliar bird coming from very near. She opened her eyes to find herself face-to-face with a large raven that had perched on the window ledge of her prison.

The bird's boldness was astonishing; what could it possibly be doing?

Not wishing to frighten the strange visitor into flying away, Rowena kept still. 'Greetings friend,' she murmured softly.

'What is it you want?'

The black-feathered bird cocked its head to one side and looked at her inquisitively with dark, beady little eyes. Then the raven opened its beak. 'Caw, caw, caw!' it called, louder this time.

The puzzled captive frowned at the raven clinging so bravely to her window ledge in the buffeting gale. It ducked the neat little head again, and still the beady black eyes were fixed questioningly on her.

'Are you lost?' she asked quietly.

The head was ducked more violently this time and accompanied by a ruffled flapping of the black wings and a 'Caw! Caw! Caw!' That was almost a screech.

She chuckled. 'A fine, sleek-feathered raven like you does not get lost, does it?'

It bobbed its head and blinked.

'Yes, that's right!'

The raven spread its wings and threw back its head. 'Caw!' it cried again, and shot a look at the watching maiden.

'Alright, perhaps you would like me to join you, so here:

I weep for you, I wait for you,
I yearn for your strong embrace and your boundless grace.
And when the west wind blows,
I say tell me pray, tell me pray,
Have you my true love seen this day?
O have you seen those angel eyes?

Another young feminine voice joined the song from the darkness below:

When my feet are bleeding and I cannot take
Another step on this weary road,

And the moon lifts her pale silver face above the mountaintop,
I say tell me pray, tell me pray,
Have you my true love seen this day?
O have you seen those angel eyes?

The two maidens were joined by a third young singer:

When I reach the dark waters of the silent lake and can go no further,
And the wild swans pass overhead,
I say tell me pray, tell me pray,
Have you my true love seen this day?
O have you seen those angel eyes?

A fourth and a fifth joined:

When the sun is asleep, in my heart a ceaseless vigil I keep,
And when the velvet darkness steals o'er the land,
I say tell me pray, tell me pray,
Have you my true love seen this day?
O have you seen those angel eyes?
For I wait for you, I weep for you,
I yearn for your strong embrace and your boundless grace.

Rowena thought she heard one more voice join the last chorus, a far-off deep, masculine voice.

And when the five maidens had finished their song, the male voice continued, coming ever nearer. The song drifted up to Rowena, still perched on her window ledge and looking at the now contentedly-silent raven. The voice seemed strangely familiar.

Rowena could scarcely believe her ears. Surely it could not possibly be? It just had to be a dream…

O she's as fair as a flower, she's as fresh as a daisy in the dawn,
O she's bright as a morning in May!
And when I saw her tripping down the lane,
When I saw her skipping down the road,
Singing tra la la lee, O sweet diddle-dee!
I called to her, I called to her: 'pretty sweeting,
O darling, darling dear!
Won't you come and be my lady fair?
I will lend an ear to your every care
And kiss you every day of the year!
Do you hear, pretty sweeting,
O do you hear, darling dear!'

The cheerful voice was now right at the prison gate, and the dearest, most hoped-for sight came into view of the delighted and incredulous young captive, who could only stare in open-mouthed amazement with eyes that glistened with tears of joy.

Sir Richard's shirt was so badly torn it revealed far more than it covered, and he was smeared in dirt, slime and blood from head to foot. But in spite of all that, he had the biggest grin on his triumphant face she had ever seen him wear. He leaned against the barred gate and linked his arms through as he continued singing to the speechless maiden perched on her high ledge.

Said she: 'O sir, I am going to the fair
To sell my ribbons and my laces,
So nay, nay, nay to your all graces and your love-sick faces'.
O fie, fie, fie!
She's as fair as a flower, she's as fresh as a daisy in the dawn,
O she's bright as a morning in May!
And she left me standing in the road all alone
While she went tripping and skipping on her way to the fair,
Singing tra la la lee, O sweet diddle-dee!

When the laughing knight had finished his song, he held out his arms to Rowena. 'I have just nearly killed myself getting up to your high tower, so aren't you going to give me something more gratifying than that stare?'

'Oh Sir Richard!' she cried, jumping down and running over to him. 'I can't believe you are really here!'

He clasped his fingers around the hands she had placed in his. 'That's better.'

'Never, never have my eyes met a more longed-for sight! I can see you have braved many terrible dangers and hardships to get this far; you are the truest and bravest of heroes!'

He gave a satisfied but rather embarrassed nod. 'You are very kind, but you have not been rescued yet, so you may want to reserve such lofty praise for later.'

She frowned worriedly at this reminder. 'The key to this gate is with the jailer—I don't know where he is.'

'That does not matter because—' he paused for a moment while he reached into his shirt, 'I have this.' He held a rusty, bent hairpin aloft.

Her frown deepened. 'If that is all you have to offer, I think you were very wise to advise me not to praise you too soon.'

'Ah, but you do not know all of my tricks yet,' came the smug reply.

Her rescuer proceeded to insert the rusty hairpin into the lock while she looked on with an unflatteringly doubtful expression.

'I'm beginning to think the ordeal has sent you mad. What *are* you doing?'

'Just a little trick a thief once showed me…' he muttered, fiddling intently with the rusty pin.

After a few breathlessly anxious moments, there was a sharp click from within the lock and the door swung open.

'Sir Richard, you are a genius!' she cried, flinging her arms around his neck.

'Ow!' yelped her rescuer, taking an unexpected step backwards.

She took a step back of her own and frowned up at him. 'What?'

'It's my shoulders,' he gasped, wincing painfully. 'They got badly bruised and grazed when I climbed up the sewer.'

She dusted herself down distastefully. 'Argh, you could've warned me!'

'No, it was disused—but thank you for your kind sympathy.'

Rowena could not help laughing at his sulky look. 'Sorry, dearest! You are quite right.' She stood on tip-toe and tried to place a kiss on his cheek, but could not reach high enough. 'Oh wretched shortness!'

He lowered himself until his face was level with hers and meekly offered her a sweat and grime-streaked cheek.

A firm kiss was unreservedly delivered. 'There.'

Looking more than satisfied, Sir Richard scanned the dark room. 'Are there any more captives with you in here?'

'Yes—' She looked around in puzzlement. 'They were right here just before you arrived...'

A pale, thin maiden dressed in a dirty blue gown stepped fearfully forward from a dark corner. 'Who...are you?'

Sir Richard turned to the lady and bowed. 'I am Sir Richard Hastings, the sheriff of Chaucy. I have come to release the captives held here.'

With her eyes glowing with a strange radiance, the pale, waif-like young lady walked slowly up to the dark knight and reached out a pitifully thin hand to touch him. When her hand met the resistance of his chest, she lifted her eyes up to him in wonder. 'So you are real after all...' she whispered.

He gave a sympathetic but bemused smile. 'I assure you, sweet lady, I am most definitely real.'

But the pale lady continued staring up at him as though he was the most magical being she had ever set eyes on. 'A brave knight…a rescuer…' She breathed the words uncertainly, as though she was saying them for the first time and hardly dared to hope that they were true.

'Yes, Celestria, it really is true,' said Rowena, who then turned to the corner from whence the blue-clad lady had come. 'Isolda, Mary, Nimue, it is safe to come out!' she called to the three pale figures huddled fearfully in the darkness.

Another blue-clad brunette maiden who looked almost identical to the pale, thin Celestria emerged hesitantly, closely followed by a gaunt but rather more robust-looking maiden dressed in the simple brown woollen gown of a peasant, and with a long, thick braid falling down her back.

'Nimue, where are you?' Rowena called impatiently.

A tiny whimper came from the darkness, where a shadowy shape huddled on the floor was just visible. 'I c-can't!' a small girlish voice sobbed weakly.

'Come, we need to go!'

'No, I can't do it! You go on without me. I will only slow you down,' came the weak, pathetically fearful wail.

'I'm afraid the poor child has been in here for longer than the rest of us, and has grown terribly frightened of the thought of leaving the dark certainty of these four walls,' Rowena explained to the puzzled Sir Richard.

'I see.' He walked over to the whimpering shadow cowering in the dark corner. 'Don't be afraid, little lass,' he said gently to the trembling figure, crouching down beside her.

The tiny shape, a musty blanket drawn tightly around her, shrunk further into the dark corner. 'I'm too weak and too frightened. I'm not coming, I'm not!' she sobbed.

He laid a firm but gentle hand on her arm, which he was shocked to discover was almost skin and bone. 'You are coming with me and that is that. I came here to release all the ladies held captive in this evil place, and I'm not leaving here until I have.'

'But I'm not a lady,' she whimpered. 'I'm just a poor, orphaned beggar-maid who nobody cares about. If you're not burdened by me you will all have a better chance of getting out of this prison alive.'

He gave her blanket an insistent tug. '*I* care about you and I mean what I said. Now come!'

'No!' she wailed tearfully.

'Very well, if you want it like that.' And with that, he caught hold of her and lifted her up as though she weighed little more than a feather.

The girl immediately started kicking and screaming, but was quickly silenced by Sir Richard clapping a large hand firmly over her mouth. 'Hush! You'll alert the guards and get us all killed.'

The painfully thin girl, who looked no more than twelve or thirteen now that Sir Richard had brought her into the moonlight, put up a feeble but determined struggle against her unwelcome rescuer, wriggling and kicking like a wild cub. But she was no match for the powerful knight.

Sir Richard carried her off with ease, and soon he and the four other pale, bedraggled maidens were making their way cautiously down the winding staircase.

'Do you know the way out of this labyrinth of a fortress?' Rowena whispered to him as she followed close behind.

'I think so,' he whispered back. 'Most castles have a fairly similar layout of the keep and main gate. But I would have had a hell of a trouble finding the way up to your prison tower if I hadn't heard you singing.'

'Yes, I was singing to a raven.'

He stopped and turned to look at her incredulously, but seemed to change his mind and started moving forward again without saying anything.

What was another ridiculous-sounding thing when so many had already been come across on this strange and perilous adventure?

Little Nimue had stopped her struggling and was now calmly letting Sir Richard carry her in his strong arms. Only an occasional whimper betrayed her presence beneath the blanket.

When the grimy fugitive band reached the bottom of the stairs Sir Richard raised his hand, silently signalling everyone to halt. He then pointed through the doorway and held a finger to his lips.

The jailer.

Rowena had been dreading this moment. But when she listened carefully, she thought she could hear snores.

Rowena and the four other maidens nodded to show they understood, and then moved off as silently and stealthily after their rescuer as they could.

The stairway opened out into a large hall with bare stone walls and a high, partly caved-in roof. And sitting on a large block of fallen stone leaning his back against the broad pillar behind him was a large, balding man with a scraggly beard, snoring like a pig. A guttering tallow candle sat on the floor beside him and an evil-looking club rested near his hand.

Keeping close to the walls to stay in the shadows as much as possible, Sir Richard led the fearful maidens slowly into the hall.

Creeping quietly along past the noisily snoring jailer was a painful ordeal. Rowena could hear her heart pounding so loudly she was almost afraid the jailer would hear it, and hardly dared to breathe lest it wake him.

The fugitives had got halfway down the hall when there was a sudden choking cough from the waif in Sir Richard's arms. He clapped a hand over her mouth while everyone froze instantly, their eyes fixed on the slumbering jailer.

The regular rhythm stopped with an abrupt grunt, and the

jailer twitched violently. To the horror of the escaping captives, who all held their breath in agonised, terrified suspense, there were a few more grunts and twitches, and then the vile figure started to blink rapidly.

Rowena took the hand of Celestria, who stood directly behind her, and prepared for a mad dash to the door at the end of the hall. But just as the jailer's eyes looked about to open, the hall was suddenly plunged into total darkness.

The wick on the tallow lamp had burnt out! Rowena wanted to laugh with joy. While the jailer uttered foul oaths and curses as he crashed around looking for a new light, Rowena offered silent thanks for this miraculous delivery.

Sir Richard took her hand and started leading her forwards, feeling his way along the wall in the blackness. With their hands joined, the rest of the maidens followed in single file.

The escaping band moved as quickly as they could in the darkness without making too much noise, desperate to get out before the cursing, bumbling jailer could light another candle. Quickly reaching the opening on the opposite side, Sir Richard dived through it, pulling the maidens behind him.

Rowena suddenly found herself outside in the silver moonlight, high up on the battlements with a strong wind tugging at her hair and gown.

Sir Richard ran along to the tower at the end, where, breathing hard, he stopped and turned to the even more breathless ladies. 'That foul swine will be onto us so we must get out fast. But there is one last thing I need to do. Watch Nimue for a moment, will you,' he ordered Rowena briskly, setting the girl down beside her.

The knight then kicked in the wooden door leading into the tower in front of them, and emerged a few moments later carrying a large barrel. He set it down and prised its lid up with the blade of his dagger.

When he lifted the lid off the barrel, the pungently awful smell of pitch filled the air. Looking on in bewilderment, Rowena covered her nose with the wide sleeve of her nun's habit.

Much to the surprise of his audience, Sir Richard lifted the open barrel high above his head and tossed it off the battlements and onto the rush-thatched roof below. His purpose quickly became clear when he seized hold of the legs of a burning brazier lighting the ramparts and threw it after the pitch.

Rowena watched with great satisfaction as the pitch splashed over the roof instantly caught fire and started burning fiercely. She was mesmerised by the sight of the bright orange tongues of flame licking devilishly around the barrel and dancing demonically over the thatch in fiendish delight.

Someone shook her shoulder. 'Rowena, I said we must go!'

'Oh,' she murmured, slowly realising that Sir Richard was urgently trying to usher the four maidens towards a flight of steps while he held Nimue in his arms.

She quickly came to her senses and hurried to the steps, which ran diagonally down the side of the castle walls to a small door halfway up. Celestria, Isolda and Mary were already hurriedly descending the narrow stone steps, keeping close to the wall and away from the sheer drop into the boiling sea far below. When Rowena started down after them, Sir Richard followed close behind her, holding Nimue tightly as she whimpered fearfully at the dizzying drop on one side of the rail-less flight of stairs.

When everyone was safely down, the five maidens looked expectantly at Sir Richard, wondering why he was looking over the terrifying plunge into the dark foaming waters below rather than getting on with breaking through the door blocking their progress.

He set Nimue down and shook his head. 'No, not that way.'

Rowena frowned. 'What then?'

He pointed to the sea far down below. 'That way. The sea is

deep enough here for us to jump.'

There was a collective gasp of horror from the five young damsels. Nimue instantly disappeared beneath her blanket and shrunk down to the floor as far back from the sea as she could.

'But Isolda and I can't swim!' gasped Celestria.

Rowena peered fearfully over the edge, not daring to go too close lest she should fall. 'I can swim a little, but the sea is so rough I will surely drown!'

'I can't swim neither,' added Mary, looking at Sir Richard as though he had just suggested she cut her own head off.

'But I can,' answered an unperturbed Sir Richard. 'And so can Sergeant Gallagher, who is waiting for us down below. Who is going to go first?'

The four visible maidens shrunk back from him and shook their heads.

Sir Richard looked at the tallest damsel. 'Mary, I think you should go first. Gallagher will pull you around to the causeway. It is just under the gatehouse, so it is only a short way.'

Rowena could see an orange glow coming from above the battlements, and smoke was starting to sting her eyes and throat. The fire might have been an excellent diversion, but it meant there was no way back now. Drowning in the sea was better than burning to death or being killed by vile, merciless villains or worse still, being imprisoned in a tiny cell for the rest of her life slowly rotting—if she didn't go mad first.

There was nothing for it.

She stepped forward. 'I will go.'

'Excellent. Who else is willing?'

Mary stepped forward. 'I also will go.'

But when he turned to the twins, the sight was more concerning. Isolda was sitting on the steps crying while her sister tried to comfort her.

'Celestria?' he prompted urgently.

Celestria shook her head. 'Isolda says she can't do it, and I am not leaving her. I'm sorry; we will have to take our chances with our captors.'

'Perhaps if you go first they may be more willing to follow?' Rowena suggested quietly to Sir Richard.

But he shook his head firmly. 'If I do that and they still will not jump, there will be nothing I can do.'

'But if they refuse to jump you cannot do anything anyway.'

He smiled grimly. 'Yes I can; I can throw them over.' And with that he turned to Mary, who stood at the edge, her chin defiantly tilted up in a firm determination not to look down at the boiling waters below. 'Brave girl, but you need to get that heavy gown off,' he said to her matter-of-factly.

Without saying a word, Mary undid her heavy woollen dress and cast it off, revealing a light, sleeveless shift.

He frowned at the long skirt of Mary's under-dress. 'Do you mind if I make a slight alteration to your garment?' he asked, unsheathing his dagger.

With her eyes still fixed on the horizon, the maiden gave a quick nod.

Sir Richard took hold of her skirt just above the knees and slit a hole in it with his dagger, then tore it all the way around until it fell away. 'That's better.' He looked down over the edge. 'Gallagher,' he shouted down, 'the first one's coming!'

The other maidens covered their eyes or looked away in horror, waiting for the splash from down below. After what seemed like an eternity, a faint, faraway splash sounded above the roar of the sea.

'Has she survived?' Isolda gasped, finally daring to peep through her fingers at Sir Richard, who crouched at the edge peering intently down.

There was an anxious pause.

'Yes, yes there she is—she's surfaced now, thank God!' He

got to his feet looking deeply relieved. After taking a few more moments to make sure Gallagher had dragged Mary to safety, he turned away from the edge and looked to Celestria and Isolda, who was still crying quietly. 'One of you ought to go next.'

Celestria locked her arms around her sister and raised her sharp blue eyes defiantly. 'Don't look at us! We are not doing it.'

Without saying a word, he immediately walked over to where Nimue was huddled against the wall cowering under her musty blanket. He whipped the rag off and threw it into the sea.

The waif, dressed only in a thin, tatty slip, was a pitiful sight to behold as she trembled and whimpered. 'No, no…' She shook her head fearfully as she looked up at the tall knight in terror.

He knelt down beside her and put his hands on her tiny shoulders. 'Now listen to me, little one. You need to be brave; do you think you can do that?'

She sniffed miserably and studied his intently serious face in silence. Then, much to the surprise of the watching Rowena, Celestria and Isolda, the wane-faced girl slowly nodded, looking up at the knight with total faith.

He smiled. 'Brave girl! I'm proud of you.'

'Ain't nobody who's ever been proud of me,' Nimue beamed shyly.

As the waif put her thin arms around his neck and held him tightly, Sir Richard looked over her shoulder at Isolda, seated on the steps behind. 'Are you still sure you want to be the damsel who doomed herself and her sister to a hellish life of slavery and degradation because she was too afraid to take the leap?'

Isolda buried her head in her hands, and did not answer.

Celestria glared angrily at Sir Richard. 'Can't you see you are upsetting my poor sister?'

Clearly biting back a hot-tempered response, he turned from the twins and looked at Nimue. 'Come, little one, it's time you left this vile prison.'

The child smiled weakly and nodded.

'Will you jump?'

'Is there anyone at the bottom waiting to catch me?' she asked falteringly.

'Yes. My brave comrade Faithful unto Death Gallagher is waiting. He never fails.'

'If he is like you, I will jump.'

He is like me but, much, much more heroic.'

Sir Richard had led little Nimue to the edge. There, she showed no sign of fear as she braved the buffeting gale and dizzying height. And without further ado, she jumped.

Rowena waited with baited breath for the splash, but none came. 'Is Nimue safe?' she asked the tensely watching Sir Richard.

He pushed away the hair blown into his face by the gale, and nodded. 'She's safe, but we are not.' He pointed up to the sky above the battlements, which was glowing brightly and streaked with showers of orange sparks. 'We must get off this doomed castle before it's too late.'

Rowena could see flames shooting above the walls overhead, and the heat of the fire was starting to reach down to where they stood. Then she thought she could hear something besides the howling of the gale and the roar of the sea.

She listened carefully. It was the sound of shouting men coming from above. 'Richard, there are men coming this way; we have to go!'

'Yes, but I'm not leaving Celestria and Isolda behind.'

'You two go,' said Celestria from her seat on the steps. 'Save yourselves and leave us!'

Sir Richard spun around to face her, the bright glow of the flames glittering in his dark eyes. 'And tell your father that I rescued every damsel except his own two daughters? I don't think so! That man has been hounding me ever since you and your sister were carried off, lady. He accused me of being a lazy and incompetent sheriff and seriously questioned my honour. So I hope you will forgive me, madam, if I am not willing to accept your refusal to be rescued. I'm not returning to Chaucy without you and your sister!'

Rowena was coming dangerously close to thinking the reluctant ladies ungrateful brats. Her eyes were running from the stinging smoke, and the sound of shouts, footsteps and clanging weapons sounded from directly overhead.

She leaned in close to the fraught Sir Richard. 'If I get hold of Celestria,' she whispered, 'and at the same time you seize Isolda, you might be able to throw her over the edge before Celestria can stop you.'

He was tensely silent for a moment, then gave a quick nod. He waited while Rowena moved in behind Celestria and crouched down.

He then sauntered casually up to the seated Isolda.

She shrunk back fearfully. 'I said, no!'

He smiled and knelt before her on one knee. 'Yes, I heard what you said. You are not willing to jump into the sea.'

She relaxed a little. 'I am glad, for I was growing tired of your bullying!'

His smile turned slightly wolfish. 'I must say, sweet lady, you are remarkably like your father; very strong-minded.' And then he gave Rowena a quick nod and had Isolda by the upper arms in an iron-fisted grip before she could even think of screaming.

At the same moment, Rowena threw her arms around Celestria and held her down with all her might. The screams of the captured Isolda were blood-curdling, but before Rowena could make out what was happening, Sir Richard and Isolda had disappeared over the edge.

Celestria's struggles and screams were even more violent than her sister's. She leapt to her feet, dragging Rowena with her, and rushed to the edge. Without hesitating, Celestria dived off after her sister.

Rowena was pulled to the edge before she could disentangle her arms from Celestria. She was so overbalanced that she teetered on the edge for a few terrifying moments before starting to fall.

The wind whistled around her as she plummeted down. Then her body was hit by a stinging slap and plunged into dark, frigid water. Encumbered by her own saturated dress and the heavy, voluminous nun's habit she was still wearing on top, she tried desperately to surface. But to no avail.

She felt herself being dragged deeper and deeper into the cold depths. Her lungs quickly became so starved of air she could not prevent herself taking in large gulps of salty water.

It was better to drown than to rot in a prison cell forever. At least she had tried her hardest, and that was the greatest thing anyone could say…

Rowena felt her life starting to slip away. Her consciousness dimmed. She was floating in a dreamy, languid state surrounded by warmth, light and colour flowing all around.

Ah…the pain was going…earthly life was slipping away…

.20.

The Face of Evil

THAT hurt. And why was someone shaking her? Rowena felt another stinging slap on her cheek. It had been nice where she was. Why couldn't they just leave her be?

She slowly became aware of a familiar sound above the muffled roar of the sea: 'Celestria, you thankless mare, if you've killed Rowena I'll never forgive you!'

It was Sir Richard, angry and shouting. Oh dear…

She was violently shaken again. 'Rowena and I were going to be married, you insolent, ungrateful b—'

She groaned.

Large hands cupped her head instantly. 'Rowena, don't you dare leave me! Do you hear?'

A wave of sickeningly salty seawater washed up her throat, bringing on a violent coughing fit.

Sir Richard's face swum hazily before her eyes. 'Rowena, thank God—I thought Celestria had killed you!'

Still splattering, she pulled herself onto her side and regurgitated a tide of seawater while firm hands steadied her.

As consciousness dawned, she realised she was now lying on the ground high up on the cliff. The prison castle was directly opposite across the chasm, with bright flames jumping high above its blackened battlements in fiendish glee as they hungrily devoured its interior.

Memory came flooding back. 'Is—is everyone safe?'

Sir Richard gathered Rowena up and pressed her to himself in a tight, watery embrace. 'Yes, everyone is safe,' he murmured hoarsely, gently rocking her and stroking her wet hair.

Rowena felt so very cold. Her limbs were numb and heavy, almost death-like. But from his skin there came a faint warmth, and the beat of his heart sounded in the ear she rested on his breast. The loud, insistent rhythm of pulsing blood, of pulsing life. No, it was not time to go yet…

The strong arms enfolding her shivering body were shaking, but not from cold. 'Don't ever leave me again, my love.'

She lifted her head and was about to answer, but something over his shoulder caught her eye. On the ruins of the causeway which had once linked the castle to the Devil's Finger stood a human figure, darkly silhouetted against the burning castle behind. He walked up to the very edge of where the causeway plunged abruptly into the sea, and stared straight at her. His long black cloak blew out behind him as the howling storm tugged at it furiously, and she almost could feel his eyes boring into her.

'Sir Richard, who is that?'

The knight turned his head to look. And an instant later he leapt to his feet like a stung lion, strode to the very end of the Devil's Finger and stopped right at the very edge of the chasm.

With his shirt hanging off him in ribbons and his black hair being whipped by the gale, the dark knight stared intently across at the other man. 'De Wintore!' he finally bellowed, above the roar of the sea far down below and the howl of the storm.

Far out to sea, dark clouds had blotted out the stars and lightning forked across the sky. Rowena pulled herself to her feet and walked over to stand beside Sir Richard.

He did not appear to notice her presence. He only had eyes for the dark, bat-like figure standing in front of the burning castle.

'It's you, isn't it, de Wintore?' he shouted again. 'You bastard!'

'Yes, it is I,' came the sinister figure's reply over the roaring storm, which was growing more violent by the moment. 'How I was enjoying our little game; hearing the reports of how you were running yourself ragged looking for the kidnappers—though I had hoped you would have been lynched by an angry mob of your own people by now. It was I who hired those thugs to worry the peasants. It was I who had your old clerk bribed into being seen about with them so Chaucy folk would think the kidnappings were the doings of their own sheriff. But the Lothbury thugs proved even more stupid than Chaucy folk, killing that odious clerk of yours because the fool wanted more money. Satan's tail, all the little fool had to do was loiter about a stinking hamlet while my thugs ruffled the locals up a bit! Those twits ruined everything by killing the fool, and they didn't even bury him properly. But I will see you wrecked yet, Hastings!'

The change which had come over Sir Richard was frightening. Lit by the silver moonlight and white lightning flashes, tattered shirt swirling and hair tossed wildly by the gale, he looked like a ghostly apparition which had arisen from the grave to seek its murderer.

'Why won't you just leave me be? You pagan swine!' he shouted.

'You killed my sister Morgana and destroyed the honour of the de Wintore name!' screamed the black shape on Skull Rock. 'I swore I would torment you until you wished you were dead, and by Satan, I will! If I'd known that that nun was your lady-love, I would have cut off her head and displayed it on the castle walls so you could watch the gulls feasting on her! As long as there is breath in my body failure and dishonour will dog you, and death and misery will be the lot of anything you love!'

The thunder clouds were creeping ever closer, lighting up the dark waters with white flashes of lightning and adding booming thunderclaps to the voice of the raging storm.

Sir Richard shook his fist furiously and looked so desperate to get his hands around the other man's neck that Rowena seized hold of his arm, half fearing he might try to jump across the chasm. 'Fight me like a man!' he bellowed.

'You don't deserve to die a hero's death in battle!' replied the bat-like figure. 'I'm going to torment you until you kill yourself and lay buried outside the churchyard in a sinner's grave like my sister, while your black soul burns in the hottest corner of hell for eternity!'

Rowena felt deeply afraid. The sinister figure that was prepared to trade threats and insults while his castle went up in flames was terrifying. And Sir Richard had a look of total recklessness as he stood right on the precipice and glowered across with eyes that were pools of black fury glittering with the reflections of flames and the lightning forks flashing across the midnight sky.

'You won't respond to my challenge because you are a cowardly worm!' shouted the dark knight. 'The de Wintores are a family of traitorous, pagan vermin who are too frightened to crawl out of their stinking holes and fight! If you refuse to give me satisfaction, I'll hunt you down and kill you! Do you hear me? You will not be refusing to stand up and face me like a man when I've got my blade at your scrawny, bastard throat!'

The dark shadow on the ruined causeway was almost hopping with rage now. 'How dare you insult the de Wintore name!'

'Talk is cheap; prove me wrong!'

'I'm going to kill you, Hastings!' came the scream from across the raging sea. 'And when I've done that, I'm going to ravish your sister and that whore with you, and sell them to a heathen brothel in Turkey!'

Sir Richard moved even closer to the cliff edge. 'Meet me in the lists at the Shrewsbury's tournament on St Valentine's day! Two men will enter, only one will leave alive.'

Rowena caught her breath in horror. 'Richard, no!'

'I'm not running like a coward any longer,' he replied quietly. 'I bring misery on everyone around me through this. It ends now.'

The hopping, fist-waving figure had gone still. 'I accept your challenge, murdering dog! My sister knew the day of her death and so now can you. On St Valentine's day, 1431, Sir Richard Hastings dies!'

Rowena pulled his arm in a desperate attempt to turn him around to face her. 'No, Richard; you can't do this!'

She might as well have been trying to pull a stone fortress around to face her. He did not move. 'If I must die so that those I love can live, so be it.'

'No, please don't do this; I'm begging you!'

But her useless words were swallowed by the howling storm unheeded by any human. Sir Richard's eyes were locked onto his long-time nemesis with a fury that was deaf to any argument, reason or plea.

* * * *

After spending the night at the Mermaid Inn, Sir Richard, Sergeant Gallagher and the five rescued maidens were ready to leave Hamlin.

It was early morning and the first rays of the sun were streaking the clear eastern sky. Merewen was very sad to bid her guests good-bye. She gave both of the Hartfield warriors many warm embraces, tender kisses and heartfelt good wishes for health and happiness.

The whole town had turned out to watch them go. Many of the other citizens also stepped forward to pass onto the two

Chaucy men their undying gratitude for vanquishing the hellish castle on Skull Rock. It had cast a dark shadow of evil and fear over them for many a long year.

By the time the travellers were finally on their way, Merewen, Bessie and Monessa's handkerchiefs were soaked with tears. They waved and called out goodbyes until the band of Chaucy folk had disappeared from sight.

'Ain't never going to forget that Sir Richard as long as I live,' sniffed Bessie.

'Aye, me neither,' said an equally tearful Merewen. 'He were a proper knight like you hear of in the tales of King Arthur.'

'True English heroes with hearts of oak,' agreed Monessa.

* * * *

The next day at noon, the houses and streets of Hamlin were empty. But the high cliffs of the Devil's Finger thronged with people. Every one of the town's inhabitants walked onwards to the smoking, blackened stones that had once been the castle of the Evil Ones. The heat of the flames had been such that many of the castle's once-towering walls had cracked and collapsed into soot-covered ruins.

At the head of his flock strode Father Jerome. His ecclesiastical robe flapped in the strong breeze blowing in from across the rippling sea, which for once looked benign as it glittered in the sunlight. Foaming white waves pounced playfully onto the rocks down below and tumbled the golden pebbles into a happy chatter.

Tall, silver-haired Father Jerome carried on his broad shoulder a wooden cross which stood higher than he. Across its horizontal beam was the inscription *They died in Christ*, and on the upright beam were inscribed the names of the fishermen who had been killed by the castle's occupants, and of the young girl who had wandered out onto the headland.

When Father Jerome reached the tip of the Devil's Finger he halted, sat the cross down in front of him, and held it upright while a group of the slain fishermen's kin piled rocks around its base until it was securely in place.

Father Jerome looked out at the smoking ruin of the once-defiant castle and, in a loud, echoing voice, addressed his flock. 'These waters have always brought life to the people of Hamlin. Their abundant fruits fill our tables with food, their swelling waves bring ships and trade to our doors, and their song that goes ever on feeds our souls. But when the Evil Ones sailed across these life-giving waters, when their demonic souls entered our cove, they polluted it. Evil lurked on the waters, malice stalked the seashore, and fear dwelt in our souls. Today, we stand before the waters in peace, our souls burdened by fear no longer; for we were blessed with a man who overcame all obstacles, who rose to lofty heights and discovered a hero within himself. This man, this knight of Saint George, was a true Christian warrior. For this warrior, and for every true warrior that came before him and will come after him, we, the people of this place, give thanks to God and to all His heavenly hosts. Amen.'

And every year from that day forth, the people of Hamlin walked out to the end of the Devil's Finger with their parson at their head on the anniversary of the castle's fall, and give thanks to God and to the two brave Chaucy men.

.21.

Hang Ups and Let Downs

ROWENA stepped lightly over the ground, the fallen autumn leaves crunching crisply beneath her feet and rustling as her skirt swished past. She held it up with one hand, anxious to keep the hem of the new gold-coloured wool gown from getting muddy as she passed across the meadow behind Eaglestone Castle.

Walter Gray had been completely overwhelmed with gratitude upon the safe return of his two daughters, and after falling at Sir Richard's feet and kissing the hem of his cloak, he had bowed repeatedly before both her and Sir Richard and offered half his worldly goods as thanks.

They had both been rather embarrassed by this, especially Sir Richard, and had graciously declined the very generous offer. But Gray would not hear of his daughters' brave rescuers leaving without accepting some token of his thanks. He had managed to persuade Sir Richard to take a well-filled purse, and Rowena to accept the gift of a lifetime discount on any cloth from his haberdashery shop.

The new gown of softest lamb's wool was among three new gowns she had sewn up from fabric bought in Walter Gray's shop. The new gowns may have been simple in style, but to the humble country maid it was enough to almost make her feel like a princess. Though Lady Sabina had been so surprised by these first-ever new additions to her cousin's wardrobe that Rowena was sure she suspected her of stealing them.

Rowena sighed and set down the basket she was carrying on a crook in the branch of an ancient oak tree at the bottom of the meadow. At least her aunt and cousin were far too busy with preparations for, and talk of, Lady Sabina's wedding to Lord Shrewsbury in a little over three months time, on St Valentine's day, to bother with the usual amusement of taunting Rowena.

She pulled herself up onto the low branch beside her basket. St Valentine's Day. The very mention of it made her heart quicken with fear and her stomach twist with dread, because the Cunninghams were not the only ones preparing for St Valentine's Day.

Rowena looked across the meadow to where the narrow towers of Eaglestone Castle soared up towards a cloudless blue sky, their brightly coloured banners fluttering lazily in the gentle breeze. Below these lofty towers, a pair of white swans glided serenely across the surface of the glittering moat, which now brimmed with clear water.

Against this peaceful backdrop, a much less serene sight was to be seen. It was now late November, and every morning the sun rose to be greeted by Jack Frost's icy workings. But despite this, Sir Richard's shirt was soaked with sweat. His black doublet lay cast aside on the ground beside him. Holding his long, glittering sword in one hand and his shield in the other, he hacked furiously at the tall wooden post set in the ground for Eaglestone's men to practice their fighting skills on. Blow after ringing blow rained down onto the pole with tremendous speed and power.

Rowena sighed again and absent-mindedly took a bite out of one of the custard and blackberry pies in her basket.

Sir Richard had been like this ever since he had arranged to meet his nemesis de Wintore at the tournament to be held by the Shrewsburys to mark the wedding of Lady Sabina and Lord Shrewsbury. He spent hours every day down in this meadow practising his skill-at-arms or riding at the tilting arm with his aimed lance.

Sir Richard seemed to have noticed her arrival at last. He slipped the shield off his arm and leaned it against the tall pole, then slid the massive blade back into its scabbard. Wiping the sweat off his brow with the sleeve of his shirt, he walked over to where Rowena sat.

'Greetings, precious darling,' he called, smiling fondly.

Her answering smile was more brave than cheerful. 'Good day.' She tilted up her face to receive the kiss Sir Richard stooped to bestow.

'Mmm, those pies you've been eating taste good.'

She bit her lip thoughtfully. 'They do taste good, but not when they are mixed with your salt.'

'What have I done now?'

She flung her hands into her lap. 'Oh Richard, I can't bear this agony of waiting! Day and night I can think of nothing else but your duel with de Wintore! Why did you do this thing?'

'Fear not, my love. I have righteousness on my side. I *will* overcome de Wintore. That man has tormented me, tried to take you from me, to ruin me and to blacken my name. On St Valentine's Day the one man leaving the field of battle alive shall be me.'

'But how can you be so sure?' she wailed. 'De Wintore is a famed warrior; he has vanquished many great knights!'

He looked at her reproachfully. 'Are you saying that you do not believe me to be as good a warrior as he?'

'No, but you have your old battle wounds; your shoulder and your knee!'

He flexed his shoulder experimentally. 'Yes, this shoulder has been giving me some bother, but by the time of the tournament I will be stronger.'

'Why do you always have to be so pig-headed? You know de

Wintore will turn up in the best armour money can buy and with an unlawful sharp sword, whereas you do not even *own* a suit of armour!'

'You are right, my love. But it is no matter. I will win a suit of armour by jousting a knight before I take on de Wintore.'

She clutched the sides of her head in exasperation. 'Have you taken leave of your senses? Joust a fully armoured knight wearing next to nothing!'

'I will pit myself against one of those vain young peacocks who turn up at tournaments only to impress the ladies. They will think a poor knight like me an easy conquest, but some of these puffed-up twits can barely lift a sword.'

'All they'll need is one lucky hit and you will be dead before de Wintore even has a chance to kill you himself!'

Sir Richard let out a long-suffering sigh and wiped his still-sweating face with the forearm of his shirt again. 'I'm going to vanquish de Wintore once and for all at the tournament. And even if you nag from this day to that one, you will not succeed in dissuading me. Now—' He perched up beside her on the log. 'Surely you have not come down here looking so rosy-cheeked and charming just to scold?'

'No,' she replied tensely. 'I also—' She paused for a moment as he started stroking her hair absent-mindedly. 'I also brought you something to eat, thinking you might be hungry after all that effort.'

He rested his cheek on her shoulder with a contented sigh. 'How thoughtful of you, sweetheart.'

'Sir Richard, stop being so familiar!' she snapped, giving him a half-hearted push. 'Someone might see us.'

He reluctantly lifted his head. 'Yes, someone might. But it is perfectly permissible for betrothed couples to be familiar.'

'But we are not betrothed!' she replied, in a voice that was almost a shout.

He smiled darkly. 'But everyone *thinks* we are…'

'Yes, thanks to you, you clever rascal,' she replied, with a look that was somewhat admiring and thoroughly cross.

It really had been a stroke of genius on Sir Richard's part. The astonished Abbess Hawisa had paid a visit to Stoatley Manor as soon as she had heard the news of the deliciously shocking betrothal. Lady Cunningham had been livid with rage at the news of her niece's sudden betrothal, which offended her on every level. She had burst into Rowena's tiny chamber without so much as knocking, and set about berating her. 'Do you not know that Sir Richard will become a commoner if he marries you?' she had screamed. 'How dare you drag a nobleman down to your level! It is an abomination, an abomination!'

Rowena *did* know that anyone of noble birth became a commoner if they married one, although a knight like Sir Richard would not lose his knighthood. Her aunt had then demanded that she break off the betrothal immediately. But Rowena had been so offended by her aunt's reaction that, before she could deny she was promised in marriage, she had told Lady Cunningham she refused to break it off. So now everyone was forever asking her when the wedding was to be, and would it be in St Luke's or St Agnes's? Had she decided on a dress? And how many guests would be invited to the wedding feast? All she could do in reply was stammer that there were no plans as yet, while the asker cooed admiringly over her maidenly modesty.

It was torturous.

Sir Richard broke the pensive silence at last. 'I have not yet asked if you will be coming to the tournament…' The question was cautious in tone, and he busied himself with reaching in her basket for a pie.

'Yes, of course I will be there,' she replied softly, after a moment's silence. Tears suddenly welled up in her eyes. 'Letting her knight die in her arms is the one comfort and service a lady can offer in war.'

He put the arm that was not occupied with delivering the pie to his mouth around her waist. 'With such a peerless lady at his side and the sword of righteousness in his hand, what knight could possibly fail?'

She sniffed miserably. 'You could.'

'If your concern were not so great a sign of your feelings for me, I should be deeply offended by your lack of regard for my knightly prowess. I used to make my living fighting at tournaments, which I had proved to be rather good at, you know.'

'Yes, *used* to.'

Rowena looked away so he would not see her tear-filled eyes. Ever since they had returned from Lothbury two moons ago, she had been berating him and pleading him not to go through with his challenge to fight de Wintore to the death. But all his answers had been in the same vein as the ones which had just fallen on her ears. Why was he so sure? The Sir Richard she had been familiar with was only ever sure of one thing: it was going to fail, disaster was sure to befall him. Now he was as confident of triumphing over de Wintore as of the sun rising the next day.

He gave her a gentle squeeze. 'I beg you, do not fear for me. I gave up jousting because I was tired of the vanity and self-seeking of many of the knights who fought at the tournaments, and decided to hang up my armour once and for all.'

'But you did not hang it up once and for all—you took it down and carted it to market!'

'Yes, but I shall be armed with the sword of righteousness.'

'You are so trying and provocative!

'Surely you will not feel my loss that much then—and just think: you would not have to worry about everyone falsely thinking you and I betrothed.'

The statement was smoothly delivered, but she felt a definite stab in his final words. It was so unfair of him.

'You are the bravest of knights but also the most insensitive!' she cried. 'If you really wished to honour me, you would not torture me with this stupid fight with de Wintore. You are always getting in my hair and underfoot—it's unbearable!'

She was surprised to find a smug smile playing on his lips when her condemnation was over. 'How can I be in your hair if I'm also underfoot?'

She gave him a shove. 'Argh! you're impossible!'

The dark smile only widened. 'My sweet darling, your doting words of love and oaths of undying faithfulness are heavenly ambrosia to my ardent heart.'

'Impossible…' she muttered, shaking her head and crossing her arms.

He hopped off the branch. 'Yes, your sweetness and grace are impossibly perfect. Now, I must go and exercise Lucifer.'

She gave a sulky grunt in reply, then quickly leaned back as Sir Richard moved towards her. But the manoeuvre was futile. A moment later she was receiving a firm kiss as she teetered on the brink of falling off her perch backwards.

'Be off with you, thieving knave!' she cried, as soon as her lips were free.

He bowed low. 'My mistress commands, I obey.' And with that, the laughing knight was gone.

Holding the empty basket in her lap, Rowena sat there like a stone. What would she do when he was gone? Spend the rest of her days living as an unwanted spinster in Stoatley Manor? It could be worse; at least she could help the poor folk and roam the woods and fields of Heathcote all day.

She angrily swatted away a hovering midge. And why was she allowing that knight to act with a lover's familiarity? Dangerous men like him should be kept away from. Why did she love him? And why, oh why did she dread his death with a lover's passion?

'Rowena...'

She was roused from her reverie by a far-distant voice which sounded like it belonged to Sir Richard.

'Rowena, come here...'

What did he want now? By St Elroy, why couldn't he manage to stay out of her hair for a single moment!

'Hell's heat, get over here!' The sound was still distant and rather muffled, but he was definitely getting bothered.

She sighed and hopped off the tree limb, then made for the woodland path Sir Richard had disappeared down earlier.

'Rowena, where the hell are you?' his bellow came from up ahead.

She broke into a trot. 'I'm coming, have a little patience!'

This time, the only answer was some inaudible dark mutterings. She kept hurrying onward. The path narrowed, branches thrust themselves into her face and heavy shade reigned.

Rowena pushed aside a large hornbeam bough —and suddenly found herself face-to-face with Sir Richard. Except that he was not the same way up as her—he was suspended upside down. Her mouth fell open.

The thin-lipped, thoroughly unimpressed expression he wore could have turned living flesh into stone. Standing rooted to the ground a mere foot from his face, she gaped in shock for a moment, and then suddenly burst out laughing. She dropped the basket and laughed until tears ran down her cheeks and her sides ached.

Some muffled twittering and giggling joined her from behind a wide-girthed beech tree near the path. But the object of her mirth did not look amused. Suspended from a beech tree's high overhead branch by a noose around the ankles, Sir Richard just observed Rowena in grimly bad-tempered silence until she finally stopped laughing.

'All right, so I've been hocked! Very funny. Now can you

please pay these ruthless vixens the ransom so they will let me down?'

Even though she had stopped howling with laughter, she still could not suppress the odd giggle. 'Well it is Hocktide Monday; women have every right to hock local men and ask for a donation for the parish. It's all in a good cause, you know.'

The knight was quite red in the face by now, though whether from embarrassment or simply being hung upside down she could not be sure. He did not look happy, of that she *could* be sure. 'The stone-hearted banshees are demanding a one-pound ransom to let me down, yet I haven't so much as a farthing on me!'

She put her hands on her hips. 'Well neither have I. Besides, it is not Hocktide Tuesday; ladies may only be ransomed on that day.'

'But they're asking one *whole* pound; it's outrageous! Have they any idea how poor I am? That damn folly of a pile—' he jerked a hand in Eaglestone castle's direction, but quickly went still again when the movement set him swinging on the end of the rope, 'eats up money like a proud wife. Half the place is empty, yet the king still expects me to maintain it even though it would be useless under siege! Folk around here seem to think I have coffers full of silver just lying about. I have barely a penny to my name!'

She looked him in the ever-reddening face detachedly. 'Be that as it may, the fact is you have managed to avoid capture every Hocktide thus far, so it is to be expected that the ransom will be higher when the women finally got your feet in their noose.'

'The slippery wenches tricked me, setting up an ambush right where only I walk—and they won't even dare show their faces!' he shouted in the direction of the beech trunk.

There was an outbreak of self-satisfied laughter from behind the tree. 'Pay up or hang up!' a shrill female voice called out.

The woman sounded an awful lot like Betty, young man-at-arms Will's new wife. After all that time she had spent working as a barmaid in the rowdy Cockerel and Cow alehouse, little could be expected in the way of leniency from her...

'But I have only got one pound and a few pennies left!' Sir Richard shouted back. 'The only damn money I get as sheriff is from the cut of the taxes and court fines I'm entitled to, but nobody has been committing any crime lately. Hell, at the last shire court the only convictions were a yokel who had his hogs roaming at large to the annoyance of his neighbours, and a couple of young twits who'd been playing tennis in the guildhall. Those offences only carry a fine of forty pennies each. The lack of crime is ruining me!'

'Our sheriff does not heed such excuses when the king's taxes are being gathered. Reap as ye sow!' came the response.

The swinging knight gave a bad-tempered huff. 'All right then, you win. Rowena, could you go get the bag of pennies in the rosewood coffer in my chamber?'

She forced the corners of her mouth down. 'Certainly.'

'It's easy to laugh when you are not the one hanging like a brace of birds in a butcher's shop,' he muttered, crossing his previously hanging arms. 'Now, you hellish imps, let me down!' The demand was loudly directed at the beech tree.

'You touch the ground when your money touches my hand,' came the unrelenting reply.

'By the Devil's hooves and very tail, I hope you fall into a ten-foot hole on the way home!' Hartfield's sheriff bellowed at the tree. 'Rowena, hurry, would you! I feel like my head is about to explode.'

'I shall run all the way.'

'God speed!' he called after her. 'Damn vermin...'

Hitching her skirt up, Rowena set off at a brisk trot. She was soon emerging from the greenwood near the base of Eaglestone Castle and skipping across the drawbridge.

As she exited the tunnel under the gatehouse, she nearly collided with a pageboy hurrying the opposite way.

'Pepin, do pardon me. I'm in that much of a flurry I didn't see you there!' she gasped, coming to a sharp halt.

Though only thirteen, the page was already taller than she was. He smoothed his neatly-bobbed golden hair and grinned casually. 'No harm done, my lady. Where are you off to in such a hurry? Perhaps I could fetch you something?'

'Well, the thing is!—' She was forced to pause when a fit of giggles overcame her.

'Oh do tell, Mistress Rowena!'

'Sir Richard was walking along the woodland path at the bottom of the meadow when!—when!—' She started laughing so hard she could barely speak. 'He was caught by both feet in the women's hocking noose and hauled five feet off the ground!'

The already widely-grinning pageboy laughed heartily. 'By Our Lady, that must have been quite a sight!'

'Yes, but there's more; he is still swinging there because he had no money on him—that's what I'm doing!'

The dapper page tried to retain some composure, but ended up laughing so hard he nearly fell to the ground. 'Let me go and fetch Sir Richard's money coffer!' he gasped, when his initial outbreak of mirth had subsided a little.

She nodded. 'But do hurry. Our valiant sheriff's mood is everything you'd expect it to be.'

Grinning broadly, Pepin raced off on his errand. Rowena did not have to wait long for the pageboy to reappear with the rosewood box in his hands. He leapt down the steps and ran across the courtyard with the grace of a deer, and the two of them were soon hurrying back to their stricken lord.

Rowena and Pepin reached the stately beech to find Sir Richard still dangling like a leg of ham. The pageboy kept behind Rowena with a hand firmly clapped over his mouth. She could tell young Pepin was barely managing to keep from laughing out loud, but was putting in a very brave effort. Doubtless the page was wary of receiving a clout around the ears from his master or being tasked with some awful job if he laughed at the hanging knight's predicament.

'Here is the money,' she called, coming up to Sir Richard.

'Christ be praised…' muttered the grim hostage, whose face was now nearly purple.

'Bring it over here, if you please,' ordered the sharp female voice from the safety of the trees.

'What do you think this is, boy, a damn cockfight?' Sir Richard growled at his page. 'Trust that maid to return with a crowd of gawkers in tow…'

'Sire, I merely came to offer you any assistance you may require,' Pepin gaffed, failing miserably at keeping a straight face.

The hostage's only reply was a black glare.

Meanwhile, Rowena had counted out the amount required for the ransom and was in the process of handing it over to the heavily-cloaked Betty. The pile of pennies was quickly counted and pocketed, and then Betty disappeared back into the thicket at the base of the beech tree whose branch Sir Richard was suspended from. A few moments later there was a creak as the rope started to move, and Sir Richard began to slowly descend.

Sir Richard's clerk and pageboy took his shoulders as he neared the ground, helping him to land on his back rather than his head.

The knight let out a groan once he was safely lying on the ground, and clutched a hand to his head. 'My head feels like there is a pair of knockers in there hammering away…'

'Would you like a hand, sire?' asked Pepin, offering a hand to help Sir Richard up.

He shook his head. 'No, let me just sit awhile. My ears are ringing and I can see stars; I'll likely fall right back down again.'

The page sat down beside Sir Richard on the leaf-strewn ground. 'I can't wait for the tournament. I've been polishing your weapons every single day.'

'Good lad—but that doesn't mean you have a God-given entitlement to laugh at my misfortune,' replied his still-sulking master.

'I never thought a boy from a tanner's family like me would ever get a chance to be squire to a renowned knight at a magnificent tournament,' Pepin continued brightly, taking no notice of Sir Richard's bad mood (the boy was learning fast, Rowena observed with approval). 'Most pages never even get to a tournament with a knight. Mother and Father will be so very proud when I tell them how I helped the valiant Sir Richard vanquish the evil Sir Roger de Wintore.'

Rowena sighed. 'You're starting to sound as bad as Sir Richard, Pepin. You do know that Sir Richard could be—could be killed?'

The page rolled his eyes. 'Yes, *of course* I know a knight could be killed in a fight; I'm not a baby! But everyone knows that good always overcomes evil in a fight to the death. Sir Roger de Wintore is a murderer and an abductor of women. He will not prevail.'

'De Wintore is indeed an evil, dishonourable man. But our Sir Richard is not exactly the lily-white Sir Galahad, is he?'

Sir Richard did not need to tell his lady that he thought she was being disloyal. The look he rested on her said it for him.

'Well you aren't!' she hastily defended herself. 'That business with de Wintore's sister was less than noble, you said it yourself.'

'Yes, but look how stupid Sir Percival was,' chirped Pepin. 'He still found the Holy Grail even though, to start off with, he did not know his elbow from his a—'

'Thank you, Pepin,' Rowena interrupted. 'I think you may wish to stop and consider the rather unflattering insinuation that line of reasoning contains.'

The pageboy grinned sheepishly at Sir Richard. 'Beg your pardon, my lord. I did not mean to imply that you were a fool, but merely that you once seem to have had a little difficulty in that area.'

Rowena raised her eyes to heaven. For such a dapper little know-it-all, that page really did have a talent for putting his foot right it.

If the young chatterbox noticed the gesture, he did not show it. 'I shall be much admired as I go about in Sir Richard's livery at the tournament,' he continued. 'Everyone will be whispering 'there goes the only trusted attendant of Sir Richard Hastings, the boldest knight in all Christendom'. As my knight rides onto the field of glory, every eye will be upon him and every lady's heart will be aflutter as she beholds his noble visage...' The page trailed off as he gazed into the distance with a glazed, dreamy look on his face.

'The very same noble warrior whom you were laughing yourself silly over as you observed him swinging by the ankles only moments before,' added the Boldest Knight in all Christendom.

Pepin patted his master's arm. 'Do not worry, I shan't tell anyone at the tournament that you got hocked by a gaggle of local peasant women.'

'I wouldn't give myself too many airs if I were you, Pepin,' said Rowena. 'You know the reason you are the sole attendant chosen to ride to the tournament is that you are the only person who could be spared.'

'Yes,' replied an unperturbed Pepin. 'But just because I am the only page at Eaglestone Castle does not mean I will not be the most attentive page at the tournament. All the other knights may well have a whole bevy of squires in tow, but I shall be just as efficient as a herd of squires, even though there is only one of me.'

Rowena smiled indulgently. 'Your ambition does you credit, Pepin. I shall be there too, though I will not travel with you and Sir Richard. My relatives are travelling by coach, so I will go with them. It would not be seemly for an unrelated maiden to be travelling alone with a knight. Tongues will start to wag if I turn up like that.'

'Indeed. A lady's role is different,' said the page. 'While a knight's attendant's task is to stand at the side of the lists and hold his horse, pass him new lances and help him if he is unhorsed, a knight's lady stands in the viewing gallery weeping and praying.'

'I see,' said a bemused Rowena. 'Is that what you wish me to do, Sir Richard?'

'Absolutely. If your lady is not on her knees quaking with terror, her love for you is highly questionable. It gets quite competitive amongst the watching ladies as they vie for the most requests for their tokens before the knights joust. And the eagerness to seem the most devoted lady is just as fierce. At one joust I fought in, my vanquished opponent's lady-love had to be prevented from throwing herself off the gallery, such was her anguish at his defeat—although I suspect she was doing it more for show than grief. She and her sister had quarrelled earlier over which of them was the most devoted lover.'

'Really. I sincerely hope that you are not expecting me to throw myself off anything if you lose a round.'

'No, certainly not. If you simply fall to the ground weeping and tearing your hair, that will be perfectly satisfactory.'

22.

The Heart of Ice and the Heart of Fire

FINE linen grown; newest crimson stockings; pointy-toed shoes of royal blue suede; silk veil. Yes, it was all there.

Rowena gathered together the four corners of the square of russet she had piled the folded items on, and tied them in a tight knot. After casting a final look around her tiny garret room, she lifted the bundle off her little bed and swung it over her shoulder. The red-haired maiden then exited her room and made her way down the attic stairs, through Stoatley's first-floor passageway, and down the main staircase leading to the grand hall.

The great hall was abuzz with activity. Servants hurried to and fro carrying coffers and bundles out to the two carts waiting outside. All the while, Lord Cunningham's overseer shouted orders and reprimands as he strutted up and down.

Rowena waited until the last of the baggage was being loaded before stepping outside, where her aunt and cousin stood on the front step.

'Careful with that, half-wit!' Lady Cunningham screeched at a thin, nervous girl attempting to heave a large chest up onto the coach's roof. 'It is worth more than your blood-price!'

Rowena drew her cloak tightly around herself as the icy breeze nipped at her already-cold body. The heavy flurries of snow that had fallen the previous night were unseasonably late, but the dark clouds had parted just as the dawn was breaking, and now the low sun smiled weakly at the sparkling snowdrifts.

Heavily wrapped in white mink and ermine furs, Lady Sabina lifted her long, full skirt of gold brocade with a white kid-glove encased hand and prepared to enter the coach after Lady Cunningham.

'What about me—where shall I put my things?' asked Rowena.

The tall, fur-clad damsel stopped, skirt still in hand. She looked down her thin, straight nose and curled her lip into a disdainful sneer, then suddenly laughed a cold, mocking laugh. 'What about *you*? Mother, silly cousin Rowena still thinks she is going to the wedding!' She let out another peal of her mocking laughter.

Rowena clutched her bundle tightly as she stared at her icy-eyed cousin. 'What—what do you mean? You said only last week that I could come!'

The regal lily put a hand over her blood-red lips to cover her snigger. 'You really are even more stupid than I gave you credit for. I have at long last succeeded in attaining my true position in life—one where you and your selfish mother can no longer drag my family down. I shall not be turning up at my noble future husband's home with a horrid beggar-girl in attendance!' She pulled a revolted face. 'Just imagine; I would have to admit that not only was I acquainted with you, but that I was in fact related to you!'

A large bank of cloud which had been creeping ever closer to the weak winter sun finally overtook it. Then a few snowflakes began fluttering down from above like ice butterflies and settling on Rowena's numb cheeks, where they quickly melted and ran downwards as tears of snow.

The red-haired damsel hardly noticed them. 'But I have to get to the tournament!'

'So you can watch dewy-eyed as your beloved fights?'

Rowena nodded dumbly.

'Ha, just look at you!' The sneering, richly-clad damsel pulled at the trim on Rowena's cloak. 'Rabbit fur. Brown, moth-eaten rabbit fur. Your Sir Richard will be so ashamed of his drab, ugly little mouse amongst all the fine lords and ladies; he will barely make it onto the field if you are present!'

Rowena looked down at the bundle in her hands. 'No, I have brought a nice dress—'

Lady Sabina was roughly snatching at the bundle before her cousin had even finished speaking. 'Indeed!' she cried, untying the cloth.

'Give that back!'

The regal lily took no heed of her anguished cousin. She held a magenta dress up as though it was the head of Medusa. 'But this gown is not even silk. I would not wear something this plain at home!'

Feeling like a tiny piece of misery and humiliation, Rowena could not think of anything to say. She had been cruelly tricked, and now Sir Richard would die alone.

Lady Sabina fixed cold eyes on her victim. Then, without looking down, she slowly turned the russet square until it was upside down, and waited while all her cousin's clothes tumbled onto the muddy, snow-covered ground. 'Now get back to the dust-heap where you belong, filthy beggar!'

And with that, the tall, lily-white damsel gave a haughty toss of the head, lifted her furs and stepped into the waiting coach, which immediately lurched forwards.

Three days. Three days it took to reach Shrewsbury Castle on foot, and the tournament was in two day's time. It was the only thought in Rowena's mind as she watched the two coaches rapidly disappearing down the road. Long after they had gone from view, she continued to stare at the tracks the carts had cut through the pristine white snow covering the ground.

'Let me help you,' a young voice interrupted Rowena's numb horror.

She looked down to find the Cunninghams' servant maid, Millicent, gathering up the clothes scattered on the ground at her feet.

'She said I can't come…' Rowena said in a stunned, barely comprehending whisper, her eyes fixed back on the tracks cutting through the snow.

'I sure am glad to see the last of that Lady Sabina,' said Millicent, joining the red-haired maiden in staring at the tracks. 'She were such a horrible thing. My old gran reckons young Lady Haughty is a changeling child or some such evil sprite.'

'I do believe she is right. Oh, what am I to do!'

'All the Cunninghams' horses are being used to pull those coaches, but you may find a passing peddler or farmer who can give you a lift on his cart—though I dare say not many folk will be out and about in this weather if they can help it.'

'Yes, if I set out on foot I might be able to beg a lift. But I shan't get there nearly so quickly as if I had travelled with the Cunninghams. They were allowing a mere day to reach Shrewsbury Castle. The wedding and the feast are to be held on the morrow, and the tournament the day after.'

'If you miss the tournament, it can't be helped.'

Rowena suddenly turned to Millicent. 'I'm not missing the tournament; I won't let it happen!'

'You'd better get going then. I think a new cloth is required for this bundle, though. The old one is well wet from lying in this here puddle.'

Rowena looked bleakly at the dripping, muddy cloth Millicent held up. 'I'll go up and see what I can find.'

Rowena then took the bundle of crumpled garments in her

arms and turned for the door, suddenly gripped by a breathless, dizzying sense of urgency.

She had promised. Promised the man who had risked everything for her in a bold and iron-willed rescue that she would be there to support him in his hour of greatest need. Promised he would die in her arms.

She hardly noticed that she was already running along the upstairs passageway until there was an almighty metallic crash. An instant later she was sprawled on her front atop a suit of armour, staring at a helmet which stared grimly back at her through the dark slits in its visor. She lifted her smarting nose from the cold steel and blinked dizzily at it.

'As if there are not enough cold, hard things around here without you as well,' she muttered crossly, giving it a shove.

Then she suddenly paused. A suit of armour? Sir Richard needed a suit a suit of armour!

The snub-nosed maiden pulled herself onto her hands and knees with a jerk, and started franticly scrabbling at the laces and buckles holding the pieces together with numb, clumsy hands. The pain in her freezing fingers as they pulled at the rusted, stubborn fastenings was so stinging it made her eyes water, but she took no heed.

She had no familiarity with armour, and every time a piece seemed to finally be free, she took a pull at it only to find yet another buckle holding it on. But her burning, blind enthusiasm was such that the job was soon done, and a pile of steel plates was all that remained of the once grimly-standing vacant shell.

Rowena ran to fetch a cloth, and upon returning to her prize, flung herself to her knees beside the dimly shining heap and begun piling it onto the outspread sheet. Once all the armour was stacked on the cloth, she deposited her own clothes in the hollow of the breastplate and tied the four corners up.

She then got to her feet, lifted—and nearly fell to the ground under the weight. Breathing hard, she set it back down with a clang loud enough to raise the dead. The thing weighed an absolute ton. She was sure it was more than half her own body weight.

'He needs armour!' she cried aloud, her mind almost blind with terrified frustration at this latest setback.

She heaved again. This time, she managed to get the huge bundle up onto her shoulder. She started staggering towards the stairs. Though the sharp steel edges cut in painfully, she pushed grimly onwards.

But a moment later she was nearly on her knees again as her foot caught something with a loud clang. The helmet—she had forgotten the accursed helmet!

Rowena set the bundle down yet again and quickly scooped up the runaway, which was then reunited with the rest of its peers. A perilous trip down the stairs followed, and soon the determined young woman and her big bundle were slowly but surely progressing down the snow-covered road.

Once the snow cover became thicker, she dropped the bundle to the ground and started pulling it along behind her. She was already breathing hard with the effort, but the iron in her will outmatched that in her bundle. She fixed her eyes on the road ahead, pulled her hood down against the blowing snowflakes placing their icy kisses on already frozen skin, and kept trudging steadily onwards with true grit and hope. Her leather-booted feet squeaked with every step pressed into the soft virgin snow, and the sound of the sharply whistling wind joined with the limp, icy slap of snowflakes hitting their targets.

Upon reaching the crossroads where the path leading to Stoatley Manor joined the road snaking down the valley, Rowena stopped. The tracks of the Cunninghams' two coaches had not been quite obliterated by the falling snow yet, but the maiden's careful scan of the road told her that no other travellers had passed that way since the snow had lightened at dawn.

What to do now? There was no hope of getting any transport from Eaglestone. All the horses would be patrolling the southern borders with their armoured riders, as they had done regularly ever since complaints about outlaws venturing forth from Glymewood to thieve started coming in. As for Sir Richard and young Pepin, they had left on horseback the previous day—and she had only offered a casual goodbye, certain in the belief they would be reunited the next day.

She had not told him how much she loved him, had not kissed that dear cheek one last time. This could not be the final earthly goodbye, it could not! A desperate sob escaped her. She heaved the dead-weight back onto her shoulder, for the road up ahead was too stony to risk dragging the precious load over.

Then she resumed the grim march. Every painful, hard-won step forward was one step closer to him. One step closer to fulfilling the most important task of her life. He could not do it on his own. He would die without her help. She did not know why, but she knew it was true.

Rowena pressed on until she reached the end of the valley, where the snowdrifts lay deep and silent, piled up against the banks and hedges at the roadside. Where the valley ended, that road ended too. The road it joined was much more frequently-travelled, and the trees had been cleared on a wide strip on either side as the law stated it must, in order to remove cover for thieves to lie in wait for their victims.

A few faint tracks were visible in the snow, so Rowena decided to put down her burden and wait a while in the hope of getting a lift from a passing cart. A stone provided a convenient if rather hard seat, and soon she was settled down, cloak drawn tightly together by frozen fingers and eyes and ears alert for any sight or sound of a fellow traveller.

Rowena had only been waiting a short while when the sound

of a horse's jingling harness and rhythmic blowing reached her ears. It was coming from the west, which meant they were going the way she wished to go. The anxiously-waiting maiden jumped to her feet and ran out into the road, desperate to see who was coming around the bend ahead.

A few moments later a furry little pony pulling a small cart came trotting into view. The heavily cloaked figure driving the cart slowed the pony to a walk and halted as he drew level with Rowena.

'Good sire,' she cried, 'I beg you to give me a lift for as long as our paths remain the same!'

Judging by the wares hanging from his cart, the man was a peddler. He pushed his hood back from his face and gave a courteous nod. 'God give ye good day, damsel. It is a blessedly rare sight for a young lady to be travelling alone in such foul weather. Are you in any strife?'

Feeling pleased with the traveller's kindly face and courteous manner, Rowena allowed herself a weak smile. 'In a manner of speaking. The offer of a seat in a cart that was to be my means of transport was hastily and cruelly withdrawn, yet my need to reach my destination was ever the same.'

'Ye are most welcome to share my humble cart, damsel,' said the old peddler. 'These here parts are not safe for a woman to travel alone. Being at the edge of Glymewood, many tales of wayfarers being robbed have reached my ears, for the greenwood offers food and shelter to many a beast and bird; if a man be turned away by his own kind, he often finds Mother Nature a less cruel companion.'

'Well can I believe that to be so. I travel this hard road by necessity, not choice.'

'I doubt any human being would pass along this road on such a day as this unless prompted by necessity,' the old Peddler replied, stepping down from his cart. 'Are these your belongings?' He pointed to her bundle.

'Yes, but they are terribly heavy, so let me give you a hand.'

The bundle was soon up on the cart, and Rowena seated beside the old peddler on the bench at the front. A sharp click of the peddler's tongue and the furry little pony was trotting determinedly down the snowy road. The next few hours passed in a silence that was only broken by the clip-clop of the pony's hooves and the rumble of the cart wheels.

It was mid afternoon when the peddler finally halted his pony at a fork in the road. 'My destination is a small hamlet a half-hour's journey up this path to the left. Your journey's end lies to the right, but surely ye will accompany me to this hamlet? It is not far off your way, and darkness will be upon us in little over two hours.'

'I thank you for your kindness, but I must leave you here and continue east. I cannot afford to lose any time,' replied the maiden.

'Damsel, I beg ye to reconsider! Many lawless and godforsaken men roam these parts; ye will be in grave danger travelling alone on foot. And where will ye spend the night? The snow lies thick and the wind blows cold. I fear ye shall freeze to death if ye are forced to spend a night out in the open.'

Rowena had already dismounted the cart. 'May God reward you for the kindness you have shown to a poor stranger, but our ways must part here. I may get a lift which will bring me closer to where I need to be, and I believe there is a little settlement not too far along the road. With luck I will reach it before nightfall.'

The old peddler begged her to change her mind, but Rowena was unrelenting. After many wishes for protection and blessing being exchanged, the two wayfarers went off on their separate paths.

Rowena set off at the fastest pace she could muster, dragging the bundle over the smooth snow. She was brightly optimistic that another traveller would overtake her before long.

But as the light started to fade so did her hopes. The only thing lying on the road ahead was a pristine, unmarked blanket of snow, and the only things behind her were her own footprints. Just when she was about to give up hope of meeting a fellow wayfarer or coming across a cottage, something caught her eye up ahead.

The exhausted maiden hurried towards it. A set of footprints came out of the forest and continued up the road—a set of *human* footprints. They were fresh, their edges still crisp in the fluffy white snow. The feet that made them could not have passed by more than half an hour ago. Perhaps they belonged to a cottager? Surely their maker could not have been far from home…

But her hopes had been raised only to be dashed when the footprints disappeared back into the forest after only a short way. Doubtless they belonged to a hunter—but a hunter of beasts or more upright prey? She shivered and glanced around nervously.

At the place where the tracks passed through a gap in the strands of bare hazel, hawthorn and birch saplings lining the side of the road, Rowena let go of her bundle and sank to the snow-covered ground. The biting north wind and freezing snow had robbed her of her warmth, and the long, weary road robbed her of her strength. What did it matter now if a bandit robbed her of all the worldly goods she had with her? She almost certainly was not going to reach Shrewsbury Castle in two days, if at all.

Seated on the cold ground, Rowena drew her knees up to her chin and hugged her legs. With fingers and toes registering no feeling and teeth chattering, she stared numbly out at the frozen whiteness all around. Although the sun was hidden by a thick veil of tumbled, watery grey clouds, the fading light signalled sunset. Now and then a snowflake fluttered down from the sky; a tiny drop of purity tossed from the heavens to veil earthly impurity with a pristine blanket of white.

It was not long before a sweet aroma drew Rowena's eye to the ground beside her. There, nestled beneath the hazel boughs in a bed of soft green moss, was a knot of violets. Smiling, Rowena reached out a numb, shaking finger to lift the green leaves and reveal the tiny purple jewels cowering modestly beneath, their enchanting little faces turned blushingly downward.

Next to the shy violets stood a bolder group; a scattering of delicate white snowdrop flowers rearing bravely up from their cluster of bright green spears. The fragile flowers were held defiantly up despite the biting, buffeting winds and frozen world above ground. Feeling cheered by the enchanting sight, a still-smiling Rowena looked up at the plump robin redbreast hopping sprightly from branch to branch above her head, chirping as he went.

As night fell on the silent, frozen land, the clouds parted to reveal a glittering dome of stars above. The twinkling stars filling the dark sky with thousands of little silver lights lit up the winter night with a pale, ghostly glow as the starlight was reflected off the snow.

Feeling tired, detached and dreamy, Rowena lay down in the soft snow. The stillness and silence were so intense that the night felt holy, and it seemed as though the pale, circling stars were resounding with the music of the spheres. No movement came to disturb the divine silence, and Rowena felt sleep start to overcome her. Her heartbeat grew fainter, her breaths slower and more rhythmical, and her eyes fell shut.

Then suddenly she was wide awake, eyes open, heart racing, breaths quick and fast. A group of heavily cloaked figures, hoods drawn low over their faces, were ringed around the maiden. Every one of the figures held aloft a burning torch. The woollen cloaks were all in the colours of the forest; there was bright green, red-brown, earthy brown, dark gold and moss.

The faces of the torch bearers were etched with curiosity and concern, and they hovered silently over the petrified young woman, who felt sure she must be dreaming. Then a trail of thick white smoke started curling towards her, she did not know from where. As she watched with terrified fascination, it snaked and trailed its way towards her face.

As the smoke reached her, she started to feel as though she was floating, and her sight became hazy. The figures crowded around her faded into a single ring of fire and then became ever fainter and more distant until there was nothingness.

.23.

Glymewood in the Red Dawn

THERE was the crackle of a fire and the sighing of the wind in the trees, and her bed seemed to have got much more comfortable overnight—wait, there was no fire in her tiny bedchamber in Stoatley Manor!

Rowena opened her eyes with a jolt.

The events of the previous night came tumbling into her sleep-dazed mind. But the torches, the figures, the snow, the cold, they were all gone. Instead, she was lying on a bed of dry leaves and fern branches with a deer pelt covering her, beside a large fire whose hot embers glowed brightly enough to light the forest glade. Yes, a forest glade, surrounded by steep rocks and banks, and atop the banks crowds of woodland giants dimly visible in the flickering shadows.

But how did she get here? Where were the mysterious hooded figures and their brightly burning torches?

Rowena sat up fearfully and looked about. There was no one there. Just the cheerful crackle of the fire and the melancholy sighing of the wind high up in the treetops overhead. Her eyes then alighted on a rough wooden platter sitting near the fire, piled with pieces of roasted venison.

Suddenly realising she was starving, Rowena reached out and took the platter. Then she paused. Surely one should not take without asking? On the other hand, who else but her could that food be meant for?

She tucked into the hot food gratefully. It was delicious, tasting of juniper berries and many more woodsy things she could not name. When the meat was finished, Rowena noticed a pot sitting in the coals at the edge of the fire. She lifted its lid and filled a tin cup lying nearby with the steaming pale green liquid inside. It smelt and tasted of herbs sweetened with honey. It too was soon gone, and Rowena started looking about her once more.

Fear crept up again. Where was she? And why was there no one here? This most likely was somewhere in Glymewood, as that was the place the road bordered. But this was little help. Glymewood was thick, virgin forest with not a single road passing through its primal wilderness, and it went on for countless miles. Except at its very edges, few dared venture in. It was said that there were still wild wolves roaming its shady interior, and even wilder men. Surely she had not been saved from a snowy death only to be lost in the forest…?

The red flush of dawn tinged the tiny amount of sky visible through the dense canopy, and light was slowly creeping into the greenwood. Her eye caught sight of another light. It was bright and flickering, and just visible amongst the trees at the top of the bank.

'Pray, if there is anyone there, show yourself!' she called.

The torch came a little closer, but its bearer was invisible. The light just seemed to hover there. 'Follow, follow!' called a distant voice.

Was this to be the guide that led her out of the wild forest? There was a chance some evil thing was trying to lure her ever deeper into Glymewood, but it was better than stumbling around the thick wood all alone, that was for sure.

She got up and started climbing towards the light. But the light never got any nearer. When she moved forward, so did the hovering light. Rowena tripped and fell in the half-light more than once as she hurried after the ever-receding beacon.

'Stop and show yourself!' she cried out to the light. 'You have nothing to fear from me.'

But the light never stopped, and after passing under kingly oak and elm, through ferny forest glade and wooded dell, over crumbling log and snow-covered hollow, she at last noticed the trees thinning and the morning light growing brighter. Just as the climbing sun was coming near to revealing the bearer of the light, she looked up at the crimson sky overhead, and when she looked again for the light she looked in vain, for it had vanished.

She burst out of the trees and onto the road, right at the place she had been the previous night when the torch-bearers and their strange, sleep-bringing smoke had materialised seemly out of nowhere. Suddenly remembering the precious bundle, Rowena looked around for it. And there it was, covered in a layer of snow and guarded by the cluster of snowdrops with their little white helmets and bright green spears.

'Friend,' she called out, 'wherever you are, I thank you! If there is ever any service I can do for you in return, send a grey goose feather to Eaglestone Castle and I will meet you at this very spot the next day at noon.'

No human voice answered, but as it sighed through the treetops, the wind seemed to say, 'Yes, yesss, yesss...'

Casting a last furtive look around, Rowena the seized the ends of her cloth-wrapped bundle and started off down the snow-covered road once more.

A very strange adventure it had been. Glymewood was said to be enchanted. Perhaps they were elves or woodland fairies? Whatever it had been, it was truly strange. She would do well to have a care whom she told about it, or folk might start thinking her mighty queer...

It was not long before Rowena was overtaken by a long-eared

little donkey that was even furrier than the old peddler's pony had been. It was pulling a small, simple, two-wheeled cart. At first she thought the short, muffled figure driving it was a child, but when the donkey halted beside her, the driver proved to be a dwarf.

She felt a little frightened by his strange and rather ugly appearance, for he had a long beard, plaited for half its length, and was dressed in a tall, pointed hat and a cloak made of small pieces of cloth of every hue stitched together. His voice proved to be as rough as his appearance, but otherwise he was a friendly fellow who introduced himself as Garroway, travelling jester.

When he told her that he was travelling to the tournament at Shrewsbury Castle, all her reservations disappeared in a flash of delight and relief, and she was soon bumping down the road on the back of the dwarf's cart with her bundle beside her.

With the exception of being jeered and pelted with stones by some drunken youths loitering outside an alehouse, Rowena and the travelling jester had an uneventful journey to Shrewsbury Castle.

Total darkness had reigned for several hours by the time they neared it. A brief but heavy shower of freezing sleet just before dusk had soaked through Rowena's thin cloak, making her gown unpleasantly damp and her dripping hair cling limply to her face.

As the little donkey trotted over the brow of the final hill, Shrewsbury Castle's brightly-lit windows could be seen twinkling down below, and from among the magnificent tents filling the field in front, the trailing smoke and glowing flames of many braziers. As Rowena had journeyed westwards, the snow had become less and less. Now there was only a sprinkling atop the higher hills. But it was still bitterly cold, and the clear, starlit night promised a lengthy visit from Jack Frost before dawn.

Once the field was reached, her bundle unloaded and the generous Garroway thanked, Rowena stood still for a moment to decide on her next move. The sound of gay laughter and merry music drifted across from the castle on the cold night air. Lady Sabina and Lord Shrewsbury's wedding had been earlier that day, and doubtless the feasting and dancing would go on far into the night.

But where was Sir Richard? As a knight participating in the tournament, he would have been invited to the feast. Although, knowing his dislike of pompous gatherings, she guessed he might have chosen not to attend. Either way, he would almost certainly be staying in one of the many tents crowding the field.

Sir Richard, who did not own such a marvel himself, had mentioned that an old friend from his tourneying days had offered to loan him one. This meant that the tent would not be in his heraldic colours, which was the usual way of identifying a knight's belongings.

Realising that the task of tracking Sir Richard and Pepin down was going to be hard enough without having to carry the armour around (for carry it she would have to, as the ground was thoroughly muddy), Rowena decided to leave it in the safekeeping of a nearby watchman until she had found Sir Richard.

There were few knights about the darkened camp, but plenty of movement was still going on as servants and attendants of the nobleman and lords went purposefully about their masters' business. Some luckier (or lazier) ones sat around campfires with pots of ale in hand, laughing, talking, eating or simply engaging in that most ancient of entertainments: staring into the flames.

Rowena hurried between the tents, dodging servants, stepping over sleeping dogs and ducking to avoid the guy-ropes that loomed out from the dark, almost always at neck height. She looked left, she looked right, she looked up, she looked down, but not a sight of her knight did she find.

Then, as she was reaching the edge of the noble encampment,

the sound of music danced across on the damp, chilly night air. She stepped out from between two tents to find herself in a small clearing amid the forest of tents and ropes, where a band of musicians stood playing.

There was a willowy, fine-fingered young man playing the viol, wearing the soulful expression that no self-respecting viol player is without; a tall, portly fellow playing the horn; and a small, fiery-eyed, lightning-fingered youth playing the recorder. Their tune was jaunty, their harmonies delightful, and their audience of three wolfhounds, two squires and one bedraggled, dripping, frozen maiden, entranced.

After Rowena had been standing silently for several minutes, the players began a new movement. The melody became slow, lyrical and sweeping. It prompted her to finally look about the clearing. Almost immediately, her eyes alighted on a shield leaning against a tent near to where the minstrels stood. The dim firelight kept many secrets, but the crest emblazoned upon the shield seemed familiar even in the half-light.

Lifting her sodden, muddied hem, she hurried over to it. And there it was: Sir Richard's fierce gold-armoured Saint George slaying the black, fire-breathing dragon with his flaming sword of iron.

A dim glow was visible through the tent's heavy cloth sides, but not a sound came from within. At the very threshold of the goal she had suffered and risked so much to reach, she froze with one shivering hand poised on the cloth hanging across the entrance, suddenly afraid to came in from the cold. To see once again that man who, since first she saw him grimly scratching out that ransom payment, had exposed her to more danger than ever she thought it possible for one lady to see…

An imminent meeting with such a man would have filled many women with horror. But the only horror Rowena felt was at the thought that it surely was the last time she would stand before his door and know she was moments away from meeting that piercing dark gaze. That countenance once so feared, and now so loved…

The minstrels' tune slipped into a slow, lilting lullaby that was like an angel's rocking of a holy cradle. As if in a dream, Rowena lifted the hanging cloth and stepped silently inside. In the centre of the round, luxuriously furnished tent sat a dimly glowing brazier, a slight haze of blue smoke hung in the warm air and—she suddenly caught her breath. For directly in front of her upon a low bed, lay Sir Richard.

Embraced by the warm, sweetly scented air and carried upon the wings of the heavenly, rocking lullaby, the cold and tiredness gripping her magically melted away. Trance-like, she undid her dripping cloak, let it fall to the ground and glided over to her sleeping knight.

Illuminated by the soft golden glow of the fire and half-covered by a fur rug, he lay with one hand beside his head on the white pillow and the other on the swan pendant lying over his heart. His linen shirt was unlaced, falling off one shoulder and revealing a cruel white scar slashed across the pale skin. The gentle, rhythmic rise and fall of his breast was the only thing that moved. Deep in sleep's holy embrace, his countenance was so beautiful and noble he looked to her like an angel fallen from heaven. With lips slightly parted, he slept so serenely she did not wish to wake him.

Love and tenderness filled her heart as she gently sat down on the edge of the bed and placed her small hand over the large one resting on the green swan. She felt the insistent, throbbing pulse of his beating heart faintly through her cold hand.

Even as she smiled, joy mingled with sadness. The heart which now beat so certainly might be still forever more by sundown on the morrow. Was this the end of his earthly journey? The man lying so vulnerable before her had come so very far since that fateful day when first her eyes had met his. Although only six months had passed since, already it seemed to belong to some other, far distant, long-ago life.

Sitting beside her sleeping knight, Rowena instinctively reached a trembling hand out to push back a stiff black lock that had fallen over the noble forehead.

But as she leaned forward, a hot tear overflowed her eye and fell onto his naked breast.

In an instant the eyelids lifted and the rhythmic breaths stopped. His enthralled eyes held her gaze unblinkingly, yet they seemed to pass right through her as though she was an apparition. Then his eyes slowly fell shut again.

But a moment later they were wide open, and in less time than it took for Rowena's heart to skip a beat, his arms were locked around her in a tight embrace while he laughed, wept, kissed her and thanked God.

'How did you get here? They said you would not come! Are you well? Why are you so cold, beloved?' The questions tumbled out as he clasped her cold face in a grip that was almost admonishing.

She just fell onto his shoulder and flung her arms around his neck.

He drew her to him and pulled the purple, fur-trimmed cloak draped across a nearby chair over her. It was warm from the brazier and smelt of the familiar mix of leather and heavy, spicy perfume particular to Sir Richard.

'Why are you so wet?' he demanded again.

'It rained.'

He pushed her back so he could wrap his cloak about her properly. 'Well I never,' he replied with a bemused smile. 'And there was I thinking that my little pixie had gone and fallen into a milk-pail.'

Now that Sir Richard had finished his attentions, she rested her head back on his chest.

He leaned back against the bed's fur-draped headboard and wriggled a little until he was comfortable, then put his arms around her. 'When the Cunninghams arrived yesterday, they told me that you'd changed your mind and would not come despite their entreaties.'

'May God have mercy on their deceitful souls.'

'Be assured that I didn't believe them for one single moment. In my darkest moments I feared that they had done you some evil; perhaps quietly arranged for an accident to befall you or slave-trader to take you. As a matter of fact, I was fully intending to cause a scene by publicly demanding to know where you were.'

'There's no need for that now. I do hope you're not too disappointed—I know how much you enjoy causing a good scene.'

He laughed softly. 'I'm barely disappointed at all, my love.'

She suddenly lifted her head. 'Oh yes—I almost forget! I brought a gift for you all the way from Stoatley.'

'That you have brought your dear self all the way from Stoatley is gift enough for me.'

'Ah, but you cannot wear *me* as protection against the blows of your opponents.'

He looked around the tent keenly. 'Now that you have got me all fired up, where is it?'

'I left it with one of the camp guards for safekeeping while I found you. Where is young Pepin? I need him to go fetch it.'

'Pepin!' Sir Richard shouted.

There was no reply.

'Pepin, where are you now that I finally want you!' he shouted again.

This at last brought a puffing, bright-eyed Pepin ducking into the tent. 'Sire? Mistress Rowena!' he exclaimed, suddenly noticing her.

'Yes, the very same,' said Sir Richard. 'Now could you go and fetch something she left with the camp guard?'

The page gave a quick nod before dashing off on his errand with an extra spring in his already bouncing step.

Puffing and soft cursing announced the page's return a rather long while before he finally appeared through the entrance. 'If I had not succeeded in tricking that guard into helping me carry this *thing,*' he muttered distastefully, 'I do believe I may have been forced to drag it here. Think how much awful mud would have got into our lovely tent then!' he finished, dropping the bundle to the floor with a final gasp.

Sir Richard threw a well-aimed almond nut at his page's head. 'You forget that all this finery is not ours, young rascal, but the property of the generous Sir Roland.'

By the time his master had finished, the boy was already smoothing his ruffled hair before a mirror and examining his forehead to see if the nut had made a mark. '*Strictly speaking,* it is not ours, but that need not be *universally* known.'

'Is this your way of saying that you have been going around telling everyone all this belongs to me?' asked his master, a dangerous edge creeping into his voice.

The pageboy squirmed slightly and smoothed his hair more vigorously. 'Maybe I might have done…'

Sir Richard fixed a chastising look on his page. 'Pepin…'

The page flung his mirror down nervously. 'It's not fair! A few squires were taunting me, saying how I was a lowly born dog whose place was the gutter, and that you were stony-broke and past your useable date. They were pinching me and pushing me around!' He looked as though he would cry if any more was said against him.

Sir Richard softened, but not before he had sent a final glare in Pepin's direction. He then turned his attention to the bundle lying on the carpeted floor. 'May I unwrap it, Rowena?'

She smiled and nodded.

The knight knelt down beside it and set about untying the tightly knotted cloth. He had a deal of trouble with the knot, but at last it gave in.

He was still for a moment before frowningly holding up Rowena's best gown. 'Thank you for the wonderful gift, dearest, but I'm not quite sure that this style would suit me, and perhaps it might be a tad on the small side too.'

She laughed. 'That's mine and you know it! Look underneath.'

He looked. 'How did you get this?'

'I...I sort of borrowed it...' she muttered, refusing to look him in the eye.

'So you stole it. Judging by the amount of rust and dust coating it, this armour was neither well-loved nor needed where it was.'

'Armour?' cried Pepin, leaping up from the chair he had been sulking in. In a flash, the pageboy was down on his knees pulling the armour out and examining it.

Pepin soon came upon the breastplate, and holding it in one hand, practically hauled his master up with the other. 'Stand up! I need to see if it will fit you.'

The tall knight complied and soon he was having a breastplate shoved against his front. 'Hold this!' the page instructed his master.

Sir Richard held it. A second plate was shoved against his back and then Pepin buckled the two pieces together at the shoulder. A helmet so coated in dust its steel was barely visible was unceremoniously thrust over Sir Richard's head. Young Pepin then stepped back to survey the result.

'Yes, very good,' pronounced the page. 'It will do nicely.'

The armour was then removed by Pepin, and without further ado he carted his prize off to the corner of the tent where the rest of Sir Richard's arms set, and started polishing and cleaning the suit of armour.

Sir Richard sunk tiredly onto a couch, leaned back against its many cushions and patted the space beside him. 'Come, sit and tell me the tale of your travels.'

She sat and started her story. He listened intently, but when she reached the bit where she had been all alone in the snowy wilderness with night falling, and the strange cloaked figures had materialised seemingly out of nowhere, she was obliged to pause while he made exclamations of horror and concern.

But once he had been assured that all turned out well, she was able to continue, though with his arms tightly around her.

The warmth and comfort made Rowena drowsy, and not long after her tale was finished, her head began to nod and her eyelids to droop, and very soon she was fast asleep.

* * * *

Lady Sabina was truly stunned. All she could do was stare in a most impolite way as her cousin swept into the viewing gallery on the morning of the tournament.

Rowena returned her gaze boldly, and gave a slight inclination of the head as she passed by. Out of the corner of her eye, the flame-haired damsel observed Lady Sabina give Lord Shrewsbury a dig in the ribs and hiss something into his ear. In response, Lord Shrewsbury tightened his lips and took a calculated step to the side that put him out of reach of his new wife.

Rowena pulled Sir Richard's purple cloak more tightly around her, revelling in its warmth and the cosy comfort of his manly scent, which clung heavily to the garment. She was grateful for the loan of it. Her own thin, moth-eaten, damp and much-maligned rabbit fur cloak would have generated stares and unkind whispers. The thought of shaming or embarrassing Sir Richard had weighed on her ever since Lady Sabina had planted her poison words, and the knight's assurances that nothing she did or wore would ever shame him had still not killed them.

The wealthy, high-born nobleman, ladies and knights thronging the grand viewing gallery in front of the lists were clad in the most costly and magnificent attire. Furs of mink, ermine and bear were to be seen at every turn, as were rich velvets, fine silks, brocades, cloth of gold, much intricate embroidery, and most dazzling of all, cloth with scatterings of precious gems attached. There was much delicate laughter, refined chatter and feminine simpering from the legions of beautiful ladies gracing the gallery.

Though present in not nearly so great a number as the ladies, a scattering of men also preened and paraded about the gallery or charmed and flattered the lovely damsels. Many of them were knights who were to joust later in the day, and were taking the opportunity to assess their opponents.

The band of minstrels who had been playing so entrancingly in the camp the previous night provided the gathering with delightfully merry music. Rowena stopped and leaned against a post to listen awhile.

But she was soon disturbed by the sight of Anne enthusiastically beckoning to her from thirty paces away. Rowena smiled reservedly and lifted a hand in salute, but hesitated about whether to come over, for Lady Sabina was standing at Anne's side, pretending not to notice her friend's vigorous flapping.

'Oh do look, darling, there is dear Cousin Rowena!' she heard Anne saying to Lady Sabina.

Lady Sabina did not look. She was far too busy pretending to be engrossed in the goings-on down in front of the gallery.

Rowena turned back to the minstrels, hoping Anne would give

up.

But Anne did not give up. A moment later Rowena was faced with the sight of Anne ploughing through the throng dragging Lady Sabina along with her.

'Oh how wonderful!' cried Anne. 'She said she was not coming—we simply *must* go over and say how do! I will absolutely die if I go another moment without knowing simply everything!'

Lady Sabina could no longer pretend not to have noticed her cousin. She had fixed a sour little smile on her face and was making reluctant noises to the oblivious Anne.

'Darling, how simply marvellous to see you here!' Anne cried ecstatically as she pounced on Rowena.

'God give you good morning, Mistress Anne,' Rowena replied in a friendly but formal manner, attempting to extract herself from Anne's excited embrace.

'Bina totally assured me that you absolutely would not come, so how come you are here after all? I was just telling dear Sabina that I would absolutely die if I did not know what happened this very instant—did I not, darling?' Anne demanded of Lady Sabina.

Lady Sabina looked as though the effort of smiling was agonising. 'Ahem, indeed, darling.'

'It is not entirely true that I would not come,' Rowena informed an over-excited Anne and an over-horrified Lady Sabina. 'I always intended to come, but at the last minute there turned out to be no room for me in the Cunninghams' coach.' She shot her cousin a steely look. 'Lady Sabina's pride had unfortunately suddenly inflated a great deal, leaving no space left. I was forced to make my own way here alone. I nearly froze to death in the snow and was lucky not to be robbed by outlaws in Glymewood, and I had a terribly strange experience which involved being drugged and carried off into the forest, but I'm here, anyhow.'

These words made little impact on Anne. 'Oh fiddle-diddums, is not this simply marvellous? All us maidens here together!' she gushed, linking an arm through Rowena's. 'This cloak, is it not Sir Richard's?' Anne asked suddenly, fingering the garment.

'Why yes, it is.'

Anne, who was a pretty but forgettable-looking damsel, suddenly went bitter. 'I see. And did you steal it from him this morning or last night, while he was sleeping?'

Rowena was rendered speechless by Anne's meanness.

'Steal what?' asked a dark, masculine voice.

Anne's feet screeched on the floorboards as she spun around to face Sir Richard, who had just appeared behind them. Her sallow face flushed crimson and she looked so mortified Rowena felt a little sorry for her. 'Steal? You—you know, I have quite forgotten what it was I said! I really am such an awful scatter-brain!'

The dark knight smiled wolfishly. 'Is that so?'

'Yes!' blurted poor Anne, squirming desperately.

Sir Richard placed a gauntleted hand on Anne's shoulder and leaned down to her ear. 'I think you will find, dear lady, that some things are better forgotten.'

Anne nodded vigorously, her already-round eyes growing into perfect orbs.

Sir Richard turned to Rowena and bowed graciously. 'Greetings, darling.'

Conscious of all the eyes that followed the famous Sir Richard Hastings, she gave a stiff, over-careful curtsy. 'Greetings, Sir Richard.'

'Lady Shrewsbury.' He bowed to Lady Sabina. 'I trust that your wedding night was not *too* dull?'

Rowena caught her breath sharply and shot a meaningful look at Sir Richard, who had a slight smile playing on the corners of his determinedly straight lips.

The regal lily gave a haughty sniff and turned her blood-red lips up into a sneer. 'Really, Sir Richard, I do not know to what you refer.'

Her face may not have given her away, but Lady Sabina's heart could be seen to quicken, as the left side of her chest, laid bare by a neckline so low it threatened to render its wearer indecent if she stooped, pulsed violently.

Anne, who appeared to have recovered from her earlier shock, giggled wildly. 'I am afraid dear old Sabina has become quite the prude since her wedding, for not a word will she utter about last night.' She jostled the haughty ice queen teasingly. 'Is that not so, darling?'

'Such things are not for the ears of little girls,' Lady Sabina hissed, stepping back from Anne with a look of cold fury.

Anne's face puckered up and she looked as if she was going to burst into tears, but then she suddenly noticed someone passing by. 'Lord Shrewsbury!' she cried, lurching towards the nobleman and seizing his arm. 'We are having such marvellously fun larks here; you absolutely must join us!'

The little lord was clearly horrified at being kidnapped in this way, but he did his best not to let it show. 'Oh indeed, how lovely for you,' he replied tightly, setting his many-plumed hat back into place. He then bowed nervously to Rowena and Sir Richard. 'Greetings...'

Sir Richard bowed politely. 'Good day, my lord. I like that chicken you are wearing on your head. Is it the latest fashion at court?'

Anne did not manage to suppress her giggle, but Rowena was coughing into her sleeve with better grace.

'It's the very latest style,' Lord Shrewsbury replied as forcefully as he could, putting a hand to his hip and looking the tall knight in the eye. 'Unlike your attire, which is *so* last year,' he added, with a haughty toss of the head.

Sir Richard's dangerous smirk grew a little more fatal. 'Yes, manliness did *use* to be quite fashionable. But this new fashion of wearing a cock on one's head; I think I shall let it pass me by. Cocks, after all, were created not merely to be decorative, but also to bring about the next generation.'

Lord Shrewsbury almost choked. 'How dare you!'

'Do pardon me, my lord, but I was merely discussing chickens. Unless you happen to be a chicken, I do not see a cause for insult, so please, do enlighten me.'

'I'm not fowl—'

'Indeed…'

Lord Shrewsbury stamped his foot. 'I meant *a* fowl! A damn chicken, cock!'

Still smiling darkly and smugly, Sir Richard gave a slight bow. 'Indeed, my lord. I can see that the events of last night have left you quite overwrought. Perhaps you ought to go and have a lie-down? I am sure you will find a pageboy to tuck you in.'

The little lord was almost hopping with fury. 'I—I—damn you, Hastings!' And with that, he flounced off to join the posse of languid, doe-eyed boys and young men lolling on the couches in the back corner.

'Name-calling is a foul response for a nobleman,' Sir Richard murmured, shaking his head. 'You must try to control your husband better, Lady Shrewsbury.'

'And *you* must try to refrain from pecking at your betters, Sir Richard!' hissed the regal lily.

But Sir Richard did not pay her any attention. He had already turned to Anne. 'Might we be hearing your wedding bells soon?'

Pained disappointment crossed Anne's face. 'Well—no. My father died some years back, and ever since then my mother has become a practical recluse. She makes no effort to find a husband for me or take me out in society. She just mopes about the house all day talking about how she yearns for death. I was only able to attend this wedding because our neighbours were going and I was allowed to journey here with them.' Her eyes suddenly lighted up a little. 'There are so many knights here; perhaps one of them will like me!'

Sir Richard smiled and placed a kindly hand on Anne's arm. 'Perhaps one will, but I would avoid Sir Percy if I were you.' He pointed to a tall man of about forty with high cheek bones and a rough but dashing air. 'He has quite a reputation for luring ladies into his bed and leaving them weeping in a puddle of ruined honour and broken dreams soon after.'

Anne's face fell. 'Oh.'

He grimaced sympathetically. 'Already been making eyes at you, has he?'

She nodded uncomfortably, before quickly changing the subject. 'Why is Sir Roger de Wintore not here yet? Surely he is going to come after all? I have been very much looking forward to your fight with him!'

'He will be here.'

'Where does he usually reside?'

'Since I burned down his castle on the South Coast, I expect his seat is somewhere in France. He is reputed to mainly spend his time fighting across Europe for whichever man will pay the most money for his services.'

'I shall be praying for your victory, Sir Richard!'

'Thank you, madam.'

Lady Sabina put haughty hand to sharp hip. 'I have no need for prayers. I already know who is going to win.'

'You do?' gasped an incredulous Anne.

'The knight who triumphs will be the knight who has chosen *me* as his lady.'

Anne leaned towards her friend conspiratorially. 'Really, darling, if you are intending to use your position as judge of honour at the tournament to favour your own knight, you ought not to tell anyone. Besides, it would be quite disloyal not to support our very own Chaucy hero.'

Lady Sabina cast an arch, venomous glance at Sir Richard. 'He might be the hero of Chaucy's riff-raff, but he is not *my* hero.' The snow queen then stepped towards Sir Richard and leaned to whisper in his ear. 'No man turns me down—especially for *that—'* she shot a poisonous look at Rowena, 'and goes unpunished. I have not forgotten your insults, Sir Richard. Nor have I forgiven them. You are going to die like a dog.' She uttered the words slowly, carefully and viciously. A final haughty toss of the head and the ice queen was gone.

Rowena suddenly felt as though icy hands had closed around her heart. She searched for Sir Richard's eyes, and found them fixed on her already.

To her surprise, he gave her a reassuring smile. 'That is precisely what I have been hoping she would do. The herald keeps tally of the points gained by each knight, but when it comes to any matters of contention such as a draw, a broken rule, or calling a halt to a fight which is getting out of hand, the judge of honour's word is law. We will be fighting with unlawful sharp swords and the fight will most certainly get out of hand. Any judge except your kindly cousin would force the fight to be stopped.'

.24.

Saint George for Justice

ROWENA had come to accept Sir Richard's imminent battle with de Wintore. De Wintore was a ruthless, dishonourable and heartless mercenary who would never forgive the young knight who had betrayed his sister and dragged the proud de Wintore name through the mud. He was a man possessed—a man who would attempt to destroy anyone loved by Sir Richard, and torment him until his dying day. She had learned to bear with composure the burden of anxiety that came with being a knight's lady.

Not one word of doubt or plea to withdraw from harm's way passed her lips as she solemnly helped Sir Richard don his armour. The knight had spent the past hour sitting beneath the towering oak tree at the bottom of the meadow, staring silently at the gurgling stream. Upon emerging, iron-willed determination and unshakable faith were firmly fixed on his countenance.

Pepin had polished the dusty armour into an astonishing shine that spoke volumes about the young page's enthusiasm. As Rowena helped Pepin put the armour on Sir Richard, silence reigned in the tent. It was broken only by an occasional softly murmured instruction between page and knight.

Once the armour was finally filled by a human form after its long years of housing nothing but dust, spider webs and musty air, Pepin knelt to attach Sir Richard's spurs.

Then the warrior was handed his trusty blade sheathed in its scabbard, and once that was buckled about the knightly waist, Pepin added the finishing touch to his knight: a cape of white silk emblazoned with Sir Richard's Saint George slaying the dragon upon the background of a red formy-fitchee couped cross, a combination of sword and crucifix symbolising unshakable faith. This was fastened on at the top of each shoulder, and after a final smooth to the cape and spit-and-polish to the already-gleaming breastplate, Sir Richard was declared ready for glory by Pepin.

Giving her own garment a final fretful smooth, Rowena followed the dapper page and his professional, know-it-all aura out of the tent. After its abuse at the hands of Lady Sabina and rough journey to Shrewsbury, Rowena's best winter gown was not in the best of states. The creases and wrinkles covering every thread of it had proved impossible to get out, and mud still clung stubbornly to it despite her best efforts, which did not amount to much as only a small quantity of water could be deployed without risking soaking the gown.

Rowena eyed the well-turned-out Pepin wistfully. How come he always managed to keep so clean despite all the time he spent around horses and armour? The page's doublet was his most prized possession. It was in the colours of Sir Richard's coat of arms and had his Saint George slaying the dragon embroidered on the back. It had been lovingly created by his proud and doting mother.

Rowena sighed. At least she had found enough of Mother Nature's free treasures even in this bare landscape, where harsh winter's reign was only just beginning to be melted by tender spring's warm breath. Green ivy there was in plenty, purple violets too, and with a little help from a blue and white ribbon, she had fashioned a garland which she hoped would draw eyes away from the less becoming aspects of her attire.

The magnificent Lucifer stood saddled by the hitching-rail in the centre of the clearing in the tents, his midnight-black fur gleaming despite it still being his longer, coarser winter coat. There was no doubting it: if you wanted something polished, Pepin was the fellow for the job.

The page hurried to the tall steed's head and took his reins in hand, ready for his master to mount. But before Sir Richard mounted, he turned back to face his fearfully following lady. Her eyes were cast down and lips tightly pressed together as she bravely fought to retain composure. An almost overwhelming urge to fling herself to the ground and cling to him whilst begging him not to go gripped her, and it took all her strength to resist.

'I'm sorry, beloved,' he whispered.

She lifted her eyes, but they did not need to come far before they met his dark gaze, as he had lowered himself almost to her height. 'I—I—' she started, but stopped as she felt her suppressed emotions begin to surface.

He placed a gentle hand on her arm. 'I know. You are the bravest of women, but even the hardiest soul reaches a limit somewhere. If it would not be blasphemy, I would curse God every day for allowing me to dwell on earth for a lifetime when I rightly should have fallen straight down from my heavenly birthplace and into Satan's hellish realm.'

All trace of hesitance was gone in an instant. She looked at him, eyes burning with a fire that dried up the dew filling them a moment ago. 'And I thank God every day for blessing me with such a loyal, brave and ever-striving knight; for that is what matters, Sir Richard. Whatever obstacle destiny places in your way you seek to overcome. Your place *is* on this earth, for it is the place from which each one of us must strive to climb up towards the heavenly and away from the hellish. You must not think you cause me grief. It is not you who cause me grief, but my love for you. I tremble for you because I love you.'

He took her tightly intertwined hands and clasped them

between his. 'Your love kindled a fire in my soul which can never be quenched. Love is a fire which burns stronger and truer than the flames of hate, and with God's grace, I will triumph. Now you must go to the gallery, my love. I need to warm Lucifer up in the field behind the lists and get the feel of this damnably heavy armour.'

'Can I come with you?'

'No, it is not safe,' he replied firmly. 'There are horses, knights and attendants milling everywhere; if you were to get run over it would be a terrible distraction.'

Biting her lip, she looked down and blinked hard. 'Very well.'

He kissed her on the forehead, and then turned to mount his horse.

But Rowena seized his steel-encased arm. 'Richard!'

'Yes?'

Heedless of all the watching eyes, she flung her arms around his neck and pressed her lips to his in a passionate kiss. At first his lips were hard with surprise, but after only a moment he yielded to her and returned the kiss. She pulled her knight down towards herself, put her hand on his cheek and sunk deeper into his intense and tender kiss.

When Sir Richard and his lady at last drew apart, the knight turned from her and swung up onto his black steed with surprising ease. Then he stooped down and bestowed a final kiss upon his beloved's upturned face, and rode away. He and Pepin were soon swallowed up by the crowd of tents, horses and men.

For several minutes Rowena stared vacantly at the busy crowd that had swallowed her knight. Then she choked back the tears threatening to overcome her, and began walking towards the arena. A knight as brave as he deserved a lady just as fearless. Whatever churned within her heart, she would not let him down by wailing like a child.

The viewing galleries were now twice as full as they had been that morning. It was a hard task to reach the front of the gallery without engaging in any ill-mannered jostling or base pushing, but after many a 'pardon me' and 'might a lady beg a place to watch her knight do battle?' Rowena at last arrived at the front rail.

A great number of other eager damsels were clustered there, excitedly chattering about whose knight was the most handsome, had fought the best or was the most likely to win. The question of which knights had or had not asked certain damsels if they could wear their favour, and which damsels had or had not accepted, was discussed with an enthusiasm that sometimes bordered on the hysterical, and many a hopeful damsel anxiously weighed her chances of being asked for a favour by her favourite.

The arena in which the knights jousted was oblong, with a barrier running down the centre but stopping before it reached the end, to allow the knights to ride around the outside of the lists. The viewing galleries were temporarily erected structures consisting of a wooden platform and frame with a roof and sides of brightly-coloured cloth. Banners bearing the coats of arms of the wealthiest and most famed knights attending the tournament fluttered from the top of the viewing galleries (Sir Richard's coat of arms was notably absent), and taking pride of place at the highest point on the gallery roof was the Shrewsbury family crest.

Rowena could not resist an ironic chuckle on seeing that their coat of arms had a cockatrice on it. The cockatrice was a mythical beast with the head and legs of a cock, the wings and scaly body of a dragon, and a long, barbed tail. It is the king of serpents, and legend had it that it came from an egg laid by a nine-year-old cock and hatched by a toad on a dunghill, and that its breath was so poisonous and its sight so foul that anyone coming within range would be killed. The cockatrice was supposed to be a fearsome symbol that struck terror into the hearts of enemies, but when borne by Lord Shrewsbury, it was more likely to inspire mirth.

Two young knights mounted on magnificent warhorses had just entered the arena. A troop of liveried attendants clustered around each, and as the herald put his trumpet to his lips and blew a voluntary, the knights rode out onto the field.

'Sir Bertram Ailetts, oldest son of the Duke of Norfolk and vanquisher of three knights already this day!' announced the herald, who then waited while Sir Bertram punched the air in victory (which Rowena thought ungracious) and took a princely bow. 'And Sir Edward Wurttenberg, youngest son of Lord Wurttenberg!' continued the herald, with a showy flourish.

Young Sir Edward gave a reserved bow.

'Sir Bertram has been unconquered in these lists, noble lords and ladies! Will this new opponent change that?' called the herald, and was answered by shouts of 'No!' from the crowd.

Sir Bertram, who was fair-haired, blue-eyed and carried himself with a proud, disdainful air, spurred his steel-grey charger violently forward whilst holding it back by the reins, causing the poor animal to prance stiffly sideways. The knight clearly wanted to make a show. He finally allowed his steed to move forward, though still tormented it so it danced tensely. Sir Bertram rode along close to the viewing galleries as he set out to ask his chosen lady for a token of her favour. He trotted a short way before suddenly hauling his horse to a stop.

He looked at a regal, stunningly dressed and bejewelled young beauty who sat surrounded by a bevy of fair companions. 'Thou art the fairest creature who has or will ever grace this earth. Thou art my heart's queen, my very life, and if any man says otherwise I will strike him down with one blow! I request, my peerless paramour, a token of your favour.'

The regal beauty seemed well pleased by this flowery speech, for she bestowed a deeply self-satisfied smile on proud Sir Bertram. 'My lord, I grant your humble request,' she said, stepping up to the rail and tying a costly gold silk veil around the knight's upper arm.

Sir Bertram cantered back with his prize, an even more self-satisfied smirk etched on his proud face than he had ridden out with.

Now it was Sir Edward's turn. He was a much less sure-looking young knight with a head of thick auburn hair. The white mare he was mounted on seemed almost as nervous as her rider, for the horse had already shied twice at the banners blowing in the breeze and was now displaying some reluctance to move forward. But a few kind words and a firm nudge later and the white mare was walking slowly onwards.

The young knight quietly halted only a few paces from where Rowena stood, and smiled bashfully up at a sleek-haired damsel with an arresting but slightly sharp beauty. 'Lady, might I beg a favour?' he asked in a soft voice.

The damsel glared at young Sir Edward for a moment before giving a disdainful toss of her head. 'Sir Edward, you please me not.'

The young man's colour deepened. 'Is—is that a no?'

She looked away disdainfully.

Every eye was fixed on Sir Edward. Being quite well acquainted with public humiliation herself, Rowena felt desperately sorry for the poor young knight.

He reeled speechlessly for a few moments before franticly searching the crowd for a kinder face. He looked left, he looked ahead, he looked right—and stopped when his eyes met Rowena's. 'Lady, is there any chance you might—'

She smiled. 'Sir Knight, I am deeply honoured by your request. You may wear my token of favour.'

A moment later she was tying the blue and white ribbon from her garland around the grateful young knight's arm.

'God bless you, kind lady,' stammered Sir Edward, as Rowena put the final bow in.

She gave him an encouraging smile. 'May virtue always dwell in your heart, noble knight.'

And with that, the knight trotted down to his end of the lists to await the herald's signal.

'The terms are: five courses with lance and shield, with the knight with the greatest number of points being victorious!' the herald announced, and blew a ringing call on his golden trumpet.

Rowena watched breathlessly as her champion charged. Sir Bertram shattered his lance on young Sir Edward, who managed a respectable hit to his opponent's shoulder. Proud Sir Bertram was handed another lance by his squire, and they charged a second time.

A hit to the shield was received by her champion, who hit Sir Bertram on the shoulder a second time. The third course was lined up and begun. This time both lances shattered.

Shouts of encouragement sounded from the galleries as Sir Bertram's large band of followers realised the match was proving more challenging than expected. The only shouts for Sir Edward came from his own small group of attendants standing beside the lists, and from his new lady. A fourth resulted in two more shattered lances. With Sir Bertram leading by only one point, his supporters' calls became louder.

'Remember Achilles!' Rowena called to her champion as he passed by on his way to lining up for the final course.

Sir Edward reined in his white mare and lifted his visor as he faced Sir Bertram across the field, lance raised. 'Sir Bertram, you have a vanity which is unmanly, and your love for yourself is greater than the love you bear for your lady!'

'Damn you, oafish runt!' bellowed Sir Bertram, lowering his lance.

This time Sir Bertram charged at Sir Edward with such mad fury that his lance was not properly aimed before it hit its target. The point glanced off Sir Edward's shield, but Sir Edward's lance hit squarely on his opponent's breastplate. A loud clang and explosion of wood later and Proud Sir Bertram was sprawled on the ground while young Sir Edward gracefully reined his steed in at the other end of the lists. Sir Edward gave a slight bow in response to the crowd's admiring applause before he quietly exited the field.

Sir Bertram's exit was rather less heroic. He had to be helped off the field by three squires.

'A most admirable and unexpected victory for Sir Edward of Wurttenberg, honoured lords and ladies!' called the herald. 'I am sure that, as a seventh son, he will be well glad of the money he receives for Sir Bertram's ransom. And now for the spectacle which you have all been awaiting with such eagerness: the fight between Sir Roger de Wintore and his hated nemesis, Sir Richard Hastings! This, I am informed by our most fair and noble judge of honour, is a grudge-match. Who will triumph? Take your bets, fair lords and ladies!'

The pleasure generated by Sir Edward's deserved victory was squeezed from Rowena in an instant as icy fear closed its iron grip around her racing heart. The viewing gallery stirred like a disturbed flock of roosting sparrows as spectators whispered and shifted, commenting and speculating on the outcome.

A whisper of 'Sir Richard is poorly equipped and well rusty; I bet you two pounds the man will not last beyond fifteen minutes' was exchanged between a pair of limpid young peacocks standing close behind Rowena.

The maiden gasped and put her hands over her ears.

Then the herald put his golden horn to his lips and sounded a majestic, ringing call. Rowena uncovered her ears and closed her hands around her thin gold pendant of the raying sun as her knight took to the field of blood and glory.

'Sir Richard Hastings of Chaucy, second son of the Duke of Melvales, winner of many past glories in the lists and on the field of battle, and famed rescuer of the ladies of the Castle of the Skull!' announced the herald, finishing with his usual showy bow and flourish of the arm.

Lucifer marched purposefully onto the field, long mane and tail flowing in the breeze, neck proudly arched and eyes flashing. Sir Richard's armour glittered and shimmered brilliantly as the sunbeams danced across it and leapt off the intricate relief of leaves, vines and sprites decorating the breastplate. His silk cape fluttered out behind him as the breeze bore it aloft like the hands of an invisible train-bearer, its icy rippling breath making determined, noble Saint George and the angry dragon seemed as though they were moving.

Pepin stood proudly at the side of the arena, his master's helmet still tucked under one arm, his shield hanging off the other, and a supply of wooden lances leaned across his shoulder. The young pageboy looked rather overloaded, but he held his fair, sleekly-groomed head high and kept up his elegant, poker-straight bearing with a success that was almost comical, as it appeared so hard-won.

A cheer sounded forth from the crowd. The magnificent warrior gave a courteous bow in response, all the while scanning the crammed galleries keenly. Rowena knew he was searching for her, but her throat was so tight she could not join in with the vocal throng's calls.

The herald blew another call on his trumpet that silenced the anticipant crowd. 'And now, fair knights, lords and ladies, the man to whom this challenge was made: Sir Roger de Wintore, only son of the late Sir Giles de Wintore, Baron of Wentwich!'

Every eye in the breathlessly watching crowd fixed onto the gap between two viewing galleries that formed the entrance to the lists. Moments passed and neither sight nor sound filled the entranceway.

But then, just as the herald was beginning to frown and fidget, a storm of flapping black and red cloth, thundering hooves, sweating horse and clanging metal filled the space. Turf flew as a fully-armed knight hauled his black warhorse to a halt in the centre of the arena like a bat freshly loosed from the gates of hell. His horse was almost entirely covered by a long caparison the colour of dried blood, with a black skull beneath a fierce bat with outstretched wings emblazoned on each side. Over his suit of sharply angular armour the knight wore a cloth jupon, in his arms of blood-red with the fearsome bat and skull. Unlike every other knight who had entered these lists, the knight of the bat and skull had his helmet on and visor lowered.

The bascinet helmet, with its pointed snout of a visor, gave the knight a disturbingly sinister appearance that had Rowena clutching the front rail like a drowning seaman.

Earlier, she had learnt from the chattering crowd that de Wintore was known as the 'Sorcerer'. The name fitted perfectly. Even his horse looked evil, with its bony head and snarling mouth. But most ghastly of all was the cruel, age-blackened battleaxe resting across his saddle pommel. It was long-handled, large-bladed and mounted with a merciless spike long enough to bite into the very centre of its enemy's beating heart. That was a weapon which had drunk away the life of many a brave and noble knight, and on this cold February morning, it was hungry for warm blood.

Rowena's lips moved in silent prayer as she begged Saint George to strengthen her knight's body and soul with iron.

Even the herald stared at the sudden arrival for a moment, but he quickly regained his wits. 'Sir Richard issued the challenge, and now it has been answered! The conditions of battle have been set forth by Sir Richard and are thus: both knights may make an unlimited number of courses. If one or both knights are unhorsed, the fighting is to continue on foot using the knights' weapon of choice. The fight is to last until one of the knights yields and declares the other man victor. Thereafter, all grievances will be considered dissolved by both parties, with the winner acknowledged as having been proven right by the divine will of God!' And with that he gave his most ornate bow yet and stepped back, giving Sir Richard a brisk nod to signal he might ride forth to his chosen lady.

Rowena was still staring at the evil storm of sharp blood-red and blackness when Sir Richard's calm, earnest face passed in front of the fearful sight. The maiden snapped out of her trance of horror and looked into the beloved dark eyes, where the low, far-distant light of the winter sun glittered like stars in the midnight sky. Her champion looked every inch the legendary warrior; a knight born of the breath of the minstrel.

'Beloved, you know my heart's deepest desire. Grant it to me.'

Though her eyes did not waver, her heart skipped a beat. What did he mean? Was this his way of asking her if he might wear her favour, or was there more?

It slowly dawned on her that every eye was fixed upon the scene in breathless anticipation, and speculative twittering was stirring through the crowd.

'Of course I will gift you a token of favour!' she replied quickly.

But then it struck her: what was she going to give? Her hands flew to her pockets. No, the handkerchief was gone—Pepin had used it to polish his master's armour without asking her leave. The little rascal.

Beginning to grow hot even on this cold day, she reached for her garland—oh the ribbon, it too was gone. Although she did not dare look around, the loud twittering told her the crowd was not oblivious to her predicament. Even a few muffled laughs could be heard.

Sir Richard waited calmly, a loving but bemused smile resting on his lips.

Even her own knight was laughing at her! Her cheeks positively burned. A sleeve, a sleeve was a most suitable favour—she seized hold of her sleeve—but a lady with only one sleeve on her gown? It would be indecent! Defeated, the hand fell back down.

Still her knight waited patiently. Those eyes were so very deep; surely she could see his heart's deepest desire written within? She trawled the glittering dark pools intently. And the answer was found.

Rowena reached up to take hold of a lock of her flaming red hair, wound it around her finger and, with one sharp tug, pulled it out. 'Give me your left hand,' she commanded her knight.

A large, metal-encased hand was immediately presented.

Silently taking hold of his gauntlet, she pulled it off and grasped his ring finger. Then she slipped the lock of hair around the strong yet refined finger and tied it in a firm knot. Still holding the hand, she looked at its owner and smiled. 'Sir Richard, I give you my hand in marriage.' She said it in clear, bell-like tones that echoed around the arena.

He wordlessly reached to pull out a lock of his own hair, then took her tiny ring finger and gently bound the ebony hair around it. When he looked up, his black eyes burned with fiery zeal. 'We are eternally one.'

'We are eternally one.'

And with that, they parted. When Sir Richard had returned to the centre of the field, the herald looked to de Wintore and indicated that he might seek a lady's favour. The sinister knight shook his head.

'Very well,' said the herald. 'Sirs, you may take your places!'

De Wintore rode his fearsome beast down to the opposite end of the lists where his bevy of squires was gathered. There he halted and turned to face his enemy.

Sir Richard did likewise, riding Lucifer up to the other end where a lone Pepin waited. The page was bravely trying not to have the appearance of an overloaded beast of burden or look intimidated by the ghastly opponents.

Sir Richard held out his hand. Pepin placed the helmet into it. The helmet was lowered into place. The hand was held out again and received the shield. This was pulled on, and he reached out to receive a lance, which was poised ready for the iron fingers to close around. The visor went down with a clang, the trumpet sounded, and battle commenced.

The two great warhorses thundered towards each other like furies riding the storm. Two lances met hard steel a moment later and burst into a hundred splinters that pelted the ground as they rained down. Without stopping, the knights took another lance as they passed their arms-bearers, turned to face each other once more, and charged.

Again and again this was repeated, until Rowena had lost count of the number of courses ridden. Sometimes an explosion of wood accompanied the moment the two knights clashed, other times the lances remained intact. The speed with which the opponents wheeled their warhorses around meant the squires who usually scurried out to clear the splintered lances from the ground were unable to carry out this task, so the lists quickly accumulated a treacherous carpet of wood fragments.

During one particularly furious charge, de Wintore's snarling black beast stumbled on a lance fragment just as the knights were about to clash. The Sorcerer's usually keen aim was thwarted and his balance thrown off. Sir Richard's lance hit de Wintore's helmet just below the visor, and the sinister tower of black and red-swathed metal teetered dangerously.

The crowd let out a gasp and Rowena fell to her knees praying the demon knight would topple. But the demon knight did not topple. An unbearably tense moment later, he miraculously pulled himself back upright and wheeled about for the next charge. Poor Pepin narrowly dodged Lucifer's flying hooves as his master dashed to seize another lance before spinning around and charging again.

Several more furious charges followed. The two warhorses were flicked with sand and foaming white sweat, and their riders noticeably beginning to tire. The lances started to droop and be aimed less true, and Rowena began to fear the knights would ride course after course until one simply fell dead from sheer exhaustion.

But before this fear could be realised, a new problem presented itself. The knights had shattered their lances against each other with a force that rung out across the arena, made the very ground shake beneath them and caused Rowena to let out a gasp of horror which was louder than usual. Then the knights had both blindly reached for a new lance, but while de Wintore's half-dozen squires had a plentiful supply, Pepin was completely empty-handed. The pageboy had tried to shout something to his master when he had handed out the last lance, but his words had been drowned by the sound of thundering hooves, puffing horses and the screaming crowd.

When Sir Richard's outstretched hand was not instantly filled by a fresh lance, he turned to look at Pepin. Rowena saw Pepin hold his empty hands up and shrug his shoulders helplessly.

The viewing gallery erupted in exclamation and speculation at the unprecedented sight. Knight and page exchanged desperately tense words while their opponents looked on laughing and pointing. The herald rushed to consult with the lance-less party, and after a quick but heated talk, Pepin was seen bolting from the arena while the rowdy crowd waited, all delighted by the scene except for Rowena, who was utterly horror-struck.

The herald held up his hand to silence the crowd. 'Fair lords and ladies, I hope you can forgive this minor delay. Be assured that battle will commence once more when Sir Richard is brought a fresh supply of lances in a moment.'

A very short while later, Pepin dashed back holding his jaunty cap on with one hand and with a light metal hunting javelin in the other.

As soon as de Wintore's party and the twittering crowd saw this, they started to roar with laughter. Even the herald laughed. Sir Richard's face was hidden beneath his helmet, but Rowena knew full well what expression he was wearing. He aimed a few words at Pepin which, although they were not audible to the crowd, were clearly not very gracious, and furiously snatched the hunting javelin from his pageboy's hand.

The mockers were still laughing as Sir Richard started a furious charge towards de Wintore, who rode at his enemy in a half-hearted way.

Lucifer was pounding along at a full gallop when the two knights neared each other. In order to get near enough to have a chance of reaching his enemy with the short spear, Sir Richard steered the mighty warhorse in so close to the barrier that his stirrup must have touched it.

A moment later a tremendous crash echoed around the arena as the javelin's sharp point hit de Wintore right in the centre of the neck-guard with such force that he was thrown off his horse instantly and landed sprawled on his back on the ground, where the fallen knight flailed feebly as he tried to regain his jarred mind and body.

Along with the rest of the cheering, applauding crowd, Rowena leapt to her feet, though unlike them, she had her hands held over her mouth in fearful suspense. The force of the clash had been so violent it had unbalanced Sir Richard, who teetered helplessly for a few moments before slowly crashing to the ground, too weighed down by his armour to recover.

While everyone's eyes were on Sir Richard's horribly slow

fall, the Sorcerer had dragged himself to his feet, drawn his murderous battleaxe, and was now rushing at the defenceless Sir Richard.

'Richard, danger behind you!' Rowena screamed, leaning so far out over the rail that a hand grabbed her from behind.

Sir Richard threw himself to one side, and a split-second later the blood-rusted blade sliced into the earth where his neck had lain a moment before.

'Mother of God, have mercy!' Rowena gasped, barely able to watch her knight face such danger, yet completely incapable of tearing her eyes away for even a moment.

By the time de Wintore had pulled his battleaxe forth from the earth's grasp and swung it high in readiness for another blow, Sir Richard had managed to get to his knees, draw his sword and lift his shield between his head and the axe's fast descending blade.

The fierce axe blade embedded itself deep into the wooden shield. And as de Wintore pulled back on it, Sir Richard allowed himself to be dragged forward and up. Barely had he regained his feet when the shield was ripped free from the axe's bite, losing a chunk with it. A furious exchange of blows began.

Although de Wintore's battleaxe had the advantage of momentum and brute power, Sir Richard was able to be quicker on his feet and deliver lightning-fast attacks with his lighter sword. But this did not save him from all of the Sorcerer's blows. Some could not be dodged or parried, and hit into his armour with a sickening thud that was complete agony to Rowena, who let out a cry of pain every time. Both knights were rapidly gaining a large collection of dents in their armour, and Sir Richard's shield soon had splits and whole pieces hacked off.

The crowd had been watching this battle enthralled, but when Sir Richard stumbled on a lance fragment and was rewarded with a crashing blow to the shoulder that instantly gushed blood, the crowd's mesmerised gasp was immediately followed by a voice demanding, 'Madam Judge, these knights are fighting with unlawfully sharp weapons. You must put a stop to this battle before one of them is slain!'

Sobbing aloud at the ghastly sight of crimson blood pouring down her knight's breastplate, Rowena turned to see who had spoken. An elderly lord in a long blue robe was sternly standing before Lady Sabina, who sat on a throne beneath a grand, cloth-draped canopy.

The regal lily eyed him sourly. 'Nay, I have no wish to stop such entertaining sport.' She smiled a glacial smile and gestured at the crowded gallery. 'Look how my guests are enjoying themselves.'

'But madam—'

A finger as thin and pointed as an icicle was raised. 'That is enough, old man! *I* am Lady Shrewsbury now. I am much more powerful than you, and this is my feast. If you insist on vexing me any further I shall be forced to ask the king to remove your head from your neck.'

The dignified lord looked so offended as he backed away muttering into his beard that Rowena was half afraid he would have a fit. But a loud crash from below brought her eyes swiftly back to the lists.

'Lord have mercy upon us!' she cried, seeing that her knight's shield had been cleaved in two by de Wintore's evil blade.

Sir Richard took his sword in both hands and the battle continued with an even more furious and brutal flurry of blows and stabs. The crash of metal on metal was deafening, and mixed with it were frequent grunts and gasps from the battling warriors. Blood now covered de Wintore's left arm and ran from his side, where Sir Richard's blade had sliced through his armour.

Rowena was now on her knees clinging to the rail, praying and sobbing. The fight seemed an even thing, with neither warrior gaining the upper hand. The blood was growing ever more plentiful; the weapons and armour of both knights were thick with it. It was now impossible to tell where it was coming from or even which knight it belonged to.

After what the sand-filled hourglass informed the crowd was another three-quarters of an hour, Rowena could tell Sir Richard was finally falling prey to fatigue. He was having difficulty parrying the murderous battleaxe's savage attack as his old wound complained, leaving his left arm ever weaker.

Exhausted herself, she leaned on the rail and clutched her arms about her head in agonised terror, silently imploring Saint George to aid her hero in his moment of need.

A sudden low swipe from de Wintore caught Sir Richard off guard, and the blood-hungry blade sunk into the place where the knee armour joined the thigh plate. Blood gushed forth instantly, and Sir Richard's leg gave way.

Rowena screamed and lunged forward, but a hand grabbed her arm from behind. 'Do control yourself, darling. It is no business of a woman to be interfering in matters of war and honour.'

She snapped her head around and was face-to-face with the limpid young peacock of earlier, now with the added irritation of an indolent, patronising smile. 'Go give your mirror a kiss, eunuch, and stop talking of things which you know nothing about!' she hissed, giving him a very unladylike shove.

When her attention returned to the battlefield, Sir Richard was fighting a desperate losing battle from a kneeling position. The ground around him was soaked with blood, and still de Wintore's blows rained down on him.

Then the Sorcerer raised his vile, blood-covered axe high above his head in what she knew he intended would be the death blow.

Time seemed to slow. She heard nothing but the beating of her heart. This was the end, surely.

The blackened blade swooped towards its prey like a diving

hawk. A dull thud rang out as the blade hit her knight on the side of the head. Sir Richard's helmet was flung to the red-stained earth, and a moment later his pale, blood-smeared head was lying senselessly beside it.

The Sorcerer raised his evil blade once more. 'Do you yield, dog?' demanded the thin, cruel voice she had heard on that stormy cliff-top.

Sir Richard neither answered nor moved. His eyes looked straight up at de Wintore, but they seemed to see nothing. He was unconscious. Perhaps even—dead.

Without a moment's thought, she leapt down from the high gallery, dragged herself up from the mud and ran towards the stricken Sir Richard, who lay on the blood-stained mud that was about to be his execution block as though it was a cloud of sweet dreams and tenderness

'He does not yield!' screamed the Sorcerer in fiendish triumph, standing over the fallen warrior and swinging his axe back for the final blow.

In a frozen tunnel ending with her knight's pale, noble face lying senseless in the mud, she flew over the ground. 'Spare him, I beg you!' she cried desperately.

As Rowena flung her body over her fallen knight, his eyes flickered. She turned to look up at de Wintore, and a shower of blood droplets sprayed off the axe as it started to descend.

Into her silent, slow-moving world rained the crimson droplets, showering her upturned face with Sir Richard's still-warm blood. Without realising what she was doing, Rowena lifted the sword lying by Sir Richard's side so its blade pointed skyward. His body felt rigid beneath her and his eyes were unseeing, but in an instant, he clamped the sword between his arm and his side.

'Help me—hold it!' he gasped.

Her hands closed around the bloodied hilt unquestioningly as the blackened battleaxe swooped in for its gory feast of blood and agony.

They were going to die together. 'God is merciful…' she murmured.

But the axe was falling no longer. It was the Sorcerer himself who was falling.

Suddenly sound flooded back into her world, and an instant later de Wintore thumped to the ground, half splayed over her and Sir Richard.

Stunned, she opened the eyes she had closed as she winced in preparation for the impact of the metal giant. De Wintore lay face down on the ground, motionless.

But why?

She squinted against the low winter sun, and saw that the light blinding her eyes belonged not only to the sun. The light belonged also to the glinting end of the sword-blade protruding from de Wintore's back.

Epilogue

'I'M hurting.'

Rowena stopped and turned.

A frustrated-looking Sir Richard gave her an apologetic smile as he limped up to her. 'Even at that slow pace, you will leave me behind shortly.' He frowned and looked down, his expression suddenly falling. 'I'm sorry, my love. A woman should not have to be burdened with such a broken husband.'

She put her hand to his pale cheek. 'Oh don't say that, Richard! We've been married for less than an hour; you are not a burden to me. It was thoughtless of me to take this long uphill path from St Agnes' to Eaglestone Castle instead of going through the woods with the rest of our wedding guests.' She took the cloak draped over his arm. 'Let's sit down for a moment and enjoy the view of the valley. The grass is nicely dry here.'

Once Rowena had spread the cloak out on the daisy-sprinkled grass, she threw herself down on it. Waiting while Sir Richard carefully, painfully lowered himself down was an exercise in self-control, as she found it almost impossible not to assist him. But she did not. Nothing was more depressing and hurtful to him than being helped by a pixie-sized lady.

To keep Rowena's mind off her companion, Nature proved a most successful distraction. The wood behind was aburst with springing, sprouting, budding growth. The fresh, tender green of the leaves almost seemed to shout with the joy of newness and sun-filled purity, of life and of harvests to come. The forest floor was a haze of bluebells that seemed to spread into eternity, their bells tolling an unheard music of magic. Here and there nestled a golden primrose or tiny, timid forget-me-not. And at the edge of the wood and all down the hedgerows danced opulent troupes of apple blossom and mayflower, their honeyed boughs a drunken feast of delight to the visiting hoards of bees and butterflies.

In front of her lay the valley, spread out in the spring sunshine. From high up here on the hill, the trees surrounding Stoatley Manor and lining the banks of the brook chattering its way down the vale could be seen, and at its far end, Willowmead's distant thatched rooftops. The brook's faint, faraway chatter was joined by a chorus of blackbirds and thrushes and, from deep within the heart of the woods, by the call of a cuckoo whose enchanting voice floated across the valley.

Noticing that Sir Richard seemed to be having little success in getting comfortable, she returned her attention to him. 'Why don't you lie down?'

Rowena's face was searched for any traces of pity.

Trying not to feel grieved, she kept her smile carefree.

'But there is no room for both of us if I spread out like that,' came the still-suspicious reply.

'There is if you rest your head in my lap.'

'But I'm too heavy; it will be uncomfortable for you.'

She rolled around so she was behind him, and took hold of his shoulders. 'Richard, stop talking and do as your wife tells you.'

He finally yielded and allowed her to pull him down until his head rested in her lap. Once settled, she sighed contentedly and smiled down at him. 'Listen to the birds in the woods. How they rejoice as the earth breathes out her golden dreams...'

He smiled fondly up at his wife and took her hand in his. 'And I rejoice too. It is not often a mortal man succeeds in winning a fairy bride.'

'And it is not often that a bride is kept waiting at the church door for twenty minutes by her bridegroom. Everyone was beginning to think you were going to jilt me! What kept you?'

'I couldn't find my comb.'

She laughed aloud at the matter-of-fact way in which he delivered this answer. 'Was that all? I thought at the very least you had had a last-moment tax demand from the king!'

'A man can't come to his own wedding with his hair a mess. It would be unseemly.'

She smoothed his elegant white damask doublet thoughtfully. 'Especially when he has come dressed all in white. You do know that penniless brides wear white to their weddings in order to signal they have no dowry to bring?'

He grinned up at her. 'Yes, I do. That is why I'm wearing white today—to signal that I'm penniless and unlike you, have nothing to offer the marriage except my useless body.'

'The Cunninghams may have provided me with a small dowry, but it was merely in order to keep up appearances. If they had not, all the other noble families would believe that they were too poor to do so. My aunt still seems to think my marriage is going to be the death of her. She has not risen from her bed for the past week. A good excuse for not attending my wedding rather than illness, I believe.'

He assumed a look of mock indignity. 'Have they no respect for my status as an illustrious knightly hero? Any decent family would welcome such a dented, rusted, penniless war-sword as I into their family like a long-lost son.'

She placed a slightly hesitant hand on his head and began gently stroking his glossy black hair. 'If you had slammed Lord Shrewsbury's head down on that table just a little harder, I may well have been the one coming to my wedding in white as a truly destitute bride, rather than in this fetching primrose-yellow gown.'

'I was in such a black mood at the time. I really wanted to do that weed an injury. But for all your admirable horror, the mirth the scene caused you did not escape me, you banshee.'

She twisted her fingers around an ebony lock and gave it a firm tug. 'Indeed, but I thought you a brutish animal—a very *brave* brutish animal.'

'Ow! Let go of me.'

She loosed her fingers and resumed the caressing strokes. 'Luckily the brutish wolf has turned into a *perfect* lapdog.'

But her smugness was short lived, as the little finger of the hand she rested on his cheek suddenly found itself held firmly captive between sharp white teeth. 'Ow! I see I spoke too soon,' she laughed.

The unsuspecting prey was mercifully released. 'You thought me a complete bastard and you were right. I, on the other hand, thought you to be a very cunning fox indeed. Being such a bear-brain myself, this made me terribly afraid. When you first started coming to the castle, I spent many sleepless hours at night pacing the ramparts trying to work out why you were there, what you were up to and how I could get rid of you. I really thought I'd cracked it when I got you down to the dungeons.' He chuckled darkly. 'The look of horror on your face as you entered the rat-infested place was priceless…'

The caresses stopped abruptly. 'You were such a beast! I really did think someone—possibly me—would not come out of that hell alive.'

He looked up at her guiltily. 'I was desperate to rid myself of you. Sorry about that, my love… After what you said about the taxes, I was truly afraid of you.'

A gratified smile spread over her lips. 'Really?'

He laughed. 'Really. I barely slept a wink for a week after that.'

The caressing hand slipped into his shirt's open neck. 'And when did you first decide that you wanted to marry me?'

'I fell under your spell the moment you first darkened my

door, but when I saw you coming down the stairs at the Cunninghams' feast in your faded, over-tight gown after your desperate last touches in the mirror, I was truly smitten. And after you proved yourself so resourceful, devious, uncompromising and fearless that night, I knew you had to be mine.'

Rowena coloured a little. 'I didn't know you were there already when I came down!'

'I stood outside while I waited for you to appear.'

She frowned at the memory. 'You really did get underfoot that evening. If you hadn't forced me to drug you I would have been much less strained.'

'Because you were afraid it might make me ill?'

'No, because I was afraid of not having enough left to drug my uncle with. I got it from a herbalist—some would say witch—who lived out in the forest.'

He rolled his eyes. 'Such kindness…'

'It was expensive and I had to walk a long way to get it!' protested the accused.

Sir Richard suddenly gasped and clutched his shoulder. 'Good God, that hurts!'

She removed her hand instantly. 'I'm so sorry; did I hurt you?'

He shook his head. 'No, it was just one of the accursed stabbing pains I've been getting lately.'

She frowned worriedly. 'These wounds you received at de Wintore's hands—they are so many!'

'Yes, but I am the one lying here in the spring sunshine in the lap of my beloved, and he is the one whose corrupted corpse is feeding the worms in Shrewsbury Church's graveyard while his sin-blackened soul feeds the fires of hell.'

With a tenderly concerned finger, she gently followed the long purple line running from his temple back into his hairline. 'Yes, and for that, I give thanks every day.'

He gave her a reassuring smile. 'You see, I did not die at de Wintore's hands as you were so sure I would.'

'Yes, but you came so very, very close…' The tender green eyes misted over. 'If you had not succeeded in kicking de Wintore's feet out from under him—I can barely think of it.'

'I had righteousness on my side; it was meant to be. Now please don't cry, dear heart.'

She managed a watery smile for his sake. 'Saint George most surely aided you in your hour of need. Any knight who did not have the angels on his side would have fallen. It truly was a miracle that you were saved that day.'

'It was, and one of those angels was you. Afterwards, when I was delirious with fever and blood loss, that butcher of a physician was all for cutting my damn leg off and bleeding me with leeches. If you had not swiftly had me taken back to Hartfield and Brother Jacob's care, I likely would never have walked again. That bastard quack, I wish I could cut *his* damn leg off!'

'Now, now, Richard…' she sighed, and was about to caress his neck but stopped, fearful of hurting him.

He pulled the opening of his partially undone doublet and shirt wider, then took her hand firmly in his and placed it on his right shoulder. 'See, it does not hurt. Your touch is not painful to me.'

She relaxed her hand a little and tentatively explored the long, deep scar running across the front of his shoulder.

A few moments later her concentration was broken when she caught his eye. The knowing glint there was undeniable.

'What?' she laughingly demanded.

'You are very good. That is *most* pleasant.'

Matching his darkly knowing smile with one of her own, she manoeuvred his head off her lap, stretched out beside him, and moved her hand back into his shirt, a little lower this time. 'Indeed…'

He let out a sigh of pleasure and settled himself comfortably against her. 'I met Lord Cunningham in Hartfield last week. After sourly congratulating me on my upcoming nuptials, he went on to say that he felt it was only fair to warn me his niece was a most headstrong and at times downright wild girl. 'Do not spare the rod,' said he, 'or you will bring trouble onto your head and dishonour onto your house!''

A distasteful sniff almost worthy of Lady Cunningham greeted this news. 'Really. And what did you say?'

'I replied that my betrothed gave me a regular hiding at chess, but was yet to overpower my person, my bodily strength being much greater than her own.'

'Hmmm…is that so? This morning my white queen took your black rook, and this afternoon…' She slipped a leg over him and moved upright to sit astride him. 'I capture the castle.'

The glittering velvet-black eyes danced with fond laughter. 'Yes, I think you have indeed captured the castle.' He looked at the gold ring encircling the third finger of his left hand. 'The cunning little fox has well and truly defeated its menacing dark lord, who surrenders unconditionally.'

'So, now that *I* am master of the castle, I shall expect—nay, *demand*—that its vanquished lord pays me the homage my exulted status is due,' said Rowena, with a princess-worthy air.

'Most noble conqueror and revered mistress, your victory is complete. Where once dark, twisted shapes flitted in the shadows of my cold halls, cries echoed from my subterranean dungeons and nameless fears cowered in my black chambers, now they are filled only with your light, with the sunbeams that dance about you, with the music of your laugh and with the scent of roses that ever surrounds you.'

She smiled archly. 'This pleases the lady of the castle. Such words will get you far, underling!'

And looking up at his wife's smiling face surrounded by the

halo of primroses, apple blossoms and mayflowers that made up her garland, Sir Richard felt happier on that sunny spring afternoon than he had ever felt before.

While he watched with deliciously drowsy joy, she slowly, teasingly undid the rest of the buttons and laces on his doublet and shirt.

'Is the conquering heroine pleased by her spoils?'

She ran her hands down the warm, hard contours of his naked torso. 'Yes, oh yes. The castle's new owner is most pleased by its fine stonework...'

'What magic spell were you born of, what elfin's charm or angel's wish, my dearest little pixie?' he sighed, placing his hand over the hand she rested on his breast.

'I was dreamed into being in the cosmic bosom, I fell to earth with the raindrops and the falling stars, I rested in earth's embrace, I grew up towards the sun with the sprouting seed and up towards the moon with the flowing sap, then I fell over you in the shadows and together we strove once more for the light...'

He smiled a drowsily bemused smile. 'Is that another of your mystic sibylline utterances which no mere mortal can unravel?'

Her laughing green eyes positively danced with mirth. 'Yes, O goose-brained one.'

'Just shut up and kiss me.'

She laughed her merry, lilting laugh and leaned forward.

'God I love you...' he breathed.

'I—love—you—too,' she murmured back, between kisses.

Lying blissfully on the warm hillside in the spring sunshine, he breathed in the intoxicating scent of nectar and crushed grass, and the violet-sweet scent of Rowena's hair, which brushed against his face as she leant over him. Feeling beneath him the firm earth of the place that now was as dear a homeland to him as ever any native soil wherein rested the bones of countless forebears was to a man, and pressing down from above the soft yet determined weight of the woman he loved, Sir Richard felt as if held between the embrace of the earth and the heavens. And the smiling face of his dearest, most beloved spouse was its life-and-light bestowing sun.

He abandoned himself to her exquisitely caressing touch and let the lingering kisses she pressed to his sighing skin set him adrift in a sea of bliss. 'Your love is to my heart what the sweetest, tenderest, most longed-for rain is to the parched dry earth…' he murmured. 'Like rain from heaven…'

The End

Note from the Author

Chaucy, 'the measliest shire in all England', is entirely fictional, as is its felon-harboring neighbor of Lothbury Shire. The topography of Chaucy and Lothbury was created mainly in the author's imagination, and is not intended to accurately mirror that of Devon.

Some of the characters in this story speak in English that is not always grammatically correct. This is deliberate. I wanted to reflect the range of regional dialects, and the differences between the speech of the wealthier, educated class and the peasant class.

65571282R00241

Made in the USA
Lexington, KY
16 July 2017